HOUSE OF CATESBY

The Complete Collection (Books 1-7)

SUNNY BROOKS

Text and Illustration Copyright © 2019 by Sunny Brooks

ISBN: 9781797438917

Publisher
Love Light Faith, LLC
400 NW 7th Avenue, Suite 825
Fort Lauderdale, FL 33302

CONTENTS

BOOK 3: THE MYSTERIOUS LORD LIVINGSTONE

BOOK 4: LADY SOPHIA AND THE
PROPER GARDENER

BOOK 5: MR. HENRY CATESBY
AND THE REBELLIOUS REDHEAD

BOOK 6: DILEMMA OF THE EARL'S HEART

BOOK 7: THE SCANDALOUS DOWAGER COUNTESS

HOUSE OF CATESBY PROLOGUE

Nothing could have prepared the Catesby clan for the unexpected passing of the family patriarch, Earl Joseph Edward Catesby. On the day of his death, in the blink of an eye, the lives of one woman and her six grown children changed irrevocably. The matriarch Countess Margaret Lilias Catesby was now a dowager countess; her strength and maternal duty the sole driving force pushing herself through the grief. Each of the Catesby children has been left to carry on their father's legacy, shown physically through their father's green eyes and spiritually through his impassioned attitude for living. Eldest son Francis had barely a day to cope with his father's death before the title of Lord Catesby was immediately thrust upon him. With Francis assuming ownership of the estate and his five siblings left to sort out the pieces, each must now find a way to navigate the world without their dear father's guidance.

WILL SIBLINGS FRANCIS, Emily, Helena, Sophia and the twins, Charles and Henry, be able to move forward into society and proudly carry on the Catesby name? There's only one way to find out...

Welcome to the House of Catesby!

BOOK 1: LADY EMILY'S ESCAPE

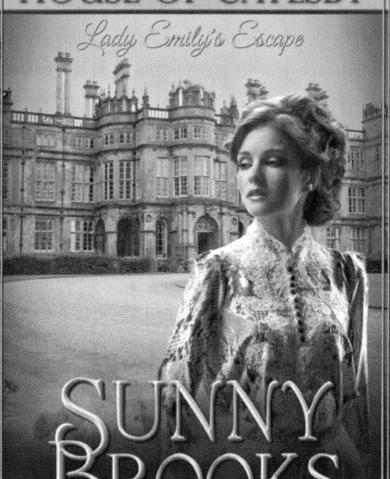

BOOK 1

HOUSE OF CATESBY

Lady Emily's Escape

SUNNY BROOKS

FOREWORD

Through the trials and tribulations of life, may we find help, may we find our strength & may we find love.

- Sunny Brooks

CHAPTER 1

F rancis wrapped an arm around his mother's shoulder, feeling her whole body shake as she wept desperately into her lace handkerchief. His mother's muffled cries were echoed by those of his sisters who all stood around the graveside shrouded in lusterless black dresses, their tears mingling with the gentle rain that was falling on them all. Their father was dead. Francis could hardly take it in. He had seemed to be in such good health, then all of a sudden taking some kind of attack and dying on the bedroom floor. The shock slammed into his chest the moment he'd heard his mother scream and seen his father's prone body on the floor. The stunned daze hadn't left him since. The funeral had been well attended, and Francis knew that his father was well liked. He had been a generous and kind employer, treating his tenants with compassion and respect. Their houses were all in a good state of repair, and he paid them well. Now Francis was stepping into his father's place, and he was not quite sure he was going to be able to do as good a job as his father.

"Oh, Francis," his mother sobbed, leaning into his shoulder. "Whatever shall I do without him?"

Francis said nothing, his mind echoing the same question. He loved and cared for both his parents deeply and had expected his father to live to a ripe old age. He had not at all expected to be taking on such a great mantle of responsibility so soon. It weighed heavily around his shoulders and Francis struggled against his own rising grief and fear. Fear that he would never be the man his father had been. Grief that he had lost his father too soon. He looked around at his other siblings, seeing their own sadness echoing in his heart: Henry, Charles, Emily, Sophie, and Helena. Of them, only Emily was married, and he was a little surprised that her husband, Lord Thurston, had not joined her. In fact, it was something of an insult. Watching her closely for a moment, he wondered if everything was right with her and her husband. It seemed most unusual for him not to be attending his father-in-law's funeral. Emily had passed on his apologies, citing some extremely serious business matter that could not be ignored. Still, it had unsettled Francis somewhat.

"Let us go home now, Mama," he urged, turning his thoughts back to his mother. "We need to get out of the rain."

"Just a few moments more," she sobbed, her tears becoming one with the raindrops. "I cannot leave my darling Joseph so soon."

Emily moved towards her mother, taking her hand gently. "Come now, Mama, Francis is right. You shall become ill if you remain here much longer. I will return with you tomorrow. I promise."

Her mother said nothing, the tears still flowing freely, and Emily's heart broke again. Thankfully her mother took Francis' arm and allowed him to lead her towards the waiting carriages. Emily watched the rest of her siblings follow suit. The procession of figures dressed in black and grey moved like a somber fog. Emily turned to take one last, long look at the grave. The earth was still fresh and as yet there was no stone. It had all been so sudden. "Goodbye, Papa," she whispered, before walking up to join the others.

THE MOOD WAS low back at the manor. As the family entered the drawing room, Francis had to keep reminding himself that he was now Lord Catesby and, as such, had all manner of new responsibilities. The world seemed very heavy and narrow at the moment, as though he could only see it through a pinprick from afar. Finding an armchair off in the corner, he stared blankly out the windows at the expanse of land before him.

"I'll ring for tea, shall I?" Emily asked, removing her bonnet and handing it to the butler. "Perhaps in the drawing room, Mama?"

"Very good, dear," her mother replied hoarsely, the sadness never leaving her eyes. Rather than ring for tea, Emily walked down to the kitchens herself, needing to get away from her family members for just a short time.

Her father had been such a vibrant and happy man, yet she had never been able to tell him the truth about her marriage to Victor. Both he and her mother had been overjoyed at her marriage, and she had to admit, so had she. Now, she looked back on the girl she had been then, too excited to see the monster behind the man who won her heart. A shiver ran through her as she wrapped her arms around herself. She gave the maid the order for tea and a light repast to settle them all.

Walking back up the stairs, she resolved that she would speak to Francis before she left. She could not return home knowing that her life was going to continue on this endless, torturous path without any hope of respite. Catching sight of her reflection in one of the mirrors in the hallway, she stared at herself for a moment. She still had the dark hair and green eyes that were something of a trait in her family, but her eyes held a deep sadness and a spark of pain that even her widest smile could not hide. It had been something of a relief when Victor had informed her with cold civility that he would not be attending. It showed her his lack of concern for her and her family, but she could not hold it against him. Ensuring she showed a proper sadness and light disapproval - the reaction he had been looking for – inwardly she rejoiced that she would be able to spend time with her family without his constant insults and increasingly frequent violence. She would get to know herself again, try to gather strength to face Victor once more. Resolving to stay as long as she could, she wondered when she would be forced to return home.

She was desperate to have a private moment with her brother, hoping that Francis would listen to her and come up with some kind of solution. It was greatly disapproved of for a woman to be divorced, but at this point, she would rather be shunned by society than remain with her tyrant of a husband. He thought he had complete power over her, and in many ways he did, but she had some mettle still within her and wouldn't allow him to extinguish her completely. The backdrop of her beloved father's funeral did even more to assure her of her decision. Her father had raised each of his children to be strong, gracious, and contributors to society. He would roll over where he lay if he were to know the truth of her life, and the notion broke her heart even further. Victor's constant abuse of her had worn her down, yes, but she was not going to remain under his thumb forever, to be treated so disparagingly whenever the mood took him. Walking back towards the drawing room, she flinched as she remembered his last display of temper.

"You're nothing but a whore," he had yelled, unheeding of the staff who remained in the room. "Thinking that I don't know about your flirtations with any man who crosses your path!" There was a lump in her throat as she remembered his words. She had sat, unyielding, refusing to cry or defend herself in any way. There were consequences for both, and she had learned how best to deflect his anger. His words had continued, making sure she realized how low in his estimation she sat. *His words are lies, his words are lies.* Over and over she'd repeated her mantra, knowing it was her only defense against his attacks. Once she gave in and started believing what he said about her, then all would be lost. She would be his for the taking, too weak to be anything other than his own little plaything that did whatever he pleased, whenever he wanted. That thought terrified her more than anything Victor could say.

On more than one occasion, he had hurt her in an attempt to get her to shrink under his control. She'd had more bruises than she cared to remember, and the frequency of it was increasing. Emily knew that it would not be too long before something drastic happened – and that was what had pushed her to speak to Francis. She was beginning to fear for her life.

Emily took a breath, her hand on the drawing-room handle. Schooling her features into a calm façade, she walked through the door to see the rest of her siblings and her mother sitting quietly. Sophie was playing some quiet pieces on the pianoforte, and she shot her a grateful look, which was met with a soft smile. Music always calmed their mother, and Emily was thankful for her sister's thoughtfulness.

"Tea will be coming very soon, Mama," she said gently, moving to sit next to her dear mother. "I am sure you will begin to feel more yourself once you are warm and dry."

"Quite," Francis replied, now up and pouring some port for himself and his brothers. "This has been a sad time for all of us, but it is also the beginning of many changes. We all need to take some time to become used to them."

Emily nodded, patting her mother's hand. Francis was now the title bearer, being the firstborn son. She wondered how he was feeling about his new responsibilities, seeing the slight crease in his forehead. There was no reason for him to worry; Emily was quite certain that he would be every bit of the man their father was. Francis had grown to be a kind and compassionate gentleman, which was exactly the characteristics their father had hoped for all of them. What an excellent father he had been. Emily's heart squeezed painfully as she remembered her father's loving smile. She was going to miss him desperately.

CHAPTER 2

A week had passed, and Francis had not yet entered his father's study. He kept telling himself that he had time, that he did not need to enter it quite yet, that his father's steward was more than capable – but it was all an excuse. He was struggling to accept the fact that he was now lord of the manor with all the responsibilities that came with it. He had an estate to run, tenants to look after, figures to look over, and a mother and sisters to care for. Thank goodness Emily was not his burden too, otherwise, he thought he would go mad! Francis shook his head, throwing back his glass of port. It needed to be done sooner rather than later, and putting it off was getting him nowhere.

A gentle knock on the library door startled him. It was late, and he had thought the others were all still abed at this hour. "Come in."

His mother appeared at the door. "Francis?"

"Mama!" He scrambled to his feet. "Come in, come in. Are you quite well?"

"I am fine, Francis, thank you. As fine as I can be." She gave him a small smile, and Francis was relieved that there appeared to be no tears as yet. There had been quite a lot of crying over the last few days, although he himself had not shed a single one.

"Could you not sleep?"

She shook her head. "It's not that, Francis. I wanted to talk to you about something."

"Of course, Mama. Whatever you need to talk about, I am always here for you."

She smiled at him gently. "Thank you, Francis. You have always been a wonderful son." She took a breath. "It is time for me to retire to the Dower House."

"What?" Francis stared at her in shock. "Mama, you cannot! Father has only been mourned a week and already you are considering –"

"I am considering you, my dear," she interrupted, her voice quiet but firm. "I know that you will need the space to run this estate as you think best, without me hovering around. It will make you constantly wonder if I am looking over your shoulder, should I stay." She patted his hand, seeing how he wanted to deny it but could not quite find the words. "I shall not be moving immediately, but I have already indicated to my maid to begin writing a list of the things I shall be taking."

"Mama," Francis said, softly, shaking his head. "I don't want you to leave!"

"I know you don't, my dear," she responded. "But in time, you will see that this was the right thing for me to do. And besides, I shall not be too far away, shall I?"

Francis gazed at her, seeing the resolve in her gentle, yet strong grey eyes. She was right, for the Dower house was less than twenty miles away, but to his surprise, he felt something like abandonment hit him. "You know how much we will miss you, Mama." It felt too soon, but she was clearly determined.

"I know." Her face softened. "One other thing, Francis. I know this will make things a little more difficult for you, but I am desirous to take my own staff with me." She shook her head. "That is not what I meant. They are *your* staff, of course, but they have been part of this household for so long that I am struggling to think of the Dower house without them!"

"Whom do you wish to take, Mama?" Francis replied, kindly. It would be something of an inconvenience to have to hire new staff, but if it meant that his mother was happier, then he would do it without question.

She sighed a little in relief. "The cook, for she knows my preference with meals, some of the longer standing maids, my personal maid, of course, and – perhaps the butler?"

Francis's eyebrows rose a little, but he pushed the look of surprise from his face as quickly as he could. The butler was a fairly new addition to the household staff and was close to his mother in years, from his guess, but it seemed he had made quite an impression on his mother. "Of course, Mama." He smiled and watched her face relax over his acquiescence. "You may take whomever you wish. Would you like me to speak to them?"

"No, I shall do so myself. I do not wish any of them to leave this place if they do not wish it!"

"You have far too soft a heart, Mama!" Francis exclaimed, shaking his head a little.

His mother smiled gently, rising to take her leave the library. "A kind heart is a wonderful quality, Francis," she replied, with just a hint of censure. "Be sure to nurture yours."

After his mother left him, he made his way to the elegantly embellished door. Letting out a long sigh, Francis stopped with his hand on the study door handle. This was the moment. He needed to go into his father's study and claim it as his own. Why then, was he finding it so difficult? He tossed and turned all night and finally rose from bed, determined to get it over with. Yet here he was, continuing the debate. He was torturing himself over nothing.

Steeling himself, he pushed open the door and took a few steps inside. The curtains were open, and the barely breaking daylight flooded the room, the smell of cigars throwing memory after memory at him. He struggled against the tears that pricked at the corner of his eyes, as he walked a little further into the room, looking around at everything. His father had decorated the study in shades of dark green and black and, whilst a little foreboding, Francis had no intention of changing it. This had been his father's room, and, at least for now, it reminded Francis of him. Moving to the table to the left of the door, Francis let his hand run over the smooth, polished surface. His father's chair was pulled out as though waiting for him to sit down. Francis' brow furrowed as he held back his emotions, sitting down heavily and hearing the leather squeak in protest, as it had always done whenever his father had sat in his study. Everything about this room reminded him of his parent, and Francis could not help but feel as though he was something of an intruder.

A sudden knock on the door startled him from his reverie and, brushing a hand over his eyes to ensure no trace of any tears were on his face, he allowed entry. The butler came in, showing no sign of surprise as though he had quite expected him to be there.

"Your steward is here, milord."

"Ah yes, thank you." Francis cleared his throat, trying not to allow the anxious panic that was clawing there to reveal itself. "Please send him in." The weight of responsibility was weighing heavily on him now and Francis tried his best to remain calm.

"Very good, sir." The butler beckoned to a small, wiry-looking man who Francis recognized as Mr. Keating, his father's steward.

"Ah, Mr. Keating. Thank you for coming. Please, sit down."

The man did so after a stiff but passable bow. "Thank you, my lord. May I say how sorry I am to hear of your dear father's passing."

"Thank you," Francis replied, a little stiffly.

"Will there be anything else, milord?"

"No, thank you – oh, wait, Jones, I forgot to ask you."

"Yes, sir?" The butler intoned, turning back to face him.

"I believe my mother has asked you to work for her at the Dower house, along with some other members of my staff."

"She has."

"And have you accepted?"

"I have, milord," the butler replied, honestly. "I do hope that is quite all right."

Francis nodded. "Of course, Jones, of course. I just wanted to say how much I shall miss you. You have been an excellent butler here in the house, and I shall struggle to find someone equal to your skills."

A ghost of a smile hovered around the butler's mouth. "Thank you, sir." With a quick, deferential bow, the butler left, leaving Francis feeling a little happier. Perhaps the kindness his mother was so keen for him to foster was going to be a beneficial characteristic in how he dealt with his staff. He truly hoped so.

CHAPTER 3

"You have a letter, ma'am."

"Thank you," Emily replied quietly, putting down her embroidery and opening the sealed envelope. Her heart began to pick up its pace as she recognized her husband's writing. Quickly reading the few lines, she felt her stomach lurch. He was demanding her return home, even if she was not ready. She would apparently be able to grieve her father just as well at home as with her family. Just another sign of how unfeeling her husband truly was.

"Is everything all right, Emily?"

Emily glanced up at her sister, Sophie, who was looking at her with slight concern.

"You have gone a little pale," Sophie continued, taking in her sister's appearance.

Emily quickly put a cheerful smile on her face. "Everything is fine, Sophie, thank you. I just received a letter from Victor who is requesting my presence back home. I had not thought he would miss me so much!" She tried to grin but failed miserably.

"What a shame he had to miss the funeral," her mother piped up from the corner of the drawing room. "And he was unable to support you when you most needed it by his lack of attendance." Emily caught her mother shaking her head in either disappointment or surprise, and she felt a wave of shame wash over her. Probably just as Victor had hoped.

"I know, Mama, and he felt quite terrible about it, I assure you," she replied, hoping her mother would not catch her bare-faced lie. "Some estate business came up, and if he had not attended to it, then we might have been quite ruined!"

"Truly?" Sophie gasped, a hand almost at her mouth. "How terrible! In that case, it is quite understandable that he should remain at home. We should not want you to be put out of your home, should we, Mama?"

Emily threw her sister a grateful glance as her mother nodded, apparently accepting both Emily and Sophie's words. She hated having to lie to her sisters and especially to her mother, but she would not let Victor's cruel behavior hurt them too. Instead, Emily had made the decision to lie and conceal Victor's true nature as best as she could, hiding him from everyone except Francis.

"If you'll excuse me, I must speak to Francis about something." Folding up the letter, she struggled not to crumple it in her hand as she left the drawing room and made her way to the library, hoping Francis would be there.

Francis was not in the library and, after questioning a couple of footmen and then the butler, Emily was pleased to discover that he was in the study. She knew that Francis had been struggling with the idea that he now took the title and all the responsibilities that came with it. Entering his father's study had seemed to be one of the greatest hurdles in his path, and Emily was delighted to find that he had, at last, managed.

Francis rubbed a hand across his eyes, tired beyond measure. His steward had taken up most of his time in the morning and, after a light luncheon which he ate in the study, he was now poring over some of the accounts the steward had left him. Then there was some correspondence to deal with, and finally, he had some letters of his own to write. Francis needed help and advice, still battling against the overwhelming desire to run and hide from all that he was now taking on. Having decided to write to his friend, Lord Thomas Markham, he hoped that he would arrive at the Catesby estate with all speed. Thomas had only taken on his own father's mantle within the year and, of all of Francis' friends, would be in the best place to advise and guide him.

A light knock on the door was followed by Emily poking her head through the gap and smiling at him. "Ah, you are here!" She walked through the door, a slight smile on her face. He could see the memories hitting her as she inhaled the scent of the room, just as he had done. "This place reminds me of father," she murmured.

"I know," Francis replied, watching his sister sit on the seat opposite him. "It is as though his very presence is here!"

She smiled at him, her green eyes a mix of sadness over their father's death and happiness over the many fond memories of him. "I am glad you are in here at last," she said eventually. "I know how difficult this was for you."

Francis said nothing, his lips twisting into a rueful smile. "Well, I am here now. And father's steward has spent most of today throwing various numbers at me until my head is quite sore!"

"Oh, dear!" Emily's voice held sympathy, and Francis appreciated her understanding. "I must apologize, Francis, for I am about to add to that pain."

Francis frowned at her words. "What do you mean?" He watched her closely, seeing the way her cheeks flushed a little and her whitened knuckles, which held something that looked like a letter, tighten a little around the paper.

Emily found it difficult to find the words, having kept her husband's mistreatment of her close to her chest for a long time. "It is about Victor."

"Victor?" Francis looked a little puzzled. "What about him?"

"He... he is hurting me, Francis."

"Hurting you?" Francis sat up a little straighter in his chair. "What can you mean, Emily?"

"Oh, Francis, I cannot stay there a moment longer!" Emily cried suddenly, feeling as though a dam had burst. "He berates me all day long, calling me things that no gentlewoman should hear!" She got to her feet, needing to pace around the room, such were the strength of her emotions. "He is a cruel, cruel man, Francis."

"Victor?" Francis said, a little incredulously. "Surely not, Emily! Are you not exaggerating a little?"

Emily froze in place for a moment, before turning slowly to look at her brother. "Exaggerating?" she whispered, shock filling her. "Francis, are you saying you doubt me?"

He shook his head, vigorously. "No, that is not what I am saying at all, my dear sister. I am just a little surprised at what you've said."

Emily walked towards him, slamming her hands on the table. "I know he was once your friend, Francis, but you do not know him as you once did!"

"I know he would never lay a finger on –"

"Well, he has!" Emily countered, her eyes flashing. "On more than one occasion! Know him though you did, you would surely not recognize the terror of a man that now walks the halls of my home."

Francis stared at her for a long moment, feeling yet more weight land on him. He heard the desperation in his sister's words, but they felt far off, as if he couldn't fully take them in. After all that had happened, this additional burden, however devastating to hear, seemed beyond his current capacity to manage. "What do you want me to do?" he asked, a little brokenly. "You are his wife, Emily. I have no right to interfere."

Her anger turning to disbelief and then to despair, Emily slumped back into her chair, feeling her limbs begin to tremble. It had taken a lot for her to tell her brother of what Victor was doing, and this was not what she had expected. Her spirit seemed to rush out of her at the reality that he was not willing to help her. She had thought he would protect her, not simply stand aside as she returned to a cruel and vicious husband. "I want you to protect me, Francis," she whispered, her eyes now filling with sudden tears. "You're my brother." She sat wilted across from him, feeling hollow as a brittle shell.

"And he's your husband," he replied, firmly. "I can do nothing, Emily." Francis simply felt as though he could not deal with anything more. This was too much. Victor was his friend, although Emily was right that he had not seen him in some time. But surely, she was exaggerating just a little? All men had times where they spoke out of turn, and it was certainly not against the law for a man to discipline his wife; mayhap Emily was simply not used to such treatment.

Emily stared at him for a long moment, before getting to her feet. "I must leave, it seems," she whispered. "My husband has demanded my return." She threw the folded letter at him, which rolled off the desk and onto the floor at his feet. "I thought you would help me, Francis," she said, in a soft voice, giving him one last, tortured look with all the piercing directness she could gather. "How you have let me down."

Her words echoed around the room long after she had left.

CHAPTER 4

I t was early morning when Emily took her leave. After pressing each of her sister's hands and giving her mother a gentle hug, her brothers Henry and Charles walked down the steps to bid her farewell. There were no tears; each of them held them back so that it would not be a sad farewell. Emily did not live too far away, and she hoped Victor would allow her to visit soon.

"Must you go, my dear?" her mother whispered, even though the carriage had already pulled up. "It seems so soon!"

"I would stay if I could, Mama," Emily replied, honestly. "But I am sure we shall see each other very soon."

"But where is Francis?" Sophie asked, a little crossly. "He should be here to wave you goodbye!"

Emily tried not to frown, knowing that their last few words had been fraught and it was little wonder that he had chosen to remain either abed or in his study. "Francis is very busy, Sophie, do not worry. Besides, I spoke to him last evening, so I have already given him my farewells."

Sophie watched her for a moment before nodding, as if she did not quite believe Emily's excuse, but accepted it nonetheless.

"I must go," Emily said again, getting into the carriage with a heavy heart, much heavier than any of them realized. "We shall see each other very soon."

She waved as the carriage began its journey, the wheels bumping over the gravel on the path, and she kept her face smiling until she was certain they could no longer see her. Only then did she give in to her grief, putting her head in her hands and sobbing aloud. Her heart was crushing, embodying the sound of the wooden carriage wheels crunching rocks into dust underneath. She was the only sibling to have married, and she felt as though she was being wrenched away from the one place in the world where she belonged. Whilst her time with her family had been marred with sadness and grief, it was still her home, and when there, she felt as though she were complete. The thought of returning to Victor tore at her soul, and the notion that she would have to accept it as her fate felt as though it may cripple her. Emily sat collapsed in her seat, so encompassed by her misery and sobbing that she did not even notice the carriage that passed by, heading back towards Catesby estate.

"THOMAS!"

"Francis!"

A wide smile on his face, Francis threw his arms around his old friend, welcoming him to the estate. "I can't tell you how glad I am to see you," Francis said, warmly, grinning at Thomas as they moved to sit in two comfortable chairs next to the fireplace. Whilst the September air was not yet too chilly, there was a still a need for a warm fire in the grate, and Thomas warmed his hands before sitting down.

"Well, I'm happy to be here," Thomas replied, seeing the exhaustion and strain on his friend's face. "I was sorry to hear about the loss of your father."

Francis nodded. "Thank you, Thomas. I must confess, I am struggling somewhat with the idea of taking on all his responsibilities!"

Thomas could sympathize, knowing that was why Francis had sent for him. "I'm happy to help you, Francis. I understand how difficult it can all appear, particularly when it happens so suddenly! At least, with my father, I had time to prepare." Thomas's father had been ill for a long time, and Thomas had slowly taken on some of his father's responsibilities before having to assume the title. It had been less demanding for Thomas than for Francis, but he was still able to advise and support Francis through his transition. "What have you taken on so far?"

Francis took a long breath, explaining everything he'd been learning from his steward, the accounts, the figures and everything that went with it.

"So you have not yet visited the tenants?"

Francis shook his head, a worried look on his face. "Should I have visited them by now?"

"They will need reassurance," Thomas replied. "But will understand that you have been taken up with other matters. Best to do it soon, however."

"Tomorrow?"

"Tomorrow," Thomas confirmed, stretching. "I shall look forward to having a ride. It seemed an age that I was sitting in that carriage!"

Francis grinned. "Best get you a drink then, Thomas! Port?"

"That would be splendid," Thomas replied, getting to his feet. He was quite looking forward to spending a few days with Francis.

Three days later, and Thomas and Francis were, once again, ensconced in the study, going over some accounts. Francis had been most reassured over his new role, and Thomas had been incredibly helpful, giving him some guidance on how to get the best from his tenants and to find ways of keeping on top of all of the steward's accounting and other duties. Far too many newly titled lords had been taken advantage of and lost vast sums of money whilst their stewards mysteriously disappeared, but Thomas was sure that Francis would not be one of them.

"And that, I think, is all of it!" he said, sitting back with a sigh.

Francis shook his head. "Thank you, Thomas," he said, knowing that he'd said the same words time and again over the last few days. "I cannot tell you how much I appreciate all of your support."

"Not at all," Thomas replied, stretching his long legs out in front of him as he ran a hand through his thick black hair. "It's been my pleasure to help." A sudden crinkling sound met his ears as he stretched his feet under Francis' desk, and he did so again, realizing that there was a bit of paper hidden there.

"Hold up," he mumbled, getting to his feet and reaching for it. "There's something under here. I hope we haven't missed something."

"What is it?" Francis asked, watching Thomas smooth out the paper. A little perplexed, he watched Thomas's brow furrow, and his blue eyes become dark.

"What's the matter, Thomas?"

"Have you read this?" Thomas thrust the paper towards him, which Francis took carefully, shooting Thomas a surprised look.

"No, what is it?" A quick glance told him that this wasn't from anyone he knew. Reading the words, he grew more and more horrified, realizing that he had just sent Emily back to this man. "Oh no," he breathed. "I didn't... I should have listened to her!"

"Listened to who?" Thomas asked, his face angry. "Francis, tell me you know who this letter was for!"

"It was Emily's," he whispered, sitting down heavily in his chair. "She tried to tell me that Victor –"

"Victor Thurston?"

"Yes, the very same," Francis replied, remembering that Thomas knew of the man, although had never formally met him. "She married him some time ago, and I had thought it a love match, but now it seems..."

"It seems he is treating her in a way no woman should be treated," Thomas replied, firmly, trying to remember which sister Emily was. They all had dark hair as he recalled, and he had not met them very often, so it was something of a mystery. Regardless, he was furious that a husband should either write or treat his wife in such a way. "Are you telling me that she came to you with this?"

"I didn't read it," Francis replied, his face blank with shock. "She tried to tell me about how Victor was treating her, but I found it difficult to believe. Everything was happening at once, and I just brushed her off."

Thomas set his mouth in a grim line, frustrated with Francis' lack of action. Whilst he could understand the man's difficulties, this kind of thing should not have been ignored. From the contents of the letter, Thomas could only imagine what might be facing Emily when she returned. "What are you going to do, Francis?"

Francis felt both guilt and shame hit him with full force. He had let his beloved sister head back to a monster and had not even tried to stop her. His failure to act might be causing her yet more trouble, and he winced at the thought. He knew he needed to think clearly, though try as he might to shake it, he still felt engulfed in a thick emotional fog. The previous few days had relieved much of his stress over his newfound position, but his head was overrun with charting and managing all the duties he had ahead of him.

"I suppose I should ride there myself and fetch her home," he said, a little slowly as his thoughts came tumbling one after the other. "But Victor is her husband after all and might very well turn me away. He has full rights over her of course, until a divorce is granted."

"*If* a divorce is granted, you mean," Thomas muttered, keenly aware of how difficult such a thing could be, particularly for the women.

"So what can I do?" Francis asked, helplessly. "I cannot leave my estate for long, given that I have only just taken on the title, and I simply cannot leave my mother and sisters either."

"What about Henry? Or Charles?"

Francis shook his head. "Whilst I love my brothers dearly, they are both hot headed and would most likely call Victor out and then be hung on the gallows themselves should they kill him!"

Thomas sighed heavily, getting up from his seat and beginning to pace the room. Francis was right. He could not leave the estate for long, and they needed time to consider how to take Emily away from Victor's clutches without his knowledge. Rubbing a hand down his face, he turned slowly back to face Francis, an idea in mind. "I'll go."

"What?"

"I said, I'll go."

Francis stared at him for a moment, a little relieved, but trying not to show it. "You, Thomas? But what about your own estate?"

Thomas shrugged. "It is in good hands; my steward is quite capable. An extended absence will not be too difficult, I shouldn't think."

"Well, that would be most appreciated," Francis replied, getting to his feet. "Emily needs to be protected, but I am not sure how you will go about that."

"I'll think of a way," Thomas replied, grimly, shaking Francis' hand. "Be assured I will write to you often until I am able to take Emily away."

"Are you going to leave immediately?"

"I am," he replied, walking towards the door. "When did she leave?"

"The day you arrived," Francis replied, a sick feeling in his stomach as he thought how much Emily would have already had to endure by the time Thomas arrived.

"Then all the more reason for me to leave with all speed," Thomas declared, pulling open the door. "Excuse me, Francis."

"Thank you," Francis called, just as the door closed. The feeling of shame had not quite left him yet, but he was slightly relieved that something was being done. He just hoped Thomas would be able to help Emily in some way, very soon.

CHAPTER 5

E mily picked up her embroidery once more, feeling the side of her face throb with pain. Her hands were shaking, and she was barely able to pull a single stitch through the material, terrified after her last encounter with her husband. Putting the embroidery hoop in her lap, she pressed shaking hands to the sides of her face, drawing in three long breaths. She felt trapped, as though the walls were slowly closing in and there was nothing she could do about it. Victor's anger had been sudden and unexpected, all because she had not come to his study quickly enough after he had sent the butler to find her. Ever since she had returned from her family's home, he had grown obsessive and suspicious of her, as though he suspected that she had told Francis or her mother about her troubles. Of course, Emily had denied it over and over again, but Victor had never once believed her. Regardless of his distrust, there was nothing Emily could do. Francis had refused to help her – refused to even believe her – and there was nowhere she could escape to. So often she had considered her predicament, wondering where she could run, where Victor would never be able to find her, but not once had she found a solution. Returning to Francis was her only option, and even then, Victor could demand her return whereupon she *and* Francis would have no other recourse but to obey his orders. The moment she'd spoken her wedding vows, she'd become just another one of his possessions. She had no rights, and, as such, no means of escape.

"Lord Markham, my lady."

Startled, Emily rose to her feet, her embroidery falling to the ground with a clatter. Brushing it under the chair with her foot, she stared as Thomas Markham walked through the door. It was some time since she had seen him, but she recognized his face, with notable piercing blue eyes and a gentleman's features.

"Lady Thurston," Thomas said grandly, sweeping a bow. "I must apologize for calling on you without any notice, but my carriage has broken down!"

"Lord Markham," Emily replied, her heart pounding furiously as she wondered with horror if he could see the bruise on her face. "Please, sit down." Indicating a chair to her left, she positioned herself so that the unmarked side of her face was towards him. "Tea, Jones, and then please insure Lord Thurston is aware of Lord Markham's arrival the moment he gets back home."

"Of course, my lady," the butler replied, turning to leave the room.

"And please send Mavis in," Emily continued, turning back to Lord Markham with a smile which she had hastily pasted on her face. Knowing that Victor would be furious to find her ensconced with any gentleman, she prayed that the maid, Mavis, would arrive swiftly. Even though she was a married woman, she did not want to further Victor's anger.

"You say your carriage has broken down?" she asked. "How terrible!"

"Indeed," Thomas replied, keeping his face cheerful. "I was coming to look over some property in the area, you see, but the mud has damaged one of my carriage wheels quite beyond repair, I believe!" Having ignored the sudden lurch of his heart on seeing the lady's beauty, he continued to study her features. He had met her on a few occasions in the past, but she had, at the time, been one of Francis' many sisters, and he had not taken much notice. Although how he could have failed to notice her was quite beyond his own understanding! Her dark auburn hair was carefully arranged, although a few small tendrils had escaped from their confinement and fluttered around her face. Her green eyes were emeralds, sparkling and gleaming, and he felt again the swift kick of desire. Her face was gentle, and there was a kindness in her eyes that had not yet been put out by the wrath of her overbearing brute of a husband. Realizing that she was speaking, he forced himself to listen carefully instead of focusing on her loveliness.

"I am quite sure Victor will ask you to stay the moment he hears of your predicament," Emily continued, catching the way he was gazing at her. "How fortunate that we are in the area!"

"I would be most grateful," Thomas replied, having decided not to share his true reason for calling on them. "My carriage will take some days to fix, but I would not wish to take advantage of your hospitality!"

She smiled at him. "Not at all, Lord Markham. It will be our pleasure to have you here."

The door opened, startling them both, and in strode Lord Victor Thurston, followed by the maid. Closing her eyes for a brief moment, and wishing that Mavis had come in before Victor, she brightened her smile and got to her feet. "Victor, this is Lord Thomas Markham, a friend of my family."

Victor did not even glance at her, keeping his eye on the intruder in his home. Narrowing his gaze a little, he took him in.

"A pleasure to meet you," Thomas began, aware of the man's scrutiny. "Your wife has been most accommodating, I assure you. She is a credit to you, Lord Thurston."

"I am sure she has been accommodating," Victor remarked, dryly, throwing an angry glance at his wife which Thomas caught. Seeing the way that Emily's face flamed, and how she looked down at her feet, his anger grew, but he kept his smile firmly on his face and directed toward Victor.

"I was just telling Lady Thurston that my carriage has broken down, which is the only reason I called upon you without any notice. I must sincerely apologize, Lord Thurston."

Victor lifted his chin, trying to get the measure of the man. "Not at all," he replied, a little stiffly. "The roads around here are often impassable."

"Quite!" Thomas laughed, the sound loosening the tension in the room a little. "How fortunate for me that I should find myself close to my friend's sister and her husband! Francis has told me all about you," he continued, wondering if flattery would break the man's icy demeanor. "I must say, I am quite interested in how you have managed to make your estate so profitable in such a short time!"

Victor frowned. "You learned this from Francis?"

"Yes, yes," Thomas continued, blithely. "I am aware that you have a long-standing friendship with the man; he speaks very highly of you."

"Does he?" Victor replied, his brows lifting a little. "I had not realized that."

"You know how Francis is," Thomas blustered. "He keeps things close to his chest. Regardless, I had every intention of sending a note to ask if I could call on you, as I have often been desirous of having an acquaintance with you of my own."

"Indeed?" Victor exclaimed, the man's adulation puffing up his pride and melting his cool regard. "In that case, I am delighted to welcome you into our home."

Thomas ensured he looked delighted, keeping up the charade. "Thank you, Thurston. It is most kind of you." He glanced over at Emily, seeing her eyes firmly on her husband.

"And you must stay," Victor continued, sitting down opposite Thomas. "Until your carriage is fixed, if not longer!"

Thomas stared at the man as though he could not quite believe the honor he was receiving. "How kind of you, Thurston! I gladly accept for I have a great many questions and would be vastly interested in learning all about your estate."

Victor grinned, feeling well satisfied by Thomas's admiration. "I am most happy to oblige." Getting up, he poured himself and Thomas a glass of port, ignoring his wife completely even though he could have easily rung for tea. Sitting back down, he began to talk about his estate, going right back to when he had assumed the title. His voice was loud and boastful, making Thomas cringe inwardly. Victor continued on and on, his presence filling the room.

Sitting back in his chair, Thomas relaxed, his first task completed and completed well. He allowed Victor to prattle on about his estate, nodding and smiling and making the usual interested sounds, whilst throwing the occasional glance towards Emily, his concern for her mounting. She was sitting quietly, her hands in her lap and head bowed as if frozen in place. He had seen her fearful reaction when her husband had first entered, shrinking back in her chair as though trying to hide herself. A sudden stream of light through the windows caught her face, and Thomas bit back a gasp of alarm. Her face was well bruised along the side she had kept turned away from him.

CHAPTER 6

Thomas did not see Emily again until dinner. He noticed that her hair had been artfully styled to hide the bruise which, by now, was probably a little more obvious. However, her beauty still took his breath away, and when she smiled at him in greeting, his heart stopped for a single moment before picking up a much faster pace than before. Being drawn to another man's wife was never something Thomas had allowed himself to feel, but with Emily, he could not push his attraction away no matter how hard he tried. He didn't even know her as of yet, but something about her compelled him to want to know what lay behind her smile. More than anything, Thomas wished to get to know Emily - but with Victor already chattering away, it appeared that he was going to have to seek Emily out at a later time.

Emily continued to watch Lord Markham, from under lowered lashes. After their earlier meeting, she had endured Victor berating her for over an hour, even though she had been sitting with Lord Markham alone for only a few minutes. Her husband had roared on and on at her, his face often only inches from hers, whilst she had sat completely still without a single word of response in the hope that he would not touch her. To her very great relief, he had not laid a finger on her, and she wondered whether Lord Markham's presence prevented him from doing so. He had ordered her to 'hide the mark,' gesturing to her face with a hint of revulsion as though she disgusted him, even though it was he who had caused it in the first place. Mavis, her maid, had come to arrange her hair, full of apology for not arriving sooner when Lord Markham had arrived. Emily had waved her apology away, assuring the maid that it was not her fault in any way. Emily supposed it was something of a blessing that she had found a friend in Mavis. Whilst she was not often allowed out to socialize, she had found her maid something of a confidante which was a blessing indeed. She had someone to talk to instead of keeping all her troubles hidden within. From Mavis, Emily learned that it was not only she who was afraid of her husband, but a tremor of anxiety and trepidation also ran through the staff. She could even now see it in the face of the footman who was currently serving Victor, an unease rooted in deep fear of his employer. Emily cringed slightly as she saw Lord Markham spot it as well. What must he think of them?

"I was sorry to hear of your father's recent passing."

Thomas's voice broke into her thoughts and, glancing for a moment at Victor, she murmured her thanks.

"He was a good man, your father."

"He was," Emily replied after a moment. "I believe my mother is due to move to the Dower house very soon." She cast another anxious glance at Victor but saw, to her relief, that he did not seem put off by her conversation.

Thomas's face grew sympathetic. "And how is Francis getting on assuming the title?" Having chosen to give the impression to Victor that he had not gone near Emily's family home, he asked the question with a completely blank expression on his face.

Emily smiled, ignoring the stab of resentment and hurt that came from hearing Francis' name. "I am sure, after a time, he will do very well."

"It always takes some time to adjust," Thomas replied, his eyes catching the flash of pain on her face. Clearly, she was still hurt by

Francis' refusal to help, and Thomas was looking forward to seeing her face when he told her his true reason for being here.

"Indeed," Victor drawled, interrupting the conversation. "I too found it most difficult when my father died, although, as you know, I have managed to take everything on exceptionally well."

Thomas managed to prevent himself from rolling his eyes, instead turning back to the man with a smile. "You have indeed," he replied, almost deferentially. "I am looking forward to learning what I can from you."

"Of course, of course," Victor replied, sitting back with an air of authority. "In fact, we have lots to discuss. Emily, why don't you retire?"

"Retire?" Emily asked, after a moment. "You wish me to retire... now?"

Victor sat up a little straighter, fixing her with a stare. "Yes. Now."

Beyond humiliated, Emily felt her cheeks heat as she rose from the table. She had not even had the entire dinner but her husband was literally demanding that she leave the dining room and retire to her room. Lord Markham said nothing, and she could not even look at him as she left.

"Just as well," she heard her husband say, as the door closed behind her. "Got very little between the ears, that one."

Thomas tried to laugh at Victor's comment, as he assumed he was expected to, but found himself barely able to do anything other than growl. The man had humiliated Lady Thurston, and the look on her face had almost made him leap from his chair and plant a facer on the man. Why he had not said anything, he did not know - perhaps the shock of Thurston's dismissal of his wife had taken him so much by surprise that he had found himself struck dumb with shock. Now he had to spend the remainder of the evening making conversation with a man he could barely tolerate, whilst pretending that he both admired and respected him. Wanting nothing more than race to find Emily - Lady Thurston, he reminded himself - he had to content himself with the knowledge that he could see her and apologize to her in the morning.

Emily covered her face with her hands, hoping it would cover the sound of her sobs as she made her way back to her room. She was humiliated, shame heating her cheeks and pushing the angry tears from her eyes. They had not often had guests, and she had not expected Victor to treat her so poorly, particularly not in front of so respected a gentleman as Lord Markham.

Managing to reach the confines of her room, she was met by a surprised Mavis, who took in her mistress's distress in one swift moment, coming over to comfort her almost immediately. Soon, Emily was sitting at her dressing table changed into her nightgown while Mavis brushed her hair with long, smooth strokes.

"What did he do, Miss?"

Emily swallowed the lump in her throat. "He dismissed me, Mavis. In front of our guest." A single tear slipped down her cheek. "Expected me to obey without a word of complaint... which I did, of course." Her fingers gently touched the bruise on her cheek, which was all the more prominent now that her hair was pulled back.

"It ain't right," Mavis commented, her eyes burning with anger over the treatment her beloved mistress was enduring.

"What can I do?" Emily continued, her face hopeless. "He is my husband." For some reason, a part of her had hoped that Lord Markham would say something, but he had remained silent. She had not looked at him but found herself wondering whether she would have seen outrage or sympathy in his eyes had she looked. She found herself quite attracted to the man, having almost forgotten what desire felt like. His dark hair had gleamed in the candlelight, and she felt herself being scrutinized by his ever-watchful blue eyes. There was something about him, as though she were a book that he was dying to read. Giving herself a slight shake, she looked at herself in the mirror, trying to rid her mind of the man. The idea of such a thing was a fool's fantasy.

"It seems Lord Markham is to have an extended stay," she said, seeing Mavis's eyebrows disappear into her hairline. "I know, I was quite shocked, to say the least, but it seems he is quite taken with my husband's estate management skills." She shook her head a little, wondering what on earth a man such as Lord Markham could learn from her husband. Whilst she knew Victor managed the estate well, his tenants and staff were all afraid of him, and that was not a trait she wanted Lord Markham to emulate.

"At least it seems my husband will not come near me whilst Lord Markham is here," she said, softly, noting Mavis' look of sympathy. "That in itself should be a blessing."

"It should not be happening at all," Mavis replied, ever defensive. "Maybe Lord Markham will be able to help you, my lady. Have you considered speaking to him? You did tell me that he was a particular friend of your brother's?"

Emily considered Mavis' suggestion for a moment, before eventually dismissing it.

"As much as I am searching for any escape from my husband's cruelty, I do not think my brother's friend would be particularly desirous to help me. Considering how much he appears to admire my husband, I do not think he would be willing to even listen to me!" If only Francis had considered her words instead of brushing her off immediately, things might be a little more hopeful, but as it was, there was nothing she could do but bear her husband's cruel taunts and violence. Sighing, she touched her cheek once more. At least there would be no more bruises, for the time being.

CHAPTER 7

T homas made an effort to rise early, hoping that perhaps Lady Thurston would be breakfasting. He was in luck. Rising to greet him, Thomas murmured a greeting, noticing her pale face and the way her eyes would not quite meet his. He felt a stab of sympathy for her, unable to imagine how she must feel having been treated so poorly by Victor. Thomas served himself a few items and sat opposite the lady, trying to send a smile her way but getting very little response.

"I must apologize to you, my lady, for ignoring your plight last evening."

Completely astonished, Emily lifted her gaze to Lord Markham's face. What had he just said?

"Your husband, if you'll forgive me, was unpardonably rude towards you and, as a gentleman, I should have said something."

Emily's mouth dropped open, and she stared at Lord Markham for a long moment. Was he sincerely apologizing?

"Th-thank you," she stammered, her cheeks tinging a little pink.

"I hope you were not too embarrassed," Thomas continued, smiling at her reaction. "I confess to being quite surprised myself, which is the reason I did not speak up sooner."

"Please, do not trouble yourself," Emily replied, her voice soft. "It is not your concern, Lord Markham although I appreciate your apology. My husband is not always a considerate man."

Thomas lifted his eyebrows. "That appears to be something of an understatement, my lady."

Emily dropped her gaze and looked away, unsure as to how to respond. She could not altogether trust this man and did not want him to repeat anything she said to Victor. It would be worse for her that way.

"Lady Thurston," Thomas began, seeing that they were almost alone, bar a footman or two. "I must speak with you in private. It is about Francis."

"Francis?" Emily's eyes once more flew to his, her face a picture of surprise. "I thought you said you had not seen him?"

"I lied," Thomas said, simply. "Victor does not need to know, I think."

Emily's mind was whirring, staring at Lord Markham with astonishment. "What do you mean?"

Thomas opened his mouth to reply, only for the door to swing open and Victor to saunter in.

"Good morning, Markham!" he cried, remarkably cheerful. "How are you this fine morning?"

"I am well, I thank you," Thomas replied, smiling broadly and back to his usual camaraderie with the man. "I was just asking your lovely wife if she would like to join me for a horse ride this morning!" He kept his gaze on Victor, hoping that Emily would play along. "After all, I am sure you will be vastly busy with the estate business this morning, perhaps you can show me what you have been doing this afternoon? I am sure Lady Thurston will be able to show me your magnificent grounds!"

Emily, still slightly astonished by all that was going on, remembered to smile just as her husband turned his gaze on her.

"Of course, I did say to Lord Markham that I would have to ask your permission first!"

Victor eyed his wife suspiciously for a moment before turning back to Markham.

"Indeed, I am busy with my steward this morning and would be delighted to see you this afternoon in my study. There is much for you to learn!"

"How wonderful," Thomas replied, sighing a little dramatically. "I am sure that, after my stay here, my estate will benefit quite remarkably from your insight, Thurston. And, of course, I will need to tell my friends about your intelligence and insight. I am quite sure a great many number of them will want to visit after I have told them what I have learned."

Victor puffed up like a peacock, all concern over his wife riding with Lord Markham completely forgotten. "Shall we say three o'clock then?"

"Excellent!"

Thomas indicated to the footman to pour him more coffee, whilst Victor strutted over to the long table to procure some food for himself.

"Shall we say in an hour?" Thomas asked, his voice as quiet as possible.

Emily looked at him, still a little confused. "At the stables?"

He nodded quickly, before leaning back in his chair, just as Victor returned to the table. Picking up the thread of their discussion once more, Thomas watched Emily as she gracefully rose from the table and took her leave.

One hour later, and Thomas found Emily already astride her mare, looking particularly fetching in a deep purple habit, so dark it was almost black as was expected from someone in mourning. Her hair was in perfect ringlets, which bounced a little as her mare stamped impatiently; however her eyes were watching him intently. Seeing that she had already asked for a horse to be prepared for him, he leaped into the saddle with ease, taking the reins and following along the path. They rode in silence away from the stables and he noticed for the first time that her hair shone with garnet jewel-tones in the sunlight.

"You said something about Francis?" Emily asked the moment they were alone. She studied his face as he responded, wondering if that was true honesty in his eyes.

"I saw Francis before I came here," Thomas replied, not holding anything back. "He told me of your predicament, and I came to help."

Emily said nothing, turning her face away from him. If that was the case, then Francis was even more of a let-down than she had first thought. "And what, exactly, did he tell you?"

Thomas shook his head at her disbelieving tone. "Lady Thurston, I should say that I found your letter."

"Letter?" She frowned at him for a moment, trying to work out what he was talking about.

"The one your husband sent you."

Her face grew red. "Oh." She wilted a little in her seat. "That was not meant for your eyes."

Thomas smiled sympathetically. "And yet, I found it. Francis and I had some heated words, and I am to convey his deepest apologies to you, my lady."

"Francis is sorry for what he did?" *Or did not do,* she thought to herself.

"Precisely."

They rode on for a few moments in silence. "Why then, is he not here?"

Thomas sighed a little heavily. "Your mother is moving to the Dower house and taking a large number of the current staff with her. This means that Francis now has more to do in order to keep the house running smoothly. And, if I may be frank, he was not coping with his new responsibilities very well."

"He did find it quite a difficult burden," Emily murmured, her heart softening a little towards him. "It was all such a shock, you see. Father seemed to be in the most perfect of health, and then, all of a sudden, Francis had to assume the title."

"That is why he sent for me," Thomas explained. "I was helping and advising him as I can understand the situation he is in, and a lot of how he feels."

"That was very generous of you, my lord." Emily studied Thomas

Markham for a moment, smiling softly at him. He appeared to be a very kind man, having helped her brother so, and now, apparently coming to help her. Although, at the moment, she could not quite imagine what he intended to do. His eyes were warm as he smiled back at her, and she felt a flushed curling in her stomach as he continued to gaze at her. Something passed between them that made Emily shiver all over and, dropping her eyes, she turned her head back to face the path.

"I cannot imagine what it is that you intend to do to help me, Lord Markham," she began, after a few moments. "Francis was correct when he said that I belong to Victor and that he can simply demand my return."

Thomas's jaw clenched. "That man does not deserve someone like you, Lady Thurston. The way he treats you…" He shook his head, his intense gaze on her once more. "However long it takes, I will take you away from this place and away from him. I promise you that."

Emily could not look directly at him with that statement, but a flutter ran through her that she could not quite define, a suppressed wellspring of tears at the idea of freedom, a hope-filled relief that she was no longer alone, and also an acute apprehension of getting her hope's dashed if he could not come through on his word.

An hour later, Emily and Thomas arrived back at the stable, both jumping down from their mounts. They had spent an enjoyable time together, and Emily was surprised to find that the man made her laugh. He was a cheerful, quick-witted gentleman, and she could not remember the last time she had enjoyed herself so much. She watched him with a shy smile as he ran a hand through his dark hair, pushing it back from his forehead. He was a handsome man, and Emily found herself quite attracted to him. Without hesitation, as she was caught up in their conversation, she took his arm and together they walked back into the house.

She did not see the scowling face of her husband at the window, nor the furious glare that fixed on her as she walked, laughing and smiling, into the house on Lord Markham's arm.

CHAPTER 8

"How *dare* you?"

Whirling around, Emily stared in the dark face of her husband, who ordered Mavis from the room and then slammed the door firmly behind her.

"I said, how dare you, Emily!"

"What did I do?" Emily asked, her voice barely above a whisper as she backed away from him slowly. "I didn't do anything, Victor."

"Oh yes, you did," he breathed, advancing closer. His eyes were narrowed, his face red and chest heaving. "I saw you with Lord Markham, flirting and toying with him!"

"Flirting?" Emily gasped. "Victor, I did no such thing."

"Don't lie to me!" he screamed, spittle flying from his mouth. "I saw you, my dear wife! I saw you!"

With her back against the wall and nowhere else to go, Emily felt herself begin to shake furiously.

"Victor, please."

Sneering, he grabbed her arm viciously, his nails digging into her skin. "Trying to make a cuckold of me, were you?"

"No," she whispered. "Victor, please, you're hurting me."

"Trying to get him to take you away from me, then," he said, his breath hot on her face. "Were you running to him with all your little tales of woe?" He grabbed her other arm, forcing them bodily behind her back, her hands scraping against the wall. "I've seen how he looks at you, my dear, and I am certain that you decided to play to your advantage!" He kissed her then, before biting her lip so hard he drew blood. "I won't be toyed with, Emily!"

He backhanded her so she fell across the bed, her face and eye screaming with pain.

"He'll not be taking you anywhere," he screamed, his eyes wide. "He's my guest! He is here to admire me and not you. Don't you go anywhere near him again. No roving eyes, no smiles, no flirtations – or it will be the worse for you!"

Emily drew in a shaking breath, sitting up carefully and wincing from the pain.

"I understand, Victor," she replied numbly, knowing that a quiet and condescending answer was the best way to get him to leave her alone. "I won't go riding with him again, I swear."

"See that you don't," he growled, his eyes still flashing. His rage taken out on her, he began to leave the room, stopping at the door. "I think you have a headache my dear. It will be best for you to stay in your rooms for the rest of the day, I should imagine. Perhaps even tomorrow as well. Just until you recover."

"Very well," Emily whispered, knowing that by ordering her to do so, it would give her face enough time to heal before she saw Lord Markham again. Watching her husband leave the room, she finally gave in to the threatening flood, deep sobs racking her body as she curled up into a ball on her bed.

Thomas was a little surprised that Lady Thurston had not joined them for luncheon or for dinner, but accepted Lord Thurston's excuse that she had a headache and needed to rest.

"Gives us more time to discuss your endeavors here," he commented, seeing the smirk on Thurston's face and the gleam in his eye at Thomas's flattery. He wanted nothing more than to excuse himself and rush to Emily's rooms to ensure she was quite well, but knew that it would be the worst thing he could do. The last thing he wanted to do was to raise Thurston's suspicions and so, he played the part and endured many, many hours in the man's company. He continued to flatter and admire the man, realizing it was possibly the only way Thurston would allow him to remain a guest in his house. The very moment Thurston suspected that he was here for any other reason that than to learn from him, Thomas was sure he'd be thrown out on his ear.

He made sure Thurston drank glass after glass of port, until, finally, Victor decided it was time for him to retire. The man could barely walk, so Thomas was more than happy to help him to his chambers, knowing that he would sleep soundly. He even helped Thurston to his bed, the man closing his eyes almost as soon as he lay down.

Thomas shook his head, his lip curling in disgust. The man was a monster, a completely heartless and selfish creature who thrived on controlling his wife and his servants with an iron rod. Pulling the bedchamber door shut, he heard Thurston begin to snore and, quickly getting his bearings, took off along one of the corridors. The estate was large but, having quizzed one of the servants earlier that day, he knew exactly where Lady Thurston's chambers were. He did not know whether or not she would be sleeping, but there had been something in Thurston's tone when he'd spoken of his wife that made him concerned. She had not complained of any headache when they had been out for a ride together that morning, and he suspected there was more to the story than Thurston was willing to share.

Emily lay on her bed, pressing the cool compress to her face. Mavis had taken care of her, as she always did, and she was under strict instructions to keep the compress against the side of her face and, in particularly, over her eye so that the bruising would be minimal. There was a bowl of cool water on her dressing table and, having just rinsed the compress, Emily closed her eyes and allowed her mind to quieten. Victor had hurt her face, arms, and hands, all because she had gone riding with Lord Markham. It wasn't safe for her here anymore. She had to stay away from the man so that Victor would have no reason to do the same again.

Any hope she had that he would be able to rescue her from his clutches died with the realization that Victor would never let her go. In fact, she suspected that he would do anything to prevent her leaving him. His need to control and possess was too great. The thought made her shudder all over, goosebumps running up and down her arms as she thought of what Victor might do to her.

She would have to find Markham somehow, convince him to leave her alone. Thinking about him made her tremble inside, the thought of his handsome face smiling at her bringing both a surge of warmth and a stab of pain. For one brief moment, she had considered him her savior, allowing the sudden attraction she felt for him to have its freedom over her mind and heart. Now, she needed to forget all of that, to put it aside, to let it wither and die within her. Whilst she appreciated that Lord Markham had come to try and help her, she needed to send him away. It was safer for them both that way.

A sudden light tap at the door startled her, as she got to her feet, wiping away an escaping tear. Had Victor returned? No. He would not tap so lightly, rather he would be hammering on her door until she opened it to allow his entry. She had sent Mavis away hours ago, so who was this knocking on her door so late at night?

"Who's there?" she called, timidly, throwing her wrapper on quickly.

"Markham."

"Markham?" she whispered, her breath catching in her chest. What could he be doing here so late at night? Why had he come?

"Please, let me in," she heard him say, his voice sounding a little urgent. "I must speak with you."

Her heart hammering in her chest, Emily walked to the door, her fingers slipping a little on the key as she turned it. Opening the door, she stepped back to allow Lord Markham entry, closing the door and locking it again just in case her husband should come knocking.

"Why are you here?" she asked, turning to face him. Her breath was coming quick and fast, both from surprise, fear and the rush of desire she felt for the man who was now standing in her bedchamber. "Has something happened?"

Thomas knew immediately that this had been a mistake. She was in her night things, and the sudden longing to take her in his arms was almost overwhelming. Taking a step closer, he noticed her face in the flickering candlelight.

"What did he do to you?" he breathed, his hand coming out to trace her bruised skin. Touching her face, he saw her eyes light with something he could not quite make out.

"It does not matter," Emily managed to reply, taking a step back and away from his tender touch. "We cannot be in one another's company again without Victor present. It is too dangerous."

"Don't say that," Thomas growled, moving closer once more. "You know we must find a solution to —"

"There can be no solution," she cried, her eyes now wet. "Victor is too possessive, too controlling. He will not let me out of his sight and certainly never alone with you." She shook her head, tears dropping from her eyes. "I thank you for your desire to help me," she whispered, her gaze dropping to the floor. "But it is quite hopeless."

Thomas looked at her for a long time, his hands curling into fists. "It is never hopeless," he replied, his voice firm. "We will find a way, Emily."

"No," she began, looking up at him with despair. "There is no way out."

"There is always a way," he replied, catching her up in his arms. Looking into her glimmering green eyes for a long moment, and seeing the wonder on her face, he lowered his head and kissed her firmly, feeling her melt in his arms.

CHAPTER 9

E mily broke the kiss, staring up into Thomas's face briefly, before returning her lips to his. There was an urgency in his kiss as a fire grew between them. Emily's breathing grew quick and fast, her heart pounding in her chest as Thomas continued to kiss her with a passion and intensity she had never experienced before.

What was he doing? Everything in Thomas's mind was screaming at him to stop, to think carefully before going along this path, but his reaction to her was too strong. She was beauty itself, inside and out, and he could not let her go. Ignoring the warning within him, he crushed her against him, allowing his strength to hold her up as tentatively, her hands moved into his hair. He groaned against her mouth, knowing he had to pull away. Lifting his head, he watched her eyes focus on him after a long moment as though she was just regaining her equilibrium. She looked dazed, her cheeks flushed and her breathing a little ragged.

"I'm sorry," Thomas began, but to his surprise, she quietened him immediately.

"I do not love my husband if that is what you are concerned about," Emily said, firmly, not lifting her eyes from his face. "Please, don't say that you regret this."

Thomas ran a hand through his hair, moving away from her to sit in a chair beside the fire. "I don't regret it at all. To be truthful, I have found you a most… interesting woman from the second we met."

"Interesting?" She regarded him with one arched brow.

He glanced away from her, his cheeks heating a little. "You are a most beautiful woman, Lady Thurston."

Emily blew out a long breath. "Thank you," she said, softly, moving to sit opposite him. She did not know what else to say, watching him carefully as he, eventually, lifted his gaze back to her face.

"Why ever did you marry him?"

"I thought he loved me, once," she said, simply. "And, foolish girl that I was, I thought I loved him. It was soon after our wedding that I realized the monster that he really was."

Thomas shook his head, his lips tightening as he saw her bruised face once more. "You cannot stay here, Lady Thurston."

"Please," she replied, quickly. "There is no name I hate more than Lady Thurston. Won't you call me Emily?"

Thomas looked at her for a long moment, his eyes betraying his feelings as he took her name on his lips. "Emily."

Emily sat back in her chair, her heart swelling with happiness. "You are my savior, then, Lord Markham, is that to be the case?"

"I hope to be, Emily," he whispered, getting to his feet and taking her again in his arms. "Can you trust me to find a way for you to escape him?"

"I can," she breathed, even though Victor's words caused the hairs to prick up along her skin. "You must be careful, though, my lord. For both our sakes."

"Call me Thomas, please," he replied, lifting her chin with one gentle hand.

Emily smiled softly, her eyes fluttering closed as she whispered his name. His tender kiss soothed her mind, and calmed her soul, and was the only thing she thought of as she finally went to bed.

Thomas walked back to his room, his steps light and a smile on his face. Hearing Victor's loud snores, he reassured himself that they had not been overhead and made his way back to his room with confidence. He had not intended to kiss Emily, but his body had responded before he could even think about stopping himself. She had been so vulnerable, and the need to protect her had overwhelmed him. He had wanted to kill Thurston for treating his wife in such a cruel manner, but sense told him that getting himself hung on the gallows for murder would not be the wisest choice. For the time being, he would have to content himself with listening to Thurston drone on and on about his amazing achievements, whilst coming up with some kind of solution that would take Emily away from him forever.

Over the next week, Thomas and Emily continued to meet whenever they could away from Victor's prying eyes. It was difficult to get more than a few moments alone, given how protective Victor was of his wife. Thankfully he had not laid another hand on her since, and Emily was at least grateful for that. Still, she was constantly aware of his watchful eyes on her, feeling trapped within her own house. Her only solace were the brief encounters she stole with Thomas, where they exchanged a few words and a brief touch or two. Anything more would put them both in danger of Victor's wrath.

"Can you meet me in the rose garden this afternoon?" Thomas whispered under his breath.

Emily glanced up from her embroidery, nodding quickly in acknowledgment as Victor continued to waffle on as he walked towards the drawing room windows. Thomas smiled in response, pretending to focus on what Victor was saying and forcing himself not to even look in Emily's direction as Victor walked back towards him.

He had been thinking hard over the last few days about how best to help Emily and could only come up with one way. She had to run away. Victor was not going to let her go without a fight, and divorce was simply not an option. Thomas knew it would be a long and arduous process and, even with witnesses such as himself, there was no guarantee that it would be granted. In fact, it might do Emily more harm than good to even attempt such a thing. Therefore, the only idea he had was that she run away with him. Thomas had a small estate in Scotland, and whilst it was certainly remote, it would save Emily from a lifetime of misery and pain. He hoped she would agree, for arrangements would need to be made soon. He was wearing out his welcome having stayed so long, and he did not want to make Victor suspicious.

"Quite, quite," he commented, seeing Victor study him as though waiting for a response. "I could not agree more, man."

Victor, apparently satisfied, then continued to talk about his recent developments in his crops and how he kept the ground fertile year after year. Thomas nodded with apparent interest, all the while wondering whether Emily would accept his proposition and escape with him to Scotland.

Victor kept up his chatter whilst keeping one eye on his wife. She was smiling to herself, although with her head bent over her sewing, he suspected that she thought he could not see her. Markham was not paying her the least bit of attention, but even that roused his suspicion. He had seen the way Markham had looked at his wife when he had first arrived, so the idea that he now did not even notice her seemed far too ridiculous a notion.

Walking over to the drawing room windows, he was sure he heard Markham mumble something but, when he turned, Markham was yawning, covering his mouth with his hand and Emily was continuing with her sewing as though nothing had happened. Keeping up his conversation, Victor wandered back over to his guest, noting with a rising sense of distrust, that his wife's cheeks were now slightly pink. Something was going on right under his nose, and the idea filled him with rage.

Ensuring his face was calm and serene, Victor proposed to fetch Markham a glass of port, pouring himself one also. It gave him enough time to calm himself, taking a few deep breaths before turning back to his guest and handing him the glass. The best way to find out exactly what was going on was to follow his wife, and Victor had every intention of not letting her out of his sight for the remainder of the day.

CHAPTER 10

Emily felt her heart beat furiously as she made her way to the rose garden, glancing all around her as if Victor might jump out at her from any direction. He had, for some inexplicable reason, wandered off to his study when he had been her constant shadow for the last few days. There was a warning in her heart that Victor was up to something, but she could not refuse Thomas. She had to see him, had to be able to touch his hands, to see his eyes smiling at her. To feel cared for, appreciated, even loved, dare she think it. It was more than anything she had ever received from Victor, and it was a whole new life for her. It made her feel worthwhile, valued, and esteemed. She just hoped that Thomas had found some way for them to leave Victor behind for good.

"Thomas?"

"Emily!" He rushed to her, pulling her into his arms and crushing her against him. He buried his face into her hair, feeling her arms around his neck and finally, in one moment, completely whole. "I've missed being able to hold you like this," he breathed against her ear, pulling back to look into her eyes. His hands moved to cup her face, and he kissed her, hard, feeling her respond immediately. Her fingers ran through his hair, and a small pool of moisture escaped from the corner of her eye.

"Why are you crying?" he whispered, feeling the dampness on his cheek. "What's wrong?"

Emily shook her head, smiling though still more tears fell. "I've just been waiting for you, for so long, it seems. It feels like an age." She wasn't making sense, she realized, trying to explain once more. "For so long I've been trapped with him, and, until you came along, I had no hope. No chance of ever escaping." Leaning forward, she rested her head on his chest. "I didn't ever expect to care for you as much as I do now. You're saving me, Thomas, bit by bit."

Thomas tried to understand, realizing that by taking her away from Victor, he was giving back more than just her freedom. She would no longer be mocked or despised, struggling against the torrents of ridicule and offense that Victor threw her way almost every day. "I want you to come away with me," he murmured, drawing her into a hidden arbor. "Come away with me, Emily."

Emily studied him for a moment. "And where would we go?"

He swallowed hard, knowing that this was going to be his only chance to convince her to be with him. "I have an estate in Scotland." He found he couldn't get any more words out, struggling to explain himself.

"You want me to live there?"

"I do," he managed, taking both her hands in his. "I want you to live there with me."

Emily frowned. "But Victor will not divorce me, Thomas. We would not be able to marry."

Thomas nodded. "You are right, my dear, we would not be able to marry for as long as Victor is alive. Perhaps, in time, he might decide to divorce you himself, perhaps not. But it would not matter to me, I assure you."

"You want me to live with you there, as a mistress of sorts?"

Thomas shook his head vigorously, dropping his hands and running them through his hair in exasperation. "I am not explaining myself very well, am I?" He threw her a rueful look. "I will do whatever it takes, whatever is needed, to get you away from Victor, Emily. I am making no secret of my desire and affection for you – but I will not press it on you, should you decide to live alone until such a time as you are free to marry again."

Emily's eyes widened a little as she finally realized what he was trying to say and what he was offering. "You would give me that estate as my own until I was free to marry you?"

"I am offering it to you outright!" he exclaimed, coming back to face her. "It is yours, Emily, to do with as you wish. In fact, I will sign it over to Francis to make it completely official, if that is what you desire!"

Emily felt her heart swell with a rush of love for the man standing before her. "You would be willing to do that for me? What if I should never wish to marry you?"

"Then that will be your decision," he replied, softly, taking her hands again. "I don't want to be without you, Emily. I find my mind thinking of you at all times of the day and night when I least expect it! I cannot rid you from my mind, or my heart, but no matter what I desire, I want you to be safe, happy, and content. I will live with you in my estate in Scotland, or you may live there alone. Should the time come when you are free to marry, then I will marry you the very same day, if I can!"

Emily laughed softly, one hand quickly covering her widening grin, the other reaching up to gently caress his face.

"Please, tell me you understand," he finished, leaning in to her touch. "Tell me that you will leave this place with me, no matter what else you decide."

"Oh, Thomas," Emily whispered, drawing his face down to hers so she could kiss him again. This time, their kiss grew in intensity, almost overwhelming them both with its passion. They clung to one another, their kiss a meeting of both minds and hearts, a new spark of life spreading through them both.

Thomas stepped back, shaking his head. "The things you do to me, Emily," he gasped, his breath ragged. "You are unlike any other woman I know!"

She laughed, pulling him to her and holding him close again. His arms slipped around her waist, and feeling the frantic beat of his heart, she rested her head on his shoulder.

"Take me away from this place, Thomas," she whispered, lifting her face a little to look into his eyes. "Take me far, far away."

"As far away as Scotland?" he quipped, seeing laughter spark in her eyes.

"As far away as Scotland," she repeated, feeling hopeful for the first time in many years. "Just promise me that you will stay with me there."

Thomas dropped his lips to hers again, just for the briefest moment. "That is my heart's desire," he murmured, holding her just a fraction closer. "I think I am beginning to fall in love with you, Emily."

Emily said nothing, just sighed deeply and, closing her eyes, let herself relax in the warmth and tenderness of his embrace. They stayed there for a long moment, until finally and ever so reluctantly, she lifted her head and stepped back. "I have to go, my love," she whispered, seeing his answering smile as he heard her words of affection. "Victor might soon come looking for me."

"I will make every arrangement," Thomas replied, still holding on to her hand. "Be ready to leave in two days. I will come to your room in the early hours of the morning."

Emily wanted to dance for joy but contented herself with a gentle squeeze of his hand, her heart singing with happiness.

"Thank you, Thomas," she said, before walking away. "I will see you very soon."

Thomas felt himself lean back against the arbor wall. He had told her so much more than he had expected, never once intending to speak to her of the love he had for her. It had been growing for some time, slowly, but surely making its way further and further into his heart. Whilst he found Emily's beauty breath-taking, her character of gentleness and kindness, even in the face of Victor's cruelty, was beyond anything he had expected to find.

She was a pure soul who had managed to cling onto that part of herself, protecting it from Victor's terrifying dominion and rule over her and his estate. Thinking that he had given her enough time, he slowly made his way out from the arbor and back towards the house, beginning to whistle a jaunty tune. There had been no gardeners or any other workers on the grounds, and he was sure that nobody had seen or heard him and Emily.

What he did not see was Victor, watching him through narrowed eyes as he stood, hidden from view, behind the trellis. Whilst he had not heard much of what his wife and Markham had said, his eyes had not hidden the truth from him. Victor was incandescent with rage, clinging onto the rose trellis so hard that the thorns cut deeply into his skin. He had to stop himself from running after Markham and smashing the man about the face, knowing that he would only ensure Emily's departure from his house. He had to be careful and he had to be cunning. That was the only way Markham would leave his house – and Emily, forever.

CHAPTER 11

"Y ou sent for me, Victor?"

Victor, by now quite calm and collected, waved his wife to a seat. Seeing the slight fear in her eyes gave him pleasure and he was quite sure that, by the end of their discussion, Emily would be doing exactly what he asked.

"Have you enjoyed our guest's visit, my dear?"

Immediately, Emily was on her guard, shifting a little in her seat.

"I have not had much chance to speak to him, Victor. In fact, you have taken up most of his time."

"Mmm," Victor mumbled, taking a sip of his port. "Are you quite sure you have not enjoyed his visit?"

Emily felt a nervousness begin to claw its way out of her stomach and up into her chest, causing her breath to quicken.

"What is this about, Victor?" she asked, firmly. Surely, he could not have seen her this afternoon! Thomas had been so careful, and Victor had still been in his study when she'd returned.

Victor sat forward, fixing Emily with a glare. "Do not toy with me, Emily." There was a warning tone in his voice, and Emily struggled to remain calm.

"I have enjoyed his visit," she replied, hopelessly. *Is that what he wants me to say?* she thought to herself. *To admit that I have enjoyed another man's company in place of his?*

"Yes," Victor continued, lifting his glass to his lips once more. He was quite enjoying tormenting her, intending to drag this out for as long as he could. "I believe that you have been enjoying his visit, my dear. Perhaps a little too much?" He arched a brow at her and was delighted to see the flash of shock cross her face. "Ah, yes, you see. I know all about his attentions towards you."

Emily said nothing, shrinking back into her seat. Her face went cold. He knew. How did he know? Had he seen them?

Victor swallowed, before flinging the glass into the fireplace, noting her gasp of fright.

"I have seen you with him, Emily," he ground out, getting to his feet and leaning over the table towards her. "Did you really think me so stupid as to not notice the way the man looks at you?"

Emily opened her mouth but could find nothing to say. Was this it? Was he going to destroy her for good? Would Thomas find her bloodied and battered body on the floor of Victor's study come the morning? Her face drained of color and her entire body began to quake.

"I will not be cuckolded," Victor spat, his eyes blazing with a sudden fury. "What has he promised you, Emily?"

"N – nothing," she whispered, trying desperately to protect Thomas. "Nothing, I swear it."

Victor stared at her, his jaw clenched and wanting nothing more than to slap her silly face until she had no choice but to tell him the truth. But he would not. A mark on her face would have Thomas questioning what he had done, and he needed the man to have no suspicions.

"I know you are lying to me, Emily," he said, softly, his tone changing so drastically that Emily's core trembled. "And you are going to have to make a choice."

"A choice?" Emily whispered, her eyes wide and staring. "What do you mean, Victor?"

"Well," Victor began, enjoying himself immensely. "You are going to have to choose, Emily. The man will not leave unless you order him to go. And you are going to order him to go." He picked up his pistol from the other side of the room and brought it back over to his desk, slamming it down with a thump. "You are going to say whatever you have to in order to get Lord Markham to leave and to leave for good." He leaned over her to look into her face. "Do you understand me?"

She nodded, her eyes on the weapon.

"He is never to return, Emily," Victor continued, running his hand along the barrel of the gun. "Never. You are to give him no expectations, no hope, nothing. Do I make myself clear?"

"You do," she whispered, her gaze frozen to the spot on the desk in front of her. Her choice was not really a choice, she realized. It was either send Thomas away or have him killed. Victor would follow through with his threat; she knew that for certain. He was calculatingly vicious and would very easily explain away a death or cover it up somehow.

Her mind raced with options as she watched Victor's fingers wrap around the walnut pistol grip, his thumb brushing over the intricate metal hammer. Every scenario that flashed before her eyes ended with a shot ringing out. She could not envision any scenario under which she and Thomas could ever leave the property together. As the anxiety of Victor's threat pounded in her chest, the only notion that seemed feasible to her was that she could at least save Thomas. He had come here and risked his safety for her, even before he even knew her truly, and the true love she felt in her heart told her that she must keep him safe at all costs. Her eyes rose to meet those of her husband. With a clenched jaw and steeled eyes, she studied his face without flinching. Going against Victor was a gamble potentially too dangerous to wager.

"Then, I suggest you go and see your beloved Thomas," Victor growled, watching her eyes break from his with a start, before fleeing from the room. He laughed quietly, sitting back down at his desk and pouring himself another glass of port. The victory was his.

"Thomas?"

Hastening to the door, he flung it open, dragging Emily inside. It was late, and Victor could still be skulking around the estate.

"Whatever are you doing here?" He pulled her into his arms, feeling her shake a little. "Is something the matter?"

Emily swallowed hard, pushing herself away from him and steeling herself for what she felt certain she had to do. "I've come to tell you that I've changed my mind, Thomas."

Thomas stared at her for a long moment, his expression changing from surprise to shock then finally to dismay. "What do you mean, you've changed your mind?"

"I mean, I'm not going to run away with you," she replied, fighting to keep her voice steady. "I've decided to stay here."

"What are you talking about?" Thomas exclaimed, trying to take her hands. "Emily, what has he said to you?"

"He's said nothing," she replied, pulling her hands away and taking a few steps back. "I've just decided that I cannot be a societal ruin."

Tension filled the room as Thomas continued to stare at her. She wasn't looking at him, looking everywhere but toward him, if he was honest.

"You would prefer to stay married to Victor than to live with me?"

"Yes."

"But I could give the estate to you, I wouldn't even be there," he began, but Emily cut him off.

"No, Thomas. It wouldn't work. The servants would talk, you know they would. Soon, it would appear that I was just your mistress, even if you gave the estate to me. I cannot have people look down on me so."

It was a feeble excuse, but it was the best she could do, given the circumstances. Her heart was being torn apart with every lie she told, with every word she was barely able to force out, but she had to do it.

Thomas walked towards her, his fists clenching. This was Victor's doing, it had to be. Emily would not have changed her mind so quickly. She was not the kind of woman who cared about such things, surely!

"I don't believe you, Emily," he muttered, pressing her back against the wall. "I know you want to get away from him. I know how you feel about me."

Emily felt her lips trembling at his nearness, but the thought of his blood-soaked body, lying on the ground, steadied her resolve. "I don't love you, Thomas."

An icy chill flooded him. "What did you say?" he whispered, seeing her turn her face away.

"I said, I don't love you, Thomas," she replied, pushing him away and escaping from his embrace. "I only said that because I hoped you would take me away from Victor, I thought it might encourage you to act more quickly." She lifted her chin, trying to look into his eyes, but only meeting them a second before needing to look away. "Now that I have decided otherwise, I think it is best to tell you the truth so that you are no longer under a false impression."

Thomas could not believe what he was hearing. This couldn't be true! He had given his heart to her, and now she was throwing it back in his face? She had played him false? Lied to him? Pretended to love him?

"What are you saying, Emily?" he breathed, his heart sinking like a stone and settling in the bottom of his stomach.

"I'm saying that I think you should leave," she replied, managing to look directly into his face. "There's no need for you to stay. Now that I've made up my mind to remain with Victor, you can inform my brother that I do not need to be rescued."

"But Victor –"

"Victor has changed," Emily interrupted, pasting a false, terse smile on her face. "We have had a long talk. He told me that he has realized how badly he has been behaving and has promised me he will no longer continue to be this way. I am quite delighted, I assure you!" She tried to laugh, but the sound died in her throat. "I am sure we will be very happy once again, very soon."

Thomas felt numb, trying to find any hint of a lie in Emily's face, but found nothing at all. Her eyes were solid, and the prim smile on her face made him feel nauseous.

"Get out," he managed to say, his lip curling. "Get out now, Emily. I never want to see your face again."

She did so at once, managing to keep the tears from spilling until she left his chambers.

What had she done? She had taken his love, his affection and torn them to shreds in front of his eyes. Staggering along the hall to her room, she kept one hand over her mouth as deep, silent sobs escaped her. The look of pain on his face had almost been more than she could bear. Her heart longed to tell him the truth with every false word she spat at him. She knew truly that she loved Thomas Markham with all her heart and soul, and she had just told him that she did not. He was going to leave her and Victor alone for good all because she had lied to his face.

"I assume it is done," Victor said, silkily, emerging from the shadows. "Ah, I can tell by your face that it is. Well done, wife." He grabbed her chin, forcing her to look at him. "Do not think that you shall ever play me so falsely again."

Emily looked back at her husband with dull, dead eyes. He had got his way and had played her well. She felt nothing but disdain for him.

"I will always love Thomas," she whispered, her eyes shimmering with tears and the slightest twinge of defiance.

"You may try to get him out of our lives, but you will never get him out of my heart, Victor." She felt his hand grip her harder, saw the lines of anger appear on his face, but felt no fear. "No matter what you do to me, or how much pain you cause me, I will never stop loving him," she continued, her eyes narrowing. "He was there for me, he loved me in a way that no man has ever done before, and I will always be grateful for that." With a strength she didn't feel, she wrenched herself from his grip and, after gazing at him for just a moment longer, walked to her chambers and slammed the door firmly behind her. Locking the door, she sagged against it for a moment, before sliding to the floor and letting her tears flow.

CHAPTER 12

Thomas flung himself into the armchair, his face dark. "Port, man!"

"Good heavens!" Francis replied, pouring him a glass. "Whatever's happened?" He had been most astonished to see Thomas arrive alone, having expected to see Emily with him, but Thomas had not said a word since he arrived.

Thomas drank the port swiftly, in only a few gulps, before asking for another. Francis obliged, but refused to give him a third glass. Thomas glowered at Francis, slamming his glass down on the desk for good measure. He had been in quite a state ever since he had left Emily behind, riding away from the estate in the early hours of the morning. Her words had been arrows to his heart, and he felt as though he were still bleeding. He knew now that he loved her deeply, and she had torn his heart from his chest and trampled on it, crushing it underfoot.

"I'm not giving you a third glass until you tell me exactly what's gone on, Thomas. Where on earth is Emily?"

Thomas grunted, shaking his head. "Wanted to stay with Victor."

"What?" Francis sat down heavily in his chair, his eyes never leaving Thomas. "What do you mean, she wanted to stay?"

Thomas shrugged. "Said that's what she wanted to do, Francis. Nothing I could do about it."

Francis frowned, shaking his head. "No, Thomas. That can't be the case. Why on Earth would she say that? You and I both read the letter that Victor sent her! Emily was terrified of him!"

A slightly uncomfortable feeling began to make its way up Thomas's spine and he shifted a little uncomfortably in the chair. "She told me to my face, Francis."

"What did she say, exactly?"

"Look," Thomas replied, getting up from his chair and pacing the room. "I offered her everything, Francis. I told her about my estate in Scotland, and that she could stay there with me or without me, and she turned me down."

"You offered her your estate?"

"What does it matter?" Thomas cried, completely frustrated. "She doesn't want it, Francis. She doesn't want me."

A knowing look came over Francis's face at Thomas's words. "Oh, I see what's happened!"

"What?" Thomas bit out, pouring himself yet another glass of port.

"You care about Emily."

Thomas said nothing for a moment, before lifting the glass of port to his lips. "I do," he said quietly, before taking a sip. Walking to the window, he looked out across the garden. "In fact, I would say that I love her, Francis." The anger was gone from his tone, his words now quiet and his face dejected.

Francis sat back in his chair, propping his feet up on the desk as he considered things. He had not expected Thomas to fall in love with his sister, but he did not consider it a bad thing. Emily needed to leave Victor, that he knew, and Thomas was clearly the best option for escape. "And how did she feel about you, may I ask?"

Thomas blew out a long breath, turning to face him. "As a matter of fact, I thought she cared for me too. But it seems I was mistaken."

"Mistaken?" Francis was surprised. "That does not sound like Emily. She would not toy with you for no reason, Thomas. That is cruel and Emily is not cruel."

"No, she's not," Thomas mumbled, walking back to his chair and sitting down opposite Francis. He thought of the way she had felt in his arms, her eyes sparkling up at him as her cheeks flushed. She had been warm and soft, gentle and tender – which had made it all the more devastating when she had told him it had all been a lie.

"Think about it Thomas," Francis began, seeing the confusion on his friend's face. "Emily does not lie; I know that to be true. She is kindness itself, although how she has managed to keep a hold of such a quality when married to Victor is quite beyond me.

"I thought the same thing only a few days ago," Thomas muttered, as an uncomfortable feeling began to make its way up his spine. Had he made a mistake?

Francis let out a sigh, throwing his head back and staring at the ceiling. "I do not know exactly what was said, Thomas, but I'd bet my life on it that she didn't mean a single word."

"Oh no," Thomas groaned, putting his head in his hands as a ball of anxiety settled in his stomach. "What have I done?"

"I suppose the question should be, what shall we do now?"

Thomas shook his head realizing now that he had reacted from a place of strong emotion when he heard her dismissive words. "I can't believe I was so stupid as to believe her without questioning."

"I am quite sure that Victor knew that by convincing her to say what she did, however he managed to do so, would cause your hurt and wounded heart to leave almost immediately."

"I dread to think what he has done to her," Thomas said, his eyes widening a little as he caught Francis' eye. "I need to go at once."

"Wait," Francis responded, holding up a hand and lifting his legs from the table. "We shall need a plan."

"You're coming?"

"Of course," Francis replied, lifting his eyebrows. "I have let my sister down once. I do not intend to do it again!"

A knock at the door interrupted their discussion, and Francis called the butler to enter with only a little frustration.

"Milord, the housekeeper has arrived."

"Oh, excellent. Send her in." Turning to Thomas, Francis tried to explain. "Mama is taking our housekeeper with her to the Dower House, and I need a new one as soon as possible. This one seems to have all the credentials." Turning back to the door, his jaw fell involuntarily as in walked a young lady, whose jet-black hair was neatly pinned up and her light blue eyes glanced expectantly at him.

"Good day, my lord," she said softly.

Francis gawped at her, finding himself robbed of speech. This was not what he had expected! Most housekeepers were of a more senior age, whilst this young lady looked as though she should still be attending balls and soirees!

Thomas cleared his throat, breaking the tense atmosphere. "Have you traveled far?"

"Just from Hertfordshire," she replied in a respectful but comfortable tone. She kept her eyes fixed deferentially somewhere near Thomas's feet. "So not too far."

"I hope you are not too tired after your journey," Thomas continued pleasantly. "This is an excellent household, and I am sure you will find it a very welcoming place." He coughed again, trying to get Francis out of whatever stupor he was in.

Everything in Francis was screaming that this beautiful creature before him could not possibly be the new housekeeper. Just gazing upon her as she entered the room, he'd felt his heart drop to his stomach before leaping back into its proper place, picking up a faster pace than he could have ever expected. He had made a dreadful mistake.

"I did not expect you to be so young," he managed, after a few more minutes of silence. Closing his eyes briefly, he realized how uncouth he sounded, trying to rectify himself immediately. "What I mean is, you have quite a reputation – as a housekeeper, I mean – given your years."

"Thank you," she replied after a moment. "I will work hard to keep your estate running smoothly, my lord."

Knowing that he could not dismiss her simply because he found her a most beguiling young woman he'd ever seen and given that he had already offered her the position in writing, Francis tried to smile.

"Thank you. Take the rest of the day to get settled in, and you may begin your duties tomorrow."

She nodded, turning to leave the room, leaving Francis staring at her retreating backside. What had happened to him? He had felt like a buffoon in front of her, and she a servant and he the master! Shaking his head, he cleared his swollen throat, trying to rid himself of the fervor that had rendered him so completely useless.

"Now," he began, sitting down once more and expelling a deep breath. "Let's get a plan in place to rescue Emily."

CHAPTER 13

E mily sat on the floor of her room with her hands pressed firmly over her ears. With her back pressed up against the far side of her bed, she sat crouched in an attempt to stay as small and quiet as possible. Victor had spent the last few hours shouting and demanding that she leave her room, but Emily had refused. He was blind drunk, and she was not going to face him when he was like this. In fact, over the last few days, she had only emerged from her room when Mavis told her that Victor was either ensconced in his study with his steward or solicitor, or when he was gone. Emily was glad for the support of Victor's household staff; without them, she was quite sure that she would be facing Victor's unrestrained wrath. It was also quite unbelievable that Victor had not yet dismissed Mavis, her maid, but perhaps he had not quite realized that it was she who was helping Emily to protect herself from him.

Slowly, Victor's demands grew less, and his voice quieter. Soon, she knew, he would stumble away and she would not hear from him until the following evening when it would begin all over again. Emily put her face in her hands and rubbed at her temples. Her face was gaunt and damp from the days of crying, and she felt as if her palms had found a permanent home nestled into her eye sockets. Was this her life from here onwards? To live in fear of her husband and hide from him until one day he would catch her and beat her beyond recognition? It was a dark thought and one that tormented her mind for many minutes as she waited for Victor to leave her bedchamber door. Finally, silence overtook as she heard his footsteps trail into the distance. She remained in her balled up position long after he left, her energy too drained to cause her to move. Hours passed, and Emily eventually made her way up into her bed, the covers cocooning her from the harsh world outside.

"My lady, your brother has arrived!" a cheerful voice burst into the room.

"My brother?" Emily startled up at Mavis, astonished. The maid's face was alight with happiness, clapping her hands together as she bustled in and made her way about the room. Mavis threw open the heavy curtains, letting in a flood of daylight.

"Yes, your brother, miss. Come now, come now, you shall need to get dressed! He is waiting in the drawing room."

Emily stood on wobbly legs, allowing Mavis to remove her nightgown and begin to dress her in her favorite day dress.

"When did he arrive?" Emily asked, assuming that it was Francis, given that none of her other brothers had any reason to visit her.

"Only just now," Mavis replied, her eyes shining. "I'm quite sure he's here to take you away, my lady. The look on his face was quite something, I'm told!"

A little unsure what Mavis meant, Emily kept her thoughts to herself. Had Thomas told Francis that she was happy here, as she'd directed him to? Had Francis come to see for himself?

"Where's my husband?"

"Out at one of the tenant's cottages overseeing repairs, or so I'm told."

Emily's chest loosened from its anxious bonds, and she took in a few deep breaths. "Then I should be quick before he returns."

Finally dressed, she left her bedchamber and rushed towards the drawing room, pushing the door open to find Francis, who had been pacing up and down the room, stop to face her.

"Emily!" he exclaimed, rushing to her and enfolding her in his arms. "Are you quite well?"

"I'm fine, Francis," Emily replied, dashing wicks of moisture from her eyes as she stepped back. "Whatever are you doing here?"

"I came to apologize." Francis took her arm and led her to the couch, sitting next to her and taking her hand. "I should have done more when you first came to me, Emily. I am deeply sorry that I did not."

"I can understand why," Emily replied, refusing to allow him to shoulder the blame completely. "Father had only just passed, and there was so much for you to take on."

"That does not excuse it," Francis said, a little severely. "Just because Victor was once my friend many, many years ago does not mean that I should have assumed you were exaggerating, my dear."

Emily gave him a wry smile. "On that count, no you should not have!"

"Listen to me, Emily," Francis continued, taking her hand. "Thomas is quite devastated."

Emily's face whitened a shade, and her hand flew to her mouth. "Oh, no," she breathed. "What have I done to him?"

"He believed everything you said, although he did not give me exact details." He smiled at her gently. "I believe that he cares for you, Emily and you for him."

"I do," she replied, her eyes filling. "Oh, Francis, I love him deeply, but I had to send him away."

Francis nodded. "I thought so. Was it Victor's doing?"

"He was going to kill Thomas," Emily whispered. "I had to send him away. It was the only way to keep him safe." She shook her head, the redness springing back to the rims of her eyes as droplets made their way down her cheeks. "The look on his face tore my soul apart."

"He does not hold it against you," Francis said softly, bending forward to look into her face as she bowed her head. "I had to show him the error he had made in thinking such things about you, but he has realized now that Victor used you to end whatever it was between the two of you."

Emily glanced up at her brother, a sudden hope flaring in her eyes. "He knows I wasn't speaking truthfully?"

"He does. He does not know why, of course, but you can explain the details to him later."

Emily's brows knitted together. "What? Is he here?"

Francis grinned. "He is, my dear sister. In fact, he waiting for us in the stables."

"In the stables?" Emily repeated, completely confused. "Why is he there?"

"Waiting for us," Francis explained, patiently. "Emily, don't you understand? We've come to take you away from Victor."

Emily clutched his hands. "You have?" Her eyes widened, her heart beginning to beat fast. "You're going to take me away?"

"Like I should have done in the first place," Francis replied, taking her hands. "We'll go back to our home, and then Thomas will take you up to Scotland after a few days have passed. Victor will not be allowed entry into our home and, by the time he engages the courts to do something about it, you will be safely in Scotland."

Emily couldn't quite catch her breath, the realization that her nightmare was finally coming to an end began to seep into her mind. "Thomas is still offering me a place to live in Scotland?"

"Of course he is," Francis replied, gently. "He loves you, Emily."

Tears ran unchecked down Emily's cheeks, her heart slowly mending. There were many wounds and many bruises, but this was the beginning of her healing.

"You will need to go and pack your things," Francis began. "Although I am sure that maid of yours has already begun."

"Oh, Francis, can I take her?" Emily begged, still holding his hand. "She has been my only friend, and I cannot dream of leaving her here."

He smiled. "My sweet, gentle, sister. Of course, you may bring her. I wouldn't have it any other way." He leaned forward and kissed her cheek. "Now go quickly. I have a feeling that Victor will not be too long away."

He watched her leave the room, feeling more anxious than he let on. He had waited to enter the house until he had seen Victor leave, muttering something about his tenants, but how long away he would be, Francis was not quite sure. Emily needed to hurry.

CHAPTER 14

Emily met Francis back in the hallway, with Mavis and her bags in tow. She had arrived back in her room to find Mavis already packing, and it had only taken them another fifteen minutes to pack only what she needed. There was not time to take everything, but Emily did not mind in the least. New dresses, bonnets, gloves, shawls, and cloaks could all be made again, and she did not need to take them with her. At Mavis's encouragement, she had changed into her traveling clothes whilst Mavis had packed all of her worldly belongings. Finally, they were both ready to leave and had found Francis waiting for them patiently.

"He has not yet arrived back," Francis said, picking up the bags with very little effort. "We must be quick. Should he see the carriage, all will be lost." He moved quickly, not wanting to think about what could happen should Victor find them. Francis was not quite sure he would be able to hold himself back, given what Thomas had told him about Emily's injuries from Victor's hand. As for Thomas... Francis did not even want to guess what would happen should they face one another. By all accounts, it was a situation best avoided, which is why he wanted Emily to move quickly.

Thomas paced back and forth beside the stables, keeping an eye open for any sign of Victor's return. The carriage had been well hidden just outside the gates of the estate, and Victor had ridden past them earlier without evening noticing, so he had no immediate concerns that it would be found. He had then returned to the stables and was now waiting for Francis to emerge with Emily.

A crunch of gravel alerted him and, turning around, he saw three figures walking from the house. Unable to contain himself, he ran towards them as fast as he could go, catching Emily up in his arms and holding her against himself tightly. She clung to him, arms flung around his neck, and her feet dangling as Thomas held her firmly, a healing in their embrace.

Francis and Mavis continued walking, making their way down the path towards the estate entrance, knowing that Emily and Thomas needed some time alone.

"I am so sorry, Thomas," Emily cried, her voice shaking as shame and regret filled her. "I should have told you the truth, but he told me he would kill you if I did not send you away."

"Hush," Thomas whispered, letting her down gently so that her back was against the cold stone wall of the estate. "It is forgotten, Emily." There were tears in his own eyes as he kissed her fiercely, feeling her melt into his embrace. There was not much time to spare, but he needed to kiss her lips again, feel her soft skin under his touch. She was there, she was real, and she was with him.

"I love you, Thomas," Emily breathed, running her fingers down the side of his face. "I never stopped, not for one second of a moment."

"I know," he replied, kissing the palm of her hand. "I understand now why you said those things. You were protecting me, and I love you even more for it."

"Take me home," she whispered, taking his hand. "Thomas, take me home."

Without a word, he began to walk alongside her, following down the path he assumed Francis must have taken.

"Wait." He frowned, seeing no sign of either Francis or Mavis. They would not have reached the carriage so soon after leaving them. "Come with me."

Moving a little further to the side, Thomas heard the faint sound of approaching hoofbeats, and with a jolt of alarm racing through him, tugged Emily further into the trees that lined the side of the estate. "We shall have to run for the carriage," he whispered. "I believe Victor is approaching."

Emily swallowed hard, a sudden terror freezing her blood. They were so close to her escape, so close to her freedom, and now Victor was threatening it all. She clung to Thomas's arm, trying her best to trust him, trying to rid herself of the fear that clung to her very bones.

"Emily!" Victor roared, jumping from his horse and storming into the house. "Emily!"

"We must run now," Thomas whispered, waiting for Victor to enter the house.

Emily said nothing, watching and waiting until, finally, she was being pulled along by Thomas, trying her best to run even though her dress often hindered her steps. Clearly, Victor was in no mood to be trifled with – what would he do when he found her gone?

"Come on, come on!"

Emily's breath came quickly as she took in great gasps of air, practically falling in through the carriage door. With no concern for propriety, Thomas practically hoisted her in, whilst Francis grabbed her arms and pulled her onto the seat. With Thomas finally inside and the door swinging shut, Francis tapped on the roof, and the carriage moved off, picking up speed fairly quickly.

"Are you all right, Miss?"

Emily nodded, barely able to get a word out as her heart refused to lessen its frantic pace. She sucked in great gulps of air, her mind still clouding with fear.

"Come here," Thomas said, firmly, dragging her into his arms. Placing one arm around her shoulders, and the other finding her hand amidst her skirts, he murmured comforting words in her ear, helping her to finally, calm herself down. Her heart began to find its natural rhythm, her breathing slowed and she slumped against the seat, resting her head on Thomas's shoulder.

"There you go," Francis smiled, reaching over and patting her hand. "You are quite safe, Emily. You have left him behind!"

"Thank you, Francis," she managed to say, giving him a tremulous smile. "Thank you for coming for me."

"Where are we going, Miss?" Mavis's sprightly voice chirped with a soothing, yet curious tone.

"Home," Emily replied, finally relaxing against the squabs. "We're going home, Mavis."

⚜

"You let me in this moment, Emily!" Victor screamed, rattling the door handle for all it was worth. "You cannot hide from me forever!" Kicking the door with frustration, he noticed it wobble and, ignoring the pain, he kicked and kicked and kicked until, finally, the door splintered and cracked, allowing him to shove it open.

"Emily?" he growled, walking in. "Don't hide from me!" Storming around the room, it only took him a few minutes to realize she wasn't here. Anger flooded him as he threw open drawers and wardrobes, realizing that her things were gone. She'd left him? "How dare you!" he screeched, throwing a small chest of drawers to the floor. "You thought you could leave me? Leave *me*!" With a scream of rage, he ran from the room, running to the stables with fury dogging his steps.

"Saddle my fastest horse," he roared, seeing the groom jump with fright. "Do it now, man, or it will be all the worse for you!"

Within moments, he was riding down the very same path the carriage had taken, his eyes blazing with rage. He would find his wife and drag her back by the hair if she were so lucky.

CHAPTER 15

They had been traveling for a little over an hour, and Emily had finally fallen asleep. Thomas looked down at her with a gentle smile, feeling whole and complete. He did not care whether they married or not, for she was his, just as he knew his heart and soul belonged to her.

"Trouble," Francis murmured, not wanting to wake Emily. He had been poking his head out of the window now and again ever since they had left Victor's estate, and whilst Thomas had found it a little annoying, it now seemed to have been worth it.

"What trouble?" Thomas asked.

Francis stuck his head out of the window once more. "I'd say someone is riding very fast towards us, and I'm guessing it will be Victor."

Thomas felt his stomach dip with a sudden fear. "What shall we do?"

Francis shook his head. "I don't know, Thomas." He looked at him steadily. "What should we do?"

"What's going on?" Emily asked, sleepily, having been woken by the sound of voices.

Thomas let her sit up completely before replying. "Victor is chasing us."

"What?" She sat bolt upright, a hand at her throat and her eyes wide and staring. "He's chasing us? Whatever shall we do?"

"We will face him," Thomas replied, quietly, seeing the alarm jump onto her face. "It is the only way, Emily. I will not hurt him," he assured her, seeing the question on her lips. "But neither Francis nor I will allow him to take you." He squeezed her hand, as Francis called for the carriage to stop.

"Stay here," Francis ordered. "And keep the doors shut."

He and Thomas leaped from the carriage, and Mavis moved to huddle next to Emily. The carriage had just rumbled over a bridge and stopped on the other side, the rushing water adding to the tumult going on in her head, instead of calming her senses.

"Don't fear, Miss. They'll protect you."

"But who will protect them?" Emily whispered.

"Get out of the carriage this instant, Emily," Victor screamed, jumping from his horse as the poor beast staggered to one side before collapsing on the grass. He had ridden it far beyond what it could manage, and it was quite done in.

"Emily is not going anywhere with you," Francis said, firmly, his voice loud over the sound of the water. "After how you have treated her, she needs protection."

"She is my wife!" Victor roared, spit flying from his mouth. "She belongs to me, and you have no right!"

"Go home," Thomas replied, keeping his voice calm whilst everything in him wanted to fly at the man and beat him senseless. "You will not be seeing her again."

"Don't tell me what to do, Markham!" Victor pulled a pistol from behind his back and leveled it at Thomas.

"Thomas!" Emily screamed, scrabbling to get out of the carriage, but Mavis held her back.

"No, no, Miss! Stay here. You must stay here!" Mavis held onto her arm tightly, and Emily could do nothing but stare out of the window with terrified eyes.

"Don't hurt him, please don't hurt him," she whispered as if he could hear her.

Francis glanced back at the carriage, relieved that Emily had been convinced to stay inside. "You can't shoot him, Thurston," he shouted, turning back to face the crazed man. "There are too many witnesses! You will be hung for sure."

"At least then, *he* won't have her," Victor exclaimed, his voice throbbing with rage as he kept the pistol pointed at Thomas's chest, beginning to advance slowly.

"Emily," he called, a wicked grin on his face. "Get out of the carriage or Markham will die. Slowly. And right in front of your eyes."

Freeing herself from Mavis's grip, Emily flung the carriage door open and stumbled down the steps. "I'm here, Victor," she cried, moving to stand directly in front of Thomas. "Don't shoot him."

"Emily," Thomas tried to put her behind him, to protect her with his body but she refused to move. "Emily, go back in the carriage."

"I lost you once, Thomas," she whispered, looking up into his face. "I will not lose you again."

"Get away from him," Victor roared, his face contorting with rage as he saw her speak lovingly to Thomas. "Get away!"

Francis, in all the commotion, managed to pull out his own pistol and, with a soft click, aimed it directly at Victor. "Emily and Thomas are going to stay exactly as they are, Thurston," he said quietly, seeing Victor's mouth drop open with shock. "And you are going to return home."

Victor was caught. He did not know what to do. More than anything, he wanted to squeeze the trigger and see the lifeless body of Thomas Markham hit the ground, but now his wife was standing in the way. To make matters worse, there was now a gun directed at him, and Victor had no intention of dying. However, neither was he about to retreat home!

"Maybe I will just kill them both, and then where will you be?" he sneered, leveling the gun. As he continued to look at Francis, he pulled the trigger, hearing the satisfying sound of a scream as he fell back. The report of the gun pushed him back, and as he struggled to keep his footing, he tripped over a tree root. Stumbling backward into the slow tone wall, he found himself falling, the air catching him and lofting him into the tumultuous icy waters beneath.

"Emily!" Francis shouted, rushing to her as she collapsed on the ground.

"She is all right," Thomas assured him. "I pulled us both to one side as Thurston took his aim and the bullet whistled straight past my ear."

"Emily," Francis said again, seeing her pale face look up into his. "Oh, Emily!" Taking her into his arms, he held her tightly, realizing just how close he had come to losing one of his beloved siblings. "Are you sure you are all right?"

"I'm just a bit weak," she admitted, smiling up reassuringly into her brother's concerned visage. Leaning heavily into Thomas, he helped her to her feet. "I got such a shock when the gun went off, I did not know whether or not Thomas was injured," she continued, attempting to right her dress and gain her composure.

"We are all quite safe, now," Thomas replied, keeping an arm firmly around her waist. "Perhaps we should go back into the carriage."

Emily stared around her. "But where is Victor?"

Francis studied her for a moment, wondering if she could take the truth. Deciding she could, he cleared his throat before answering. "He fell into the water."

"Oh." Emily's eyes grew wide. "He cannot swim."

A somber silence overtook them as they realized what had most likely happened. Emily felt relief, mingled with shock, staring into the face of her brother and realizing the truth: she was free.

CHAPTER 16

"The funeral went very well, I thought."

"Yes, it did." Emily kept her hand in the crook of Francis' arm, feeling as though the final chapter of her life with Victor had been closed. "Although notably, there were not many there."

"He was not very well liked, it seems."

"Indeed."

Francis looked down at his sister, patting her hand. "You have done very well."

"Thank you, Francis."

The funeral had been only a few days ago, and it was only now that the hubbub was settling. Victor's body had been found downstream, and thankfully, the constable had not seemed particularly interested in investigating. They told him that he had tripped – just as he had – and that was all the constable needed to hear.

Emily continued to walk in the garden, with her brother, smiling gently. "I'm glad to be back home."

Francis smiled back at her. "I'm glad too."

"Emily!"

Turning, Emily saw Thomas stride towards them. "Thomas! When did you arrive?"

"Just this very moment," he replied, kissing her thoroughly and completely ignoring Francis. "I could not wait to see you."

"So it seems," Francis replied, dryly. "I feel I am not needed here!" He walked back to the house, hearing Emily laugh as he went. There was a smile on his face and happiness in his heart as he realized that he could not remember the last time he had heard his sister laugh. He had Thomas to thank for that.

"How are you, my love?"

"Better now that you are back beside me," she murmured, pulling him in close for another kiss. "I have missed you."

"And I you," he replied, fervently. "These last few days without you have been torture!"

They had decided it best that Thomas return to town and distance himself from them – and from Victor's death – just for a time. It had been a precaution and had seemed like a good idea at the time, but both Thomas and Emily had felt the separation keenly.

Emily smiled. "Well, it is all over now."

"And I hear you are a very rich widow!"

"I am," she replied, shaking her head. "The estate passes to Victor's brother, but much of the wealth remains with me. Why he put that in his will, I shall never know. Perhaps he did care for me a little back when we first married." She looked up into Thomas's face, seeing the sympathy and concern in his eyes.

"You have been through a great trauma," he said softly, running a gentle hand down her cheek. "And just look at you now! You seem more alive than ever."

It was true. Her eyes were bright, and there was a peaceful glow about her face that had not been there before.

"You are more beautiful than I have ever seen you, Emily."

"That is all thanks to you, Thomas," she replied, accepting his compliments. "You are the one who came for me when I did not think there was another way out."

"And fell in love with you in the process!"

"Indeed," she laughed, her eyes twinkling.

"So," Thomas began, his voice suddenly serious. "I know that it is but days since the funeral of your husband, but I must know, Emily. Will you have me?"

Emily let out a light peal of laughter. "Must you ask, you foolish man? Of course, I will have you! There is nobody else in my heart but you!"

Thomas let out a sigh of relief, crushing her against him. Whilst he had been quite hopeful that she would accept, there had been a part of him that worried that it was too soon or that she would relish her freedom too much. How foolish he was, indeed!

"Although we will have to wait a year."

"I can do that," he replied, knowing it would be difficult but necessary. She had to have her mourning period first.

"But, must we live in Scotland?" Emily asked, a hint of mirth in her voice. "It is so far away, and I hear you have a lovely estate quite close by!"

"We will live wherever you wish," he laughed, taking her hands. "So long as I am with you, Emily, any place will be home."

"I love you, Thomas," she whispered, tipping her head back for his kiss.

"And I love you, Emily," he replied, pressing his lips to hers.

჻

FRANCIS MADE his way back to the study, a smile on his lips. It had been a difficult few weeks, but he was glad that his sister was now happy. He was quite sure there would be an announcement within the family quite soon, and he was quite delighted with that fact. Thomas was a dear friend and he knew that he would never treat Emily in the way that Victor had. In fact, he would cherish her always. Pouring himself a glass of port, he toasted to the happy couple, even though he could not see them.

"My lord?"

Slightly startled, Francis spun around, splashing his port all over his shirt.

"Oh!" his new housekeeper cried, pulling a cloth from her pocket. "I am terribly sorry, my lord, I did not mean to startle you."

"It is quite all right," he mumbled, a little surprised to see her begin to dab at the spots on his shirt with the cloth. "I was lost in thought."

She shook her head, a few tendrils of black hair coming loose and curling around her face. "This shirt will be quite ruined if we do not wash it immediately."

Francis said nothing, her nearness causing him to feel a sudden heat rush up his neck. He licked his dry lips, wondering what on Earth was going on. Why did his tongue feel so heavy? Why was his throat like sandpaper?

"There," she murmured. "I think I have the worst of it, my lord. If you would be able to change, then I shall have the maids wash the stains immediately." She glanced at him with those clear sky blue eyes he sometimes caught himself daydreaming about and flushed. "I must apologize if I am too forward, my lord."

"Not at all," Francis managed to say, trying to collect himself. "You have done an admirable job, thank you…" He trailed off. To his utter disgrace, he found he could not recollect her name. "I shall change immediately. He walked to the door and allowed her to pass in front of him. "Was there something you wanted?"

"I can come back later," she replied, softly, her eyes now back on the ground. "I am sorry for the mess I caused."

"Think nothing of it," he said, as off-hand as possible. Almost unconsciously, he watched her walk away, her heavy gown not quite managing to hide her womanly curves. "Forgive me," he called after her. "But I have quite forgotten your name."

"Oh." She turned to face him. "Mrs. Hannah Reece," she said, bobbing a curtsy. "If you'll excuse me, my lord."

He nodded, her name searing into his mind. Why they had such tricky customs as to call the housekeeper Mrs. regardless of marital status, he couldn't fathom. He tried to shake off the absurd line of thinking and focus on the ornate crown moulding above the doorway in front of him. "Hannah Reece," he said, under his breath, as his eyes flickered down and he watched her walk away.

ॐ

The End

ॐ

ACKNOWLEDGMENTS

It has been such fun beginning to craft the world of the Catesby family. This book would not be at all possible without the help of the ever brilliant Isabel, who I know I am beyond lucky to have along for this ride. *Thank you Izzy, for your time, your energy, your vast knowledge and the spirit that infuse into these projects!*

I must also thank my dear friend Caroline, who provides me tireless support day in and day out. *I wouldn't be here without you.*

I am endlessly thankful for Ellen, whose unwavering support lies at the foundation of my writing career. *Even when you are far away, you are with me.*

I want to send love and gratitude to my family, who make me want to do better ever single day. It's through these books that I am able to support them, and not a moment goes by that I'm not grateful for that opportunity!

And lastly, I want to thank you, dear reader, for taking the time out of your busy life to spend with me. You allow me to live a blessed life!

BOOK 2: CHARLES AND THE INTRUDER

BOOK 2

HOUSE OF CATESBY

Charles and the Intruder

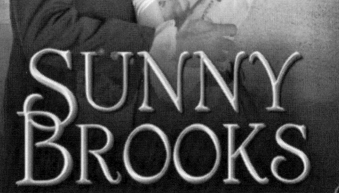

SUNNY BROOKS

FOREWORD

When something unexpected shows up in your life, take pause, listen
to your heart, and trust your instincts…you never know what adventure
awaits you.

- Sunny Brooks

CHAPTER 1

A knock interrupted Charles' sonata in A major, and he looked up from the piano with irritation. He never appreciated anyone disturbing his practice, and now it was more frustrating than ever.

"Yes?"

"Sorry to intrude on you, brother, but it appears that the solicitor will be here soon." Charles' older brother Francis passed through the doorway, walking in with the look of a man carrying a great weight on his shoulders. "I thought it best that we meet in the drawing room. The solicitor can read the will there."

"I see," Charles replied, resting his fingers gently on the soft, ivory keys. "Very well, I shall be along in a moment."

Francis studied his younger brother, seeing the despondence on his face. Charles had spent much of his childhood alone, choosing to spend his time practicing the pianoforte or reading quietly in the library. He was, of course, inordinately clever and his skill at the pianoforte outshone all of his sisters, much to their chagrin. His dark, brooding hair was mussed, and Francis knew from the state of it that Charles had been running his hands through it – probably from frustration over a few poorly played bars or a missed note. Though the undertone of mourning had everyone in a deep state of profound grief, Francis recognized that his brother's grief manifested by him being even more hard on himself than usual.

"How are you keeping, Charles?"

"I should be asking you, that, Francis," Charles replied, beginning to play once more. "After all, you are the one who has had to take on father's helm!"

Their father's death had been a swift and sudden blow, and, whilst he had been a wealthy man and had, no doubt, left them all a suitable living, it was his great character and loving nature that they missed the most.

"It has been a struggle," Francis replied, honestly. "I have never felt so overwhelmed in all my life!"

Charles nodded, his fingers moving smoothly over the keys as he played. "I saw Thomas here a few days ago. I didn't see much of the man, but I assume he was here at your request?"

"Yes." Francis swallowed hard, unwilling to share too much about his friend Thomas's current whereabouts. "He was giving me some advice as regards to the estate. I found him to be a great help."

"I am glad," Charles replied, pleased that Francis had someone to turn to. "Seems to be a good friend, that man."

"A most excellent one," Francis said softly, half to himself. The fact that Thomas had both rebuked him and then taken on the responsibility for his sister, Emily, had been both difficult to stomach and a relief for his already burdened shoulders.

"But you did not answer my question, Charles. How are you?"

Charles sighed, the music stopping abruptly. "How well can one be when their dear father has departed too soon?" His heart clenched as he spoke, his voice trembling a little. He had loved their father dearly and was not yet truly able to talk about his passing. It was like a vast chasm had opened up in his life, and he was not sure what he was meant to fill it with.

"I understand," Francis replied, coming around to place a gentle hand on Charles' shoulder. "One thing Thomas taught me was that I should be there for my family. You are most welcome to come and talk to me, any time you should need to. My door is always open to you, Charles, just as father's was. I have no intention of ever filling his shoes, but I should like to have that openness and frankness that was so important to him."

"Thank you." Lowering his familial green eyes back to the music in front of him, Charles began to play once more, putting everything he felt into the music. Out of the corner of his eye, he saw Francis leave a few moments later, pulling the door closed behind him.

Stopping abruptly, Charles leaned his head back and stared at the ceiling, refusing to allow any tears to fall. The ache he felt over his father's death had been growing steadily and, with no-one to speak to, he had fallen into a deep melancholy. Whilst he appreciated Francis' offer, Charles knew that his brother already had a great many things to deal with. There was the estate to care for, accounts to look over, and many new skills to learn. Charles' twin brother, Henry, was arranging their mother's relocation to the Dower House, preferring to keep himself busy rather than dwell on his grief. Charles' sisters all had one another to lean on. He would often find them ensconced together in the library, their cheeks damp. They had always welcomed him, of course, but females and their tears were not something he felt particularly able to cope with, even if they were those of his sisters. Finally, his mother was working with Henry to move both her belongings and some of the staff to the Dower house. The speed at which she had decided to move had come as something of a surprise, but it made sense. Francis was now Lord Catesby and, whilst many widows remained with their sons until their sons married, his mother was quite the sensible woman. She wanted Francis to have the full run of the estate, without her influence or input. Smiling lightly at the thought of his mother, Charles felt his unshed tears run down the back of his throat, and he was once more able to look at the sheet music in front of him. Knowing that he was soon expected in the drawing room, Charles threw himself into the piece, playing it one last time without a single mistake and with a great swell of emotion.

"AND TO CHARLES, I leave the London townhouse and all its contents."

Charles bolted upright, staring first at the solicitor and then at his mother. The townhouse? He'd thought his father had sold it long ago. It hadn't been used in a great many years, given that all his sisters were out. If ever they'd gone to town, they'd rented comfortable lodgings, and even at that, the family had not gone often. His father, in particular, had not visited London in quite some time.

"With a yearly living, so that he will remain both comfortable and eligible," the solicitor finished, giving Lady Catesby a slight smile over her husband's gentle wit. Lady Catesby returned the smile, dabbing the corner of her eye with her handkerchief. Her husband's greatest wish had been for all of his children to be happy and settled, but they had often fretted over Charles. His quiet nature and tendency towards preferring his own company had not exactly made him an eligible bachelor. In fact, Charles had only gone to dances at Almacks and the like because his father had, quite literally, forced him to go. To his father's dismay, even that had not lasted long. Charles' determination to remain home beside the fire made him glaringly poor company at balls and soirees.

"Then to my daughter –"

"Wait a moment, if you please," Charles interrupted, getting to his feet. "He's giving me the townhouse, Mama? I thought that had been sold!"

She shook her head, smiling at him with unshed tears sparkling in her maternal grey eyes. "We thought about selling it, Charles, but your father decided that it would do much better to be left in your hands. He thought you enjoyed town life and would be the best one suited to living there."

"You knew he was going to give me this?"

"Why, of course!" his mother replied, softly. "Although I must confess, I did not think it would be happening so soon."

Seeing the pain on his mother's face, Charles sat back down, barely hearing the solicitor continue with the reading of his father's will. He had a home, and a living – but what to do with it all? His father and mother had been quite correct, he did indeed greatly enjoy town living, for there was a much greater collection of books in London than in the countryside. He was able to read in peace, finding a wide variety of subjects to capture his interests. There were a number of scholarly men to meet with, to discuss topics with, and Charles felt his heart grow a little lighter with the prospect. Returning to town might be a way to help him out of his despair, give him a course for his life. At the moment, he felt lost – adrift on a sea of emotions. Were he in town, then he would be able to work through his grief slowly, finding solace in the company of others and in the great many books he was sure to read.

"Charles," his mother whispered, leaning over to him. "I do believe the townhouse has a pianoforte." She smiled at him as his sage eyes lit up, and he thanked her quietly before sitting up once more. His mother never ceased to amaze him, for it was as if she knew exactly what he had been thinking, and had known just what to say to convince him once and for all that this was a good thing.

"That settles it, then," he muttered to himself as a miniature flutter began in his chest. "It seems I'm going to London."

CHAPTER 2

"Thought I'd best come and wish you farewell."

Glancing over his shoulder, Charles spotted Francis walking down the stone steps of the estate, a resigned look on his face.

"I hope you don't feel like you're not welcome here, Charles. You know this is your home for as long as you choose to stay."

Smiling, Charles slapped his brother on the back. "Nonsense, Francis. In fact, I feel brighter than I have in months! Although I thank you for your concern."

"Then I am a little relieved," Francis replied, his face clearing. "I should not like you to feel chased away!"

"It is precisely the opposite, I assure you," Charles replied, watching the staff load the last of his luggage. "You know how much I adore being in town. It seems father appreciated that as well."

"He knew you well," Francis responded, a distant look in his eyes. "Father wanted us all to be happy and content in our lives, to make something of ourselves. It seems he is giving you that opportunity, Charles. I do hope you will make the best of things."

Trying not to feel as though his older brother was lecturing him, Charles glanced away, seeing the gate and the wide open road waiting for him. "I am going to take some time to get settled, before deciding what it is I want to do with my life," he said, quietly.

Francis nodded. "I understand that feeling. It was quite some time before I was prepared to even enter father's study. I simply needed some time to prepare myself for what was ahead."

"You have your responsibilities laid out for you, Francis," Charles replied, immediately. "It is somewhat different for someone in my position. I do not want to spend my life drinking and gambling, leg-shackled at some point, and then producing a few squalling children. That life has no purpose. I need a purpose in my life."

"Perhaps you should write a few books," a light but confident voice broke into the conversation.

Charles looked up, surprised to hear the voice of his mother as she walked down the steps. "Books, Mama?"

"Why not, Charles? You are clever enough, I am sure, and the world could always use a few more books."

"I shall certainly consider it, Mama," Charles replied slowly as his brow furrowed in a quick contemplation. He had not ever considered writing, but perhaps his mother was right. It would be a good use of his time, and he would enjoy putting his thoughts and knowledge to paper.

She smiled at him, the grief still evident in her eyes being hidden as best she could. "Good. Now, ensure that you take great care when you get to the townhouse. If I remember rightly it should all still be under covers."

"There is no staff to speak of, Mama?"

Shaking her head, she gave him a bright smile. "But I am quite sure you shall be able to find some suitable staff very soon. I have made a few inquiries, and a butler, a maid, and cook should be with you tomorrow morning. The rest you shall have to hire yourself."

"And you'll need a valet," Francis interrupted, smiling broadly. "If you are to be in London, then you shall certainly need to have an impeccable wardrobe, and I know how difficult you find it to tie your cravat!" Francis tried to stifle a smirk, though he delighted in teasing his rather sensitive brother.

"Only on occasion," Charles replied, somewhat crossly. "But yes, I take your point. I shall make every effort to find a suitable valet once I arrive" Francis' guffaw made Charles smile, and even his mother let out a small chuckle.

"Take care, my dear." Leaning forward, she kissed his cheek, pressing her hand to his face for a moment before stepping back. "Write to me soon, let me know you are settled."

"I will," he promised, catching the light sheen of tears in her eyes. "Although I am quite sure you shall be very busy setting up the Dower house, Mama."

Francis shot him a glance. "Yes, indeed," he commented, a little gruffly. Francis was slightly unsure as to how he felt about his mother leaving the estate she'd called home for so long. It would be strange not to have her around, as Francis would often seek her input on things he was unsure of, wanting to know how his father had run the estate. The idea of whether he could manage on his own had been haunting him since his mother had first announced her intentions to move.

"I do hope all goes well for you both," Charles continued, opening the carriage door and getting in. "Mama, I will write again very soon. I promise." With a wave, he tapped on the carriage roof, and the wheels began to move across the gravel road.

"Goodbye, my dear!" his mother cried, waving to him. "Goodbye!"

Charles shouted a final goodbye, before sitting back in the carriage, a smile on his face. It would be a good few hours before they reached London, but already the anticipation was thrilling him to the core. Pulling out a book from the corner of his bag, he began to read, hoping the time would pass swiftly.

"WE'RE ALMOST THERE, SIR."

"Oh!" Charles sat up, rubbing the sleep from his eyes as the book he'd been reading toppled to the floor. He hadn't meant to fall asleep, but his eyes had grown heavy as he'd been reading and eventually, he'd allowed them to close. The hours had passed quickly as he'd dozed, and now they were deep in the heart of London. The sound of the passing carriages and hooves on cobbled streets hadn't woken him, only the shout of his driver as they approached the townhouse. Picking up the book carefully, Charles sat up tall, looking out of the window.

It was growing late, and the London streets were looking a little less than welcoming, but that didn't dampen Charles' enthusiasm. Recognizing a few areas, Charles grinned into the burgeoning darkness, as a feeling of happiness wrapped itself around him. He was here. He was home. A new beginning to a life he was yet to know.

"Here you go, sir."

"Thank you," Charles replied, exiting the carriage on tired legs. The journey had been long, and his entire body complained about the cramped position he had been sleeping in. Glancing around and seeing no-one about, Charles indulged himself in a long, deep stretch, loosening the tight muscles in his neck and shoulders.

"You have the key, Guv?"

"Yes, thank you." Pulling the keys from his pocket, Charles gave instructions to his groom about unloading his belongings and then gave directions as to where the nearby mews was so he may see to the horse and carriage. Glad to finally be at his new residence, Charles bid his driver goodnight and continued towards the house alone.

A large, heavy front door greeted him, almost intimidating by its height and heft. Charles studied it for a moment, a vast array of memories assailing him all at once. Memories of being here with his father and mother, helping his sisters make their first promenade into the whirling social activities of their very first Season, of time spent with his brothers as they gathered around the fire. Truly grateful that his father had given him this beautiful place to call home, Charles put the key in the lock, hearing it grate and squeak as it turned. Then, he pushed the door open.

CHAPTER 3

The door led to a seemingly never-ending darkness, and Charles grimaced as he realized he had no source of light with him. The curtains would all be pulled in the house, of course, given that it had been locked up tightly for such a long time. Taking a few steps in, Charles stopped completely still, feeling a little disorientated in the darkness.

"Can I help you, Guv?"

Turning back to see the lamplighter passing by the townhouse, holding out a candle for him. Charles accepted it with thanks, giving the man a couple of coins for his trouble. Grateful that he now had at least one candle with which to begin to explore the house, Charles walked a little further into the pitch-black, hearing the lamplighter whistle as he walked away down the street. Pushing the heavy door shut, he tried not to shiver as the sound echoed through the empty hallway. He was not exactly afraid of the dark, but there was something about being alone with absolutely no bearings that shot a cold shiver directly up his spine.

Walking ahead, with a lot more confidence than he felt, Charles eventually made his way down a single flight of stairs and into the kitchens. Thankfully and expectedly, they had no curtains in the windows. Finally able to see a little more clearly, he found a few more candles and one candlestick, lighting them immediately. "Much better," he breathed, walking around the kitchen to inspect the interior. It seemed to be in fairly good order, although he had expected to find a thick layer of dust over almost every surface. Instead, he found that even the wooden table in the middle of the kitchens was remarkably clean. Frowning slightly, he held the candlestick a little higher, realizing that some of the crockery that was to the side of the large basin was clean and slightly damp to the touch. Was someone here?

Walking to the pantry, he looked for more clues but could see no evidence of any perishables being kept there. Making his way to the kitchen door, he rattled the handle, but the lock held fast. The windows in the kitchens were all in good condition, with no evidence of any nefarious activity. Shrugging, he turned to walk back up the stairs and along the long, narrow hallway.

Coughing a little, Charles felt an incredible sense of gratitude toward his mother for arranging both a cook, a maid, and a butler for the morning. He had everything he needed for one night, but there would be much to do once day broke and he would be sure to set his staff to work almost immediately. Then he had the trouble of finding at least two more maids and a couple of footmen. Given how large the townhouse was and that he intended to do at least some kind of entertaining, he would need a decent staff. Returning to the front door, Charles found all of his belongings neatly pushed to one side beside the front door, just as he'd instructed the driver. Wondering for a moment whether to heft them all to his bedchamber himself, Charles chose not to, realizing that he had not even decided on where he would sleep. There would be no fresh sheets either, given that he had no clue as to where the linen cupboard was and, on top of that, he did not even know how to make up a bed for himself. Charles found the small bag filled with only his essentials, and, hoisting it under his arm, climbed the staircase that led up to the bedchambers and the study.

Finding the main bedchamber where his mother and father had once slept was not too difficult, even in the gloomy light. Charles' memory served him well, and he looked around the room with a mix of emotions. This would be his room now, of course, but the reminiscences of his father swept over him in a wave. Even though he reasoned that the house now belonged to him, he felt a strong intrusion into his parent's privacy. In his mind, this was still his father's room, and Charles felt uncomfortable staying in it.

Thinking perhaps he would do better to stay in the room he'd usually slept in, Charles closed the door tightly and made his way, a little more carefully, along the hallway. A sudden sound stopped him in his tracks. Standing as still as he could, he listened hard. The candlestick rose slowly as he examined the darkness ahead for any sign of movement, hearing only a slight 'click' from somewhere to his left. Padding forward, Charles held his breath as he walked, a ball of anxiety twisting in his stomach. Reaching his old room, he turned the door handle quickly and let the door swing open wildly as though he hoped to startle someone within. Of course, it was empty.

"It must have been a mouse," Charles muttered to himself. He made his way over to light the candlestick that was still on the mantelpiece from last time he had stayed here. The candles caught quickly, lighting the room just enough for Charles to look around.

"Good gracious!" Walking towards the bed, Charles stared at the mess of sheets. They had been pulled back, the pillow dimpled from the weight of someone's head. Someone's been staying here, he thought to himself, as he whirled around in case an intruder held a knife at his back. He was useless in the shadow-flecked room and completely without protection. Feeling a little afraid, he reached for the only weapon he saw at hand – a large, heavy book that was sitting on a small table beside the bed. Not even glancing at the title, he walked a little more cautiously around the room, holding it firmly in his grip. The weight of it gave him some reassurance, knowing that it would give an almighty thump to whoever it was that was residing in his home, should they attack him. His eyes noticed the fresh ashes in the fireplace, the bucket of coal that lay next to it. Pausing for a moment, Charles tried to think carefully about his next plan of action. His heart was thudding in his chest, and he forced long and even breaths in an attempt to counteract the fear that was beginning to overtake him.

"I need to get to the study," he whispered to himself. "It has a key." The study was the only place in the house that had a fully functioning lock, and Charles took himself there with great speed. As his hand reached for the door, he realized that he hadn't yet pulled the keys from his pocket. Putting down the heavy book, he glanced around warily as he frantically attempted to find the correct key, placing it in the lock with slightly trembling fingers. As the door opened, Charles quickly stepped inside and closed the door behind him. His back resting against the large door, he let out a sigh of relief. The wave of anxiety slowly began to ease from his chest at the very same time that a ferocious growling rose up from his empty stomach. Realizing he could not go all evening without sustenance, his mind jumped to the basket his mother had given him. Throwing back his head in despair, he exited the door and locked it again, before racing back down the stairs, his heart beating frantically.

ONE HOUR LATER, Charles was sitting beside a roaring fire in the study, surrounded by the remains of what had been a delicious meal. He would miss his mother's cooking, that was for certain. Making a mental note to write to his mother and thank her for her thoughtfulness, he sat back in the overstuffed chair, awash with relief. He felt secure now, knowing that no-one could come through the study door without the key. There had been neither further sight nor sound of any stranger who had taken to living in his home and given that he had servants arriving in the morning, he had nothing to fear. Hopefully, whoever it was would grasp that he had come to claim the house and would leave at once. And, should they not, Charles was quite happy to summon a constable who would help them depart his premises.

Resting his eyes for just a moment, Charles smiled lightly. Things were beginning to look a bit brighter. There would be challenges ahead, but he felt he was prepared for them. All he needed now were just a few moments rest.

CHAPTER 4

"Who are you?" a voice boomed, assaulting Charles' dream.

His eyes were blurry with sleep, but his brain fought through the grogginess to reconcile the angry voice breaking through the beautiful sonata he was performing in his dream.

"I'm going to ask you again. Who are you? Did he send you?"

Blinking hard, Charles sat upright in the overstuffed chair. His vision cleared and focused on the gleaming tip of what appeared to be a very sharp sword pointed directly at his throat. "I say, what on earth –"

"I suggest you answer my questions before I run you through."

Running his eyes along the shining steel of the sword, Charles was even more confused to find a slightly disheveled young woman at the far end of it. Her long, blonde hair was tied to one side in a ribbon, and her penetrating blue eyes were balls of ice that were currently attempting to freeze him with just a look.

"What is the meaning of this? Who are you?" he spluttered, attempting to get up but discovering that he was not even allocated the tiniest of movements. "Drop that sword at once!"

"Did he send you?" she asked again, her eyes narrowing. "If he did, then it will be all the worse for you!" The sword bobbed a little closer to his throat, and Charles pushed himself a little further back into the chair. The young woman clearly knew how to use such a weapon, for she was holding it correctly and had the correct stance to boot. The weapon must surely be heavy for such a small woman to be holding, but she showed no sign of weariness.

"Answer me!" she cried, her cheeks flaming with anger. "Did he send you?"

"I have no idea what on earth you are talking about!" Charles exclaimed, his eyes focused on her face. "My name is Charles Catesby, and I own this townhouse!" He saw the flicker of doubt in her eyes, as the sword began to lower just a little. "Now drop that weapon and let me free!"

"How do I know you're not here to capture me?" she fired back, the sword lifting once more. "Why should I believe you?"

"Because I do not know who on God's green earth you are!" he exclaimed, exasperated. "Although I should dearly love to know how you got into my home and why you are pressing a sword to my throat!"

Charles waited for a long moment as the woman studied him with her sharp eyes. It seemed like an eternity for his muscles holding himself taught back against the armchair wavered, before watching in relief as she took a step back and dropped the sword to the ground.

"Very well," she said, keeping her gaze fixed on him. "But no tricks. I shall have this at your throat again in an instant!" She raised the sword a bit threateningly to punctuate the point.

"Thank you," he managed, rubbing his throat even though the sword hadn't touched it. Getting up from his chair, he stretched carefully, seeing her jump in alarm at his movements and height.

"I am not going to hurt you," he said, a little more gently. "You do not need to be afraid of me."

She chuckled darkly, a wry look in her eye as she placed the sword carefully against the wall. "That tells me that you are being truthful, sir, for otherwise, you would know why I should be afraid."

Without completely turning his back to her, Charles walked over to the fire, stirring the coals to help the blaze get going again. The dull gloom at the windows told him that it was early morning, which explained the chill in the air.

"Would you like something to eat?" He gestured to the table, where the remains of his meal from the previous evening still sat. "I do not think I have eaten everything my mother sent with me."

Her eyes flickered toward the hamper of food, then back to Charles, as if deciding whether it was truly safe to let her guard down.

"Thank you." Sitting down gracefully, she accepted some cold meat pie from him, eating it with nimble fingers.

"My maid will be bringing tea soon enough," she offered politely.

"You have a maid with you?" Charles' eyebrows rose. "Goodness me!"

"I must apologize for the intrusion," she said, honestly. "I had nowhere else to go."

With a rush, Charles realized that she must have been the one moving around the bedchambers the previous evening and that her presence also explained the reason the kitchen had been so clean. "I think you had better start at the beginning, Miss...?"

"Miss Abigail Sidmore," she replied, primly. "How do you do?" She nodded politely in his direction.

"I think the time has passed for such formal introductions," he replied, with a cocked eyebrow and a slight grin. "Why are you in my home?"

Sitting back in the chair rather dramatically, she let free a wretched, frustrated sigh. But as she stared up at the ceiling, her eyes glazed with tears.

"You would not believe it if I were to tell you..." She paused for a moment as her face hardened with the words she was about to speak. "But I have been sold." She returned her gaze to Charles', having come to terms with the reality of her situation, at least conversationally.

"Sold?"

"Indeed. My father has been given an excellent price for me!"

Charles frowned, his eyes darkening at the thought of a woman being traded like cattle. "You are to be married then?"

"Yes. To Lord Kettering."

Abigail watched to see if there was any recognition in his eyes, but he simply shook his head.

"I do not know the man, I must confess. It has been an age since I have been in town."

"Better for you that you do not know him," Abigail replied, darkly "His cruelty knows no bounds. He spends his time ridiculing any lady he chooses, whilst happily taking both money and possessions from the green young men who dare play him at the tables."

Charles's mouth twisted. A gentleman knew not to play hard against any young newcomer, for they had to learn the ropes before being able to play seriously. It was simply common decency. A man who had no regard for the youth was not someone Charles would be particularly enamored with.

"He whips his staff, or so I am told, and everyone is afraid of him."

"So why is your father forcing you to marry?"

Taking a breath, Abigail collected herself before replying. "He is in debt. Lord Kettering has had his eye on me for a long time, but I have continually rejected his advances. Now that my father is in debt and simply cannot pay –"

"Lord Kettering has used it to get what he wants, which is…you."

With a bleak look, she nodded. "Precisely." She shrugged her shoulders and continued matter of factly, "I had to get away. I had to escape. There is no love lost between myself and my father, and with no mother or siblings to speak of, I had no qualms in leaving him to his own folly."

"You would leave him in Lord Kettering's mercy?"

"Why should I not?" she asked, a little defensively. "My father chose to gamble, and I will not be used as a bargaining chip in order to bring him relief!"

Charles nodded, slowly. The girl had a point, and he could not imagine the thought of being forced into marriage. "So you ran away?"

"Yes."

"You do realize your reputation –"

"Is quite ruined, yes."

He thought for a moment. "You have your maid with you?"

"Yes, she should be bringing us some tea in a moment."

"I see." Charles thought hard. "We have much to discuss, Miss Sidmore."

"Abigail, please." The hardened expression that had relayed her predicament melted away. Her eyes softened into a smile and Charles was surprised to feel his stomach flip under her gaze.

"Being a stowaway in your house puts us on first name terms, wouldn't you agree?"

He let out a light chuckle. "You are quite unconventional, Miss Sidmore – Abigail, I mean. And yes, yes, you are quite right. First names it is. Now, why don't we see about that tea and then think about what we are going to do with you."

Abigail nodded, trying for the moment, not to be concerned with the uncertainty that this new stranger brought. Was he going to send her back to her father? Or would he help her escape from her cruel fate?

CHAPTER 5

"**G**oodness!"

"It is quite all right, Bess, do come in."

Charles raised an eyebrow as the maid came in, carrying a tea tray that was laden for two.

"I normally take tea with Bess in the morning," Abigail explained, seeing him study the tray. "Although I think Bess would much prefer to have her own in the kitchen today, wouldn't you, Bess?"

Reddening a little, the maid mumbled something incoherent in agreement, before casting a suspicious look at Charles and turning to back out of the room.

Charles cleared his throat, catching her attention. "There should be some new staff appearing this morning, Bess. Please ensure they make themselves at home. You are able to find them suitable bedchambers, I presume?"

Bess threw a glance to Abigail, before nodding.

"Excellent." Sitting back, Charles stretched out his long legs, crossing them at the ankle. "That saves me a task this morning. Given that I already have so much on my hands…" He trailed off, giving Abigail a meaningful glance which she merely rolled her eyes at.

"Thank you, Bess. I'll come down later to speak to you. I'm quite safe, I assure you." Giving Bess a wide smile, Abigail waited for her to leave before turning back to Charles who, to her surprise, was already pouring the tea.

"Shouldn't I do that?

Charles merely grinned in reply, handing her a cup so she could add whatever she wanted to it. His eyes were keenly aware, watching the way a wayward tendril slipped from its confines and rested loosely across her forehead before being tucked away. She was a beautiful woman, and he could easily imagine that she would command a room simply by her presence. She was obviously made of strong stuff, given that she had basically run away from home, with very little money or support. Lord Kettering must indeed be a dastardly scoundrel for her to go to these lengths.

"What are you going to do with me?"

Tipping his head to one side, Charles considered his answer. "Did you plan to come here?" he asked, ignoring her question. "How did you know this house was empty?"

"Bess," she replied, simply. "The staff know everything."

"Of course," Charles mused, thinking hard. It would have taken some time for the maid to discover which houses nearby could be used. If he were to demand that Abigail leave his home at once, there would be no other recourse for her other than to return to her father's house – or find another vacant lodging, which would be quite difficult on the spur of the moment. However, Charles wanted to assure himself that this woman was exactly who she said she was. He did not trust strangers, no matter how fine their sparkling eyes or how dazzling their figure. As his mind ran through the situation, he realized uncomfortably that finding answers would mean going out again into society. No doubt there would be invitations to balls and soirees now that he was back in town, but this new twist of events meant that he would actually have to attend many of them if he were to discover the truth.

Abigail struggled to read the man sitting across from her, his gentle green eyes perusing her carefully as his thumb ran over his bottom lip again and again. He was obviously thinking about what to do with her, and she found it difficult not to beg him to help her, re-pleading her case to him until he relented. Begging would do nothing for her, she told herself firmly. Keep your mouth closed tightly. At least he appeared to be quite friendly, for most other men, she was sure, would have had her out on her ear the moment she lowered her sword. Polite society had strict rules, and no-one wanted to break one for fear of being pushed out of the sphere where gentry and nobility dwelt. By running away, she was certain that her reputation was completely ruined. Add to it that she was now temporarily living with an unknown gentleman with neither maid nor chaperone to guard her, and the fact was absolutely certain. Not that it mattered, for anything was better than being chained to Lord Kettering. A slight shiver went through her as she considered his vile face for a moment, knowing that she would be quite happy as an old maid, should she manage to escape him.

"I suppose you may remain here for a time," Charles began, seeing the surprise and delight spring onto her face. "I cannot yet decide what I should do with you, nor what my next course of action should be, so you are welcome to stay here until such a time as I decide what to do."

"I am truly grateful," Abigail murmured through the hands risen to prayer at her lips.

"However, that does leave the issue of my staff," Charles continued, grimacing. "As you say, the staff know everything. I have a butler, a cook and a maid arriving this morning and I am quite sure one of them will know of the tale of your absconding from your father's house."

Thinking for a moment, Abigail turned to him with a wide smile. "Then I shall be your ailing sister." Her smile turned to worry, "You do have a sister, do you not?"

"Yes, yes I do," he replied, his brow furrowing. "But how shall that keep your presence hidden?"

Beaming, she let out a light chuckle. "I am your ailing sister and must keep to my room and not be disturbed by anyone other than my own, personal maid."

Charles' eyes roved around the room as he considered her suggestion. It had merit, he concluded, nodding in agreement. "Very well. You may also use the library when I am not at home if you wish. I am quite sure Bess can make sure the staff does not bother you."

Clapping her hands together, Abigail could not help but show her delight. "How can I ever thank you, Charles? I shall remain out of sight, I promise. You shall not even know that I am here!"

"You are quite welcome," Charles accepted, then his brow furled into a subtle frown. "Although -" he paused as he tried to find appropriate words to get across his feelings, "you would be most welcome to join me some evenings in either the study or the library, should Bess be willing to remain with you."

Her eyebrows lifted.

"I am quite sure that you will not wish to spend all your time in your room alone, for you would become quite bored," Charles blustered, seeing her expression. "Whilst I am not always fond of company, I suppose an hour or two might be amenable."

What are you doing? He chastised himself. *Surely you have not been so easily seduced by a pair of bright eyes and a perfect rosebud mouth?*

Apparently, he had, given the way his heart squeezed as she smiled at him, thanking him for his invitation. Watching her as she left the room in search of Bess, Charles shook his head to himself, realizing how easily he had been taken in by her guile.

Not that there was anything to suspect her of not truly being who she said she was, Charles thought, as the door swung closed. She appeared to be exactly who she said she was, someone running from an unwanted marriage. So long as she kept to herself, then he would have no immediate concerns over his own future. Nobody would talk, there would be no calls for them to marry in order to save her reputation. He had nothing to worry about.

It was funny, Charles mused, how the idea of marrying such a lady did not immediately fill him with dread. Shaking his head to himself once more at the preposterous thoughts overtaking him, he poured himself another cup of tea and sat back to enjoy a few moments of peace.

CHAPTER 6

C harles wandered into Whites, seeing a few eyes on him as he walked through the doors of the exclusive gentleman's club. Not many would know who he was, a mere second son, and particularly one that had not been in town for a long time. "Port, please," he murmured, throwing a couple of coins into the waiting hands. Taking a seat at a quiet table, glass in hand, he sat back and let out a long breath. The events of the previous day were already catching up with him. His mind was almost foggy with the number of thoughts trying to bring themselves to the fore. All he wanted was some peace and quiet, a chance to try and think about what he was to do with the lady currently in hiding in his home.

"Charles, my boy!"

His silence interrupted, Charles looked up to see his good friend Richard beaming down at him.

"Goodness me, Richard!" Getting up immediately, the two friends slapped one another on the back, both talking at once.

"I did not know you were in town! When did you arrive? Are your sisters with you?"

Knowing that Richard had his eye on Charles' younger sister, Helena, Charles was not surprised to see the slight sadness in his friend's eyes when he shook his head. "Sorry, old chap. Although I'm quite sure Helena would be delighted if you were ever to pay Francis a visit."

"You think so?" Richard mused, his dark eyes lighting for a moment. "Anyway, that is beside the point. Why are you in town? When did you arrive?"

Charles hesitated for a moment before replying, knowing that he would have to keep all mention of his surprise guest to himself. Richard knew his family well and wouldn't believe the 'ill sister' story for tuppence. Either that or he would not see it as a reasonable enough excuse not to visit Charles' home. "Just recently. Father passed away, as I'm sure you've heard."

Richard's eyebrows shot to his hairline as he looked up in surprise. "No, I hadn't heard. How awful. I'm truly sorry, Charles."

"You didn't hear? It was in the papers, I am sure."

"I - uh - have been a little distracted lately," Richard replied, a little off balance. "Been away from society – and from town - for a while."

"Oh?"

Richard shrugged, unwilling to give away any details. "You know, family, business, that sort of thing."

Briefly, Charles wondered what it was Richard had got himself mixed up in this time, before mentally shrugging and carrying on the conversation. "Regardless, Francis is now the new Lord Catesby and father left me the townhouse, as well as a modest living."

"I see," Richard replied, his eyebrows still lost in his hairline. "And what do you intend to do while you're here?"

"That I do not know," Charles answered, honestly. "I feel a little at sea, to be frank. I hope to spend some time back in my old haunts, and work out what it is I should do with my life."

"Perhaps seek out a few eligible ladies?" Richard queried, a grin on his face. "I could introduce you if you like."

"No," Charles replied, immediately. "Nothing like that. You know how much I prefer my own company." To his surprise, a vision of Abigail floated in front of his eyes for a very brief moment, but he instantly pushed the errant thoughts away.

Richard shrugged. "Then how about I keep you company whilst you are in town? You know how much sage advice I have to give!"

Charles snorted inelegantly, fully aware of just how little Richard had to offer. Richard stumbled from one mishap to another, his life meandering in any given direction. Whilst they had not seen each other in some time, Charles could not imagine that Richard had changed much. For some reason, his friend seemed to enjoy his ridiculous life, never making any particular changes or seeking any direction. It was not a life that Charles wished for himself, but, despite their differences, they were the closest of friends.

"Perhaps a visit to the library this afternoon, then you are welcome to my home for dinner?"

Aware that Richard had a townhouse near to his, Charles shook his head. "Thank you, Richard, but I have some new staff to see to."

"Very well, we shall just dine at yours." Sitting back, Richard took a swig of his drink before grinning at Charles.

Charles did not know how to respond, knowing that Richard would find any excuse he came up with a little less than believable. But what was he to do about Abigail? Could he trust Richard enough to tell him the truth or would that be too dangerous?

"Tell me," he began, after another moment's thought. "What's the gossip these days?"

"Gossip?" Richard asked, astonished. "You never were one for the rumor mills, Charles!"

"And that is still the case, of course," he replied, smoothly. "Just in case there is anything of note that I have missed, that is all. Is there anyone, in particular, I should be avoiding?"

Richard's brow furrowed for a moment as he thought. "As I said, I have only just returned to town and to society myself." Thinking for another minute or two, his face suddenly cleared. "Ah yes, well, a Lord Kettering has only recently been making his mark around town. One to be avoided, apparently."

"Oh?" Charles ensured his face was blank, even though his ears had pricked up at the name of the man Abigail had mentioned.

"Why is that?"

"Something about greed and fleecing some green youngsters, if I'm not mistaken. Seems he's quite an arrogant chap."

"I see," Charles mused. "If he is wealthy, then he surely has no need for extra funds. So why take money from those just learning their way around the tables?"

Richard shrugged. "I have no other knowledge about the man, I must confess. Someone mentioned that he had his eye on a particular young lady, but she has been hiding at her father's house, I believe. No-one has seen hide nor hair of her in over a week."

Charles hid his surprise by lifting his glass to his mouth. Apparently, Abigail's father was doing an excellent job of pretending that his daughter wasn't missing but was rather, in fact, simply hiding from society. Whilst the rumor of her hiding from society was embarrassing, it meant that her reputation was safe at the moment. However, that wouldn't last too long for surely someone would notice soon that she was gone from the house. Her father could not keep up such a ruse for weeks on end.

Diverting Richard from the topic, Charles began a fresh conversation over the latest additions to the London Library, still not quite sure how to avoid having Richard at his townhouse where he could, very likely, run the chance of running into Abigail.

CHAPTER 7

C harles had not managed to find a single excuse for Richard not to visit his home and had been quite unable to put him off. Mentions of his new staff, yawning constantly, or talking about how much he was looking forward to doing some reading this evening had done little to dampen Richard's enthusiasm. Charles could quite understand it. Had Abigail not been hiding in his townhouse, then he would have been more than delighted to spend time with Richard. Neither had Richard forgotten that Charles had some new staff to see to, so they had meandered along the cobbled streets to his townhouse, whilst Charles tried desperately to think of some reason to get rid of his friend.

Unfortunately, he was not struck with any particular idea, so he was simply left hoping that Abigail would make good on her promise not to be seen. Opening the front door, he heard Richard chuckle.

"Something funny, old boy?"

Richard grinned. "You need to get that new butler of yours on the go immediately, Charles. You cannot be seen to be opening doors and hanging up coats yourself."

Rolling his eyes, Charles took Richard's coat from him without a word.

"It's a little chilly too," Richard commented, rubbing his hands.

"The library will be warm," Charles replied, without thinking. Closing his eyes tightly for a moment, he turned back to Richard with a bright smile. "Although, how about we go and see if the staff has arrived? I shall need to greet them and give the cook instructions for dinner." Hoping that Richard would be persuaded to stay away from the library until Charles could be sure that Abigail was not within its confines, he was swept with relief as Richard agreed. Walking down the back stairs together, Charles was met by Bess, who looked up at him in surprise. It was not usual to see the master of the house below stairs.

"Ah, Bess. Have my new staff arrived?"

She bobbed a curtsy. "Yes, Milord. They are all in the kitchens I believe, taking a little rest. They have traveled quite some distance, it seems."

"Very good," he replied, glancing at the kitchen doorway. "My friend, Lord Livingstone, will be dining with us – me, this evening." He widened his eyes slightly, hoping that she would catch his meaning. Relieved at her somewhat startled look, he nodded briefly, before continuing on down the stairs.

"Is she the cook?" Richard asked, a little confused.

"Oh….no," Charles replied, searching for an answer. "She has been cooking for me the last day or so – I simply forgot that she would not be doing so any longer."

"Ah!" Richard exclaimed, apparently satisfied.

Walking through the kitchen door, Charles saw three heads swivel toward him before there was a sudden scraping of chairs as they all got to their feet at once. Quickly making the necessary introductions and ensuring they were all settled in their rooms, Charles explained to the cook that Richard would be dining with him this evening and what time he expected the meal. The cook nodded and bobbed a curtsy. After a few more instructions to the butler and the maid, Charles and Richard took their leave, knowing that a tea tray would follow them shortly after. Once Richard was settled in the library, Charles intended to make his way down back below stairs to explain about his 'ill sister' to the staff. This was already becoming quite the difficult situation.

"Wonderful," Richard commented, as they walked into the library. "I've missed this place, you know."

Charles glanced around the high shelves, hugely relieved that there was no trace of Abigail anywhere. "My father loved this place."

"Indeed he did," Richard replied, quietly, taking a seat beside the roaring fire. "So, tell me, how many more staff do you need? I can get a few recommendations for you if you like?"

Sitting down, Charles thought for a moment. "Certainly two footmen and a few more maids. This place is large enough to merit a fair amount of cleaning, given that most things have been under dust covers for some time."

Chuckling, Richard grinned at him. "And a valet?"

Charles blew out a breath. "Yes, I suppose. I cannot keep tying my own cravat, now, can I?"

"No, Charles, you can't," Richard replied, a smirk on his face as he eyed Charles' fairly rumpled cravat.

"Now that you have mentioned it, I believe I forgot to speak to the butler about something," Charles moaned, shaking his head in a show of irritation. "I shan't be long."

Richard waved a hand. "Go ahead. I'll find a new title for myself whilst I await your return" Getting up from his chair, he meandered over to one of the book-laden shelves, as Charles left the room.

Closing the door behind him, he turned and bumped straight into Abigail. "Goodness," he exclaimed, grabbing her to steady both her and himself.

"Charles?" Richard called out. "Was that you? Is everything all right?"

Dragging Abigail by the hand, he flung open the nearest door and pulled her inside, closing it immediately, surrounding them in near pitch black.

"What were you doing?" he hissed, his brows knitting together. Holding up a hand, he heard Richard open the door to the library, presumably to look around for any sign of trouble. They listened to

Richard's footsteps as he paced a few steps out before finally retreating back to the confines of the library. The door closed with a thud. Heaving a sigh of relief, Charles turned back to Abigail, seeing only the outline of her face in the sliver of light that snuck in from the hallway.

"For goodness sake, woman!" he whispered. "Whatever were you doing wandering the hallways? Didn't Bess tell you that I had company?"

"I haven't seen Bess," Abigail replied, her own voice quiet. "I was just returning from her room down below." Her breath was coming quickly, but it had nothing to do with the fright he had just given her. His arm was still clutching the back of her dress, their faces frightfully close. Something in her stomach began to unfurl, his nearness to her causing all kinds of inexplicable sensations.

"What were you doing below stairs?" Charles demanded, his voice still an angry whisper. "We could have seen you!"

"I didn't know you were bringing company," she replied, her own anger sparking. "I was just fetching her needle and thread. That was all!"

"Thank goodness we didn't see you," he let out, leaning his head back against the wall. "That would have ruined everything."

Abigail said nothing, wondering if she dared move just a fraction of an inch closer to him. Her hands were still pressed against his chest, and she tilted her head slightly, considering whether or not he realized how intimate an embrace they were in. Wanting to explore these new feelings, she inched the smallest bit forward, only to hear Charles let out a long breath. The strong hand that had bunched the fabric at her back as he'd hauled her inside slowly loosened its grip – but he did not move it away. Rather, it rested there, as though he could not find either the will or the strength to do so. Boldly, Abigail moved her hands a little further to either side of his chest, near to his shoulders, feeling the strength of his muscles beneath the fabric of his shirt. Her heart picked up its pace, as darkness surrounded them both like a cloak. It kept them exactly where they were, concealing them from prying eyes. Here, their actions could be hidden – a secret between the two of them.

Lifting her gaze up to his, she only just managed to make out his eyes, light eyes that were desperately searching her face.

Charles couldn't help but feel torn. Here he was, his arms around a woman he barely knew, with his friend in the next room. Of course, as a gentleman, he should have moved away from her immediately, but his body was refusing to respond. Instead of letting her go, his arms tightened a fraction, letting out a long breath as her hands spread across his chest. A brief thought of kissing her swept through his mind, but then everything that could come with it washed over him like an icy flood.

One kiss. A betrothal. Marriage.

Charles wasn't ready for that, wasn't even sure if that was what he wanted in life. Until yesterday, he was fairly certain that he didn't. Fractured thoughts raced through his mind. He hardly knew this woman and wasn't even sure that her story was true. So why was he finding it so difficult to move away?

"Charles," she breathed, tipping her head back, their eyes meeting through the slim fraction of light.

With an effort, he pulled away. Looking at her for a long moment, he turned on his heel, opened the door and walked through it. It swung closed behind him, leaving her encased in darkness.

CHAPTER 8

C harles did not see Abigail again that evening, even after Richard had departed. He sat in the library for some time before retiring to his own room. For some inexplicable reason, he wanted to see her again, even though he knew that his previous behavior had been most unlike him and it worried him on several levels. Whilst a few ladies had caught his eye in the past, he'd never done anything particular about it. He supposed that they simply hadn't intrigued him enough. Neither had he ever once held a woman in his embrace, nor run his hands over her gentle curves. The thought of it brought a slight flush to his face and a punch of desire coursed through him as the memory of her came to mind.

You still don't know if her story is true, he reminded himself. That's your first task. Get back into society and discover for yourself if she is being honest with you. Then you can decide what to do next. A little more resolved, Charles took himself to bed, far too aware that Abigail was only a few doors down.

Unfortunately, Abigail was not asleep either. She had tossed and turned for many hours but had not once managed to keep her eyes closed for more than a few seconds. Charles' shocking behavior earlier that day had exhilarated her, not appalled her as it should have. In that moment, when his grip on her had loosened and they'd drawn a little closer, the rush of attraction she'd felt had almost catapulted her further into his arms. He was certainly nothing like the type of man she was normally attracted to, given what she knew of his nature. By his own account, he was quiet and reserved, not particularly enamored by the colorful social events going on around him. The library was full of books that she was quite sure he'd have read at one time or another, and, as she'd crept along the corridor back to her room, she'd heard him talking to Richard about walking to the London Library come the following morning. Charles was apparently quite the scholar. Abigail sighed, turning her pillow over and slamming her head back down in frustration. She could not get the feeling of his arms around her out of her mind.

He was a kind and compassionate man too, she had to admit. The way he had so willingly accepted her presence here had spoken volumes about who he truly was, and she could not have been more thankful that she had chosen his house to hide in. Perhaps fate had guided their steps towards each other.

"Stuff and nonsense," she muttered to herself, pushing the thought away immediately. Charles still had to decide what he was going to do with her, and that in itself was a reason to be cautious. There could be no more thoughts of him, no more wondering what his lips would have felt like against her own, or recalling the way his fingers had almost seared her skin with their heat. It would have to be put from her mind and forgotten. She was being far too hasty in her trust of him. He could decide to turn her out or return her to her father at any given moment. Reminding herself of this, Abigail succeeding in dampening her longing for him, managing, finally, to drift off into a dreamless sleep.

"Miss! Miss!"

Sitting up, Abigail rubbed her eyes, seeing Bess's frantic face. "Goodness, Bess! What time is it?"

"The Master wants you to breakfast with him," Bess exclaimed, ignoring her question. "Come now, you must be dressed!"

"The Master?" She frowned for a moment, before recollecting her situation. "Oh, you mean Charles?" Throwing back the bedclothes, she started to scramble into her clothes with Bess' help. "Why does he want me to meet him? I thought I was supposed to be discreet."

"We've all been told not to disturb the Master this morning," Bess replied, buttoning up the back of her green day dress. "He caught me on the stairs and told me he'd be waiting for you as soon as you were ready."

Trying to rid herself of the ball of anxiety that was currently settling in her stomach, Abigail let out a long breath. "I'm sure he just wants to talk about the present situation," she assured Bess. And perhaps to talk about what happened between us yesterday. That thought sent a spear of anxiety shuddering through her veins, forcing her to take a few deep breaths.

"Sit down, Miss, and I'll do your hair. Pinch your cheeks for goodness sake!"

Obliging, Abigail did as she was directed, giving Bess a fond look. Her maid could be somewhat sharp with her tongue, but Abigail knew it was for her best interests. Bess had been with her for as far back as she could remember and Abigail considered her more of a confidante than a servant. Bess knew practically everything about her and had come with her willingly when Abigail had decided to leave. "I don't want to attract the Master, Bess. You don't need to do anything too ornate," she said, gently. "Just a simple style will do."

"Want you to look your best," Bess said, eyeing her handiwork carefully. "There." She pulled a few tendrils from the chignon, softening the severity of the style a touch. "Elegant as always. Now, off with you!" A soft smile lit Bess' face as Abigail kissed her maid's cheek before leaving the room.

CHARLES PACED BACK AND FORTH, wondering when Abigail was going to show. He had just received this morning's paper and had been utterly astonished by what he'd read. Of course, the paper – as always – had been very careful not to splash Abigail's name about, but it was undoubtedly about her. What he'd read had been somewhat different to Abigail's story, and he hated the thought that he was being lied to. It didn't help that he reacted every time he thought of the lady, hating the slowly unfurling attraction to her. She was certainly out of the ordinary, for he did not know many women who would ruin their reputation by running from their parental home. But could she be trusted?

His thoughts were interrupted as Abigail stepped through the door, her color high. Was it from the memory of what had passed between them only yesterday, or did she suspect that he had, somehow, found her out?

"Good morning, Abigail," he began. "Please, sit down."

CHAPTER 9

"Thank you." With as much grace as she could muster, Abigail took a seat opposite Charles, folding her hands neatly in her lap. Lifting her chin, she looked him directly in the face, as a shudder of nerves rippled its way through her. There was something different about him this morning, a thinness around his mouth that had not been there before. His demeanor seemed a little severe, his eyes slightly narrowed. Something was wrong.

"Tea?"

Abigail nodded, murmuring her thanks as he served her a steaming cup. Leaning forward, she added a little milk, stirring it carefully before sitting back and fixing Charles with a stare.

"I can tell that something is bothering you, Charles, so you might as well tell me."

Charles glared at her. Her impertinent words only added fuel to the fire burning in his chest, as he slammed the teacup down on the table with such force that Abigail jumped.

"I have been reading the paper this morning." He looked at her meaningfully, but Abigail simply shrugged.

"And?"

"And I have read some things that put you in a very different light, my dear."

"Oh?" Abigail tried to remain nonchalant. "You are telling me that the old biddies have finally managed to get a rumor about me into that old rag?"

"It is not a rumor," Charles bit out, his eyes displaying a rolling thunderstorm. "It tells me, in no uncertain terms, that you have been lying to me, Abigail."

Her mouth dropped open as she gasped. "Lying?"

"Yes, lying."

Abigail was stunned for a moment, staring into Charles' red face. His anger was clearly evident but was soon matched with her own.

"You think I have been lying to you, Charles? Lying that I am running from a man who wishes to possess me so that he has someone to beat black and blue, whenever he feels like it? You truly believe that I have taken advantage of your good nature somehow?"

A flicker of doubt crept into Charles' mind, but he picked up the paper regardless. "Let me read it to you, shall I?"

His sarcastic tone brought sparks to her otherwise calm eyes, but he ignored her completely, clearing his throat before beginning.

"A Miss A- S- has, it seemed, run from the confines of her home in an attempted elopement. Much to her chagrin, her intended chose to leave her at the nearest coaching inn, after realizing he would sooner marry respectably than run off with a Lord's daughter. It seems that Miss A- has gone into hiding, although she must by now be aware that her reputation is utterly in tatters. One must feel for her doting father who must be beside himself over her disappearance. It may be that a quick marriage to a respectable man will be her only way to salvage some of her once spotless reputation. It is rumored that a Lord K- would be quite willing to do so, should he find Miss A-, so besotted is he with her. One must wonder what Miss A- could be thinking, and hopes that she will return to the safety of her parental home very soon."

A white hot anger raced up Abigail's neck, bringing a hot flush to her cheeks. Her heart began to hammer against her chest as she glared at Charles, who was staring at her with something akin to vitriol.

"Can you explain this?" He held the paper firmly in his hand, and his sight was locked into hers.

"What is there to explain?" Abigail bit out, her hand curling into a fist. She had absolutely no doubt who had told the papers about this ridiculous rumor, for it could only be one person. For Charles to disbelieve her story over this brought a sudden, sharp pain to her stomach.

"You are not hiding from a failed elopement, then?" Charles asked, his voice icy.

"No!" Abigail cried, thumping the table with her fist. "I thought you were meant to be clever, Charles! But it seems all that reading has done very little to help your intellect!"

"There is no reason to insult me," Charles replied, a slow flush creeping up his neck. "What else am I to believe? The writers of the paper –"

"Are spiteful, no-good busybodies who seek nothing more than to make other people's lives a misery!" she interrupted, angrily. "Don't you know that these society pages are filled with nothing more than fabrications and gossip? Isn't that the kind of thing you shun?"

She did have a point, Charles thought to himself, his color still heightened. "So you are telling me that you are not hiding from a failed elopement?"

"No!"

"What you told me about Lord Kettering –"

"Is quite true."

"And your father's gambling debts?"

"Again, absolutely true."

Charles said nothing, sudden doubts assuaging his mind. Had he been too quick in his judgment of her?

"Don't you realize," Abigail began, her voice softening a little. "That the very thing you have just read proves my story?"

Shaking his head, Charles frowned heavily. "I can't see how."

"Lord K, which is, of course, Lord Kettering, is 'quite willing' to marry me, with great haste, so as to preserve my reputation."

"Yes, I read that." Still unclear as to the point Abigail was trying to make, Charles studied the paper again, re-reading the short paragraph.

"And who am I trying to hide from?"

"Lord….Kettering," Charles said, slowly, the truth finally dawning. Of course. Lord Kettering could have put the rumors about, attempting to force Abigail's hand.

"Lord Kettering is used to getting what he wants," Abigail finished, her voice quiet. "And, as it stands, I am what he wants. Although I am quite sure that my father is equally as desperate for the marriage to take place, given what is at stake." There was no hint of triumph on her face, just unadulterated sadness. She sat back in her chair, completely despondent. Whilst she knew very little of Charles, it pained her that he had believed the poorly written article over her. She had no reason to expect him to take her at her word, of course, but the pain was still there. Now that the anger had left her, anguish slowly filled her until tears pricked at the corner of her eyes.

"I must apologize," Charles muttered, glancing up from the paper. "I believe I may have been a trifle hasty." When there was no response, he looked at her again, seeing the tears she was attempting to wipe away. Guilt wracked him. This woman had sought refuge from what seemed to be a terrible situation, and he had almost condemned her after only a few lines in a newspaper. Was he truly so quick to disbelieve, to judge? Those tears were his fault.

"Abigail, I am truly sorry." Getting to his feet, he walked around to stand beside her. She did not look up, so he crouched down, feeling entirely awkward. "I am awfully sorry, Abigail. Please, do not cry." Charles was lost, unsure as to what to do with a crying woman – particularly when the tears were his fault.

Abigail sighed, her heart still sore. Wiping her cheeks furiously, she shook her head. "It is quite all right, Charles. I am still a stranger to you, and you have been so kind to me already. I should not blame you for having your doubts." Fresh tears fell as she grasped the desperate situation she was in. "Lord Kettering will not stop, I don't think." Burying her face in her hands, she sobbed aloud, her shoulders shaking with grief. "Whatever am I to do?"

Charles stood then, pulling her up and into his arms as he had done the day before. She cried for a long time, and he did the only thing he could. He held her.

CHAPTER 10

I t was quite some time before Abigail's tears slowed and her
sniffles stopped. Her head was still on Charles' chest, and she
could hear the slow beat of his heart as it gently soothed her. In
her heart, Abigail knew she could not blame Charles for what he had
said, but the reality that she had no idea of what to do or where to go
from here left her surrounded by questions she couldn't answer. She
couldn't remain here indefinitely, nor could she return home to where
her father would, no doubt, be waiting with Lord Kettering in the
wings. What was she to do?

Looking up into Charles' face, she made to step back – only for
Charles to lower his head, catch the back of her head in his hands and
gently kiss her upturned lips.

Charles didn't know what had come over him, but he knew he
couldn't stop. The sadness that swam in her sky blue eyes had been too
much to bear, the protective urge he felt as he held her demanding that
he do something. His heart, mind, and body were all reacting to the
feeling of her body molded to his, and the longing to kiss her had
forced him to act. Her startled gasp had been swallowed by his kiss
but, to his very great relief, she had responded almost at once. Her
hands rested on his chest, with one hand clinging to his shirt as he

pressed her against the table and deepened the kiss. It was a strange kind of euphoria – one where he did not quite know what he was doing but was thrilled nonetheless.

"My, my! What's going on here, then?"

Jumping back from Abigail, Charles spun around to see Richard looking at them both with a slightly bemused expression on his face. "Oh, Richard, I –"

Abigail turned her back to them both, as Charles spluttered and stammered his way through some kind of ridiculous explanation. Her cheeks were hot, and she was quite sure her neat chignon was now slightly less than elegant. A panic ran through her as she realized that, for the moment, she was quite compromised. Should Charles' friend tell anyone of what he had just seen, they would be forced to marry, and she did not want that. It was not that the thought of being wed to Charles was a particularly awful one, more the idea of forcing him into matrimony. Indeed, that was precisely what she was running from! Abigail had always promised herself that she would marry for love if that were ever possible, and she had absolutely no idea what Charles felt for her. To be frank, she was barely able to give a name to her own emotions. Taking a breath, she turned to face the stranger, placing a bright smile on her face.

"Good morning, sir. I am Miss Abigail Sidmore. I am very pleased to meet you." She bobbed a curtsy, well aware that it was far outside the realms of propriety for her to introduce herself to a gentleman, but, given the circumstances, she supposed it was for the best. Thankfully, the man seemed quite at ease.

"I am delighted to make you acquaintance," he replied, bowing with as much grandiose as he could muster. "Lord Livingstone at your service." His eyes swept over the lady, noting the blush to her cheeks and the slightly mussed flaxen hair. She was certainly pretty, but what had Charles been doing with such a lady?

"I must say, I am quite parched this morning. I don't suppose there's any hot tea left?"

"Please," Abigail smiled, gesturing to the table as though it were her own. Both she and Richard took seats at the table, leaving Charles to stare at them both, open-mouthed. He had been attempting to find some kind of reasonable explanation for why he had been kissing a lady in his dining room, only for her to put Richard quite at ease, as though nothing had ever happened. She appeared neither flustered nor put out, although there was still a slight tinge of pink to her cheeks. After what had just occurred between them, Charles was a drowning man, trying desperately to grab hold of firm ground.

"Aren't you going to sit, Charles?" Richard grinned, quirking an eyebrow.

"Suppose I should," Charles mumbled, sinking into a chair. "Seems you have both made yourself quite at ease."

Richard shook a finger in Charles' direction. "Don't think I am about to let you off so easily, my man! I must know exactly what is going on here between you and Miss Sidmore..." He trailed off, his eyes on Abigail. She looked at him steadily, seeing the flicker of recognition in his eyes.

"I see that you have only just now, recollected my name," she said, primly. "You are quite right. I am the missing daughter of Lord Sidmore."

"Indeed" Richard replied, throwing Charles an astonished look. "Whatever is going on? Why are you in Charles' residence?" His eyes widened slightly as a shocked look appeared on his face. "Charles! Never tell me that you are the runaway groom, who spurned his future bride at the last moment?"

"No, no!" Charles exclaimed, holding up his hands in defense. "Nothing like that, I assure you!"

Abigail gave a slight chuckle, relieving the sudden tension as Richard sat back in his chair, his face filled with a look of relief. "I must say I am glad to hear it. Otherwise, I am afraid I should have had to horsewhip you, Charles."

Charles grimaced, his eyes trailing over to Abigail before turning back to Richard.

"Miss Sidmore has been seeking refuge from Lord Kettering," Charles explained shortly. "Fortunately, she found my house."

"I was here before Charles arrived," Abigail explained, thinking that she quite liked Lord Livingstone. "Once Charles…ahem… discovered my residence in his house, he allowed me to stay for a time. I have my maid, Bess with me too."

Richard frowned, a crease appearing between his eyes. "You are in hiding, then?"

Sighing, Abigail nodded. "I am afraid so. My father wishes me to marry Lord Kettering and, to be frank, I cannot think of anything worse!" Her heart grew heavy as she remembered her father's orders, and she managed to suppress a shudder. "My father was quite adamant, I'm afraid." She chose not to speak of her father's debts for the moment, quite sure that Charles would make him aware of that fact soon enough.

"How dreadful," Richard replied, sympathetically. "So what are your plans now, may I ask?" *And do they include Charles?* He wanted to add, only just managing to refrain.

"That, I'm afraid, is not a question I can answer at the moment," she said, throwing a quick glance to Charles, who was studying his piece of buttered toast with great deliberation. "We are yet to discuss it."

Charles nodded. "Ah, yes, well I'm afraid I was a little harsh with Abigail – Miss Sidmore – this morning. The paper, you see."

"I've not read it," Richard replied, cheerfully. "Of course, it's all absolute tosh in there anyway, isn't it? Society gossip and what not."

"Yes, absolutely," Charles commented, faintly.

"Then may I suggest we put our heads together and see if we can come up with a way to keep Abigail out of Lord Kettering's clutches? It is not as if she can stay here forever."

There was a brief moment of silence before Abigail enthusiastically agreed.

"No, I suppose she cannot," Charles murmured, wondering why the thought of her leaving his home caused his heart to sting with pain.

CHAPTER 11

"My dear sir! How delighted we are to see you again!"

"Thank you," Charles smiled, pressing the hand of the older lady. "Glad to be back." From the corner of his eye, he caught Richard's indolent grin, clearly aware that nothing could be further from the truth.

"And how is your dear mother?"

"As well as can be expected," he replied, wanting to take his leave of this conversation – and the lady – as soon as possible.

"Of course, of course," the lady smiled sadly, giving a slight shake of her head. "How awful it must be to lose one's partner so unexpectedly."

Charles grimaced. "Indeed," he replied, shortly.

The lady did not seem in the least put off by his quick reply. "May I introduce you to my daughter, Miss Sarah Ponserby?"

Attempting to keep the sigh from escaping his lips, Charles went through the motions, thinking that the reason Miss Ponserby had yet to find a suitor was because she looked so extremely disagreeable. There was no smile on her face, nor a hint of warmth of any kind. Perhaps she is simply tired of being paraded about by her mother, Charles thought, attempting to treat the girl with a little kindness.

"And....is your dance card full this evening?"

Charles stared at the brazen woman for a full minute, her propriety severely lacking. No-one asked a gentleman to dance with their daughter, no matter how keen they were to put their precious child directly under his nose.

"I'm afraid you will not get a dance from this man," Richard interrupted, smoothing over the situation at once. "In fact, I must beg you not to endanger your daughter's gentle feet!" He laughed, and Charles slowly began to relax, seeing the curiosity on Lady Ponserby's features. "Despite numerous lessons, Catesby here has two left feet. He has often left his partners in agony, to the point that now he refuses to dance completely, for the sake of the beautiful young ladies and their delicate feet."

"Truly?"

Charles could tell by the way the lady was studying him with slightly narrowed eyes that she was not altogether convinced by the tale.

"I should hate to break your daughter's toes," he announced, with a wince. "It would not be the first time…"

That did it. The lady gave a horrified gasp and, hastening her farewells, made off at once, dragging her daughter with her.

"Very well done there, Richard," Charles proclaimed, slapping his friend on the back. "I was quite at a loss. The impudence of the woman!"

"You have been away from town too long," Richard laughed as they made their way through the crowd. "I'm afraid those with unmarried daughters have become quite a bit more brazen."

"But I am only a second son," Charles protested. "Why should they want me?"

Richard grinned. "You have a modest living, a townhouse and, of course, being the second son, a chance of the title."

Catching his meaning, Charles blanched. "But that would mean that Francis –"

"Yes, of course," Richard replied, waving a hand almost as to disregard the notion. "But that is still a chance for the conniving mothers. You must be on your guard – although, by now the rumor of broken toes and two left feet should be making its way around."

"Then I am greatly in your debt," Charles commented with feeling. "Shall we play some cards?"

"Indeed," Richard replied, following him. "Perhaps there we shall find our quarry."

THEY DID INDEED FIND Lord Kettering in the card room, laughing aloud as he pulled yet more coffers from reluctant hands. His dark features gave him an almost maleficent air.

"There he is," Richard uttered lowly, turning his back so that the man wouldn't get a hint that they were watching him. "I don't know what you intend to do, Charles, but I'd advise not becoming too friendly with him."

Charles wasn't listening. The thought of Abigail in the arms of Lord Kettering was pushing anger into his veins. Here he was, faced with the man who had smeared Abigail's name through the mud in the hope that, somehow, he could force her into marriage. The man was abhorrent. Unfortunately for Charles, none of them had managed to come up with much of a plan, other than to at least meet Lord Kettering and attempt to find a way to pay off Lord Sidmore's debts. Perhaps if the man had nothing more to ask of Abigail's father, he would loosen his demands for her hand. Although it is not as though I hold much respect for her father either, Charles grumbled to himself, beginning to stalk towards the table.

"Ah, Catesby!" An old acquaintance got up and shook his hand, clearly delighted to see him. "When did you come back to town?"

"Only a short time ago," Charles replied, evenly. "I was hoping I might join you?"

"Of course, of course," his friend replied, as both Richard and Charles seated themselves. "I'm quite sure we can deal you in. Let me make the introductions."

Charles nodded and attempted to smile at the men around the table, forcing his eyes not to linger on Lord Kettering.

"And this is Lord Sidmore."

Managing to suppress his gasp of surprise, Charles nodded at the older man on the opposite side of the table, as Richard coughed frantically beside him. The shock had come quickly, realizing that Abigail's father was amongst the players. Things are getting a little more serious now, Charles thought, picking up the cards that were dealt. Keep your head and your cool, Charles. Show this man what you've got!

A COUPLE OF HOURS LATER, and Lord Kettering was staring at Charles with a look that would have sliced him open, had such a thing been possible. Charles had played well, but fairly and had managed to, not only clear the table of the rest of the players, but had won a substantial amount in the process. Gambling had never been his forte particularly, but it seemed fate had her gaze on him tonight. Whilst, unfortunately, it had meant taking a substantial amount from Lord Sidmore, there was now only himself and Lord Kettering at the table.

"I shall play for everything I have on the table," he said, calmly. "What have you there, Kettering?"

Kettering scowled, staring down at his meager pile. "I shall have to write you a dun, should I lose."

"Or you could turn over some of your other duns," Richard said, helpfully. "Goodness, don't scowl at me so, man! Everyone knows you hold many a man's duns at the moment. Although tonight, it appears that you are not particularly on a winning streak."

"So it seems," Lord Kettering said, tightly. "Very well. I hold duns for almost every man that was sitting at this table. I shall add them to my pile. Should you lose, then you shall give me everything you have at the table. Should I lose, then you may consider those duns my payment. The men shall pay you instead of me." His eyebrow quirked as he glared at Charles. "What say you?"

Charles frowned heavily, trying his best to put on the demeanor of a man who had not quite made up his mind. "I am not quite sure –"

"Come along now!" Lord Sidmore protested, the first words he had spoken in their presence. "You can't just give away my dues, Kettering! It isn't right!"

"I accept," Charles interrupted, smoothly. "Shall we get to it?"

Completely ignoring Lord Sidmore's gasp of dismay, followed by some ominous mutterings, Charles watched the next hand dealt, hoping that luck wouldn't leave him at the very last moment.

It didn't.

"Mine, I think," he uttered cooly, trying not to show any hint of victory. He didn't want to make an enemy of Lord Kettering, who was currently scowling at him with vitriol. "I'll get those duns from you, shall I?"

"Tomorrow," Lord Kettering bit out, his dark eyes flashing. "I'll send my man around with them."

"Excellent," Charles replied, getting up from the table. "This has helped me pass a pleasant evening, gentlemen. Thank you." Giving Kettering his townhouse address, Charles slowly meandered his way out of the room, swiftly followed by Richard.

"You did it!" Richard exclaimed, but Charles hushed him immediately.

"Not so loud, man! Kettering is not exactly best pleased to have lost so heavily. I do not wish to appear to be gloating."

"Nonsense," Richard declared, slapping him on the back. "The man doesn't know a fig about you! He has no suspicions. Other than being peeved over his loss, you shouldn't have any concerns as regards to your…guest."

Charles was not as relaxed, however. "Still, I feel we must be careful."

Shrugging, Richard fixed him with a beaming smile. "What shall your lovely guest say when she discovers that you hold her father's duns?" he asked, quietly. "I am quite sure she shall be immensely grateful." He gave Charles a large wink, which Charles could not help but chuckle at.

"Grateful to be sure," he agreed, a light smile on his face.

CHAPTER 12

Abigail's eyes widened in surprise. "You have my father's duns?"

"Well, I shall," Charles corrected. "Lord Kettering's man should be round with them – and the others, sometime today." He smiled at her surprise, feeling a warmth in his heart over what he had managed to achieve.

"I can barely believe it," Abigail whispered, shaking her head. "I did not take you for a gambling man, Charles."

"Oh, I assure you, I am quite the opposite," Charles refuted at once, catching the flicker of disappointment on her face. Given how she'd ended up in this situation, he could hardly blame her. "I am nothing like your father, I assure you. Richard and I only joined the game to try to get to know Kettering a little more and I simply never expected to do so well. Given that we had no kind of plan in place, joining him at cards seemed to be our only option."

"And what did you discover about him?"

Charles shook his head. "I can see why people are afraid of the man. He is almost darkness itself." Recalling the way the man had glowered at him, Charles couldn't imagine Abigail in the man's arms, not even for a moment. She was light, and he was darkness. "No longer can I blame you for running away."

Her face turned joyful. "I cannot tell you how relieved I am to hear you say that, Charles."

"I should never have doubted you," he confessed, taking her hand. "I hope that your father will relent, once I tell him his debts are torn up."

"You are going to tear up his duns?" Abigail repeated a blank expression on her face. "But Charles, they are sure to be quite substantial!"

"I have no need of additional funds," Charles replied with a smile. "I intend to do it for all those men, not only your father."

Abigail did not know what to say, staring at Charles for a moment. He was the kindest man she had ever come across, and his attempts to remove Kettering from her life were more than anyone else had ever done. "Thank you," she whispered, getting to her feet and leaning down to kiss him on the cheek. "Truly, Charles."

She did not pull away, her mouth dangerously close to his.

"You are most welcome," he breathed, his senses swimming with her closeness. Her lips curved into a gentle smile, and Charles was lost. Pressing his lips to hers, he pulled her onto his lap. She went at once, soft and malleable in his arms. Charles dug his fingers into her silken hair, disregarding her carefully set style completely. Her arms tightened around his neck, and he kissed her more deeply, struggling to keep a hold of his own erupting desires.

The door flew open.

"I suppose I should be used to this by now," Richard commented, drolly, watching with amusement as Abigail extracted herself from Charles' affectionate hold.

Abigail blushed hotly, sitting down on the chaise longue and attempting to smooth her skirts. "Good afternoon, Lord Livingstone."

"Good afternoon, my dear. I see Charles has told you the news!"

Charles couldn't help but feel both amused and embarrassed at the same time. "Indeed I have, thank you for your concern."

"Has the man arrived yet?" Richard asked, sitting down opposite

Charles and stretching his booted feet out across the floor. "With the duns, I mean?"

Shaking his head no, Charles glanced over at Abigail the precise moment her eyes flicked to his. A semblance of a smile played around her mouth, and Charles immediately felt himself relax. She was embarrassed to have been caught kissing him, yet again, it seemed, but apparently did not regret it. That was something of a relief, for he was already imagining what it would be like to kiss her again.

Wait a moment, Charles, he thought to himself, his heart almost stopping for a moment. *What do you feel for this woman? Do you love her? And if you love her, are you prepared to marry her?* The realization that the inevitable consequences of what they were doing hit him squarely between the eyes. Even if he did not love the woman, he should at least marry her regardless, given their behavior. It would be a simple enough matter, and it would mean that Abigail would be safe from Kettering forever. I need a little more time to think about this, Charles concluded, the idea of being married to the delectable Abigail bringing him a mix of both joy and sheer terror.

Bess appeared at the open door, knocking once. "There's a man at the door," she said, looking at Charles. "The butler's training one of the footmen, so I answered it for him. Says something about notes or something?"

"Thank you, Bess," Charles replied, getting to his feet. "I'll come at once."

"Do you feel this is now all at an end?" Richard asked the moment Charles had left. "I mean, now that he holds your father's duns, Charles has effectively removed the necessity for you to marry Kettering."

Abigail's smile was brittle. "My father will not stop gambling, as you may have seen yourself. Already he has lost so much to Lord Kettering, yet you both found him at the very same table he was playing at!" She shook her head. "Undoubtedly, my father will soon find himself back in debt and shall wager me off to the highest bidder."

The agony on her face made Richard's heart swell with sympathy. "There is always Charles, you know."

Her eyes flew to his face. "Charles?"

"Yes. Charles." He looked at her with one eyebrow quirked, as though he expected her to understand what he meant immediately. "Come now, my dear. Surely you cannot seriously believe that he is kissing you for no other reason than sport!"

Her blush was immediate. "I – I had not considered –"

"Charles is a quiet man," Richard continued, fully aware that he was landing his friend in the parson's trap. "But I must confess, I have never once walked in on him kissing another female in my life. In fact, I do not remember him ever being even the slightest bit enamored with a woman."

"Is that so?" Abigail's heart was beating faster and faster, grasping exactly what Richard was trying to say. Wedding Charles would keep her from both her father's and Lord Kettering's clutches, and it appeared as though Richard had also considered the same possibility.

"Not once, my dear," Richard replied, with feeling. "If I may be blunt, I fear you have quite stolen his heart."

Silence filled the room as Abigail took in his words. "I see."

"And does he hold yours?"

"That is enough now," she replied, shaking her finger at him although her cheeks were still pink. "You may tell me all you like about your friend, but my own feelings are absolutely private!"

He laughed, throwing his head back. "I see I shall not be able to get anything out of you."

"Quite," she replied, primly. "Unless you care to tell me about your own heart…?"

"Ah, my heart is quite lost, my dear," he said, suddenly serious as he pressed a hand to his heart. "For quite some time, I must confess."

"Truly!" Astonished at his frankness, Abigail continued the conversation, more than content to keep the discussion away from her own feelings towards Charles. "And why have you not told the lady?"

He shook his head, shadows flickering in his eyes. "I am not quite suitable for her, I'm afraid?"

"Oh? You seem quite the respectable gentleman to me."

"Alas, I am not all that it seems," he replied, quite mysteriously.

"Then tell me, who is the lady in question? Do I know her?"

A far off look came over his face, as he lost himself in thoughts and memories of his beloved. "It is the lovely Miss Helena Catesby."

Nonplussed for a moment, the name became all the more clear to Abigail the more she thought on it. "Wait a moment! You do not mean to say you are in love with Charles' sister?"

"Indeed," he replied, a smile on his face although sadness crept into the corners of his upturned lips. "Charles is aware that my feelings turn in that regard, but he does not know that I have quite lost my heart to her."

"Then you should tell her!" Abigail exclaimed. "For what lady would not wish to know the depths of feeling a gentleman holds?"

Hearing Charles' footsteps along the corridor, Richard sat up a little straighter and pinned her with a look. "And one might ask, what gentleman would not wish to know the depth of feeling a lady holds for him? What do you say to that, Miss Sidmore?"

CHAPTER 13

Abigail found she could not take her eyes of Charles all through dinner. Richard had joined them, of course, but Charles seemed more relaxed than ever before, happier almost. The duns had been returned to each of the gentlemen, her father included, and, for the moment, Abigail felt free. It was a strange kind of freedom, given that she would have to remain in Charles' home for some time, but that did not seem to matter at the moment.

"So what are we to do with you now, Miss Sidmore?" Charles said, drolly. The wine had been plentiful, and he was beginning to feel quite light, the serious matters he normally thought about dissipating as the liquor made its way through his veins. "Are you going to stay at my house forever?"

"If you will have me," Abigail replied, a light smile on her face.

"I'm quite sure he will have you," Richard interrupted, chuckling. "What say you, Charles?"

He shrugged. "I must confess myself quite at a loss. I do not know what to do with you, Abigail."

"Perhaps I shall take on employment," Abigail said, suddenly. "Perhaps move to the country and become a governess. I am quite well trained, you know, in all manner of –"

"Absolutely not!"

The sheer force and volume of Charles' exclamation had her jumping almost right out of her seat, whilst Richard managed to spill his glass of wine in fright. Being completely out of character, Charles didn't know what to do with the explosion of feelings that suddenly hit him. With the liquor blurring his self-censorship, he could not control the frustration that rose up so ferociously from within. Wanting desperately to return to his previously playful tone, the words came out instead with direct seriousness. "You will not be seeking employment anywhere, do you understand?"

Something about the way he spoke riled Abigail. "May I remind you, Charles, that I am not your property? I shall do as I think best."

"You are beholden to me!"

"Beholden!" Her eyes widened, her lips thinning in anger. "And you think that this allows you to dictate what I do?"

"Time for me to go," Richard quipped, getting up from his seat. "Don't mind me. I'll come by tomorrow. I believe the two of you need to discuss this without my presence."

Abigail stumbled over her goodbyes, aware that Charles had neither moved nor spoken. His eyes were fixed on her, his face growing crimson as he held onto his anger. The thought of Abigail leaving his home, of taking employment where he might never see her again, was like the stabbing of a knife deep into his chest. He could absolutely not, *would not*, let her consider it. His thoughts turned in a circle as his words raced out ahead of them.

"*As* I said," he continued, while the door closed behind Richard's retreating form. "You shall not be taking employment, Abigail. I will not allow it!"

She got to her feet then, stamping her foot. "I am not yours to order around as you please, Charles! I am most grateful that you have allowed me to stay here, to hide from Lord Kettering, but I must look to the future." What Richard had said to her only that very afternoon sprang to mind almost at once, but Abigail refused to listen. She would not force the man to marry her, no matter how much she desired it. She would not trap him. If he were to offer for her, that would be entirely different, but the idea must come from him, not from her own mouth. Until then, she would think about her next step.

"I cannot imagine a future without you!" Charles shouted, his voice echoing around the room. "Can you not understand that, Abigail?"

Her heart was pounding as she stared into his eyes. "I think you have had a little too much to drink, Charles. We should speak of this when you are entirely sober."

"I am sober enough!"

"Goodnight," she said calmly, walking out of the door and up to her room. What she did not expect was for Charles to follow her out of the room and up the stairs.

"Abigail! I must speak to you!"

Grasping her door handle, Abigail turned to Charles with a fierce look. "Charles, I have made myself quite clear! We shall talk on this in the morning, perhaps. Now is not the time to enter into such discussions!" Although her heart was pounding, Abigail was quietly pleased at his fervor over her suggestion of leaving his home. It spoke more to her about his feelings that perhaps he was willing to admit.

Charles couldn't help himself. The thought of her leaving had driven him almost to insanity, where he couldn't seem to think clearly. She would no longer be in his home, no longer be there at the breakfast table with an easy smile that brightened his morning. Her kisses would just be memories, fading away into the back of his mind. He simply could not consider that fact. "I cannot let you go, Abigail," he breathed, moving closer and leaning over her so that one arm rested against the door on either side of her face. "Say that you will marry me."

Abigail blinked twice, her heart slowing as she tried to make sense of his words. "Marry you?"

"Yes, marry me."

"Why?"

"Because I cannot think of my life without you," he exclaimed, a shadow on his face. "You have filled my world with color and to go back to the gray cannot be considered!"

It was not a declaration of love, but neither had she confessed to him her own feelings, as mixed as they were. She was already on her way to falling in love with the man, Richard's words from this afternoon ringing in her ears. Abigail had always promised herself that she would marry for love, and from Richard's observations, that was what she could have, should she agree.

"I suppose I am quite ruined already," she fumbled, unable to say more. She looked deeply into his lovely sage green eyes, watching his face clear.

"Then that is a yes? You will stay? We will marry?"

As she nodded her assent, he dropped his head to hers immediately, capturing her lips with such a ferocity that she gasped in astonishment. The sound was hidden by his kiss, pressing her against the door so that she was flush against his body. His hand twisted the doorknob, and they went through together.

Charles did not stop kissing her, his hands roving up her back and onto her shoulders before his fingers began to pull the pins from her hair. One by one, they fell to the ground, and Abigail did not have the heart to stop him. In truth, she did not want to. When her hair fell loose around her shoulders, cascading like a golden waterfall toward her waist, he took a step back to admire her. "You are the most beautiful and beguiling creature I've ever seen," he whispered, then clutched her to him, kissing her once more. She gave into the rapturous kisses, raking her hands through his dark, thick hair.

Her whole being was crying out for him, wanting to belong to him entirely. He was going to be her husband, and she would be his wife. Then, not only would all of her pain and struggles with her father and Lord Kettering be at an end, but she would reside in the safety and comfort of this gorgeous man's strong arms. Out of the corner of her eye, she spotted the bed nearing. Her mind fought ferociously with her body, quarreling between want and reason. Before she knew it Charles' back was at the edge of the bed, and she could see that he was lost in a world beyond sense; a threshold that she was moments from crossing if she didn't stop herself. She dropped her hands from around his neck, sliding them down to his firm chest.

"The most reluctant words I have perhaps ever spoken, but I think we must both go to bed now," she managed

A smile lazily crossed his face. "I most agree."

She pushed down the thick lump in her throat, alternating between the urge to laugh at his words or cry at the sheer intensity she was feeling.

"No, my darling, I think we must go to sleep. But not together. Not yet."

As the words sunk in, he flung himself back onto the bed and let out a loud groan. Though his eyes remained closed, he still kept a hand gripped on her bodice.

"I cannot wait to marry you Abigail Sidmore. If the Church were open at this hour, I would carry you up the stone steps in my arms, racing the entire way."

His grip loosened and she took his large hand in hers, smiling all the while at his words. Bringing his hand to her lips, she kissed his palm and allowed her heart to stop racing a bit.

"Crawl into bed, you silly man. We shall continue this conversation in the morning."

Charles rolled into the bed and was fast asleep within a minute. Abigail scanned his peaceful features before moving in closer to cup his face in her small hands. Brushing back his hair she kissed his brow and gave him one final kiss on the lips before retreating down the hall to the room she had originally called her own.

🌺

IT WAS pitch dark when Abigail woke. Something was scuffling around in the room. Hoping it was not a mouse, she pulled the covers up tight and tried to locate the proximity of the sound. Dreamily, she wished that she could simply scoot closer to Charles, draping her hand over his chest and resting her head on his shoulder. Some night very soon, she thought, she would have him to protect her from all the scary sounds of the night.

She tugged the blankets up even higher, thinking that the room had suddenly turned particularly cold.

Burying her head into her pillow, she closed her eyes. The cloth suddenly pressed to her mouth silenced her scream, her senses swimming as she struggled for air. Her struggles grew weaker and weaker until she could no longer fight against the person overpowering her. By the time she was lifted from her bed and hoisted over a hulking shoulder, her body would no longer respond to her commands. She tried futilely to scream, to wake Charles from his alcohol induced sleep down the hall, but all she could hear were the light thudding footsteps of her captor. Then everything went black.

C harles woke to a thunderous knocking on the door, his head feeling as though it would split in two.

"All right, all right," he groaned. Swinging his legs to the side of the bed, he put his head in his hands as the world swam for a moment. He'd clearly drank too much last night.

"Come in," he yelled, wanting nothing more than for the knocking to cease.

Richard came in at once, his face pale. "Charles?"

Charles glanced at him, as the maid behind Richard giggled and looked away.

"For heaven's sake, put some clothes on, man!" Closing the door on the maid, Richard shook his head at his friend. "Whatever are you doing in here? We've been looking for you all over!"

He frowned, pulling a blanket over his lap. "Why wouldn't I be here?"

His friend stared at him. "Because this is Abigail's room."

It all came back to him in a rush. Dinner last evening, their argument, his proposal and at least some of their night together. Whipping his head around, he stared at the bed, wondering where she had gone. "My betrothed, you mean," he commented, getting slowly to his feet and taking the clothes that Richard had been helpfully collecting from the floor.

"Your betrothed?" Richard asked, astonished. "My goodness! When did that happen?"

"Last evening," Charles replied, rubbing a hand down his face. "Although I may have imbibed a little too much."

"I hope you don't regret the asking," Richard said at once, his face darkening slightly. "Abigail is a good woman, and I have never seen you as happy as you are with her around."

Charles shook his head. "I must confess I have been toying with the idea for some time. When she told me of her plans to leave this place…." he shook his head. "I could not stomach the idea of her no longer being in my life. I had to say something to get her to stay!"

"You are telling me that you do not love her, then?"

"Does it matter?"

Richard shook his head. "Of course it does! You must be honest with your wife to be, Charles. Besides, I have seen the way she looks at you and you at her. There is more than just a friendship between the two of you."

Recalling the way she had felt in his arms the night before, Charles could not speak for a moment, his heart swelling with some untold emotion. "Perhaps you are right," he considered for a moment, before gruffly adding. "Where is she? Have you seen her?"

His brows knotting together, Richard shook his head. "We came here to ask Abigail if she had seen you," he confessed. "We did not think that you would be in here in her stead."

"She was here," Charles commented, wondering where she might be. "I cannot imagine where she would have gone off to so early."

"Early?" Richard chuckled despite his concern. "It is almost noon!"

"What?"

"Too much brandy has never agreed with you," Richard replied, shaking his head. "Breakfast is still waiting, I believe. Coffee?"

"I'll meet you there," Charles grumbled. "I won't be long."

"A new shirt and a shave would do it," Richard replied with a grin, walking out of the door and closing it behind him.

. . .

CHARLES DRANK his hot cup of coffee, but it rolled in his stomach unsettling him even more. Abigail had not been seen or heard from, and Bess was almost at her wit's end.

"She wouldn't have run off, sir!" she exclaimed, her face pink and eyes wide. "She would have told me, if she had meant to, I'm sure of it!"

"I'd have to agree there," Richard commented, leaning back in his seat. "None of her belongings are missing, and we know how much she trusts you, Bess."

"Trusts me with everything!" Bess agreed, her hands wrapped in her apron. "I can't think what would have happened to her."

A sudden thought hit Charles right between the eyes. Ice ran through his body, his heart slowing right down in shock.

"What is it?" Richard asked, seeing his change in demeanor. "What, Charles?"

Charles looked at him, the coffee cup slipping from his fingers and rattling in the saucer. "The man."

Richard stared at him. "What man?"

"The man. Kettering's man. The duns."

"Yes, he came yesterday to hand them to you."

Charles' eyes swiveled to Bess. "You answered the door."

"I did. The butler –"

"Was training the footman."

Out of the corner of his eye, Charles saw Richard let out a long breath, his eyes closing as he realized what had happened.

"He recognized you, Bess."

"What?" Her eyes filled as she stared at him. "I did this? How?"

Richard got to his feet, patting her hand. "No, no, it is not your fault. Charles and I have much to discuss, Bess. Please, can you ensure that the houseboy is sent to us at once? We shall have an errand for him."

Seeing Bess out of the room, Richard turned back to Charles with a glare. "You cannot beset the woman, Charles! She is practically

Abigail's mother, the way she has taken care of her and for her to think that she had anything to do with her disappearance will be heartbreaking."

"I spoke without thinking," Charles said, with a nod. "Thank you for your consideration."

Accepting his compliment with a nod, Richard sat back down at the table. "So the messenger recognized Bess."

"I believe so," Charles said, heavily. "Kettering has been searching for her for many days, it is little wonder that he would have informed all of his staff of her disappearance, and that of her maid."

"And do not forget our sudden appearance at the card table," Richard replied, with a shake of his head. "Winning all those duns, I am quite sure he would have discovered without too much difficulty that you returned them to Lord Sidmore."

"Enough to raise his suspicions?"

Richard nodded. "Remember, the man is used to getting what he wants. Abigail is what he wants."

The thought of her held captive by Lord Kettering had fury flooding Charles' veins, his eyes darkening. Thumping the table with his fist, he got to his feet and began to pace. "What are we going to do?" he practically yelled, running a hand through his hair. "We have no idea where she is, or where he has gone!"

"First things first," Richard said, calmly. "Let us do some spying of our own." The houseboy entered, and Richard gave him some swift instructions and a heavy number of coins from his pocket, watching him run off almost immediately.

"What did you tell him?" Charles asked, wondering how on earth Richard was managing to remain so calm.

Getting to his feet, Richard poured himself and Charles a small brandy each before replying. "I told him to go and ask Lord Kettering's staff where he's gone."

"The staff?"

Richard nodded, throwing back his brandy in a few small gulps. "Don't you remember that saying, 'The maids know everything'?"

Charles shook his head.

Shaking his head, Richard loudly lamented how little Charles knew about polite society. "Where do you think most of the gossip comes from, Charles? From the staff! This maid sees Lady so-and-so in her master's house, alone and unchaperoned, and the next day, it's in all the rags!"

Charles' brain was working overtime, trying to keep up. "So you're saying that Lord Kettering's maids will know where the man is?"

"Well, someone will," Richard promised. "Gave that lad a small fortune in guineas, just so that he'll have something to barter with. Promised him the same for himself, should he return with information."

"How exactly did you know what to do?" Charles, asked, resuming his pacing. "I mean, I am practically a blubbering wreck whereas you have taken almost complete control of the situation. Goodness, Richard, you're not some kind of Bow Street Runner, are you?"

Richard's grin was just a fraction of a second too long in appearing. "No, nothing like that. I suppose I've just been around society a little more than you, Charles. Now," holding out the brandy, he refilled Charles' glass. "The best thing you can do is remain calm and wait, as hard as that may be. We'll hear soon enough, I'm quite sure."

CHAPTER 15

I t appeared that Richard had been quite right, for soon the boy was back, red in the cheeks and puffing and blowing for all he was worth.

"I say!" Richard exclaimed, handing the child a glass of water. "Drink this and sit down before you collapse where you stand."

Charles opened his mouth to say that he didn't think servants should be allowed to sit anywhere but their own quarters, but shut it again almost immediately. This was not the time for propriety.

"Know where 'e is," the boy managed to say, through great gulps of air.

"Where?" Richard encouraged, holding up a hand to silence Charles' many questions.

"Scotland," the boy replied before drinking thirstily out of the glass. "Stopping somewhere on the way, they said. The Master was mighty angry, the maid said."

"And why was that?"

"Something about wanting to get hitched as soon as he could," the boy replied, his eyebrows darting to Charles who was cursing under his breath.

Richard smiled, pulling yet more coins from his pocket and handing them to the boy. "You have done a wonderful job," he said gently. "Now don't go spending this all at once!"

"I won't, sir, thankee!" His fists were almost too small to hold the sheer amount Richard was giving him. "My ma, she'll be needing these. Thankee, sir."

Richard smiled again, dismissing the boy.

"You need to treat your staff better, Charles," he reprimanded. "Or at least pay them a little more! That boy's bringing home the only income his family has if I'm not mistaken."

"Not now!" Charles exclaimed, a wild look in his eye. "Kettering's taken Abigail to Scotland! To wed her!"

"I can't see her allowing that," Richard mused, walking towards the door. "Undoubtedly, we shall have to find her at once. If they have stayed overnight, then there are only a few inns I know that Kettering would find good enough to stay at."

"We cannot check them all!" Charles expelled with dismay.

Richard shook his head. "We may have to," he replied, grimly. "Besides, we will have to change horses at some point."

"Then what are we waiting for?" Charles roared, adrenaline flooding his veins.

"We should leave at once," Richard agreed, mildly. "Two riders will be faster than a carriage, but we have a large amount of ground to cover. You'd best go change. I'll have the horses readied."

Walking down the long corridor, Richard finally allowed the worry he felt to show on his face. He'd remained calm and collected in front of Charles, not wanting to concern his friend further. Whilst Abigail would refuse, there were ways and means for Kettering to ensure she became his wife, and Richard was quite sure the man would do what he had to in order to get what he wanted. That was the focus of Kettering's existence. He prided himself on having everything he wanted, for no-one was ever able to refuse him. His cruel nature made sure of that. Abigail had been the first one to defy him, and Kettering's determination not to be shamed in front of all society had forced his hand. He had taken her right out from under Charles' nose. *Why didn't I see it? I should have realized the moment the man saw Bess that she was in imminent danger!* Squaring his shoulders, Richard tried to remember that berating himself would do no good. He had to focus on the task at hand, using all the skills he had. He would help Charles find the woman he loved and then, so help him, he would insist that Charles tell her about his feelings. And he fully intended to be the best man at their wedding.

Charles readied himself as quickly as he could, urgency pushing him on. He cursed himself for his own foolishness, drinking too much last evening had meant that they'd taken Abigail almost right out of his arms. It had been daring, foolish even, but they'd managed to get away with it. Now he had very little idea of where she was, or even if they'd find her in time.

Striding from the room, he spoke quickly to the butler in short, clipped tones, making sure that Bess was to be informed about their plans. "Tell her that I intend to bring back her mistress without delay. And prepare the master bedrooms. I shall be moving there upon my return. Miss Sidmore and I shall be married before we return to this house."

"Very good, Milord," the butler intoned, a slight look of relief playing about his features. Charles nodded and walked away, trying to force his legs to remain at a walking pace and to not break into a run in front of his staff.

He was going to marry Abigail the moment he had her back in his arms, safe. She would be his wife and never again have to face the terrors Kettering had put her through. *Why did I never tell her the true depths of my feelings?* Cursing himself yet again, Charles made his way outside, only to find Richard standing beside two readied horses.

"Shall we go?"

"Lead on, please," Charles replied, mounting quickly. He followed Richard through the cobbled streets of London, itching to push his horse to a gallop before they were outside the city. It seemed to take an inordinate length of time before they were finally free to do so, and even the horses seemed to enjoy the chance to run at full pace.

෨ඁඁඁ෩

ABIGAIL DIDN'T KNOW where she was. All she knew was that her head hurt and she had no desire to open her eyes. Low voices murmured in the background, and, on instinct, she kept her eyes shut, remaining perfectly still.

Kettering. She recognized his voice.

It all came flooding back to her. She'd been taken from her room, away from Charles and, when she'd woken, laudanum had been forced down her throat, knocking her out almost immediately. Kettering's face had stared into hers, his dark eyes boring holes through her as he let out an almost maniacal laugh.

"Thought you could escape me," he'd said, his voice low and threatening. "Don't you understand, my dear? I always get what I want, no matter how much a certain Catesby wants you for himself!"

As her eyes had slid shut, she'd fought the fog long enough to hear him say something about Scotland, complaining about how long it would take, and she'd felt panic rise in her chest. Then she'd been lost to the oblivion.

Pressing down with her fingers, Abigail felt straw underneath a cotton sheet, realizing that she was lying on some kind of bed. Were they at an inn somewhere? If so, where? And how was she going to get away?

"She's still out," she heard Kettering say. "Maybe we gave her a little too much of that laudanum"

A second man laughed. "I can stay here with her."

"No," Kettering replied. "You'd like to have your way with her, unconscious or not, and I won't have that. She's mine. Not to be touched by anyone else. Understand?" The threat in his voice was real, and Abigail only just managed to suppress a shiver. "You sit outside," Kettering continued. "If she as much as tries the handle, I want to know about it."

"Yes, sir."

"Good."

Two pairs of feet made their way out of the door. The door was shut, and then creaking and scraping followed as a stool was pulled in front of it. Two male voices became one, as Kettering made his way down the stairs to get himself something to eat.

Abigail opened her eyes.

CHAPTER 16

S itting up, Abigail looked around the small room, pushing the two thin blankets off her legs. There was one window and, from the look of it, not much else. A basin with water, a small fire that was already dying, and that was it. Not even a table and chair. Swinging her legs off the side of the bed, Abigail had to pause for just a moment as everything started swimming. Blasted laudanum! After her world had righted, Abigail took a slow breath and got to her feet, realizing that she was not even wearing shoes. There were stockings, at least, which she did not remember putting on, and already her feet were beginning to nip with cold. Frowning heavily, she pulled the corners of the heavy cloak she was wearing over her thin nightgown, wondering when Lord Kettering had put it on. Not that she wasn't grateful for it, although it felt strange to be beholden to the person who had kidnapped her.

Glancing out of the window, staying as much out of sight as possible, Abigail realized that she was much too far from the ground to jump towards freedom. Recalling the clatter of Kettering's feet on the stairs, she scowled darkly, frustration rising within her. It was becoming more and more apparent that she was at his mercy. Oh, but I will not be so easily trapped, she determined, looking around the bare room once more.

⚜

LORD KETTERING WAS in good spirits, knowing that his bride to be was upstairs with no means of escape. He would have her by tomorrow night, he thought, grinning widely. *But why should I wait until we are wed?* He thought, his addled brain giving him pause. *You could take her now, couldn't you? No matter how much she screams, Joe is behind the door. No-one, not even her, could stop me.* With the drink sloshing in his hand, he raised a toast to his own prosperity, throwing it back in a few gulps before getting to his feet and staggering up the stairs.

"I'm going to be spending the night, Joe," he grinned, swaying a little. "Don't come in, no matter what happens."

"Yes, sir," the man grinned, his eyes crinkling with dark humor. "I'll be right here till dawn."

"She'll come willingly by morning," Kettering boasted, turning the door handle. "Now, hand me that candle and make sure this door is closed behind me."

Walking into the room, Kettering couldn't see anything but the faint moonlight coming through the window. Holding the candle aloft, he heard the door click shut behind him, a wicked smile spreading across his face. "Alone, at last, my dear," he murmured, staggering towards the bed. "I hope you have not been waiting too long..." His words died in his throat as he saw the empty bed, his mind only just grasping that she wasn't there.

"Not at all," came a sweet voice, and he spun on his heel only for a hard object to hit him not once, but twice, on the head. With a grunt, he crumpled to the ground, the candle rolling away along the floor.

Abigail grabbed it up, dropping the basin with a clatter. Her breath was coming fast, her terrified eyes searching for a pulse in Kettering's throat. *Please say I haven't killed him.* To her utter relief, she saw the rise and fall of his chest, letting her know that he was still very much alive.

"Now what?" she murmured, not sure what her next step was. This was the only thing she could think of, and, while it had worked well, she didn't know what to do next. Getting to her feet, she managed to build a small fire in the grate, glad when it caught fire. She had put it out in order to make sure the room was completely dark for when Kettering returned, but she had missed the slight warmth it had brought. Shivering, she turned back to study Kettering's prone form. She had no idea how long he would be out for and, from what she'd heard from their conversation, his man would be right outside the door for the rest of the night. Her mind raced wildly for what to do next. No, now was not the moment to panic, she reprimanded herself as she squatted in front of the small fire. Now was the time to gather every bit of calm she could muster and come up with an escape plan.

෴

"WE'D BEST STOP, CHARLES."

"No!" he retorted. "Absolutely not. We haven't found her, Richard!"

"And we're not going to at this rate," Richard replied, calmly. "Your horse is tired, and I don't particularly fancy attempting to ride in the dark."

Charles didn't care. All he could think about was Abigail. "What if we're too late because we stopped, Richard?"

His friend bit his lip. "Then we will still save her, Charles. Married or not, we won't allow her to stay with Kettering. No matter what it takes."

"I'll run away with her abroad, if I have to," Charles vowed. "Even if she's legally his wife, she'll never belong to him."

Richard nodded. "Appreciate your fervor, Charles, but that still doesn't help us with the matter at hand. We have to rest, old boy! We have to eat. Keeps the senses sharp. I swear we shall be out again at first light."

Despite every bone in his body wanting to do otherwise, Charles assented. "Very well."

"Good." Richard stared straight ahead, his eyes struggling to make out what they were approaching. "Looks like another inn to me. Not the best, but then again, I'm sure it shall not matter too much."

"No, not in the least," Charles replied, thinking that he probably wouldn't get more than a few winks of sleep given how distraught he was over Abigail's disappearance.

"Listen to me, Charles," Richard said, sternly. "You simply must stop being so morose."

"Morose?" Charles glared at his friend. "The love of my life has gone missing, and you're criticizing me for being miserable?"

Richard shrugged. "Why not be a little more positive, old chap? It would buoy both our spirits, I'm quite sure. You'll get her back, in the end, I've no doubt about it."

"I'm delighted to hear it." Charles' voice dripped with disdain. "Until your heart is fully enamored with a woman, don't try and dictate to me about how I should feel and behave over a woman."

The words cut deeply. Charles knew that Richard favored his younger sister, Helena, but what he did not know was that Richard's heart was quite lost to her. Circumstances had kept him from her, and he'd never had the chance to begin to pursue her properly, but that did not mean that he loved her any less.

"I'm just trying to give you some hope," he said quietly.

A harsh laugh left Charles' mouth. "As to what? What exactly is she going to do?" he asked, as they approached the inn. "Hear us coming and run right into my arms?"

Just as he said those words, the front door of the inn flew open, and Abigail ran straight out towards them, her pale hair and dark cloak flying behind her.

CHAPTER 17

Abigail did not know what to do, eventually deciding to drag Kettering across the floor so that he would be out of sight of the door. He had shown no sign of wakening, but, just to be sure, Abigail tore one of the rough blankets into long strips, hastily tying a rough gag around his mouth. Then she tied first his hands and then his legs together before ensuring that he was also secured to one of the wooden legs of the rickety bed. She didn't think it would hold him for long, but it would certainly give her enough time to attempt an escape should he wake.

Listening at the door, she heard nothing for a long time. The minutes slowly ticked by, until Abigail felt as though she'd had her ear pressed to the door for hours.

Eventually, she heard what she'd been waiting for – the slow, quiet rattle of a man deep in sleep. Holding her breath, Abigail reached for the door handle, turning it slowly and carefully until the door loosened. Every time it creaked, even just a little, she paused, her heart beating so loudly she was sure it would wake the man on the other side of the door.

Deciding to open it in one swift motion, she pulled the door back as far and as wide as it could go. A large arm swung wildly toward her like a wayward pendulum, and Abigail's heart jumped into her throat! Abigail bit back a shriek, clamping her lips together as she stared at the man with wide, terrified eyes. To her astonishment, he didn't move. Didn't even wake. There was no sudden roar of rage as he scrambled to his feet, no strong hand grabbing for her. Nothing. His head lay buried in his portly frame, lightly snoring and deeply asleep. Abigail took a few moments to allow her heart to calm its frantic pace, taking deep, steadying breaths as she pressed herself against the side of the doorframe. As she made her way towards the wooden stairs, she almost tripped over the man's boots which were strewn haphazardly beside him. He'd clearly had no intention of staying awake all night, never thinking that the woman inside would try and escape when Kettering was in there with her.

Pulling them on, even though they were clearly far too big for her, Abigail made her way down the stairs as fast as she could, seeing only a few drunkards lying across the tables in the area below. There was no proprietor that she could see, in fact, no-one was moving at all. Heading straight for the door, Abigail threw it open with all her might and ran, as fast as she could, out into the cold dark night.

"Abigail!"

For one horrifying moment, Abigail thought that the two figures on horseback were yet more of Kettering's men, but the second time her name was spoken, she recognized Charles' voice.

"Charles!" she cried, rushing towards him as he jumped from his horse. She flung herself into his waiting arms, relief warming her entire body as she clung to him. "Whatever are you doing here?"

"Looking for you," Charles replied, completely astonished. He hugged Abigail tightly to him, hardly able to take in what had just happened. "Thank God we stopped here! We've been searching for you all day! We'd thought to go on –"

"What he means is, he wanted to continue on, but I persuaded him to stay," Richard replied, dismounting smoothly and coming over to pat Abigail on the shoulder, albeit a little awkwardly. "How glad I am to see that you are unharmed."

"I am so very grateful to you both," Abigail sniffled, trying her best to stop the tears from falling. "I thought….I was afraid that…"

Charles ran his hands through her hair and tilted her face up towards his, kissing her gently. "You're safe now," he said, softly. "You don't need to be afraid anymore. He'll never get near you again!"

"Speaking of," Richard replied, calmly. "Where is the brute?"

"Kettering?" Abigail asked, resting her head on Charles' shoulder. "He's upstairs in the bedroom. I knocked him out and tied him to the bed." Her eyes closed as she wrapped her arms around Charles, allowing his strength to consume her, encasing her in the security and warmth of his embrace.

Charles blinked, looking down at her. "You did?" Quite amazed at her tenacity, he shook his head. "It appears you didn't need our help after all," he smirked, pulling her in a little closer. Now that she was safe, Charles was quite determined to ensure that she never left his side again.

Richard let out a low whistle. "Well, there seems nothing more for us to do than to return home!"

"Not quite," Charles interjected, shaking his head. "We shall need to find a bishop. We must get a common license, Abigail. Then a carriage to my brother's estate."

Abigail shook her head. "Charles, we cannot!"

"We are, and we will," he said firmly. "I am not taking you back to town unless you bear my name, Abigail." A small smile crept into his heart as he said the words aloud.

"You will need some clothes, also," Richard commented practically. Meeting eyes with Charles, he continued, "But let me give you two a moment of privacy, if I may."

Seeing Richard turn and amble away, Charles stepped back, took her hands and looked her directly in the eye. ""We must marry soon, Abigail. A common license means we shall not need to concern ourselves with the banns, and we may marry back in my home parish."

"But your mother and sisters!" Abigail exclaimed, fully aware of her lack of dress. "What will they think of me? I have quite ruined my reputation, and they will think that I have somehow seduced you into marriage!"

Charles shook his head. "No, my dear, they will not. Abigail, when I found you were gone, my entire world collapsed. You were in my every thought, my entire being calling for you, longing for your return." He smiled at her gently, as she raised a hand to his face, her eyes glistening in the moonlight. "You have become everything to me, Abigail. You know that I wish to marry you, but I promise you here and now, that it is because I love you and not because of some gentlemanly notion that wishes to do right by you. I want you with me always. To raise children, should we be blessed with any. To help me pull myself away from the books I surround myself with and to find enjoyment in other things. My family will see how you have changed me for the better. Indeed, I would be the proudest man in all of England to have you on my arm!"

Abigail pressed a finger to Charles' mouth, to stem the flow of words.

"Charles," she said, simply. "Did you say that you loved me?"

"I did."

She smiled up at him, her eyes shining. "Then that is all you needed to say, my love. I always hoped I'd marry for love and now, it seems, I will." Brushing away her concerns over what her prospective sisters-in-law would say, she smiled up at him, ready to receive his kiss.

Charles caught her lips once more, holding her tightly under the silver moon. His heart slowly healed, the fear and terror he'd felt for many hours evaporating as Abigail kissed him back. She was his, now and forever. All they had to do now was find a church.

The sound of a gunshot punctured the air, forcing them both apart.

"What was that?" Abigail whispered, gripping Charles' arm.

"I don't know," he replied, grimly. "But we'd best be off."

Turning around, Charles couldn't see Richard anywhere, wondering where on earth he'd got to.

"Here," he said, tugging Abigail after him. "Up you go. I'll ride behind you."

"No need," came a sudden voice, as Richard appeared out of the gloom. "There are horses in the stable. You take mine, Charles, and I'll fetch another one. I can have my man return him later."

With no time to argue, Charles jumped up onto his horse and, together, he and Abigail clattered up onto the road.

"Back the way we came," Charles said, hoping Abigail wouldn't freeze in that time. "The next town is not too far, and I'm quite sure we can get both a license and a carriage there."

"And some clothes," Abigail muttered, tugging the cloak around her shoulders with one hand, as the other held tightly to the reins.

RICHARD WALKED BACK into the stables quietly but quickly, his eyes darting everywhere. There was no sign of anyone. Apparently, he had been too late.

CHAPTER 18

By the time they had found a carriage and paid a tired bishop for a common license, it was already growing light. It didn't take much to find someone willing to sell them a respectable looking dress and slippers for Abigail, even if she did have to don it on top of her nightgown.

"Quickly, quickly," Richard hissed, hurrying Charles back into the carriage.

Pulling the door shut behind him, Charles handed Abigail the slippers and rapped on the roof to tell the driver to pull away.

"Do you think Kettering will find us?" Abigail asked as she put the delicate slippers on in place of the over-sized boots. "Surely, he must have woken by now. And if not him, then the oaf that he hired to sit outside my room."

There was a short pause. "No doubt he will be looking for you somewhere on the road," Richard replied, grimly. "We should be careful when we pass other carriages."

Charles said nothing, tugging Abigail back against him and pressing her head into his shoulder. He did not want her to worry. The shadows in her eyes were enough to convince him that she had been through quite enough. A knock on the head, followed by laudanum would make anyone sick. She needed sleep and lots of it.

"You should rest," he said, softly. "Close your eyes and sleep."

Abigail did not protest for a moment, taking a deep breath as she snuggled against him. Her eyes closed immediately, and she allowed her body to relax completely. She did not need to worry anymore, for she knew that Charles and Richard would be more than capable of keeping her safe. Her lips curved into a smile as she felt the tender kiss Charles placed just beside her ear, and she drifted off into a welcoming sleep.

ABIGAIL WAS ASLEEP IN MOMENTS, her whole body limp against him. As the carriage rumbled on, Charles fixed Richard with a stern look. "Richard, you are not keeping anything from me, are you?"

Turning to face Charles, Richard had the decency to look surprised. "What do you mean?"

"There have been a few things that have surprised me of late," Charles replied, honestly. "You disappeared from town for goodness knows how long, but have never explained to me where you were. When Abigail went missing, you seemed to know exactly what to do, and then –" He frowned, not wanting to suggest anything untoward. "The gunshot back at the inn."

"What about it?"

"You weren't with us when it happened, only to appear out of the gloom a few minutes later."

"I didn't shoot Kettering, if that's what you're asking, Charles!" Richard's face darkened at the suggestion, his brows knotting together.

Charles shook his head. "I didn't mean that, Richard." Sighing, he rested his head on the squabs. "I don't know what I am asking."

Richard calmed his mind and his mild anger, aware that he had revealed more about himself than he had ever intended. "I am not mixed up in anything, Charles. I swear to you that I had nothing to do with the gunshot back at the inn and the only reason I knew what to do about Abigail is because I have spent more time in town than you. I know that servants gossip and that the best way to find something out is with guineas."

Something about the way Richard spoke warned Charles that, not only was he not telling him the truth, he was trying his best to keep Charles from knowing it.

"Very well," Charles muttered, hoping that whatever it was Richard was keeping from him, it was nothing too serious. "You know I am here to listen to you, should you need to talk, Richard. I do not like secrets between us."

"I know," Richard replied quietly, grasping that Charles was willing to let the subject lie. "Thank you, Charles."

⚜

"MAMA!" Pressing a kiss to her cheek, Charles presented Abigail to his astonished mother with great grandiose. "Mama, this is Miss Abigail Sidmore. We shall be wed tomorrow."

"Tomorrow?" his mother said, astonished. "Goodness!"

Abigail blushed scarlet, aware of her lack of formal dress, untidy hair, and bleary eyes. "I am delighted to meet you, ma'am. Please excuse my appearance."

"Not at all," Charles replied, wrapping a strong arm around her shoulders. "Now, I insist that you have a bath and a short rest before you meet the rest of my family. We do not want to you to be overwhelmed, not after everything you have gone through." Shooting a look at his mother, he saw, with great relief, that she understood his words completely.

"Of course, my dear," the dowager countess replied gently. "Charles can escort you. The purple room, Charles, I think."

"Wonderful. Perhaps the drawing room once Abigail is settled?"

His mother nodded, turning to greet Richard who was slowly meandering up the steps towards them.

"Do you think she considers me quite terrible?" Abigail asked,

174

anxiously. She had been woken only a few moments before arriving, berating Charles at once for not giving her more time to prepare. He had only shrugged, a smile on his face as he pressed a kiss to her brow. Her nerves had come thick and fast on meeting the dowager countess, whose eyes had glanced at her mussed hair before Charles had explained everything in one single sentence.

"Not at all," Charles replied at once, slipping an arm around her waist as they walked into the bedchamber together. It was a beautiful room, if not a little cold, although Charles knew that a maid would be up in a trice to set a fire in the grate. "She will understand everything once I explain."

"Are we really to be wed tomorrow?" Abigail asked, turning in Charles' arms so that she faced him.

A slow smile spread across his face. "Indeed. If you are willing."

"I am most willing," she whispered, a happiness in her soul spreading warmth to the very tips of her fingers. "I love you, Charles."

"I love you," he whispered, kissing her with a sweet passion that sent shivers through her soul. He felt her hands twine around the back of his neck, and pulled her closer, angling his head so that their kiss deepened. It was only when the maid rapped on the door that they stepped reluctantly apart.

"They'll bring a bath up for you in a moment, and please don't worry about coming down again until dinner. I'll make sure some fresh clothes are sent up for you, and a maid also. Just rest until then."

"Thank you," Abigail replied, trying not to feel anxious over the thought of eating with Charles' family. "I'll make sure I look presentable."

"You'll be beautiful as always," he murmured, pressing a gentle kiss to her hair before taking his leave.

EPILOGUE

Charles' brief but detailed explanation about all that had gone on brought looks of horror to the faces of his family members. Francis shook his head, sitting up a little straighter in his chair.

"Goodness, Charles!" he said, astonished. "It is most unlike you to get yourself mixed up in this kind of thing!"

"Meeting Abigail has certainly changed me, if that's what you mean," Charles replied with a smile. "All for good, I assure you."

"That poor girl!" his mother exclaimed. "When I first met her, I must admit I was a little shocked at her appearance, but it all makes sense now. How wonderful it was that you should be there to help her, Charles."

"Not just me, Mama," Charles replied, throwing a look towards Richard who, unsurprisingly, had his eyes on Helena. "I could not have done it without Richard."

"How good of you," Helena breathed, her green eyes meeting Richard's, a slight blush to her cheeks.

Richard shook his head. "It was not much, I assure you. I am just glad that the lady is safe."

"And you are to wed tomorrow?" Francis asked, studying his brother.

Charles nodded, unable to keep the smile from his face. "Indeed. As soon as possible. I shall go and speak to the bishop today, and I already have a common license."

His mother looked from Charles to Francis and back again. "Then we shall have to make sure we make the day very special for you both," she said, gently. "After what you have been through, it is the least we can do!"

"Thank you, Mama," Charles said, gratefully. "Richard will be my best man, of course." He grinned at his friend, all concern over Richard's curious behavior gone in a moment.

"When do we get to meet your lovely bride?"

"At dinner," Charles replied. "She is tired and needs a good rest. Although she has no clean dresses to wear, Mama."

"She is about Helena's height and build," his mother replied, giving her daughter a look.

Helena got to her feet. "I'll go at once and find something suitable in my wardrobe for her."

"And we shall have to order the dressmaker tomorrow."

"The day after, Mama," Charles replied with a grin. "Tomorrow is my wedding day, and I intend to enjoy it!"

There were smiles on every face, and Charles sat back in his chair with a feeling of contentment. There was no more danger to contend with, and the woman he loved was safe in his brother's home. Tomorrow she would become his wife, and then no-one could ever take her from his side again. Remembering the very first time they had met, Charles let a smile play about his lips. She was truly the most amazing woman he had ever met. He would spend the rest of his life thankful for the day she'd pointed a sword in his face, demanding to know who he was.

Richard got to his feet, excusing himself. He needed to send a letter at once, to let them know what had happened back at the inn. Whilst he had not been able to verify it, he was sure that Kettering now lay dead, but he had not quite been able to catch the shadowy figure running out of the room.

Who was he? Why was he doing this? And most of all, would Richard be able to catch him?

The End

ACKNOWLEDGMENTS

I want express my deepest gratitude to my wonderful and supportive loved ones, my incredible Love Light Faith publishing family, my fantastic editor Nicole, and the unmatchable, ever brilliant Isabel. Each of you has helped to make this book a reality. Thank you for being my partners on this journey!

And thank you, dear reader, for being here with me, reading these words, sharing in my life, and partaking in the adventure. Without you, this wouldn't exist, so thank you, thank you, thank you.

BOOK 3: THE MYSTERIOUS LORD LIVINGSTONE

BOOK 3

HOUSE OF CATESBY

The Mysterious Lord Livingstone

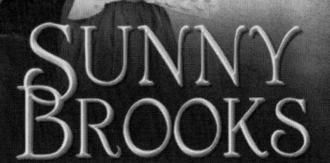

SUNNY BROOKS

FOREWORD

The greatest mysteries of life often unveil some of the greatest personal
treasures. Persevere, investigate, question, learn, and grow.
And never be afraid of sharing your deepest, or your darkest, secrets
with someone else. They may surprise you in the best possible way. We
are not meant to navigate life's journey alone.

- Sunny Brooks

CHAPTER 1

L ord Richard Livingstone glanced at Miss Helena Catesby, seeing her answering smile. He dropped his eyes immediately, wishing he could linger on her beautiful face. Her long, dark tresses had been piled elegantly on her head, with only a few strands sweeping around her face. Green eyes sought to meet his over the crowd, and for a moment, he allowed his gaze to linger. She had a yearning in her eyes that he craved to answer, but Richard knew he could not allow himself to stay. He had work to do and, once more, he had to pull himself away from Helena.

Giving her a slight smile, he raised his hand to her in farewell, seeing the immediate confusion lines cross her face. Wrenching himself from her was going to cause him considerable pain, but it had to be done.

Walking over to Charles, he turned his back on Helena, focusing on his friend. "Congratulations," he boomed, settling his hand on Charles' shoulder. "I wish you and Abigail a lifetime of happiness."

"Thank you," Charles replied, shaking his hand firmly. He frowned, a crease appearing between his eyebrows. "Are you heading back to town so soon?"

"Afraid I must, old boy!" Richard grinned, trying not to let his despair show. "Responsibilities and such like."

Charles shook his head, thinking that this was simply typical of Richard's behavior. He often disappeared at a moment's notice, citing some forgotten business or another such thing. He was quite possibly the most forgetful man of Charles' acquaintance.

"Must you go so soon?"

Richard looked at Charles' new bride, Abigail, giving her a slightly rueful smile. "I'm afraid so. Charles will tell you that you must come to expect this of me."

"Indeed," Charles grumbled, grimacing.

"Then you must call on us the moment we return to town," Abigail said, looking up at him affectionately and ignoring her husband. "We shall not be gone long."

"A month or so, I think," Charles replied, taking his new bride's hand and forgetting all about Richard. The thought of taking his new bride on honeymoon was quite a delightful prospect. "And then we shall return to London." At Abigail's sharp look, he turned back to Richard. Abigail had spoken to him previously about needing to keep in touch with his friend, despite now being a married man. "I will send a note to you the very moment we arrive back in London," he followed.

Richard nodded. "Very good, Charles. Enjoy your honeymoon trip, you both vastly deserve it." Charles and Abigail had struggled through some particularly difficult circumstances, but the love they had for one another had helped them forge a way through. Richard was utterly delighted that they had married, knowing that Charles was much happier with Abigail by his side. She managed to pull him from his quiet ways, making him laugh and smile much more frequently than Richard had ever seen before.

"Thank you for all your help, Richard," Charles said, shaking his hand again. "I do not know what we would have done without you."

"Not at all, my friend." Taking his leave, Richard walked out of the drawing room, forcing himself not to search out Helena for one last look.

HELENA SIGHED TO HERSELF, watching Richard leave the room. She had no idea where he could be going at this time of night, but his lengthy absences were always a painful trial. She had loved him almost from the first moment that Charles had introduced him as one of his dear friends. At times, he had come to stay at the family estate, and over the years had become a dear family friend. Even her father had liked him! Helena sighed again, wandering to the window in a futile attempt to catch one last glimpse of him. She knew that he would be leaving again, never able to stay more than a few days. With the excitement of Charles and Abigail's hasty marriage, there had been very little time for her to spend with him.

"Are you quite well, my dear?"

She smiled, turning to face her concerned mama. "I am quite well, Mama. Just a little fatigued."

The anxiety did not drop from her mother's face. "You are pining after someone, I think."

Heat bloomed in Helena's cheeks. "I'm sorry, Mama."

"Don't be sorry, my dear!" her mother exclaimed. "Lord Livingstone is a good man."

"Am I really so obvious?" Helena muttered, resting her head against the cool glass.

"Well, I am your mother, my dear. I do know some things." Giving her daughter a gentle hug around the waist, her mother withdrew back to the festivities, leaving Helena alone.

Helena's breath caught as she spotted a figure leaving the estate. She could barely see him in the darkness since the lanterns gave out only a little light, but she knew it was him. Watching him, Helena felt a piece of her heart break off and leave with him. Why did he never say anything to her about his feelings? She had little doubt that he felt something for her, given the way that she would often catch his eyes on her. Why were there only ever gentle looks and soft smiles, with only brief conversations on banal topics such as the weather? A sob caught in her throat as she watched him ride away, leaving her feeling completely dejected.

☙❧

RICHARD GLANCED up at the window, seeing Helena's silhouette. He could barely make out her features but knew in his heart it was her. No other of Charles' sisters would watch him ride away.

Gritting his teeth, he turned his face to the wind, wishing that he could stay. The horse tossed its head as he rode slowly out of the gate, leaving the woman he loved behind.

Richard remembered all too well the first moment he had laid eyes on Helena. It had been a good few years ago now, but he'd never forgotten. He'd met Charles in town, at some ball or another, and they'd hit it off at once. They were both equally disenchanted with the ton and the grasping mamas that only had eyes for wealth and titles. Instead, they'd spent their days either riding, walking or exploring the large library. Evenings had been spent at White's, often shunning the soirees and balls that they had been invited to. Richard was a titled lord and, unfortunately for him, had many more interested parties than Charles, given that Charles was only a second son. What Richard had never been able to disclose to Charles was that he was not merely another lord, seeking to hide from glassy-eyed chits who cared only for his status. He had another reason to keep himself on the fringes of society. It was the reason he had never been able to show Helena the true depth of his feelings.

Feeling utterly dejected, Richard rode on into the night, unable to remove her from his memory. They had never spoken of their feelings, and he had never been able to tell her how much he truly cared for her. It had always eaten away at him, a gnawing ache that he could never quite get rid of. His arms longed to hold her, but his desire could never be fulfilled. Certainly not now and certainly not yet. He would have to continue to play the fool, keeping the truth to himself and only ever being able to admire her from a distance. There were times he truly hated the life he had chosen, despite being fully aware it was for the greater good. It kept him from telling his dear friend the truth and, even more than that, it kept him from telling the woman he loved exactly how he felt. Frustrated, Richard forced his eyes to the road ahead and pushed all thought of Helena from his mind. He had to be focused for his meeting with Blake. His next mission was at hand.

CHAPTER 2

Helena looked up from her drawing as her mother entered with a cheery welcome.

"Good morning, my dear."

"Good morning, Mama," Helena replied, getting up to kiss her mother's cheek. "How are you?" Her mother was preparing to leave the family estate and take to the dower house. By the end of the following week, she would be gone - although the house itself was not far from the estate. The decision had not been welcomed, by Helena's eldest brother Francis, the new Lord Catesby, but their mother had insisted. Her one request had been that she would take her beloved household staff with her, and Francis had immediately obliged.

"I am well, I thank you, dear." Her mother sat down opposite her. "Francis is busy checking that the new staff is settling in so I thought it best to stay out of his way."

"Did you wish to speak to him?" Helena inquired, aware that the new housekeeper, valet, cook and other staff had been busy shadowing the current staff to ensure they could take on their new roles with ease.

Her mother shook her head. "No, not particularly. I just wished to inform him that I have received a note from Charles."

"From Charles?" Helena repeated, her interest immediately piqued. "He and Abigail have returned to town?"

"Indeed," her mother smiled. "It seems they have had a vastly enjoyable trip. They have a specific request, however, Helena."

"Oh?"

Her mother's smile widened. "They specifically asked Francis if he can spare you and your sister."

Helena dropped her pencil, leaping to her feet. "I am to go to town?"

Her mother laughed. "If Francis agrees, then yes you are. You and your sister have never truly had a Season now, have you? I believe Abigail and Charles wish to rectify that." Both she and Sophia had been enjoying their come out but, to their chagrin, it had been cut short. Their father had been called back to their country estate due to severe flooding that threatened to ruin the crops they relied on, and they had never managed to return to London. Now, it seemed, she was to have her chance.

"Oh, Mama, how wonderful!" Helena exclaimed, whirling around the room. "Do you think Francis will agree?"

"Of course he will," her mother replied. "Both you and Sophia deserve some enjoyment, and I am quite sure spending time in town will be simply wonderful for you both."

Helena wanted to hug herself with excitement, hoping Sophia would be just as interested in the trip. Sophia had been quiet of late, often taking long walks within the estate and saying very little. Perhaps a trip to town would shake her from her long, pronounced melancholy.

"You shall see Lord Livingstone too, I am sure," her mother said casually, once Helena had finally stopped whirling around. "It is the Season after all."

"Do you truly think so?" Helena exclaimed, clasping her hands together. Her aching heart began to lighten at the thought of seeing him again. "What shall I say to him?"

Her mother studied her daughter for a moment, her eyes softening. "Do you desire my advice?"

"Yes, Mama," Helena said, honestly. Sitting back down, she decided to be frank with her mother. "I believe I have loved Lord Livingstone for a long time, but I have never been able to share with him how I truly feel."

"Then listen to what I have to say," her mother said. "Enjoy your season, my dear. Dance as often as you can, and accept as many invitations as you can."

Helena's face fell. "Mama, I only wish to dance with Lord Livingstone."

"And that is precisely why you must not," her mother countered. "To show such a regard would be immediately pounced on by members of the society and it would immediately become gossip. You may care only for Lord Livingstone, but you must not show it, my dear. Besides," she continued, a gleam in her eye. "The man may become jealous when he sees just how many gentlemen vie for your hand."

Helena gasped, staring at her mother in shock. "Mama, you cannot be serious," she exclaimed.

"I'm afraid I am, my dear," her mother responded, hiding a smile. "I have seen the way he looks at you, but he has never spoken to you of how he feels. I cannot imagine how trying that must be for you." Reaching across, she took her hand and patted it gently. "This may be the one way to get him to speak of his love for you."

Swallowing hard, Helena blinked furiously against the hot tears that sprang to her eyes. "You believe he loves me, Mama?"

Again, that gentle smile. "Of course he does, my dear. No one could doubt it."

"Then why does he not speak to me of it?" Helena burst out, frustration rising. "He looks and smiles, and looks again, but that is all!"

"That is precisely why you are going to do what I have told you," her mother said, firmly. "Find out the truth from your Lord Livingstone and tell him of your own heart. I do not expect you to return here a still eligible young woman."

Helena smiled slowly, acknowledging that what her mother said was what she truly longed for. "Thank you, Mama."

◎✦◎

HELENA WAS in town by the end of the week, although a little sad to be leaving her sister behind. For whatever reason, Sophia had chosen to stay at the estate, making the excuse that she wished to stay with Mama for as long as she could. Helena had not quite understood her sister's desire to stay at the estate, but no amount of persuading had convinced her to come to town.

"How delighted I am to see you!" Abigail exclaimed, throwing her arms around Helena the moment she stepped through the door.

"Thank you for inviting me," Helena gushed, greeting her sister-in-law and then her brother. "I am sorry that Sophia could not come."

"Is she well?" Charles asked, a little concerned.

Helena nodded. "I believe so. She is taking father's death quite hard, I believe," she said. "Perhaps she just needs a little more time. She does not seem keen to leave Mama."

A frown flickered over Abigail's face. "Isn't your mother moving to the dower house very soon?"

"By next week's end," Helena confirmed. "I think Sophia wants to ensure she is settled before returning to the estate."

"Well, it is good that your mama will have company," Abigail replied, taking Helena's arm. "Come through to the drawing room, and we will order some refreshments. I am sure you must be quite parched."

"Indeed," Helena agreed, chuckling at her rumbling stomach. "I am never able to eat when I am traveling."

"Dinner will be a little later, this evening," Abigail began with a smile. "So we will make sure you have a light repast with the tea tray."

"Richard is coming," Charles interrupted, walking alongside them. "He does not know you are here, Helena, although I'm sure he will be delighted to see you."

Helena's heart slammed into her ribs at the words. Charles had no notion of her feelings for Richard, so she attempted nonchalance the best she could. "It will be lovely to see him again, Charles." Turning back to Abigail, she smiled brightly at her sister-in-law. "Now, you must tell me all about your trip, I am desperate to hear what Italy is like."

CHAPTER 3

Richard slammed through the door, sweat pouring down his face but, alas, he was too late. Lord Davis was slumped over his desk, his eyes frozen in shock and staring, although Richard knew he could see nothing. The man was dead.

Groaning, Richard thumped the top of the desk, hard.

"He is dead, then?"

"Yes," Richard responded, not turning to look at his sometimes valet, sometimes bodyguard.

"We are too late."

Gritting his teeth, Richard turned to face his companion. "So it would seem."

"Blast."

"My sentiments exactly, George." Grimacing, Richard walked around to the dead man and sniffed. "Almonds."

"Cyanide again, then."

"So it appears we *are* dealing with the same killer."

Richard nodded, walking around the desk once more towards the window. "I only wish I knew how he chose his victims. That would give us the surest way of stopping him."

"If we knew that, then the case would be over by now," George chuckled, grinning. "It is precisely because we do not know that you were given the task of finding him."

"Yes, I know," Richard grumbled in agreement. Many years ago, Richard had been approached by a man called the Duke of Riverford, who had recruited him almost immediately. The Duke, as he preferred to be called, took on a number of requests, or cases as they were, from what seemed like a colorful assortment of people. Although, given the Duke's required level of secrecy, Richard was not very sure how these clients found him in the first place. But, then again, it was not his place to ask. The Duke never got involved in his investigations, leaving that to Richard and the others he had recruited. Richard reported back to the Duke, the Duke informed the client, and payment was made.

Richard had found himself a little short of funds all those years ago, partly due to his dearly departed father's gambling habits and partly due to his own inexperience in handling money. When the Duke of Riverford told him just how much he would be given at the close of each case, Richard had grasped the opportunity with both hands. However, it had meant that he had been forced to keep this new part of his life completely and utterly secret, for that was one of the Duke's requirements. He had always enjoyed his investigations for the most part, but he had not enjoyed hiding the truth from his friends. Money was no longer an issue in his life, and at times, Richard had wondered about leaving the Duke's service, but had never been sure what he would do with his life if he were to. Truth be told, he enjoyed the thrill of the chase, but the ache in his heart for Helena was growing stronger and stronger each time he saw her. Perhaps one day soon, he would have to make a choice.

Sighing heavily, Richard began to make his way around the room, looking for anything that might alert him to who the killer was. This particular person had been killing men of the highest ranks, although he could not work out why. At every murder had been the presence of cyanide, which he could smell from the dead men's mouths. And, at every location, there had always been a glass of liquor, which would, they presumed, carry the cyanide. This was no different.

"Whiskey this time." Richard pointed to the glass on the table.

George grunted. "Better get rid of the contents, in case some poor fool at the constabulary chooses to drink it."

Richard grimaced, pouring the glass of whiskey into the cold fireplace. The constable would have to be alerted soon. "I wish he would not toy with us so," he grumbled, under his breath.

"He likes to play games," George reminded, leafing through some papers. "He enjoys sending us these notes so that we will chase after him, only to realize we have been bested, yet again."

George often liked to restate known facts about their cases, but Richard had come to find the habit soothing. Richard thumped the desk twice for good measure, despite the pain it caused him. The killer had not been murdering men for long, but each time he had left Richard a note, with a clue as to who his next victim might be. Apparently, the man was aware of who Richard really was and what his job entailed. George was correct, the man did like to play games. By the time Richard and George had worked out who the target was, it was already too late. If somehow, he was able to work out *how* this killer chose his victims, then he would be able to stop him with ease.

"We will catch him one day, milord," George said, calmly.

"Unfortunately, one day is not today," Richard ground out, between clenched teeth. He despised the killer, whoever he was. His pointless games were causing more families to lose loved ones, and Richard felt the weight of their deaths on his conscience. If only he were able to work out these confounded notes in time!

"Now wait a minute," he heard George say, his ears pricking up in excitement. "What's this?"

"Found something, have you?" Richard asked, walking over to him.

George frowned, the lines in his forehead deepening. "Perhaps," he groused, studying the paper in his hand. "It merits a closer look, that is for sure." Folding it up, he handed it to Richard. "Not here, however. There is no saying who might be lurking nearby."

Knowing that George was correct, Richard placed the paper in his pocket without looking at it, although he itched to know what was inside that had caught George's attention. "Let's go back to the townhouse," he said, walking to the door. Stopping short, he thumped his forehead with the heel of his hand. "Blast, I quite forgot. I am requested at Charles's residence for dinner."

George ran his eyes over Richard's dusty and crumpled clothes. "Then I suggest we return at once so you can change," he said wryly. "For you cannot be seen in such a state. I should not allow it."

Letting out a snort, Richard walked from the house, knowing that George was once again back into his role as Richard's valet. The study of the document in his pocket would have to wait.

◈

ONE HOUR LATER, after a hasty change of clothes, Richard entered Charles's drawing room right on time.

"Lord Livingstone," intoned the butler, and Richard walked in immediately, giving Abigail a quick bow before grasping his friends' hand.

"May I say how delighted I am to see you, old boy," Charles grinned, as he shook Richard's hand.

"How was your trip?" Richard asked, walking to sit across from Abigail. "You are both looking very well."

Abigail smiled at him. "It was lovely, thank you. I am glad to see you again, Richard."

"And I you," Richard replied, truthfully. He and Abigail had bonded over her time in Charles' care, long before Charles had declared his love for Abigail. Of course, by that time, it had been more than apparent to Richard that his friend had fallen deeply in love. It had just taken Charles a little more time to realize it.

"What have you been doing in town?" Charles asked, handing Richard a glass.

Richard shrugged, knowing that, as ever, he could not tell his friend the truth. He was sworn to secrecy and, on top of that, Richard knew that keeping the truth from his friends was the best way to keep them safe. "I have visited my tailor on a few occasions," he answered nonchalantly, as Charles groaned.

"You do not need yet more suits, Richard," Charles chastised. "Your current wardrobe is more than suitable."

"One never knows when a new cravat might be in order," Richard tossed out with a grin.

"I could not agree more," Abigail interrupted, throwing a mischievous look at her husband. "Especially since Charles has decided that, since matrimony is apparently a most blessed state, you too should enter into it."

Richard's mouth fell open in shock as he gazed at Abigail. This could not be true! His friend had never once suggested that he marry, and he certainly did not expect him to start matchmaking now.

"That is not quite it, Abigail," Charles began before Richard could find his voice. "Simply that I had mentioned that you have never truly sought a bride before, Richard and that perhaps now might be the time."

"I see," Richard managed, his voice a little hoarse. "And had you anyone particular in mind?"

At that precise moment, the door behind him opened once more, shutting again with a soft click.

"Good day, Richard," came a soft voice. "How delighted I am to see you."

Richard felt his heart practically stop in his chest, before beginning to beat frantically as he recognized Helena's voice. Getting hastily to his feet, he turned around to see her shining eyes looking at him. Without the chance to hide it, a wide smile crossed his face.

"Helena," he uttered almost breathlessly, dropping to a quick bow. "Whatever are you doing here?"

CHAPTER 4

Helena smiled into Richard's eyes, glad that she had been able to surprise him. The look on his face was one of astonishment and confusion, which made her smile. "I am here visiting Charles and Abigail," she replied, lifting her hand so he could take it. "They invited me to come on their return to London."

Richard took her hand, before warmly pressing it to his lips. Her skin was soft and smooth, and he could feel a trickle of excitement run down his spine as he looked into her eyes. She was smiling gently, her eyes almost glowing with delight, and for a moment, there was only the two of them in the room.

Charles cleared his throat, breaking the spell. "Indeed, we invited Sophia *and* Helena, but Sophia declined to come."

"Oh?" Richard mumbled, dropping Helena's hand and sitting back down once she had taken a seat opposite him. He had been on first name terms with the rest of Charles' family for a number of years, giving him a sense of familiarity with the family.

"Something about wanting to be close to Mama," Helena explained, a flicker of a frown crossing her face.

"Mama is to move to the dower house," Charles explained. "Even though Francis is not exactly ready to marry."

Richard frowned. Lady Catesby would not be expected to move to the dower house until her eldest son, the new Lord Catesby, was to marry. It was quite unusual for a widow to do so before that time.

"I believe she misses Papa greatly," came Helena's soft voice. "She has commented that everything in the house reminds her of him and that her grief is, unfortunately, being prolonged by being there."

"You are only just out of mourning clothes yourself," her brother reminded her gently. "That is the only reason you are allowed here for the Season."

Helena frowned at once, and Richard caught himself wishing he could smooth the lines in her forehead away with his fingers.

"I am aware of that, Charles," Helena retorted. "I am simply repeating what Mama has expressed as the reason for her departure to the dower house. Besides, a year has gone by, and now Mama wishes to live in a place of her own."

"She is taking the household staff with her," Abigail smiled, informing Richard and simultaneously breaking the tension between brother and sister. "Francis, apparently, has been interviewing a great many new staff recently."

Charles let out a chuckle. "Francis was not enjoying that part of his responsibilities, that is for sure! He kept muttering something about the new housekeeper."

"They are all in place, then?"

Charles nodded in answer to Richard's question. "The new staff have been working alongside the old so that the transition will be seamless."

"When I return, she will be in the dower house, and calm will be restored," Helena smiled, thinking just how much of a difference there would be in the only home she had ever known.

Richard nodded, his eyes on Helena as her gaze drifted off to the corner of the room. She was clearly deep in thought and, for a moment or so, he allowed himself to look at her. To his mind, she grew more beautiful each time he saw her. Her jet black hair had been piled on her head in the most elegant of styles, with a few wisps gentling her features. Her green eyes were almost cloudy as she lost herself in thoughts, her lips pursed delicately. Richard had to drag his eyes away before he lost his senses completely. His arms ached to hold her, his lips longed to kiss her, but he knew he could not. No matter how much he cared for Helena, there could be nothing between them. Not unless he was willing to give up the work he was doing for the Duke, and he could not make that decision until he completed his present assignment.

"We are to attend Lord and Lady Simpkins ball in two days time," Abigail said, looking directly at Richard. "Are you to be in attendance?" Her slightly raised eyebrow and light smile told him that she had noticed in which direction his interest turned, but he refused to acknowledge it.

"The Simpkins ball?" he repeated, casting his mind back to the many invitations he had received. If he had declined it, then he would make sure to make his apologies and accept it instead. If Helena were planning to attend, then he would attend too. "Yes, I believe so. You must promise me a dance, Abigail."

She laughed. "Yes, of course, I shall promise you that, so long as Charles does not mind."

"He will not," Richard assured her, grinning at his friend. "And Helena, of course, you must promise me a dance also." He tried to keep his tone nonchalant, although the thought of having her in his arms sent a thrill straight through him.

"I would be delighted," Helena replied, her voice soft. "It has been some time since I danced, I am not sure I will remember the steps."

Richard smiled at her reassuringly. "I am quite sure you will do very well, Helena. Although, if you wish, I am more than happy to give you a short lesson beforehand. Perhaps tomorrow afternoon? That way you will be quite ready for the ball."

Helena blushed, her eyes sparkling with delight. Richard was Charles' closest friend, so his offer was not particularly unexpected and certainly not unwelcome, but she could not help but feel a rush of excitement. "I would be greatly in your debt."

"Are you sure you can dance, Richard?" Charles commented,

dryly. "I should not like my sister's feet to be tread on before the ball has even begun."

Richard shook his head, giving Helena a quick smile. "You must ignore your brother. I am a wonderful dancer, I assure you."

Helena let out a light peal of laughter. "Charles is the one who has trod on my toes on a number of occasions, Richard, so he has very little ground to be warning you from."

"Is that so?" Richard grinned, as Charles muttered something incoherent and looked away. "How strange it is that in as many years as we have known each other, I have never managed to watch you traipse around the dance floor at any of the balls we've attended."

"That is because you are always forgetting something and having to rush back to town," Charles shot back.

Richard took a breath, giving his friend a lazy smile in spite of the sudden tensing of his body. "Then I shall be delighted to show your sister just how a dance ought to be done, by someone who will not stand on her toes. Abigail, you must be *very* careful at the ball."

"I will," Abigail replied, with a wry smile. "I'm afraid I have already learned about just how ungainly Charles can be."

"This is not to be tolerated!" Charles complained, coming over to sit beside his wife. "I am a prolific dancer."

"Of course you are," Abigail agreed, smoothing back Charles' hair with one hand. Richard watched them for a moment, his heart lifting at the clear love between the two of them. He was truly happy for his friend that he had found someone like Abigail. It had brought happiness back into Charles' life, and for that, Richard was profoundly grateful.

His eyes drifted back towards Helena, who had been watching the proceedings with a light smile on her face. When she looked back at him, Richard did not immediately look away, allowing his gaze to linger. He took in her sharp, green eyes and the color that suddenly blossomed in her cheeks. There was no doubt in his mind that she returned his regard in some small way, and, despite the warning in his heart, Richard could not help but feel a growing excitement over the prospect of having Helena in his arms.

CHAPTER 5

Helena sobbed quietly, hoping no one would hear her. The piece of music she was practicing at the pianoforte was incredibly moving, but it did not normally make her sob so. Tears ran down her cheeks and, lifting her hands from the keys, she picked up her handkerchief from where she had left it and delicately dabbed at her eyes.

"Excuse me, Helena," came Abigail's sudden voice. "For the ball tomorrow, I was wondering if – "

Stopping short, Abigail stared at her sister-in-law. "You are crying, Helena," she breathed, before rushing over to her. "Whatever is the matter?"

"Tis nothing," Helena sniffled, attempting to stop the heavy flow of tears. "The piece I have been playing is very emotive, that is all."

Abigail frowned, sitting down next to her on the piano stool. "And that is all? Truly?"

Helena did not answer immediately, struggling through her mixed emotions. She was not quite sure why she had burst into such distraught tears, but she *was* sure that it was something to do with Richard. "I did not sleep well last night. Perhaps that has something to do with it."

"Oh?" Abigail asked. "And why was that? I thought we all had a most enjoyable evening."

"Oh yes, I had a wonderful time," Helena replied, quickly. Their dinner had been delicious and the short time of entertaining afterward had been delightful. "I do not want you to think I am complaining, in any way."

"No, not at all," Abigail responded, taking Helena's hand. "This has nothing to do with Lord Livingstone, does it, Helena?"

Heat crept into her cheeks. "Why should you think that?"

"Because," Abigail cautioned gently. "I could not help but notice the looks you both shared. Is there an attachment between you?"

"No, there is not," Helena whispered, as a lump caught in her throat. "Although...I wish there were." Her head dropped, her eyes on her lap as she realized what she had just admitted. "Please, do not tell Charles," she quickly added, a small fear creeping into her voice.

Abigail let out a long breath. "Charles will not be angry if there *is* an attachment between the two of you," she promised, wondering if Helena was telling her the truth. "You need have no fear of that."

Helena shook her head, firmly. "There is no attachment, Abigail!" Her voice grew in fervor. "All there is are looks and glances. That is all."

"So he has never spoken to you of his feelings?" Abigail asked, surprised.

Helena shook her head. "I am not even sure he feels anything for me," she admitted. "We have barely spoken."

Abigail stared at her sister-in-law for a moment. "Helena," she said, firmly. "I am quite certain that Lord Livingstone – Richard – is in love with you."

Helena's head shot up, and she gazed at Abigail for a long moment. Her heart began to beat quickly, hope rising in her chest. "Do you truly believe so?"

"I do."

"Then why does he not speak to me of it?" Helena asked, growing a little angry. "For years, it seems, we have danced this peculiar little dance around each other, and nothing has ever been said. He does not stay long enough for anything to be said, either. At any given moment, he is away and gone, with little or no explanation. It is very perplexing."

"And this is why you have never danced with him before?"

Helena closed her eyes briefly. "Precisely. It is not the proper thing for a woman to ask a man, is it?" She shook her head, her features drowning in sorrow. "And he has never once approached me," she continued, her voice melting into a whisper. "So, you see, I am quite muddled over the entire situation."

"Yes, I can see that," Abigail commiserated. "Now that you are here for the Season, perhaps you will finally have the opportunity to take things further with him."

"Whatever can you mean?"

Abigail gave her a slight grin. "Well, I am not best placed to advise you, Helena, given my own slightly scandalous reputation. I am certainly not the epitome of womanhood, with all its rules and requirements."

"That matters very little to me," Helena declared, smiling at Abigail's wry expression. "Please, I would greatly appreciate any advice."

Thinking for a moment, Abigail pursed her lips. "The trouble with men is that they are not particularly keen to share their feelings," she muttered. "So you shall simply have to press him to be honest with you."

"And how do I do that?"

A slow smile spread across Abigail's face. "You must get him to kiss you."

Helena gasped, her eyes widening in shock. "What? I cannot!"

"Yes, you can," Abigail insisted. "Then, and only then, will he be honest with you about how he feels."

Helena shook her head, her hand going to her mouth as she thought of Richard kissing her. The idea shot sparks straight through her, making a warmth begin to unfurl in her chest. "I do not know how to do such a thing, Abigail."

"Oh, it is simple enough," Abigail responded, with a light chuckle.

"Since you are to be dancing with him, then there will be ample opportunity for you to attempt it."

Seeing Helena's shocked expression, Abigail hid her amusement. Helena was still a fairly innocent young woman, and certainly not as bold in her character as Abigail was. She would need to take a fairly cautious approach in guiding her young ward.

"Helena," Abigail began, attempting to explain. "When he is dancing with you, you will need to look deeply into his eyes. Allow yourself to be held fractionally closer than appropriate, and ensure a few gentle sighs to catch his attention."

Nodding, Helena committed every word to memory. "And then?"

Abigail shrugged. "And then he will kiss you." She stated it so matter of factly that Helena's eyes grew round.

"You are quite sure of it?"

"Oh yes," Abigail assured her with a smile. "And it will be one of the most wondrous experiences of your life."

CHAPTER 6

As Richard approached Charles' townhouse, he cursed under his breath and shook his head in reproach. Last evening, he had thought the idea of giving Helena a dance lesson or two had been a wonderful notion, but now he regretted ever mentioning it at all. The thought of holding her in his arms brought both excitement and agitation. He knew that he could not tell Helena of his work for the Duke, for that could put her in danger. On top of that, if she discovered the truth, she then might reject him completely. That left him needing to shield so much of his true self that he often felt ridiculous with the way he had to behave to cover for his actions. It was an irresolvable situation. Grimacing, Richard muttered darkly to himself. There was no getting out of it now. He would simply have to give Helena a few turns about the floor and attempt not to be affected by her closeness.

To add to his mood, he had discovered that the document George had found interesting was merely a short note to a Lord MacDonald, congratulating him on some success or other. Considering he had no idea who Lord MacDonald was, Richard had been forced to disregard the note as anything of either help or interest. It was most frustrating.

Handing his hat and gloves to the butler, Richard was shown to the drawing room which, to his surprise, had been prepared for their dancing. Abigail was sitting beside Helena, their heads together in deep conversation. Clearing his throat, he smiled as both ladies jumped in surprise, a rosy blush hitting Helena's cheeks.

"Good afternoon," he smiled, as they got to their feet. "I do apologize for the interruption."

"Not at all, Richard," Abigail smiled. "We were merely discussing the ball tomorrow."

"Ah," Richard replied, walking a little further in. "Is Charles around?"

"He is, but he is catching up on some business matters," Abigail said quickly. "Perhaps we can all have tea together, once you have completed your lesson?"

"Very good," Richard mumbled, suddenly feeling a rush of nerves. As Abigail walked out of the room leaving the door wide open, he turned and gave Helena a quick bow. "Are you well, Helena?"

"Very well, I thank you," she responded, her voice soft. In truth, she had been quite startled at his sudden appearance, having completely lost track of time. She and Abigail had, in truth, been discussing the ball, but their previous discussion had brought a flush to her cheeks. "Shall we begin?"

Richard glanced around. "Is there a maid or…?"

Helena lifted her eyebrows, surprised. "A maid?"

"For propriety," he explained, as Helena let out a soft laugh.

"Richard, I had not thought you a stickler for such things. I can fetch one if you wish, but Charles and Abigail trust you – and I – completely."

He cleared his throat. "I see."

"Should you like me to fetch one?" Helena inquired, making to walk towards the door, but Richard shook his head.

"No, forgive me, you are quite right. We are longtime friends, are we not?"

"Indeed," Helena smiled, walking back towards him.

Richard felt as though he could not breathe, his chest constricting as she approached. He resisted the urge to pull at his collar, suddenly aware that they were quite alone. Yes, the door was open, but there was no one else around. He had thought that either Charles or Abigail would be in attendance, but it seemed he had been wrong on that count. "There is no music, I am afraid, but –"

"That does not matter," Helena said, with a quick smile. "I just need to rehearse the steps, that is all. I do not want to make a mistake and bring shame on myself!"

"Of course," Richard answered, understanding completely. "Then, shall we begin?"

Holding his hand out to her, he caught his breath as she took it in her own. Neither of them wore gloves and the heat of her skin on his sent a swift kick of desire ricocheting through him. He cleared his throat once more. "Now," he began. "Which dance shall we start with?"

Helena's face bloomed with color, but she steeled her resolve. "I have only danced the waltz on one occasion," she murmured. "And that was a few years ago now."

"The waltz?" Richard repeated, his voice sounding hoarse to even his own ears. "You were granted permission, I take it?"

"But of course," Helena assured him, smiling gently. "I have made my come out, after all, Richard."

Those words reminded Richard that Helena was now a young woman, no longer a child. Her womanly curves made his face burn with awareness, and, as he placed one hand on her waist and took the other in his hand, his breath caught in his chest. "As I said, there is no music, so we shall simply have to count to three." He attempted to take a step, but stumbled in the process, almost toppling Helena.

"Careful!" Helena laughed, as some of the tension left her body. "I thought you said you were good at this!"

"I am," Richard defended, his face hot.

She laughed again, as he held her again, a little more firmly. His stumble had made her relax, and, as much as she wanted to follow the directions that Abigail had given, Helena decided that she would simply enjoy the moment.

"1, 2, 3, 1, 2, 3," Richard muttered, beginning to swing her across the floor. He kept his voice firm and his steps sure, not wanting to make a cake of himself yet again. His stumble had simply been from anxiety, for Richard was truly a proficient dancer. His counting became the tune for them both as they continued to dance across the floor, and finally, Richard relaxed.

Braving a glance down at Helena, he saw the way she was looking at him with an almost dreamy expression. Suddenly becoming aware of just how soft and warm she felt under his hands, Richard swallowed the lump that appeared in his throat. Everything in him wanted to stop the dance and press his lips to hers, pulling her tight against him. Blood began to pulse in his veins as he tugged her slightly closer, hoping she would not protest. Helena's coy smile grew as he did so, as though she too desired a closeness with him.

The whispered counting died in his throat, as he looked deeply into her eyes. He did not think that she truly did need dance lessons after all, for she moved perfectly well across the floor. Was this her way of having a short time alone with him?

The thought forced him to a standstill, making her start with surprise.

"Richard, whatever is the matter?"

He took a step back, dropping his hands from her waist. "Helena, I –" He could not put words to what he felt. On the one hand, he wanted desperately to show her the depths of his feelings for her, hoping she would return them in kind, but on the other, he knew that it could potentially be dangerous, deadly even, for her to be involved with him. That was the last thing he wanted.

"Richard," Helena said again, moving closer to him – so close that they were almost touching. "Why did you stop dancing with me?" Nervous anxiety was rippling through her, but she refused to step away. She wanted to know why Richard had never spoken to her of his obvious feelings, and why, just when they were beginning to get a little closer, he had stepped back as though he'd been burned.

Richard could barely think straight as he looked into Helena's deep green eyes. His hands itched to touch her until he had no choice but to give in. Almost unwillingly, his hand reached out towards her face, letting his fingers run down the side of her jawbone. "Helena," he breathed. "I –"

"Sir!"

Richard dropped his hand at once, staring at his valet who had suddenly appeared in the doorway. Clearly, he was needed.

"I must go," he mumbled, hating the confusion and upset on Helena's face. "My sincerest apologies, Helena. Please save me a dance tomorrow evening. Perhaps, the waltz?"

He watched her give an almost imperceptible nod, before hastily bowing and leaving the room. Helena stared after him, completely and utterly baffled.

CHAPTER 7

"You are very quiet, Helena."

Startled out of her daze, Helena glanced up at her brother with a somewhat guilty look. She knew she had been quite terrible company this evening, given that her thoughts were completely taken up with Richard.

"My apologies, Charles. I am just a little tired."

"No doubt after your dancing lessons with Richard," he commented with a wry grin. "I hope they went well, Helena, and you are quite prepared?"

"Yes, of course," she offered, her stomach tightening at the sound of Richard's name.

Abigail shot Charles a warning look, which was met with complete confusion. Sighing at Charles' complete lack of insight, Abigail turned the conversation to the upcoming ball.

"Have you decided what you shall wear, Helena?"

"No," Helena grumbled, discontentedly. "Perhaps I should wear white, or cream since I am returning to society to complete my come out."

Abigail shook her head. "No, you should not. With your coloring, you need something vibrant. Something that will help you catch the eye of...some of the gentlemen."

"So long as they are worthy gentlemen," Charles interjected.

Helena said nothing. There was no gentleman other than Richard that she wished to notice her. She was completely confused over his earlier behavior. It was as if he wanted to kiss her, but would not allow himself to do so. Of course, gentlemen did not go around kissing various ladies, so perhaps Richard merely wished to behave with all propriety, but that did not mean he could not speak to her of his feelings, did it? Wishing she could bury her head in her hands, Helena sighed again, heavily. What was she to do about the man?

🐲

RICHARD WAS PACING around his drawing room, his chest heaving with emotion. Berating himself for touching Helena in such an inappropriate manner, he could not forget the softness of her cheek or the way her eyes had fluttered closed for just a moment. Heavens above, he was a man tormented.

"Is something the matter, sir?"

"Yes," Richard bit out, as his valet-cum-bodyguard lifted an inquiring brow.

"Something to do with that lady you were dancing with?"

Richard snorted. "Unfortunately, yes. As well as the fact that we have, yet again, been outsmarted by our cyanide killer." Frustrated, he picked up the note that had been sent to his address, a puzzle that they had worked out to mean Lord Bentson, who was within the uppermost circles of society. They had thrown open the door to his townhouse, ignoring the shouts of the butler, and had found Bentson lying in his library, dead. They had been too late.

"We shall catch him soon, I am quite sure," George replied, in an attempt to bolster Richard's sinking spirits. "We simply need to work out these blasted clues."

"We *do* work them out," Richard returned. "Just not quickly enough."

George let out a long breath. "Perhaps we should seek someone else's counsel."

Richard arched an eyebrow. "You mean, involve someone else?"

George nodded, but Richard shook his head at once. He was not about to put anyone else in danger. For whatever reason, the killer seemed to enjoy sending Richard clues as to who was his next target, but, as yet, had not seen fit to threaten him directly. "I will not put anyone else in harm's way," Richard explained. "One day, I fully expect the killer to target one of us."

"Yes, I am aware of that, sir," George said, a little dryly. "Although we are on our guard, of course, which is more than can be said for Lord Bentson."

"That is true," Richard murmured. Sinking into his chair, he thumped his desk with his fist, ignoring the pain. He was growing tired of this. Tired of failing, tired of being two steps behind at almost every turn. "If only I knew why the killer was targeting these men."

George threw himself into a chair in front of the desk and contemplated Richard for a moment. "Do you wish for my theory?"

Richard nodded, spreading his hands. "Please, share it."

George let out a long sigh, shaking his head before speaking. "The men who have been killed are all entirely at random, yes?"

"Yes," Richard confirmed.

"Then, perhaps that is exactly what he is doing."

Richard stared at George for a moment, not entirely sure what he was getting at. "You believe the killer is choosing men in the upper circles of society, entirely at random? Poisoning them for no particular reason?"

"Oh, I am sure he has his reasons," George exclaimed, sitting up a little straighter. "Mayhap he has been wronged by someone of great import, or perhaps he has a grudge against society in general. For whatever purpose, I believe he is choosing his targets out of nothing more than whimsy, which is what is making it so difficult for us to work out who his next target might be."

Richard nodded slowly. "This is nothing but a game to him. He is enjoying besting us, by sending us these almost indecipherable clues, knowing that we will, most likely, always be too late."

"He believes that his intelligence will always be greater than ours," George continued, rubbing his hands together. "That is why he has begun sending you the clues. Despite receiving them, we are always too far behind him. You are correct when you suggest he might see this as a game - but, unfortunately, it is one that he is currently winning."

Richard took in a long breath, rubbing his chin with one hand as he thought. "At least now we have a greater understanding of our killer. Whilst I am frustrated that these killings seem to be without reason, accepting that he is doing that purposefully gives the entire situation a little more clarity."

"Then all we need to do is attempt to work out these clues a little more quickly," George responded, with a wry smile.

Richard huffed out a breath, knowing this was where they struggled the most. The notes contained clues as to who the next victim would be, but would never give the man's name. Instead, it gave clues as to their status in society, their family, their fortune, as well as their vices. Not all of which was readily available knowledge, considering the sheer amount of society men in London. Lord Bentson, it seemed, had a penchant for brandy, and, sadly for him, that had been his downfall. According to the butler, the man had rarely been seen without a glass in his hand.

"What are we to do, then?" he asked a little helplessly. "What is our next step, George?"

George's face remained stoic, as he spread his hands. "I am not sure, sir. In fact, I find myself at something of a loss."

Richard wanted to thump his desk again, hard, but refrained. This was one of the most frustrating cases he had ever been assigned, and, given his complete lack of progress, he would not be surprised if the Duke demanded an explanation soon. "It is so very confusing," he groaned, rubbing a hand down his face.

"Indeed it is, sir," George agreed. "And, if you don't mind me saying so, you'd best be careful with that young girl of yours. The last thing we want is for the killer to take notice of someone you care about."

Richard's blood ran cold. "He's never targeted a woman before."

George shrugged. "Doesn't mean that he won't, sir." He steepled his fingers, studying Richard as though choosing his words carefully. "If we believe that the killer is playing a game with you - and enjoying it, I might add, then you must be extremely cautious. As you said yourself, we have no idea who he will be targeting next."

A tight band of anxiety crossed Richard's chest as he thought of Helena. He was in love with her, he admitted, but was George correct in his assumptions, that love could potentially bring about her death.

"The killer could be watching us, - watching me," He felt a hand squeeze his heart. The image of Helena lying dead on the floor flashed into his mind, bringing on a wave of nausea.

George nodded, getting to his feet. "We have no idea who he is, sir. He could be watching you, and watching those you care about. You'd best be on your guard."

CHAPTER 8

Helena was more than anxious when she entered the ballroom. She had thought of nothing but Richard since their dance together, wondering just how close he had come to kissing her. When she had spoken of it to Abigail, she had agreed wholeheartedly that, had they not been interrupted, Richard would have made his feelings quite clear.

"Whatever was he doing?" she wondered to herself, trying to figure out what it was that had pulled Richard away from her so quickly. Indeed, he had not even said a word to Charles but had left the house at once. He had no family to speak of, given that his parents had already passed away some years ago. In addition, he was an only child so had no siblings to care for. Helena was quite at a loss as to what had occurred. Lifting her chin, she smiled at the first young gentleman who came to sign her dance card. She had quite a few names there after only a few minutes, with only a few dances left available.

"Ah, Lord Franks," Charles announced, making the introductions. "May I present my sister, Miss Helena Catesby."

"Miss Catesby," the man echoed, bowing low. "How lovely to make your acquaintance."

"Lord Franks," she acknowledged, bobbing a curtsy. The

gentleman was handsome enough, standing tall and strong, with just a hint of laughter in his dull gray eyes. His smile was genuine, but Helena felt not even a spark of interest. Her heart belonged entirely to Richard, whether or not she wished it.

"I was hoping I might secure you for a dance," he continued earnestly. "Perhaps, the waltz?"

Helena opened her mouth to say that she was saving that dance for Lord Livingstone, but a slight nudge from Abigail forced her to close it again. It would not do to show her partiality for Richard in such company, for that particular tidbit would spread like wildfire around the room and then she would be in the suds!

"That would be lovely," she said, weakly. "But I –"

"Did you not promise that waltz for me, Miss Catesby?"

Helena's breath caught in her chest as Richard appeared at Lord Franks' side, his brows knotting together. He looked almost irate, and Lord Franks quelled under his angry stare.

"I – I quite forgot," she stammered, throwing a helpless look at Abigail. "Perhaps the quadrille, Lord Franks?"

The man nodded, recovering himself. "Indeed, the quadrille it is." Lifting her card, he signed his name boldly, before giving her a quick bow once more. "Until then."

Helena watched him go, indignation slowly building in her chest.

"My turn, I think," Richard interjected, his fingers reaching for her wrist. His gloved hand held hers for just a moment before taking her dance card in his hand and writing his name down on not one, but two waltzes.

"Richard," Helena hissed, tugging her hand free almost at once. "What do you think you are doing?"

"I am signing your dance card," he announced, suddenly affable. "What else do you mean?"

Gritting her teeth, Helena glared at him. She was quite sure that Lord Franks would not be slow in telling other guests exactly what had occurred.

"You should be a little more discreet, Richard," Abigail breathed with just a touch of admonishment while putting a calming hand on

Helena's arm. "Lord Franks was quite disconcerted by your behavior, and Helena does have two waltzes. You could have had one and Lord Franks the other. Unless –" She tipped her head and regarded him carefully, a twinkle in her eyes. "Unless there is a particular reason that you wanted both dances to yourself?"

Helena's frustration grew as Richard glanced away from her and Abigail. He stayed silent, refusing to give any kind of explanation. She was just on the verge of giving him a harsh set down for his lack of discretion when she was borne away by her very first dance partner, a Lord Haddington. Throwing one last angry glance over her shoulder towards Richard, she took three deep breaths to calm her frustrations. It would not do her any good to allow her irritation and upset to show.

"Richard," Abigail said quietly. "Whatever is going on? I am quite aware that you hold Helena in your affections."

"You are?" The words slipped from his mouth before he could stop them, turning searching eyes on Abigail.

"Yes, I am," she replied with a smile. "You all but confessed it to me back before Charles and I were married. Do you not remember? Why you have not already told her of them is quite beyond me."

Richard let out a heavy sigh, looking out over the dance floor and letting his eyes rest of Helena. He had seen the way gentlemen flocked to her, and the moment he had seen Lord Franks approach, he had found himself making his way towards her at once. Lord Franks was handsome, genteel, rich, and in search of a wife, and Richard did not want him to receive even the slightest bit of encouragement in regards to Helena. She was not going to be Lord Franks' wife that was for sure. "I cannot tell her," he said, eventually. "At least, not yet."

"Why ever not?" Abigail inquired, curiously. "She cares for you, Richard, but I am afraid that if you continue to pull yourself away from her, she will find someone else. Not that I am saying she is fickle, for I believe her affections to be real and true towards you."

"Then what are you saying?" he asked, the thought of Helena in another man's arms making him grow hot with anger.

"I am saying," Abigail continued softly. "That she will not wait forever. If you continue to deny your feelings to both yourself and her, then she will not always be there waiting and hoping for you to declare yourself." She shook her head. "Believe it or not, Richard, but you are making her heart tear with agony over you."

His irritability dissipated in a moment as he turned his head to look out at Helena once more. She was incredibly beautiful this evening, her perfect smile making his heart ache. Her long, dark tresses were piled up in an almost ornate fashion, with some tendrils falling around her cheeks. The deep green of her dress made her eyes sparkle like emeralds. He was pulled towards her like a man who had found treasure. He wanted to hold her in his arms, to kiss her soft lips and to declare his intentions towards her, but his work would not allow him to do so. Not yet, at least.

"I do not wish to hurt her," he said, his years of regret dousing him in shame.

"Then can't you give her *some* kind of explanation?" Abigail implored quietly. "Give her hope? Or else give her the freedom she needs to seek another gentleman?"

Richard thought for a long moment, his heart constricting. "I'll speak to her," he said eventually.

"I think you should," Abigail replied gently. "Tonight, if you can."

Richard nodded slowly, then lifted his head as a sudden thought had him jerking in fright. "Does Charles know?"

Abigail laughed airily, a wide smile spreading across her face. Looking over to where her husband was talking to a friend of his, her eyes gentled as she shook her head. "Come now, Richard. You know Charles and what he is like. If you remember, you had to push him into considering his own feelings when it came to me."

Relief made Richard want to sag against the wall, but he remained standing. Charles would have had him hung, drawn and quartered if he ever suspected Richard was toying with Helena's affections. But Abigail was correct. Charles was not an emotive man, and very rarely had the instinct to consider what others felt. Richard had practically had to prod him into accepting that he was in love with Abigail, a fact that Richard found glaringly obvious.

"He will have to know at some point, however," Abigail continued.

"Perhaps once you have made your intentions clear to Helena, you might think about speaking to Charles."

"I will consider it," Richard said firmly. The thought made something akin to fear swirl in his chest, for Charles was quite protective of his younger sisters. One thing was for certain; he could not continue to pull himself away from Helena without giving her some kind of explanation. He did not want to hurt her, and certainly did not want her to begin to seek out another potential husband. "I will speak to Helena this evening," he promised, seeing Abigail's smile of relief. "Thank you, Abigail."

Helena had danced four dances in a row before she was able to return to her seat. She was quite parched and was sure that her cheeks were rosy from the heat. Thankfully, her irritation over Richard had slowly begun to ebb away, and she had been able to bat away Lord Franks' questions over him with some ease. The quadrille did not give much time for conversation either, which she was grateful for. At the very least, she had been able to ensure Lord Franks was aware that Richard was a dear friend of her brother, which explained their familiarity at least.

"Here," came a voice, along with a hand holding out a glass of ratafia.

Helena glanced up, seeing Richard's contrite face. "Thank you," she managed, taking it from him and looking away almost at once. She did not know quite what to say to him. Abigail and Charles were talking to various acquaintances, leaving her quite alone with Richard. Lifting the glass to her mouth, she drank thirstily, as he sat down next to her.

"Helena," he said, delicately – his tone causing warmth to burst through her core. "I'm sorry."

"And so you should be," she retorted, although a slight smile touched her lips. "I would not like for there to be any rumors whispered about us," she finished, glancing away.

Richard sighed inwardly. He had reacted to Lord Franks' presence and behaved with a lack of decorum. "Should you care for some fresh air?" he asked after a moment. He saw the surprise in her eyes but kept his face calm. He wanted to walk with her, to feel her hand on his arm. He was not quite sure what he was going to say to her, but he would ensure that she was quite aware of his feelings, as well as the fact that, for the moment, he was unable to express them in the way he desired.

"I should ask Charles," Helena managed, heat coursing through her. The terrace would be quite within sight of the other guests, but she had a feeling that Richard might wish to walk in the gardens beyond. Normally such things were discouraged, for a lady's reputation could shatter in a moment were it discovered that she had been out walking alone with a gentleman, particularly when it was dark. However, a frisson of excitement raced through her as she thought of walking along with Richard, wondering if this would be the moment he would express his feelings towards her.

"I have mentioned to Abigail that I wished to speak to you," Richard continued. "I do not think Charles will mind."

Right on cue, Abigail turned her head and saw both Richard and Helena looking over at her. Her eyes crinkled approvingly, and she gave a slight nod before turning back to her friends.

"It appears Abigail has given me permission," Helena marveled, getting to her feet. "Shall we go?"

"What of your next dance partner?" Richard asked.

Helena shook her head. "I have none for the next dance, and I believe the one after is the first waltz of the evening." She raised one enquiring eyebrow. "Unless you prefer to stay?"

We can dance in the garden, Richard wanted to say, but contented himself with a quick smile, before leading the way towards the terrace.

CHAPTER 9

As they made their way outside, it was with a little surprise that Richard found Helena wandering down the steps towards the garden, instead of remaining on the terrace, but he followed without delay. Abigail's words came back to his ears - *I believe her affections to be real and true towards you.* He had always believed that Helena returned his affections in some way, but Abigail had only confirmed what he had long hoped. He now worked to remind himself that his feelings for her were returned.

"Are you going to speak to me then, Richard?" Helena asked after they began to walk along the path. Reaching up, she took his arm, aware that her heart was already beating faster. His presence always had the same effect on her, although his current closeness was making everything a little more intense. She was tingling from head to foot, as gentle butterflies began to flap their wings in her belly.

"What do you wish me to say, Helena?"

She looked up at him, surprised. "You are truly asking me that?"

He glanced at her, before looking away. The gardens were lit only by a few soft lanterns and, in the dim light, Helena was sure she could see his face reddening. "You left me without a word," she said plainly, though without accusation.

Richard swallowed hard, aware she was referencing their previous dancing lesson. "Yes, I am aware of my behavior, and I must apologize. I should not have done so without explanation."

"Then what is it?"

"What is…what?"

"Your explanation?"

He let out a long breath, not sure what to say. "Helena, I am afraid I cannot tell you."

"Why not?"

He shook his head. "I simply can't. It is for your own benefit, I swear it."

"My benefit?" she asked, tugging her hand from his arm and turning to face him. "What benefit is that?"

"Hush," he begged, aware that there were other couples walking the path. Taking her hand, he all but dragged her into a small arbor, sitting her down on a stone bench. Dragging a hand through his hair, he threw his head back and groaned aloud. This was more difficult than he had anticipated. "I know this is a lot to ask of you, Helena, but I simply need you to trust me that what I am keeping from you is of the greatest importance." Reaching over, he placed one hand atop of hers, glad that he had already removed his gloves. Her skin was soft, and a spark shot into her eyes almost at once as he looked at her.

"You confuse me greatly, Richard," Helena replied, refusing to be distracted from what they were discussing. "In one moment, you seem almost unable to take your eyes from me, then the next you disappear without nary an explanation!"

"I can hardly ever take my eyes from you," he admitted, a touch ruefully. "I think you know that I have long held you in my heart, Helena."

She looked at him, honestly. "Yes, I have, Richard. I mean, I always hoped that one day you would speak to me of these feelings, but as the years have gone by, you have never said a word."

He leaned a little closer, looking deeply into her eyes. All thought of what he was going to say, of what he was going to explain, left his mind completely. All he could see was Helena. "I have longed to speak to you, Helena, but I have never been able to."

Helena wanted to ask why. She wanted to seek out his explanation but found she could barely even breathe, never mind form any coherent words. He was drawing ever closer, his breath fanning across her cheek. His soulful eyes were darkening in the gloom, and a wave of excitement and nervousness flooded her all at once. All she had to do was close her eyes, lean forward and...

The first touch of Helena's lips against his sent such a heady sensation through Richard that he had to hold onto the stone bench with one hand in order to keep steady. He'd been desperate for this for so long, had needed this for what felt like a lifetime, and now, finally, to be touching her in such an intimate way almost overwhelmed him completely. Her lips were soft as she attempted to kiss him back. Her hesitancy endeared her to him even more, and he lifted his hand from the bench to clasp her closer to him. One hand settled on her waist, whilst the other wrapped around the nape of her neck.

Helena sagged against Richard at once, weak with happiness and relief. Finally, he had kissed her, and it was everything she had hoped for. Lights were exploding in her head, and shivers ran down her arms as he pulled her tighter. When Richard angled his head just a little, nipping at her lower lip gently, Helena gasped in surprise, allowing him entry. His tongue twined with hers in a most intimate fashion, and Helena could do nothing but cling to Richard.

Richard knew he had to stop, but couldn't bring himself to tear his lips from hers. Her hands had slowly left his arms and had made their way around his neck, her fingers channeling into his hair. Time seemed to slow. Everything in him told him he should be dropping to his knees in front of her so that she would be secured to him forever.

"Lord Livingstone?"

Richard dropped his hands at once, pulling back and staring into the evening haze. That voice had sounded like that of George. *Not now,* he begged silently, turning around to shield Helena from whomever it was who had come searching for him.

"Lord Livingstone?"

Clearing his throat, Richard got to his feet and nodded at George, who entered the arbor with a desperate look on his face.

"You're needed, sir."

"Needed?" Helena asked faintly. Stars were sparkling in her vision, and she felt numb all over. To have Richard so close, only to pull away so suddenly, had left her in something of a fog.

Richard turned to her, an apologetic look on her face. "I have to go."

A sharp pain raced through her. "What do you mean, *go*?"

"I mean, I have to leave the ball at once."

"Please, sir," George interrupted. "We must hurry."

Richard was torn between going with George to decipher the next note, or staying with Helena to explain what was going on. She was staring at him with a lost look in her eyes, not at all understanding the urgency. For heaven's sake, he had just kissed her and was now about to leave her completely alone. Guilt warred in his soul, but his dedication to his work urged him from his seat. He had to at least *try* and prevent another man's death.

"Come with me please, Helena," he urged, reaching for her hand. "Let me return you to Abigail."

Helena withdrew her hand at once. "You cannot mean to leave me, Richard, after all, that has just passed between us."

"I swear that I would stay with you, Helena, if the matter did not need my immediate attention."

Anger began to mount as Helena stared back at him in shock. He had just kissed her – the first kiss she'd ever received – and now he was leaving her, in much the same manner as he had done the previous day?

"You cannot do this to me, Richard," she whispered, her face draining of color. "Please."

Richard swallowed hard, rubbing a hand over his face, a desperation threatening to choke him. "Let me return you to Abigail, Helena."

Helena shook her head defiantly. "No," she said firmly. "If you must leave, then leave. I will be quite all right here alone. Besides," she continued, looking up at him. "I need to think about what has just occurred." Her voice was icy, letting him know exactly what she meant.

His heart tugged him back towards her, but Richard forced himself to turn from her. He knew that, should he leave her again, he might very well be throwing away his chance of a happy future with her by his side, but he had very little choice. "Forgive me," he whispered, watching a single tear tracking down her cheek before turning away and walking briskly into the gloom beside George.

Helena watched him leave, her hands clenching into fists. She was moving somewhere between anger and agony, feeling as though she were about to cry at any moment. She could not believe that Richard had left her, despite her pleading. Whatever it was that had occurred, he had sworn it was of the utmost importance, but she struggled to accept that it was more important than the magnificent kisses they had just shared. She had been so wonderfully happy. Richard's kisses had been the culmination of the years they had spent growing infinitesimally closer and, at that moment, she had seen her future. It was a future with Richard, where they kept nothing from each other and were as close as two people in love could be.

But what was left of that now? Richard was clearly hiding something from her. Was he truly the man she thought he was? Had she fallen in love with only the façade he presented? Her heart began to twist as she leaned back against the stone back, looking up at the starry sky and blinking back tears. She couldn't go on like this. Her upset would only eat away at her, plaguing her mind. Richard had to know that he couldn't keep pushing himself away from her like this.

Thinking hard, Helena made a decision. She had to find out the truth if there was going to be any hope for their future. Richard apparently wanted to keep the truth from her for her own good, but it wasn't doing her any particular good. In fact, it was making things much worse. There was a chasm opening up between them both, the longer he kept things from her. She would simply have to convince him to be honest with her. Her mind made up, Helena took in a few long breaths, as the moisture left her lashes. Feeling a little more settled, she got to her feet and brushed her hands down her dress, smoothing out a few creases. Lifting her head high, she took a deep breath and began to walk back towards the ball, hoping she could slip in unnoticed.

CHAPTER 10

Georgia handed Richard the note the moment they reached the carriage.

"Arrived shortly after you left," he said, by way of explanation. "Same as always."

"A child?"

George nodded. "I asked him, of course, but it was the same story. A gentleman gave the boy a few coins to deliver the letter to your home. He hid his face in some kind of scarf."

"Exactly the same as the other beggar children," Richard huffed, unfolding the letter and beginning to read the few lines.

'The wealthy must eat, it seems. Their corpulent bodies will line the streets, stuffed with caviar and sherry. Men with more money than sense throw it away on horses and cards, but they can take none of it with them. The daughters will be left weeping, knowing that the most precious thing in their lives has now departed this earth.'

Richard blew out a long breath, re-reading the lines. "Have you any idea, George?"

To his surprise, George gave him an uncharacteristic grin. "As a matter of fact, I have!"

"Who?" Richard asked, a shot of adrenaline jolting through him.

This might be the very first time they would find the victim before the killer got there.

"From the note, we are looking for a gentleman of quality, with a penchant for frivolous gambling on horses and cards, who enjoys caviar and sherry and has daughters."

Richard lifted his shoulders. "That narrows it down, certainly, but I cannot think…." He trailed off as he remembered something of import. A certain gentleman had, only last week, lost a vast amount of money on a simple game of cards, but had laughed it off immediately. In fact, he had then gone on to lose even more money on the horses. Whites had been abuzz with the news of his losses. "You are thinking of Lord Wallace."

"I am," George said, almost cheerfully. "He is beyond wealthy and has often lost money gambling, but it does not seem to bother him in the least."

"And he lost a great sum last week, on two separate occasions." A frown crossed Richard's face. "And he has daughters?"

"Two, in fact," George said. "Although whether they think him the 'most precious thing in their lives', I am not sure," he continued, quoting the note. "By all accounts, they despise his gambling."

"Perhaps we should let the killer do his work, then," Richard quipped, a smirk-ish grin spreading across his face. He had no intention of doing such a thing of course, but he could not resist the jest. When George had appeared, his heart had sunk into his boots at the thought of another note. He had expected failure, whereas now, it seemed, they were about to have their first ever success.

The carriage eventually stopped outside Lord Wallace's townhouse, and Richard and George threw themselves from it the moment it came to a standstill. Racing up the steps, George rapped loudly on the door, over and over, until the butler finally appeared.

"We must see your master at once," George boomed, pushing the door open and forcing the astonished butler out of the way. "I –"

"George!" Richard shouted, catching sight of someone out of the corner of his eye. Rushing down the steps, he began to give chase, as the cloaked figure broke into a run. Richard had no idea where this man had come from, nor exactly what he had to do with the murders, but on instinct, he gave chase. After all, an innocent man would not run away now, would he? Unfortunately, for him, the cloaked figure was fleet of foot, lengthening the distance between them. Richard's lungs began to burn as he dragged air into his chest, determined not to give up. The man turned into a small park to his left, with Richard but a few steps behind him.

The park was completely dark, and Richard jogged to slow his steps and walk slowly along the path. There were no lamps of any kind, so Richard had no idea where he was going. *Foolishness,* he thought to himself, gritting his teeth with frustration. The man had clearly chosen this place to hide, knowing that Richard would not easily be able to find him. Standing still finally, Richard took in great gulps of air, trying to catch his breath. This was no good. He had lost him. Vexed, he turned back towards the dim light of the street ahead of him, knowing he had no other choice but to walk back to Lord Wallace's home. He just hoped George had managed to prevent the man's impending death.

A sudden blow threw him backward, knocking him harshly to the ground. All the air left his lungs as two strong hands wrapped themselves around his throat. Stars began to sparkle in his vision, as Richard gasped for air, grappling with the strong hands at his throat. Already dazed from the two separate blows to his head, Richard tried to stay conscious, suddenly aware that he could be in a battle for his life.

Gathering what strength he had, Richard threw his entire body weight to one side, managing to unseat his attacker for just a moment. The grip around his throat loosened briefly, giving Richard enough time to grab them and pull them away. Pulling in a huge breath of air, Richard let out a great bellow of rage as he continued to fight against the strong hands that were trying to make their way back around his throat. A sudden vision of all the men he had seen lying dead in their homes filled his mind, pulsing a sudden rage through him. With another roar, he threw the man to one side, managing to then scramble to his feet. His hands reached for his attacker, as he simultaneously kicked out with his feet – only to be met with air. The man had apparently run from him, realizing that he was not going to achieve his goal. His breath coming in short, sharp gasps, Richard placed his hands on his knees and pulled in as much air as he could into his burning lungs. It was frightening how close the attacker had come to killing him. Richard had no doubt in his mind that this was the man responsible. This had been the murderer they had been searching for.

Stumbling back towards Lord Wallace's home, Richard hoped desperately that George had found a living man instead of a dead body. The cloaked figure had left at almost the same moment they'd arrived, which meant he could not have been long ahead of them.

"George?" he called, as the still shaken and confused butler let him in. "George?"

"The library, sir," the butler muttered, opening the door to let him in.

George and Lord Wallace looked up the moment he entered, both pairs of eyes widening in shock.

"Goodness, Richard," George exclaimed, coming over to help him into a seat. "Whatever happened?"

"I didn't catch him," Richard lamented, as Lord Wallace ambled over and handed him a brandy. "This isn't poisoned, is it?"

Lord Wallace, who looked quite pale, shook his head. "A fresh bottle, I assure you," he replied, with a shake of his head. "Although, if you had not arrived when you did, I believe I would be on my way to glory!"

Richard lifted one enquiring eyebrow at George, ignoring the buzzing pain in his head.

"Poisoned, yes," George said, nodding. "The gardener had caught some rats recently, so we tested it on them."

"And?"

"Dead."

Richard let out a long breath of relief. Finally, they had managed to prevent the murderer from achieving his goal, albeit just on this one occasion. There was no guarantee they would do so again. Taking a long draught of the brandy, he rested his head back on the chair. "How do I look?"

"Terrible," George commented, wryly. "You have a dent in your head, it seems, as well as various scratches and bruises around your throat." He shook his head, studying Richard's injuries closely. "Oh, and there appears to be bleeding coming from the *back* of your head."

"That sounds about right," Richard murmured, letting his eyes slide closed. "At least I am – we are – alive."

"I'll drink to that," came Lord Wallace's gruff reply, refilling Richard's glass, which now sat empty on a small table beside him. "I can't thank you both enough for saving my life."

"Don't mention it," Richard replied, managing to open his eyes and look at the man in front of him. "It's just what we do."

CHAPTER 11

Once morning broke, Richard knew he had to see Helena straight away, despite his dreadful appearance. There was much he had to say, the least of which was to apologize profusely for leaving her alone in the gardens the evening before. His face grew hot with shame every time he thought of it.

Ushered into the drawing room, he attempted a smile as he heard gasps from the three occupants of the room.

"Whatever happened, old boy?" Charles exclaimed, getting to his feet. "You look...."

"Hideous, yes," Richard interrupted, waving away his concern. "It is of no consequence. I was simply knocked down by a would be thief on my return home."

"Did they take anything?" Abigail asked, her face lined with concern.

Richard shook his head, wading deeper into his lie. "No, not at all. I had a friend with me, who was able to subdue him."

"I presume you caught him?"

Helena's voice was icy, and Richard shivered involuntarily. "Caught who?"

"The thief."

"Ah – well, no, we did not, I'm afraid. It was very dark, you see."

Helena rolled her eyes, not caring whether or not Richard saw her. She did not believe his story at all, although his appearance still concerned her greatly. Whatever had he been doing?

Ever since the moment he had left her, Helena had wavered between anger and frustration. She had attempted to enjoy the rest of the ball, but her heart had simply not been in it. Her smiles had been few, her conversation stilted until she was practically begging Charles to return home. Yet, even then, she could not get Richard from her mind. His kisses had woken something primal in her, something that could not be easily satiated. She wanted more – more of him. She desired for him to be truthful with her, instead of simply leaving her without explanation. Why he was not open and honest with her, she simply could not understand.

Sleep had not come easily. Tossing and turning all night, she had determined that she would speak to Richard as soon as she could, without appearing indiscreet. There had to be an end to this impossible situation, for she was not about to allow this relationship to continue in the same vein. She would not allow him to kiss her and then disappear without explanation, or to start telling her about his feelings, only to then pull back.

"Would you care for a stroll in the park, Helena?"

She glanced up at him, noticing the slight desperation on his face. He clearly wanted to discuss things with her, which was something of a relief.

"I suppose," she agreed, looking away.

"Capital idea, we shall all go," Charles announced. "Abigail?"

Abigail glanced at Richard before turning back to Charles. "I had been hoping we might have a quiet morning," she began, hiding a yawn. "After all, we were back very late last evening."

Charles frowned. "That is true. If you are too tired, my dear, then I can accompany Richard and Helena."

Abigail's voice turned sultry. "Would you not rather stay here with me?"

Richard barely managed to hide his amusement at seeing Charles' face turned a bright red as he took in Abigail's meaning. Coughing to cover his chuckle, he caught the twinkle in Abigail's eye. She was clearly quite aware that he and Helena needed some time together. Whatever Helena had told her, he was grateful that she was attempting to help.

"I can take a maid, if you think that best," Helena offered casually, walking towards Charles. "But it is only Richard."

"You are quite right," Charles blustered. "Off with you, then. It is a fine day after all."

৩৯৫৫

"I SUPPOSE you are quite cross with me."

Helena glanced up at Richard, one eyebrow cocked. "*Cross* is not quite the right word, Richard."

"Oh?"

Helena's jaw tightened. "Richard, you practically kissed me senseless, and then left me with no attempt at an explanation." She looked up at him again. "It is not as though I have been kissed before," she continued, her voice lightly pleading, "Do you not understand just how momentous that was for me?"

Shame rose up in his chest. "No, I confess I had not considered that."

"Why can you not be truthful with me, Richard?" she implored of him, her breath coming out in a huff of air. "It is most frustrating and, to be truthful with you, your behavior upsets me greatly." She waited with bated breath for his explanation, but, to her displeasure, it was not forthcoming.

"I am sorry, Helena."

She paused in her steps and crossed her arms, turning to face him. "That is all you are going to say? You are not going to tell me why you left me, or why you have bruises on your throat and forehead?"

He pressed his lips together. "As I said to you last evening, Helena, it is for your own good that I keep these things to myself."

"Then how can there be any kind of future for us?" she exclaimed, her cheeks growing pink. "You told me that you have long had me in your heart, are you now confessing that you do not, in truth, love me?"

"No, I am not saying that at all!" Richard exclaimed, his heart beginning to hammer as he attempted to find a way to explain himself. "I do love you, Helena, truly."

His words fell around them, the world slowing as they gazed into each other's eyes.

"You do love me," Helena repeated, her voice a breathy whisper. Helena's shoulders felt as if they melted with his confession. "I have longed to hear you say those words to me, Richard."

"I have longed desperately to say them," he replied.

"And why have you not?"

Richard threw his head back, letting out a frustrated breath as he squeezed his eyes tightly shut. What could he possibly say that would let her understand?

Helena watched him, aware that he was troubled with something he refused to speak of. She wanted to help him, wanted to share the burden, but he was refusing to allow her to do so.

"Richard, please," she begged. "We have been apart for so long. I beg you not to lengthen that time by keeping silent."

"I have to keep you safe," he barked, making her jump, but she could hear the pain in his voice. "Can you not see what was done to me? How he tried to kill me? I will not put you in danger, Helena!"

Her eyes broadened with both shock and surprise. "Someone tried to kill you?" she whispered, the blood draining from her face.

Richard grasped her arms, seeing her sway a little. "I should not have said such a thing," he backtracked, irritated with himself for letting such a small detail slip. "You must understand, Helena, I want to give myself to you, to share my life with you, but at present, I cannot."

Helena could barely breathe, realizing that the marks around his throat, the ones she could see in spite of his cravat, were from a life and death struggle. Richard changed almost in front of her eyes. Instead of the slightly forgetful, humorous and jovial gentleman, he became a man who was involved in deep and dark things. Mystery surrounded him like a shroud, and Helena could not tear it from him easily.

"I feel as if I do not know you," she whispered, stepping back from his arms.

"You do know me," he promised, reaching for her again. "Helena, don't run from me, please. I know that this is a lot to accept but – "

Helena did not wait for his explanation, choosing to leave him behind. To her relief, he did not follow. Her mind was already full of thoughts and questions, each tumbling over one another in a fight to get to the front of her mind. Richard had been in a fight for his life, a fight that could have ended with tragic consequences. She might never have seen him again, and might never have known his true feelings for her. Whatever he was caught up in was of a much greater consequence than she had even imagined, and she did not quite know what to do with that knowledge. The man she thought she knew, thought she had loved, was keeping a large part of himself and his life away from her, and that was not something Helena could easily accept.

CHAPTER 12

Helena retired early, choosing to take a tray in her room rather than dine with Charles and Abigail. She had exchanged pleasantries with Abigail but refused to give her any details of what had occurred with Richard. She did not want to discuss their situation with anyone, not even her dear sister-in-law. The only person she wanted to discuss things with was Richard.

Looking at herself in the mirror, Helena cringed inwardly at her red-rimmed and puffy eyes. Her long hair curled around her shoulders in an unruly mop, and she looked altogether much too pale. However, a calm serenity was in her eyes. Now that she had worked through everything Richard had told her, Helena had decided on a path ahead. A peace entered her soul as the last of her tears dried on her cheeks. Richard was not going to be as calm as she, however, but Helena was now quite determined that he would not have his way. Whilst she hated that Richard was keeping something from her, the knowledge that he was doing so in order to protect her mollified her frustration somewhat.

Helena lifted her chin with a boldness she did not quite feel. Richard was going to have to accept that Helena was not about to give up. The love they shared was worth more than that. He might be utterly desperate to keep some part of his life a secret from her, but Helena was not so easily satisfied. They were meant to have a life and a future together, she was quite sure of it, and Helena was not about to enter into any kind of intimacy with him without knowing everything about him. There had to be trust between them, did there not? Love and trust came hand in hand. She gave a wane smile to her reflection, utterly determined to find out the truth.

But what could she do? Her smile faded, and a frown creased her brow. She was not exactly able to speak at length with Richard at a ball or soiree, for they could easily be interrupted. *Or he could be summoned away again,* she thought, ruefully. She could ask him to call on her, of course – but then, should he not like her questions, he could easily take his leave, and she would have no other recourse than to let him go. It was not as if she could run down the street after him.

Her frown deepened. The only place she could speak to Richard at length would be his own home. That was not too far from here, by all accounts, although she had never called on him before. What would he say if she turned up in the middle of the night, asking to see him? Would he turn her away, send her back to walk alone on the streets of London? Helena shook her head, knowing that Richard would have no choice but to take her in, although he might very well bundle her in a carriage soon after.

What would Charles think? A small smile played around Helena's lips. Charles' potential outrage would make Richard think very carefully about how he treated Helena. He could not exactly turn up at Charles' door with Helena in his carriage with no explanation. The more she thought about it, the more Helena realized that this would be the only way to ensure Richard's cooperation.

Rising from her chair, she found a brush and began to quickly tie up her hair. Her nightgown was discarded, and she attempted to dress herself in one of her warmest walking dresses. The back ties were a little difficult to manage on her own, but she got there in the end. Her sturdy boots were on her feet, and a high-rimmed bonnet on her head as she approached the bedroom door.

Her heart began to thunder, as the door opened with a gentle click. She assumed Charles and Abigail would already have retired, given the hour, and whilst there might be a few household staff around, most would be abed. Swallowing hard, she walked the length of the hallway on her tiptoes, before descending down the servant stairs.

No one saw the slim shadow slip through the back entrance, leaving the latch unlocked. Her footsteps made barely a sound as she stepped out of the town house and onto the cobbles. Filling her lungs with night air, Helena began to walk as fast as she could in the direction of Richard's town house, hoping that no one would stop her. She had no plan about what to do should someone attack her, other than scream.

The lanterns were lit, but their dim light barely made a dent in the fog. Helena walked as quickly as she could, keeping her eyes on the street ahead. There was barely a sound, other than the random shriek of an owl or the squeak of a rat. Shivering in the cold, she tugged her shawl a little tighter around her shoulders, practically running towards Richard's home by this point.

To her very great relief, she found his town house with no trouble whatsoever. It helped that his name was emblazoned on the large wooden door, helping Helena's anxiety to settle somewhat. Wrapping quietly with her knuckles, she cringed as the sound echoed through the streets, not knowing what she would do should she be required to use the knocker.

To her very great surprise, the door opened almost at once, and a burly looking man looked down on her. His eyes opened with surprise, but Helena simply gave him a quick smile and pushed past him into the house.

"Good evening," she said evenly. "I am here to speak to Richard."

The man stared at her for a long moment, before finally closing both his mouth and the door. "You're here to see the master? At this hour?"

She nodded, removing her gloves and shawl and handing it to him. "And you may tell the master that Helena Catesby will not be leaving until I speak to him."

"Ah." A look of understanding swept over the man's face. "This way, please."

Helena followed the man towards another door, presuming it was the study, and wondering where the butler was. This man was clearly not the butler, yet was clearly somehow in Richard's employ.

"Just go on in," the man said, indicating the door to her left. "He's having a drink, I believe."

"Thank you," Helena extended, casting him one more curious glance before walking to the door, knocking on it lightly and turning the handle.

On entering the room, she found it blazing with light. Richard had various candles lit, and a roaring fire was in the grate. Heat washed over her.

"Close the door, George," came a voice from the chair in front of her. "You're letting in a dreadful draft."

Slightly nonplussed, Helena shut the door behind her, completely at a loss as to what to say. What had seemed like an excellent plan now had her doubting herself. She was in a room, alone, with Richard, in the dead of night, and no one except the man outside the study was aware of her presence. What was she doing?

"Pour me a whiskey, will you?" Richard asked, flinging an arm over the side of the chair and motioning toward the small table to his left where the decanter sat. "I've not had one all evening. Get one for yourself, too."

Helena walked forward, attempting to keep her nerve.

"Whiskey's not quite my tipple," she replied, jumping as he launched himself from his seat and stared at her wide-eyed. "In fact, I'd prefer a cup of tea."

CHAPTER 13

Richard could hardly believe what he was seeing. He blinked furiously to ensure he wasn't dreaming. Helena was standing in his study, her cheeks red and rosy from the crisp night air.

"Wh – what are you doing here?" he stammered, staying exactly where he was.

Helena could hardly tear her eyes from him. He'd long discarded his cravat, his shirt was pulled from his trousers, and a few buttons were undone at the neck. Clearly, he'd thrown his hands through his hair on a few occasions, and it was now a ruffled mop. It was possibly the most unrefined state she had ever seen him in, but a wave of attraction suddenly flooded her.

"This was not a good idea," she stammered, turning on her heel and making for the door. "I should not have come."

"But you have," Richard interrupted, practically running from behind his chair to stand in front of the door, blocking her exit. "Why did you come, Helena?"

Trying to answer only made her tongue stick to the roof of her mouth. He was entirely beguiling, and she found she could not look away.

"Helena," Richard said again, more softly. "What are you doing here?" Stepping forward, he drew closer to her, knowing that every minute she spent here was putting her reputation at stake. Not that he cared. All he could think about was that Helena was here, that she had come to his home. It was ridiculous and foolish, but here she was, standing in his study. Her cheeks were flushed, and her eyes were bright as she studied him. Immediately aware of his lack of proper dress, he averted his eyes for a moment, feeling slightly foolish. "I must apologize for my appearance," he hastily added, when she didn't answer his question. "It is late, after all."

"I had to see you," Helena eventually blurted out, her words suddenly pouring out in an unfiltered rush. "I don't know what's happening. I have to understand! I –"

Richard couldn't help but kiss her. Her eyes had lingered near the open collar of his shirt, a slow blush infusing her cheeks. When she'd looked at him with a mixture of confusion and love, he couldn't have kept himself from her for the world.

His secrets had forced them apart for so long and, deep down, he knew he should still be keeping himself from her, but his heart could not be denied any longer. He kissed her fiercely, with all the pent up passion he felt. Her hands reached around his neck, and he pulled her tighter against him, finally feeling whole.

"We have to stop," he whispered, eventually tearing his mouth from hers. "You could be compromised simply by being here, Helena."

"I know," she admitted, breathily. "But I had to see you." Her face took on a slightly pleading look. "What is happening, Richard? Why are you pushing yourself from me, when I know how much you care for me?" Her fingers reached up, tracing the bruises at his throat. "What are these marks from?" Helena trembled as he shook his head, desperation filling her. "Please, don't deny me the truth, Richard. I must know. Can't you tell how much this is tearing me apart?"

He groaned aloud, his arms still around her waist. "I am trying to keep you safe, Helena."

"I know that," she whispered. "But if we are to share our lives together, then you cannot keep this from me."

Looking down at her face, Richard sighed heavily. "All I have ever wanted is to have you by my side, Helena," he breathed, brushing a hand down her soft cheek. "I have been unable to tell you until now. And that is only because my heart will no longer let me keep myself from you."

Helena's smile lit up her face. She was finally going to have the truth from the man she loved. The final obstacle in their path was going be shattered. "I love you so very much, Richard," she said, as a sheen of tears glimmered in her eyes. "I have longed for this."

"That's why you came?" Richard asked.

She gave a slight nod. "I became determined not to allow your secrets to push me away any longer. You have to understand, Richard, I am quite determined. I will no longer be kept out of your arms." Her face and words grew resolute.

Richard pulled her tighter against him once more, letting her rest her head on his shoulder. "I have tried and tried to stay away from you, Helena," he professed. "But my love for you has grown regardless."

Helena looked up at him, pressing her lips to his for a brief kiss. A long sigh of happiness left her, finally secure in the love they shared.

Eventually, Richard stepped away, keeping one arm around her shoulders. "Charles will have my head, should he find out about this."

"Not if you make your intentions clear," she suggested, with a mischievous grin. "Although I am quite sure he will suspect very little. You know how Charles is."

"Yes, indeed I do," Richard agreed, knowing that Charles would be astonished to hear that there was any kind of intimacy between them. "I must promise you now, Helena, that my intentions are honorable."

His seriousness made her laugh. "I have no doubt that they are, Richard. And, when the time should come, I promise you that I will accept."

Richard couldn't help but kiss her again, making a silent promise to himself that, once this murderous affair was over, his first thought would be to propose to Helena.

Helena drew in a ragged breath as Richard broke their kiss, blinking a few times before regaining her composure. She saw Richard grin at her reaction, bringing another blush to her cheeks.

"I shall have to get you home," she heard Richard say, bringing a frown to her face.

"Richard, you know why I am here. Do not push me away again. I will not be so easily distracted!"

He blew out a breath of frustration, dropping his hands from her waist. "It is too dangerous, Helena."

She lifted her brow. "And nevertheless, I will not be put off."

Richard opened his mouth to answer, only to be interrupted by a sudden knock at the door. Without even calling the man to enter, the door opened to admit George, who was holding a stack of notes in his hand.

"I know this is terrible timing, sir, but I've assembled the old notes for us to go over. I fear that you are right, we need to tackle this tonight, before the next one arrives."

Throwing a glance at Helena, he nodded. "I'll come to the drawing room."

"And I'll come with you," Helena announced, refusing to be pushed aside. "And you may as well introduce me to this man, as I'm quite sure he is not your butler." Placing her hands on her hips, Helena waited for Richard to respond. He was in something of a bind, she could tell, but that still did not put her off in the least.

Finally accepting that he was not able to keep Helena from the truth any longer, Richard eventually nodded and held out his hand to her, which she took with only a momentary hesitation.

"Helena, this is George."

"Very nice to meet you, ma'am."

Helena inclined her head, studying him with an obvious curiosity. "And what do you do, exactly?"

George grinned, his face lighting up with a mischievous humor. "I'm Richard's valet, ma'am."

She narrowed her eyes, quite sure he was not telling her the complete truth. A valet did not answer the door, nor did he come into a room without invitation. This man was something more than a simple valet. "And what else?"

"And," George continued, giving Richard a slightly resigned look, "his bodyguard."

CHAPTER 14

Helena could hardly believe what she was hearing, staring, aghast, from one man to the other. Richard needed a bodyguard? She had known that Richard had been in a fight for his life the other night, but the man's familiarity with Richard clearly showed that this was a relationship of long standing. What was Richard involved in that required a bodyguard? Growing a little faint, she leaned heavily against Richard who pulled her tightly against him, his face growing concerned.

"You have a bodyguard?" Helena whispered as he led her to a nearby chair. "Why?"

"Because of my work," he replied, carefully seating her. Taking her hands, he nodded to George to fetch her a small glass of brandy. Her color was not good, and he cursed himself for allowing George to reveal the sometimes deadly nature of his work in such a brash manner. "Forgive me, Helena. I should have been more gentle with you in discovering this."

"I was quite determined," she said in a weak but playful tone, attempting a smile. "I shall not hold a grudge on that regard." Holding his gaze, she continued to watch him, seeing the concern in his eyes.

"Here you go," George mumbled, his behavior suggesting he felt more than a little foolish over his bold introduction moments before.

"Drink a little," Richard encouraged, as Helena screwed up her face with distaste at the smell. "It will help you recover." He watched as she did so, gasping in surprise after she took her first sip. "I have had good reason to keep things from you, Helena," he continued. "I did not want to put you in harm's way."

"Perhaps you should start from the beginning, sir," George commented, stepping away for a moment. "I will fetch a tea tray for the lady, despite the hour. I have heard it is quite fortifying in trying times."

Helena settled back in her chair, finally releasing Richard's hands. Strength was beginning to infuse her again, reminding her of her task. "You were going to tell me about your work, I think."

Richard rose to his feet. "Please, Richard, don't hold anything back. Knowing that you have had a bodyguard for some time makes me more than anxious."

His brow rose in surprise. "How do you know I have had George with me for a long time?"

She shrugged, braving another sip of her brandy. "He appeared very familiar with you. Obviously, your relationship is one of long standing."

"Indeed," Richard reflected thoughtfully. "Very astute, Helena."

A sudden thought hit him that perhaps she might be able to assist them with the decoding of the mysterious notes – but he pushed it away almost at once. He did not want to involve her any more than he had to.

"Richard," Helena huffed, growing a little irritated by his pausing. "You still have not explained to me what it is that you are involved in! I had thought you a simple gentleman of the realm who, at times, seemed both distracted and forgetful, often leaving at a moment's notice. Now, I presume, your hasty retreats have all been to do with…." She waved her hands around the room, "…whatever this is."

"You are right again, Helena," Richard continued, focusing entirely on what he had to say. "You must promise me not to breathe a word of what I tell you to anyone, not even Charles."

"Of course I will not," she retorted, a little hurt at the implication. "I would not betray you, Richard."

He gave her an endeared, knowing nod in an attempt to mollify her. "It is simply that my work is of the utmost secrecy, Helena. That is why I have kept it from you for so long." He shook his head, looking away from her. "No, it is why I have kept *myself* from you for so long."

"But no longer," Helena cautioned softly.

Meeting her eyes, Richard smiled tenderly. "Yes, of course. I am glad of that, Helena. The truth is that I work for a Duke."

"A Duke?" Helena exclaimed, astonished, and also a bit perplexed. "Does not a Duke have enough work to do already?"

"Apparently he finds the requirements of a dukedom a little… insipid," Richard replied, dryly. "He sets me various…tasks, and I complete them."

"Tasks," Helena repeated, squinting dubiously at him. "And what kind of *tasks* are they exactly, Richard?"

Richard sighed, knowing she was not going to take the simple explanation he had been hoping to give her. "It could be anything, Helena. I have dealt with robberies, muggings, affairs, and murders."

"I see." She placed her glass down on the table to her left and folded her hands in her lap, still looking at him intently. "You are not a Bow Street runner, are you?"

"No, nothing like that," Richard retorted, fully aware that the Runners had a less than stellar reputation. "Often I am assigned cases where there appears to be a dead end – or where the constable simply cannot find the culprit on his own."

"And the case you are involved with now?"

"Murder." He watched her closely, as emotion flickered across her face, but still, her gaze remained resolute. She was determined to be strong, and not wilt like a flower in the heat. In a strange way, he was immensely proud of her for that. "In this particular circumstance, I receive notes as to who the next target it, but by the time we have deciphered them, we are often too late."

"And you are attempting to catch whoever is doing this?"

He nodded. "Precisely. However, we are, as yet, not entirely successful. There have been numerous deaths, unfortunately. Although, we did manage to save our last mark."

Helena's thoughts raced with his words. "These notes, they are what have been calling you away recently," she offered as more of a statement than a question.

"I have had to leave wherever I am almost as soon as George comes to me with the next note," Richard explained. "It is truly a matter of life or death."

Helena nodded, slowly. Her mind was working through each thing that Richard had revealed, chewing over each word carefully. Gone was the image of him she had carried with her for so long. Instead of being the slightly ridiculous, forgetful man she had fallen for, she now realized that he had been hiding behind that persona for a long time. Instead, he was clearly extremely intelligent, quick witted and not in the least forgetful. It was quite a startling revelation, were she honest, although it did nothing to dim the love she held for him.

"I am sorry I kept this from you, Helena," he said, truthfully. "I pray you can understand why."

"I suppose I do," she said thoughtfully. "But how I wish you had been able to tell me, Richard. We have been kept apart for so long that, at times, it felt as though you were torturing me."

He swallowed, as shame trickled into his features. "I know," he whispered. "I felt it too." Looking up at her, he tried to smile. "But no longer."

"No," she agreed, looking at him with a loving look that beckoned him towards her. "No longer."

Richard couldn't stop himself from walking over to her and dragging her into his arms. He was pulled to her like a magnet, unable to resist the force of his attraction. Attempting to be soft and sweet in his kisses, he was astonished by the fervency of her response. She wasn't holding back in the least, pressing her mouth against his in the most passionate way, twining her fingers through his hair and angling her head just a little. He felt as if they were finally one. His body burst into life, his heart beating even faster in his chest as he held her, aware now that no other secrets stood between them.

CHAPTER 15

The door swung open with such force that it hit the wall with a great crash, causing Richard and Helena to jump apart, completely startled.

"Another note!" George cried, not even apologizing for the interruption. "When I went to fetch the tea tray, there was a boy at the door."

Immediately focused, Richard took the tea tray from George's hands and handed it to Helena. "Stay here," he said, firmly. "I'll be back soon."

"Why, where are you going?" Helena asked, a trifle put out at being so quickly dismissed.

"If there is a note, then I must study it at once," Richard said, his brain switching gears. "It is life or death, Helena."

"I have placed it in your study. I will meet you there," George said, before walking towards the door.

Richard nodded, turning back to Helena and taking in her furious expression. "I will return as soon as I can," he promised. "Please, Helena, I –" He halted, mid-sentence, as she shook her head at him.

With great deliberation, Helena put the tea tray down and walked towards the door. There was no doubt in her mind that she was going to assist Richard with this matter, despite his protestations. "Now, where is the study?" she asked, as Richard attempted to block her.

"Helena, you cannot –"

"Yes, I can and I will," she interrupted, her brows gathering. "You need as much help as you can get, by your own account, and perhaps a fresh mind might be just the ticket."

Richard's shoulders slumped in defeat, and he led her to the study against his better judgement. Everything she'd said was true, but that did not mean that he liked it. In fact, he wanted Helena as far away from this as possible, but it seemed it was not to be. His dear Helena was clearly quite stubborn when she needed to be, but he had to admit that he admired a determined mind. George threw him a slightly astounded look as they entered, but Richard simply shrugged his shoulders. Given that Helena was going to be a part of his life from this point onwards, it was probably best that George got to know her.

"So, where is this note?" Helena asked.

Richard walked past her and sat down at his desk, ripping open the seal.

"It is always delivered the same way," George explained, as Richard read the few lines. "A beggar child delivers it."

"Then, can you not ask them what the man looks like?"

George shook his head. "He disguises himself well and never uses the same child twice. It is what makes him so difficult to catch."

Richard let out a low groan, running his hand through his hair before resting his forehead on his broad palm and placing his elbow on the table. The note was an indecipherable as before. "I don't think we'll work this one out in time, George."

"No?" George replied, his face falling. "And we did so well with the last one."

Helena looked at them both, seeing the discouragement and despair. "Why don't I read it?" she asked. "Perhaps I might know."

"I doubt it," Richard commented, handing it to her. "You have not long been in London, and all of our targets have been gentlemen of the *ton*."

"Never a woman?" Helena asked, taking the parchment from him.

Richard shook his head. Thumping his fist on the table in frustration, he rose and walked over to the window. The drapes had not yet been drawn, despite the late hour, and he stared out into the darkness. The gloom seemed to pervade his very soul, dragging him down into the depths. Richard bit his lip, frustrated with how little he'd managed to decipher of the note. All he could see was that the target was yet again, another gentleman of the ton, who had very little family or friends. "That could be any number of men," he grumbled, resting his head against the cool glass.

Helena read the note once, then twice. *'There is a method to my madness, as you will no doubt see. Calculating and plotting, my work is never done. The man who leads a lonely life will not see me coming. His attentions are always elsewhere, hiding in shadows. Not many will miss him. Then I will succeed, no longer troubled by his presence.'*

She frowned to herself, working through the sentences once at a time. "How does he normally....kill people?" she asked, suppressing a shudder.

"Cyanide," George responded. "Usually in whatever the man's favorite liquor is. It is well known that most men take a drink after dinner, whether that be port, whiskey, or brandy. And those who can afford it tend to drink copious amounts."

"Speaking of," Richard muttered, walking from the window and pouring himself a small amount of whiskey. "This has been something of a trying day."

"Indeed it has, sir," George agreed with a slight grin, before throwing a glance at Helena.

Helena let their conversation flow over her, thinking hard about the note. "A method to my madness," she repeated to herself. It meant nothing to her. Moving on, she bit her lip as she read the next few lines over and over. Her heart seemed to stop as she suddenly hit on a possibility. "The man who leads a lonely life will not see me coming," she read aloud, anxiety flooding her. Richard gave all the appearances of being a lonely man, and he would not ever think that the murderer might make him a target. That would mean that he would *'not see me coming.'*

"Richard," she said, alert slowly registering in her tone, but her eyes still on the parchment. The words made their way into her mind, beginning to slowly make sense. *'His attentions are always elsewhere, hiding in shadows.'* Richard was forever looking to his work, being pulled from whatever social occasion he was attending at a moment's notice. *'Not many will miss him.'* Richard did not have many friends and certainly no family to speak of. *'Then I will succeed, no longer troubled by his presence.'* With Richard gone, the murderer could make as many victims as he chose, knowing that all the work Richard had done would die with him.

Her heart slammed into her chest, as she stared at the parchment. It all made sense now. "Richard," she shouted, pushing herself to her feet. Her eyes turned to him, taking in the glass in his hand and the way he was moving it towards his mouth. There was barely enough time to act. The chair toppled backward as she turned, throwing herself at him and knocking him to the ground. The glass shattered and the liquor trickled out of the glass, soaking into the carpet.

Richard's breath slammed out of his body as Helena threw herself at him, landing on top of him. His body hit the carpet, knocking his head backward. Shock filled him as he stared up at her, trying to catch his breath.

"You didn't drink any did you?" she asked frantically. "Richard, did you drink any?"

"No," he gasped, finally catching his breath. "No, why?"

Helena's eyes filled with tears and she sank her head onto his chest. "Oh, thank goodness," she sobbed, her entire body shaking. "Thank goodness, Richard. I don't know what I would have done."

Completely and utterly confused, Richard wrapped his arms around Helena's shaking form and held her for a few moments, staring at George who shrugged in bewilderment and turned to pick up the pieces of glass on the ground.

"Helena," he sang lightly, trying to get her to stop crying. "Helena, can you stand up? I don't know what's going on."

Helena tried to stop her sudden rush of tears. The moment Richard confirmed he'd not taken a drop of his liquor, relief had flooded her and made her dissolve completely into sobs. She had come so close to losing him. Slowly becoming aware of the awkwardness of her position, Helena pushed herself up, taking George's outstretched hand to help her rise to her feet. Gratefully, she allowed him to guide her towards a chair by the fire, sinking into it on unsteady legs.

"Now," Richard said, getting to his feet and rubbing the back of his head. "Can you tell me what all that was about, Helena?"

"The note," she explained, looking from one man to the other. "The note was about you."

As she watched, Richard's face slowly lost a bit of its color. "Are you sure?"

"No, I am not sure," Helena countered, a little crossly. "I made an assumption, but one worth making. After all, Richard, you fit the description entirely."

George threw the pieces of glass into the fire, frowning heavily. "Can you explain?"

Briefly, Helena went through each sentence of the note, seeing the dawning comprehension in Richard's eyes. "And so, you see, this has to be you."

"By jove," Richard whispered, leaning one hand on the study table for support.

George, ever practical, walked to the side table and picked up the bottle of liquor. "There's only one way to be sure. I've got a few rats in the cellar. I won't be long." The door slammed shut behind him, leaving Richard and Helena alone.

"I'm sorry if I hurt you," she said, after a few seconds of silence. "And if I am wrong, I am even more sorry for it, but I could not take the chance."

Richard made his way around to his desk chair, still leaning heavily on the table. Small beads of perspiration were on his brow, as he mentally went over the words of the note and what Helena had deciphered. It did sound very much like she was correct. "But why would he come after me? "I am not a high standing member of society. It does not quite fit." He sat down, thinking hard.

"Did you not tell me that you managed to foil his last attempt?" Helena reminded him. "And that you were in a fight for your life?"

Richard nodded, slowly. "But I could not identify him."

"I don't think that matters," Helena replied. "It is more the fact that you have foiled him in one of his attempts. Don't you remember what the note said?" She screwed up her face, trying to remember it exactly. "*'Then I will succeed, no longer troubled by his presence,'*" she recalled aloud. "With you gone, then all your hard work will come to naught. He will be able to continue his killings with no one to stop him."

"The Duke would have another man on his case almost at once," Richard said, firmly. "The chase would continue."

"It would, but they would not have the experience that you do at this point," Helena ruminated. "It would be as though they had to start all over again, with a blank slate in front of them. You know a great deal about this man, but should you die, then that knowledge dies with you. Unless, of course, you have it all written down somewhere?" She gazed at him sidelong, already aware of what his answer would be. Richard was not a man who was either tidy or practical. Having a journal or various notes of some kind was not something she imagined him doing. He looked at her and glanced away, confirming her theory.

"No," she considered, "I didn't think so."

Silence grew between them as they both considered what she had said. There was no doubt in Helena's mind that the man who had been killing high members of society had now targeted Richard. Richard had managed to save one of his targets, and that had been seen as unacceptable by the murderer. With Richard out of the way, his murderous hands could find and kill anyone he chose, completely unhindered. This Duke, whoever he was, would be able to find someone new, should Richard have been killed, but Helena assumed that would have taken some time.

The door suddenly slammed open as George rushed in, holding a dead rat in his hand.

"She's right!" he shouted, staring at Richard. "Look! Look!"

Helena turned her face away, not wishing to stare at the dead creature dangling from George's meaty fist. Her stomach rolled as his words entered her mind, securing themselves there. She had been correct. The glass had been poisoned. Richard could have been murdered.

"By my stars," she heard Richard say in something of a weedy voice. "I could have been…."

"Poisoned," George's loud voice echoed through the room, bouncing off the walls.

Helena closed her eyes, willing herself not to dissolve into tears of relief once more. She had been right in her assumption and had managed to save Richard. A cold hand of fear slowly wrapped itself around her heart as she thought on the murderer. What would he do once he discovered Richard was safe? Would he attempt to kill him again? How could she keep him safe from here on out?

CHAPTER 16

Richard felt his entire body go from hot to cold and then back again as he stared at the dead rat in George's hand. He hadn't wanted to admit to himself that Helena's conclusion had made sense, but now it seemed he had no choice. For a moment, he saw himself lying on the floor, white as a sheet, with a glass shattered next to his hand. He had been so close to taking a mouthful, having had such a trying evening. Had it not been for Helena, George would have been making arrangements for the coroner and sending a note to the Duke to tell him of Richard's passing. The thought sent a tremor through his body, as he sank lower into his chair.

"Open a fresh bottle of whiskey, George," he muttered. "And throw everything else away. And I mean everything. Anything that is open needs to go, be it liquor or water or milk."

"Right away," George replied, picking up the tray with the offending brandy and walking from the room.

"Helena," Richard whispered the moment he left. "You marvelous, marvelous girl. You saved my life." He watched as the corners of her mouth turned up, feeling nothing but awe and gratefulness for her quick mind and even quicker action. "Had you not been here, had you not insisted on coming in, then I might now be...." He could barely bring himself to say the words aloud.

"But you are not," Helena interrupted, unwilling to think about it anymore than she had to. "And we have stopped his plan, yet again."

Richard threaded his hands into his hair, resting his elbows on his knees. Every breath he took was suddenly a gift, making him ever more aware of the blood pumping through his veins. A single sip could have stopped his heart. No more air would have entered his lungs. The thought was chilling. But Helena, sweet, clever Helena, had seen what he had not, stopping the murderer's evil intentions. A thrill of dread ran straight through him as he thought of what had just occurred. Should the murderer discover that he was still living, then Richard was sure he would attempt to discover who it was who had managed to prevent his death. He could not allow Helena to be implicated, for then she too might be in danger.

"Oh, Helena," he uttered with dread, lifting his head to look into her eyes. "What am I to do with you?"

A slightly hurt look jumped onto her face as she frowned. It was enough to force Richard to his feet and walk toward her. He crouched down and framed her face with his hands. "That is not what I meant," he whispered. "I am so terrified for your safety that I do not know what it is I should do with you in order to keep you safe." He saw her face relax and a small smile appear in place of her frown. "That is simply what I meant," he reassured her. "I can barely believe how close I came to losing my life, and it is only because of your quick thinking that I am still here. How can I ever thank you?"

Helena smiled at him openly now, as a single runaway tear tracked down her cheek. He wiped it away with his thumb before leaning towards her, catching her mouth with his. She clung to him desperately, and he could not help but respond in kind. There was something about coming so close to death that was making him realize just how much he had.

Richard eventually lifted his mouth from hers, but continued to hold her close. "You are my one true love," he whispered in her ear. "I cannot imagine life without you, Helena. Say you will marry me."

Stunned, she lifted her face to his, her face registering with surprise.

"I know this is not the best place, nor even the best time to ask you," Richard continued, aware that there was still the dead rat on his study table. "But I must know, Helena. Will you be my wife?"

"Oh, Richard," Helena managed, her eyes glistening with tears once more. "How long I have waited for you to ask me such a thing. Of course, I will marry you!"

Richard's happiness overflowed from deep within him as he crushed her in his arms, the dampness of her happy tears on his cheek. Here he held his future bride, his life stretching out before him. He imagined them sharing a home, talking for hours by the fire, with some beautiful children at their feet. It was an idyllic picture.

The idyllic picture was quickly shattered by the presence of George who, once again, threw open the door and walked in without even considering Richard and Helena. Neither did he react in any way on seeing them ensconced together, but instead put down a fresh tea tray in front of them both, followed by pouring a glass of newly opened whiskey into a glass for Richard.

"Thank you, George," Richard bowed, slowly extracting himself from Helena.

"Not at all, sir," George replied cheerfully. "Although I feel I should warn you that dawn is soon to be on us." He gave Helena a pointed look.

"Ah." Richard frowned as he thought for a moment. "I shall have to speak to Charles."

Helena giggled. "Yes, you will. He will be quite astonished, I am sure."

"Not unless he tears my head from my shoulders first" Richard ruminated darkly.

George sat down heavily opposite them, his own glass in his hand. "I tasted it first, sir, so I can assure you that it is quite safe."

Taken aback by both his consideration and loyalty, Richard inclined his head. "I thank you, George. Most considerate. Remind me to increase your salary."

Grinning, George took another swig. "So, what are we to do, then? By all accounts, you should be dead, and the murderer, I am quite sure, is hoping that you are."

"And if he discovers that I am not, then he might attempt to do so again," Richard added, thoughtfully. "Or worse, seek retribution." He could see from Helena's face that she understood what he meant. "I do not want him to come after Helena."

Nodding slowly, George's smile slowly left his face. "I can understand that, sir. But how are we to catch the culprit, if he relieves you to be dead? He will no longer send any notes or the like. So what can we do?"

Silence fell over them like a blanket.

"What do you know of him so far?" Helena questioned, breaking the quiet.

Richard shook his head. "Not too much, I'm afraid. He is slightly taller than me and strong to boot."

"We believe him to be attacking the members of high society, simply because he was either wronged in some way or because he is jealous of their status."

"Or," Helena interjected. "Because he once was a member of high society, but has since fallen on harder times. Perhaps he has been rejected, due to his lack of funds. He feels wronged and, since then, has taken revenge in the worst possible way."

"Upon my word," Richard whispered, as Helena's theory slowly made its way into his mind. "You are quite something, Helena. I should have told you of this long ago!"

"You think I might be correct, then?" Hope was in her eyes, and Richard's smile began to grow.

"I think you have got it in one, my dear," he exclaimed, turning delighted eyes onto George who was similarly beaming at Helena. "I have never even considered that before!"

"Well done, Miss Catesby!" George boomed. "This requires us to go over all our information again, Richard. We will need to think of those who have recently fallen out of high society, and who might be connected to all our current victims. Perhaps we might even come up with a name this time."

Richard shook his head, completely astonished at how easily Helena had been able to come up with something that had completely escaped him. He was going to be the happiest man in all of London with her as his wife. "Helena, I do hope you will stay and discuss with us what we have found? You have been the one to both save me and come up with a working hypothesis! I can't imagine what other help you might be." He watched her blush, but she nodded in agreement.

"May I make a suggestion, sir?" George asked, getting to his feet. "If you are meant to be dead, then it would be best if you took Miss Catesby home – and remained there."

"Remain there?" Richard frowned.

George nodded. "The murderer expects you to have passed, sir. Therefore, I can give all the appearances of a man – and a house – in mourning, while you discuss with Miss Catesby what it is you have learned so far. That way you will be well hidden, and Miss Catesby will be safe."

"Charles would not mind in the least," Helena chimed in excitedly, supporting George's proposal. "And since you have already told me that you keep much of this information in your head, Richard, I would expect it will take some time for us to write everything down."

Richard nodded slowly, agreeing with them both. "You are quite right. I suppose we should make haste at once before the sun comes up."

"And you must keep yourself hidden," George warned. "There's no saying who could be watching the house."

Rising to his feet, Richard held out his hand to Helena. "The servants entrance it is," he announced. "George, please fetch my cloak and something for Miss Catesby. We have work to do."

CHAPTER 17

"I should rip your head from your shoulders!" Charles exclaimed, his normally calm face now bright red with anger. "How could you keep this from me?"

Richard swallowed hard, having never seen his friend in such a state before. "It was not unkindly meant, Charles. I have had to keep this part of my life away from all those I care about." His eyes met Helena's, who smiled at him in spite of Charles' anger. "It was the only way I could keep you from harm."

"Charles, sit down," Abigail interrupted, crisply. "Your behavior is quite ridiculous."

To Richard's utter astonishment, Charles drew in one long breath, before sullenly sitting down beside his wife. He did not stop glaring at Richard, however, muttering something under his breath.

"Charles," Helena began, catching Richard's eye and giving him a slightly impish grin. "There is something else we must tell you."

Richard drew in a long breath as he saw Charles narrow his eyes. As yet, Charles didn't know about their engagement - or anything that had occurred last night, and given how he'd reacted to Richard's confession of his life as a spy, Richard wasn't quite sure how Charles would react to any additional news.

"What is it?" Charles bit out. "Never tell me he has *you* mixed up in this, Helena!"

Helena let out a light giggle, apparently completely unperturbed by her brother's ire. "Unfortunately, I am mixed up in this, as you put it - but entirely by my own less than appropriate behavior."

Charles sat forward, his attention entirely fixed on Helena. "Behavior? What behavior?"

The confusion in his voice could easily be understood. Richard knew that Charles thought very highly of his sister, who had never once done anything even remotely questionable.

"I went to Richard's residence last evening."

The silence in the room grew thick.

"We are engaged."

Richard's entire body tensed as Charles stared at his sister, only for his head to swivel around to face Richard. Swallowing hard, Richard struggled to know what to say, eventually choosing to stay completely silent.

"You are engaged to Richard?" Charles asked slowly, even though his eyes were fixed on his friend. "You left this place alone, unsupervised, to seek him out?"

Helena's voice was clear and unconcerned. "Yes, I did. Quite frankly, Charles, I'm astonished to realize that you had absolutely no notion of any growing attachment between myself and Richard. After all, it has been ongoing for some time."

Charles staggered to his feet, thrusting his hands into his hair. "What is going on in this house?" he gasped, turning to face Abigail. "First of all, I find out my best friend is, in fact, a spy, and now I discover that my sister, who has never done anything wrong in her life, has snuck out in the middle of the night to seek an alliance with said best friend!"

"I have loved her for some years," Richard interrupted, as caringly as he could. "But have never been able to declare my feelings. Until now." Feeling a little bolder, he got to his feet and walked over to Helena, putting a gentle hand on her shoulder. "You will be angry with me, of course, for not speaking to you first, but given the circumstances, I felt you would - eventually - understand."

Charles' face grew ashen as his gaze moved from one to the other. "Circumstances?" he asked, throwing his hands in the air. "What circumstances are these?"

"He's dead," Helena interrupted.

"Who is dead?" Charles asked, his eyes widening once more.

"Richard is," she replied calmly. "What I mean is, of course, he is not dead, but it is important that the killer thinks he is."

Charles let out a strangled sound, looking up towards the ceiling and bunching his hands into fists.

Abigail got to her feet and placed one gentle hand around Charles' waist. "Sit down by me, my love. Let me get you a drink." Her bright eyes bore into Richard's, making him a little more uncomfortable. "Perhaps you should start from the beginning, Richard, before we all become thoroughly confused."

He nodded, glad that Charles wasn't immediately going to throw him from his house. "It all started when I first received a letter."

TWO HOURS later and Charles appeared to have calmed down almost completely. Now that everything had been explained to him in a clear and organized manner, he was able to take everything in and was, surprisingly, agreeing that Helena's plan was a good one.

"Although I must say," he confessed, clutching what was now his third brandy. "I do wish you had not taken matters into your own hands, Helena. Why did you not talk to me?"

Helena let out a light chuckle. "Charles, you were barely able to recognize the feelings you had for Abigail, without help from Richard, so I am told. So what kind of advice do you think you would have been able to give me as regards the state of my own heart?" One eyebrow lifted quizzically, although her lips curved into a smile as Charles stumbled for an answer.

"I, for one, am glad that you did go," Abigail broke in, her eyes shining with happiness. "Today might have brought about very different circumstances, had you not."

"Indeed," Richard echoed, his heart swelling with emotion as he thought about what Helena had done. "Charles, I am sorry that things came about as they did and you must believe me that this was never my intention, but it has happened now, and I do hope you can be happy for us both."

There was a brief silence, which made Richard more than a little anxious, but, eventually, a smirk broke out on Charles' face.

"Of course I am happy for you," he finally conceded, getting to his feet and walking towards Richard. "In fact, I cannot imagine anything better than my closest friend marrying my dear sister. You shall be family in every sense, Richard." He bent to kiss his sister's cheek, before holding out his hand to Richard.

Richard grasped it firmly, his body growing weak with relief. Finally, the truth was out, and Charles was, somehow, not intending to throw him out on his ear.

"You will have to write to Francis and mother at once," Charles continued, walking back to his seat beside Abigail. "They will be delighted."

"No!" Helena cried in unison with Richard. "We cannot, Charles. Everyone must think that Richard is dead, for then the killer will believe he has achieved his goal."

"And that will give me time to write down everything I have kept up here," Richard continued, tapping his temple. "So that, with just a little bit more like, we can identify who this mysterious murderer is and stop the killings for good."

"I see." Charles frowned. "So this man of yours, George, he is going to do all that is required to give the appearance of your death?"

Richard nodded. "Yes, at once. There will be a note in the paper, the house will be dressed appropriately, and I would appreciate it if you visited him perhaps later today, to pay your last respects. George is expecting you."

Charles nodded slowly. "Very good."

"I shall have to stay away from the windows and the like," Richard continued. "There is no telling who might be watching the place."

Richard felt himself grow weary as he stood beside Helena. The night's events had taken their toll, and now that he and Helena were both safe, his body was calling for rest. Realizing that he had not slept a wink in the last day and a half, Richard struggled to contain a yawn. Helena glanced up at him, and he saw the concern on her face. "I am simply tired, that is all," he reassured her with a smile.

"Then, of course, let me show you to your room," Helena offered, getting to her feet and taking his arm. "The blue room, Charles?"

Charles opened his mouth with a frown on his face as though he were about to object, but closed it again as Abigail nudged him gently. "Yes," he said, shaking his head. "That one has been prepared."

"Very good," Helena replied smartly.

"Thank you, old boy," Richard said, genuinely. "I know this has all come as quite a shock and you have taken it very well, on the whole." Before Charles could reply, Richard allowed himself to be walked out of the room by a very determined Helena. He wondered if she was just as desperate to be back in his arms as he was, hoping that it was not far to the blue room.

As soon as they were alone, Richard took Helena in his arms and hugged her tightly against him. The events of the last few hours had brought about a change in him, one where he now realized the true depths of his feelings for the woman in his arms, as well as a deep appreciation for everyone he held dear. "We shall be wed as soon as possible, I swear it," he breathed, closing his eyes tightly. "I am so proud of you, my love."

Helena looked up at him, her eyes bright. "I am glad that Charles took that so well."

"So well?" he exclaimed, stepping back. "I thought he was going to call me out for a duel!"

Helena laughed, shaking her head. "You know what Charles is like, Richard. He was simply surprised, that was all. I was glad that Abigail was there, however."

"Indeed," Richard agreed fervently. "She makes him a better man, in the same way, you do me."

Pressing one hand to his cheek, Helena lifted her face to his, standing on tiptoe so she could reach him. Richard obliged at once, slowly pressing his lips to hers for a few moments, before stepping back with a groan. "I must go to my room. You are irresistible my dear Helena. Our wedding cannot come soon enough."

Her eyes sparkled. "It is so wonderful to finally be able to do such things, Richard. I do not think I shall ever tire of kissing you."

He smiled softly, dropping one more kiss on her pert lips before opening the door to his room. "Get some rest, my dear," he whispered, squeezing her hand. "I shall see you soon."

CHAPTER 18

"A nd you're sure that's all you can remember?" Charles pressed, scrutinizing the parchment.

Richard rubbed one hand over his eyes. "Yes, I'm quite sure." He had slept for a ridiculous number of hours, and now it was the second day he had spent at Charles' residence. Not that he minded, given that George was doing an admirable job of appearing to be in mourning for his master. Charles had visited yesterday and had been most impressed.

"Well done," Helena declared, also reading through what she had written down. "I'm sure we can come up with a name or two from here."

Richard had done very well in listing all the information he knew about the murderer, to the point that Helena had been amazed over what he had kept in his memory for so long. Now, at long last, they had written details about each death, as well as the dates and times of each occurrence. She had to admit that some details had been a little difficult to write, given the subject matter, but she steeled herself against it and continued on.

"So now, we shall need to think about whom, if anyone, is connected to all these men," she announced, handing the parchment to

Charles. "They will no longer be a member of high society, but will have been in the past."

"Perhaps they were wronged in some way," Richard continued. "Lost money gambling, or perhaps in a bad bet."

Abigail nodded, thoughtfully. "If they are strong, as you stated, Richard, then they must not be old."

"He was fast, too," Richard added, recalling how the man had run from him. "So we are looking at a youthful man, who has fallen out of society within the last few years."

Charles shrugged, looking helplessly at Richard. "I confess I take very little notice of such things, Richard. I will not be of much help, I'm afraid."

"Nor I," Helena agreed. "Since I have only just arrived in town."

Richard opened his mouth to reply, only for Abigail to gasp aloud.

"What?" Helena exclaimed, getting to her feet. "What is it, Abigail? Have you thought of someone?"

Abigail nodded slowly, her eyes fixed on the parchment. "I believe I might have done." Thoughts calculated in her head before she continued, "Perhaps it could be my old suitor."

Charles' face darkened immediately. "Not Lord Kettering, Abigail? Surely not!"

Richard pressed a gentling hand on his friend's shoulder, in an attempt to quiet him. "Let her speak, Charles."

Abigail sank back in her chair, her eyes drifting up to Richard's. Her face was quite pale, and Helena noticed that her hands were shaking slightly.

"Lord Kettering was known as a rogue and a wastrel, cheating people wherever and whenever he could. He was cruel and callous and my father, for various nefarious reasons, chose to hand me over to Lord Kettering in marriage."

"But I married you before he had the chance," Charles growled, filling in the story, but clearly still angry over how she had been treated.

Giving him a slightly wobbly smile, Abigail nodded. "Yes, you did. Although, I had no intention of marrying Lord Kettering regardless."

Helena gave her sister-in-law a gentle look. "Charles told me about how you both met."

A bark of laughter came from Richard. "Ah yes, I remember. The sword pointed at your throat, Charles."

Charles gave a wry grin. "Yes, she was quite formidable, I must confess."

Helena looked from Richard to Charles to Abigail.

Charles looked up at the ceiling with an almost sheepish expression. "I may have left that part out of the version of the story I told you, dear Helena."

The tension slowly eased as everyone laughed.

"Kettering has since fallen out of favor," Abigail continued, after a few moments. "Gentlemen were tired of being fleeced by him so, together, a few of the older members of society gathered together and found a way to rid Kettering of his wealth."

"As payback?" Richard asked.

Abigail nodded. "Yes, I believe so, and also because they wished to rid society of him. He was a proper menace, after all."

Helena glanced at Richard, seeing the understanding creep over his face. "These gentlemen, the ones who attempted to take Lord Kettering down, they were successful?"

"Yes."

"And," Helena continued, pointing to the parchment. "Their names are on that list?"

Abigail swallowed hard, before nodding. "Yes, all but one. A Lord MacDonald, who came from Scotland. He spends the Season in London each year, apparently on account of his wife's desire for parties and dancing."

Richard's mouth dropped open, as he remembered the note he had found some time ago, at Lord Davis' home. He had been writing to Lord MacDonald, congratulating him on some scheme or other. If Abigail was correct, then that scheme could have been the one to drive Lord Kettering from town.

"Do you know where he resides?" Richard asked hurriedly. "Lord MacDonald is in imminent danger, and we must get to him." Finally, he might be able to put an end to this terrible situation. Richard's entire body began flooding with tension and adrenaline.

As Abigail shook her head, Richard let out a low growl, his face darkening. He steadied his emotions; now was not the time to be gotten the better of. This case had drained him, and ground down his usually sharp instincts, but time was passing, and he had to find the man regardless.

"Perhaps one of the servants might know?" Helena asked, tentatively. "Either that or perhaps we could –"

Charles got to his feet and rushed from the room, cutting off her conversation.

Richard turned back to Helena with a small twinkle in his eye. "Once again, my love, you have shown yourself to be quick witted. How lucky I am to have you."

Helena smiled, although tension gnawed at her. "You think Abigail's theory might be correct?"

Richard nodded. "It certainly has merit and, from what I know of Lord Kettering, I can well imagine him carrying out these deeds. He was not a man who took well to having his plans foiled. I cannot imagine he simply accepted his exit from society and slunk off into the country somewhere."

Helena glanced at Abigail, who was agreeing with every word Richard said.

"He was greatly displeased when I attempted to hide from him," she added. "It was as though if he could not have me as his wife, then no one would." A shiver ran through her body, making Helena rush to her side and press her hand over Abigail's.

"Perhaps ring the bell for tea," Helena suggested to Richard, who did so at once.

Abigail gave a wane smile. "I am quite all right, Helena, please do not concern yourself. It is simply that bringing back old bitter memories makes me a little shaky."

"After what you went through to escape from him, I am not in the least surprised," Richard said firmly, sitting back down.

At that moment, Charles burst through the door, his face alive with excitement. "It's Arlington Street," he exclaimed, slapping Richard on the back. "The servants know everything!"

Richard got to his feet at once. "I must get a note to George immediately," he replied hurriedly. "I'll have to hail a hackney."

"We'll take the carriage," Charles said briskly. "I'll be coming with you, Richard."

"And I," Helena echoed stoutly, before remembering Abigail's poorly state. "Although perhaps I should remain with you."

"Of course you should," Richard regarded her firmly. "I will not put you in danger, Helena."

Abigail patted Helena's arm. "I am quite well, Helena. Of course, you must go."

"Abigail!" Charles spluttered, as Richard's face took on a horrified look. "You cannot be serious! She will be –"

"An asset to you," Abigail stated firmly, her voice boding no argument.

Whispering a quick, 'thank you,' Helena got to her feet and smiled at her brother and her betrothed. "I want to see this through," she said. "After all, this has become my fight too, Richard. But I promise I will do everything you say."

"It appears that I do not have much of a choice," Richard resigned. "Promise me you will stay out of sight, Helena. Kettering – if that is who our murderer is – cannot see you."

"Of course I will," Helena exclaimed, walking past him towards the door. "I will be like a shadow. Let me go and fetch my cloak."

"And we need to hurry," Charles followed, walking out behind her. "Let us hope we are not too late and that Lord MacDonald is still alive."

"Indeed," Richard sighed, scribbling down a quick note before following after Charles.

CHAPTER 19

T hankfully, Lord MacDonald was still alive and well by the time the party arrived. He admitted the parade of visitors at once to his study, nodding to Richard, Charles, and George, although he did cast a curious eye over Helena's presence.

"Lord MacDonald," Richard began, hoping the man would believe him. "We think your life is in danger."

The older man frowned, as the wrinkles beside his eyes deepened. "Oh?"

"You were involved in a scheme to bring down Lord Kettering, were you not?" Helena asked, determined not to be ignored. "I know it was some time ago, but was it vastly successful?"

Lord MacDonald nodded. "Yes, it was." A small smile played around the corners of his mouth. "We drove that man out of town with barely a few pennies to rub together."

"And well he deserved it," Charles muttered under his breath.

Lord MacDonald's keen blue eyes landed on Charles, flaring with recognition. "Ah, so you're the one who got in his way, then?"

Charles nodded. "Yes, I married the woman he was attempting to force into matrimony."

"Then I commend you," Lord MacDonald replied, nodding his approval. "That man was a cruel, selfish rogue."

"And a murderer," Richard added, seeing the shock register on Lord MacDonald's face. "At least, we believe so." Quickly, he listed the names of the other victims, aware of Lord MacDonald's increasingly paling face.

"Those were the men who were involved in the scheme?" he asked in a calm, compassionate tone, needing confirmation.

Lord MacDonald nodded, now leaning heavily on the back of his study chair. "Yes, they were," he stated, his voice now hoarse. "I have not long returned to town, so I was not aware of their deaths."

Richard drew in a long breath, feeling a mixture of relief and sadness. "We believe Lord Kettering is the man who has been killing these men, in retribution for what was done to him."

"I see." Lord MacDonald ran a slow hand down his face, apparently quite taken aback. "May I ask how they died?"

"Poisoned," Richard responded tersely. "What liquor do you have here, Lord MacDonald?"

The man reached for his glass on the table. "Brandy, usually," he replied.

"And have you drank from it this evening?"

The man nodded. "Of course. This is my third glass of the evening, I must confess."

Richard felt his body sag with relief. "Then we are not too late. Lord MacDonald, you must sit by the fireplace, with your back to the door and all other candles extinguished. The rest of us will hide ourselves within your room and be ready to capture the man when he arrives."

"Arrives?" Lord MacDonald repeated, looking alarmed. "Will he not simply knock me on the head if I am alone and vulnerable?"

George cleared his throat. "Without being crude, my lord, Kettering seems quite interested in poison. He's done it that way since the beginning, and I don't think it likely he'll change his ways now. He likes to wait around to see his victims die, from what we've established

– all except for Richard, of course. He didn't wait around for him, which is just as well."

Lord MacDonald looked from George to Richard and back again, evidently nonplussed. Sighing inwardly, knowing that every second counted, Richard quickly sketched out the details of what had happened to him, giving Helena a quick, appreciative glance as he did so.

Lord MacDonald nodded slowly, taking in a deep breath or two as though to calm his nerves. "Very well," he agreed. "Just make sure that man doesn't best me, won't you? I'd quite like to see my grandchildren."

"Of course," Richard assured him, guiding him over towards the comfortable chair next to the fireplace. "There is nothing to worry about, Lord MacDonald. It may be some time before he appears, but we will remain vigilant. Please, do not become anxious."

Lord MacDonald mumbled something under his breath, but sat down next to the fireplace, glass in hand. Richard walked back towards the others, speaking quietly.

"There are various different ways for Lord Kettering to enter," he said, looking around the room. "There are those two large windows, overlooking the gardens, which can easily be reached should he have a ladder."

"Or be a good climber," Charles added.

Richard grimaced. "Regardless, there is also the side door below the stairs, as well as the servant's entrance. He could be up here in an instant, so long as he remains unseen. I suspect that the only notice we will have of his arrival will be his sudden presence in the room."

"And then what?" George asked. "We just grab him?"

A little unsure as to what would be the best plan of attack, Richard paused. "I think we should simply use the surprise of our presence here as an advantage. Given that he thinks I am dead, he will not be suspecting any one. Now, all that remains is to find a place to hide, although make sure that you have a full view of the windows and doors."

CHAPTER 20

Helena held her breath as the room descended into silence. She couldn't even see where Charles and George were, but Richard was pressed beside her into the small alcove in the corner of the room. The intimacy of their situation would have set her heart a flutter under ordinary circumstances, but given how much rested on capturing this man, she could think of nothing else.

It seemed like hours passed before a single noise was heard. Helena squeezed Richard's fingers as the door was pushed open a crack. It opened almost soundlessly, and Helena held her breath as a tall, dark-cloaked figure slowly entered the room. She was amazed to see how quietly the man moved, watching him slowly drip some clear liquid into the carafe.

"Stay here," Richard whispered in her ear, before launching himself from the alcove, swiftly followed by George and Charles.

Helena and Lord MacDonald followed hesitantly, hearing the shouts of the men as they grabbed at the shadowy figure.

"Is it him?" she asked, breathlessly, as Richard finally managed to get a hold of his quarry. "Is it who you thought?"

"Lord Kettering," Richard exclaimed, as he pulled the cloak back while Charles and George grabbed Lord Kettering's arms and held him tightly. "It is as we thought."

Lord Kettering's face dark with anger, his eyes blazing fury. His mouth was twisted with rage, as he struggled against the two men who held him. "You're dead," he hissed between clenched teeth. "I killed you."

"You tried to," Richard retorted coolly. "It appears that we have finally managed to outwit you, Kettering."

Lord MacDonald stepped forward, his face a mask of disgust. "You killed my friends," he said with quiet composure, although his fists were clenched. "You hideous man."

"You took everything away from me," Lord Kettering spat, glaring at Lord MacDonald as though a look could knock the man dead. "I do not take such slights without retribution."

Richard stepped forward, visibly trembling in anger as he attempted to keep a hold of his temper. "Retribution will bring you only the gallows, Kettering." Turning to George, he nodded, tersely. "Take him away."

Relief flooded Helena as George began to frog-march Lord Kettering away, despite the vehement curses that poured from his mouth. Charles, relinquishing his hold, gave the man's custody entirely over to the more than capable George, staying back with Helena, Richard and Lord MacDonald.

"Where will he take him?" Helena asked quietly.

Richard sighed, wrapping an arm around Helena's waist and pulling her against him, despite the presence of Lord MacDonald and Charles. "To the cells," he responded, his entire being flooded with relief. "He will be tried in due course, once I have completed my report."

"You think he will be hanged?" Charles asked, opening the window and pouring out Lord MacDonald's carafe of brandy.

"No doubt," Richard stated firmly.

Helena felt him sag slightly and realized that Richard was finally able to relax after such a long and harrowing case. "You have done it,

Richard," she whispered to him. "You caught him. I am so very proud of you."

He rested his head on top of hers, his voice hoarse as he spoke. "Without your help, Helena, I might never have found him. If he had taken his retribution on Lord MacDonald, then I am not sure that I would ever have caught him. He would have retreated back to the country, having satisfied his need for revenge, and I would have been left entirely empty-handed."

Helena took a satisfied breath in, glad that they had managed to capture Kettering and that the investigation was at an end. It was the close of a difficult chapter, but one that had eventually brought them together. Finally knowing who Richard truly was made her feel as though she knew him all the better. Now she could look to the future with hope, knowing that there was nothing hidden between them any longer.

"Thank you," Lord MacDonald said, holding out his hand to Richard. "I am more grateful for each breath I take now that I have been kept from death."

"I know exactly how that feels," Richard commiserated, shaking Lord MacDonald's hand firmly. "Miss Catesby here had a great deal to do with not only my survival, but with yours."

Lord MacDonald's face registered surprise for a moment, but he quickly turned to Helena and bowed low. Helena bobbed a curtsy, smiling at the older gentleman as he rose from his bow. "Thank you, my lord," she said. "I wish you many happy days with your grandchildren."

"I must confess, I look forward to that, with great delight." His face transformed, breaking free a blissful smile as he thought of happier things. "Thank you, both."

Helena looked up at Richard, seeing both the weariness and the relief etched on his features. "It is over," she reassured him. "Come, Richard. We should return home. You need to rest."

"Yes, indeed," Charles agreed, walking over to them. "Home, where Abigail will be eagerly waiting for us, I'm quite sure."

Richard nodded, and together they gave their farewells to Lord MacDonald before exiting the house.

❦❧

ABIGAIL RUSHED towards them the moment they arrived, her face filled with anxiety.

"All is well," Helena soothed before she could begin her barrage of questions. "He is in custody."

"Oh, thank goodness," Abigail nearly collapsed, throwing her arms around Charles' neck for support. "And Lord MacDonald?"

"Alive, thank heavens," Richard confirmed, sitting down heavily in a chair by the fire. "It is over."

"Over," Helena repeated resolutely. She walked over and sat down beside him. "I am so happy to hear those words from your lips."

"Indeed," Richard chuckled, dropping a kiss on the top of her head. "And now we can think of the future. Our wedding, our life together."

Helena beamed happily, resting her head on Richard's shoulder, his arm wrapped around her shoulders like a blanket. Her body grew tired, the heat of the fire only adding to her weariness. Here she was comfortable, here she was safe. Next to Richard, the man she loved, knowing that their future was filled with possibilities.

"I have never loved you more," she whispered before her eyes slowly fluttered closed.

CHAPTER 21

One week later, and Helena and Richard were back at the Catesby estate, their mother thoroughly delighted to see them both. She clasped Helena to her chest as though she were a long lost daughter.

"How wonderful," she breathed, evidently thrilled that Helena and Richard had managed to find their way together. "I am truly delighted for you both."

"The banns will be announced this Sunday hence, for the first time," Richard smiled, thoroughly relaxed now that the heavy weight of the last few months had dropped from his shoulders. Helena had commented that she had never seen him so happy, and Richard had agreed at once. He had never felt this happy before in all his life.

"Then we have a great deal of planning to do," Lady Catesby replied, an invigorated grin gracing her face. "And I am sure your sister will be delighted to help you."

Helena frowned slightly at the mention of her sister. "Where is Sophia?"

Lady Catesby shook her head slightly. "There is something upsetting that child, and I am afraid I cannot quite work out what it is. She refuses to tell me, of course, stating that all is quite well."

"Perhaps she is still struggling with father's passing," Helena said warmly. "It affects us all in different ways."

"Tis more than that," Lady Catesby pondered aloud, contemplating her daughter's strange mood of late. "Whatever it is, I do hope she can speak to me about it soon. Although perhaps now that you have returned, she will tell you what it is on her heart."

Helena nodded, worry shining in her eyes. "Yes, of course, Mama. Hopefully, it is nothing more than a spell. I do hope she is not ill." Clearing her melancholy thoughts, she smiled at her mama again. "And how is the dower house?"

"Wonderful," her mother exclaimed, almost exuberantly. "And I believe Francis is quite glad to have me out from under his feet."

Richard laughed, seeing the mischief twinkle in Lady Catesby's eyes. "Francis is probably more than likely missing your wisdom and guidance, my lady. Although I believe he has taken on new staff?"

Lady Catesby confirmed that with a nod. "I took the household staff from this house with me, thanks to Francis' generosity and understanding." Her face softened. "I confess it has made the entire transition much easier."

"I am glad to hear it," Richard responded with a smile. To lose the patriarch of the family must be quite a burden to bear, especially when it was one's beloved husband. He could not imagine life without Helena.

"And where will you stay, once you are wed?" Lady Catesby asked, glancing from one to the other.

Richard laughed, looking down at Helena. "In truth, we have not yet fully decided. I have a house in town, of course, and we will reside there for the remainder of the Season – "

"And we are hoping Francis will ask us here for the Christmas festivities," Helena interjected, making Lady Catesby nod fervently.

"But we have not yet fully settled on where we are to live permanently," Richard finished. "I have a country estate, of course, but perhaps we might reside in town for a few more years."

"Oh?" Lady Catesby replied, evidently surprised. It was often expected that newly wedded couples would live in their country estate for a time, as so often there would be a child expected very soon after a wedding. Richard was not quite able to find the words to explain their situation, looking down at Helena with a slightly helpless look on his face.

Helena grinned, her eyes dancing. She knew precisely what Richard wanted to say, and could tell he was quite flummoxed with how to explain it.

"Mama," she began, squeezing Richard's arm. "Richard has a rather interesting vocation. We had discussed whether or not he would give it up completely, but we have decided that, for the time being, he should continue with his work."

Lady Catesby now looked thoroughly confused. "A vocation?" she asked curiously. "I did not know this about you, Lord Livingstone."

"Nor I," Helena laughed, making Richard chuckle. "It came as quite a surprise, I must tell you!" Looking up at him again, her eyes sparkled. "As it stands, Richard will now take on less dangerous cases. I would not like him to come so close to death again."

Turning back to her mother, Helena couldn't help but giggle as she saw her mother's mouth opening and closing soundlessly. It had taken a long time, but finally, she and Richard had come to an agreement. He would continue to work for the Duke, keeping George alongside him, since he admitted that it was something he did enjoy. Helena had felt for him, knowing that he didn't particularly want to give it up, but that he would do it for her because of his love for her. Helena, because she loved him, did not want him to be miserable, giving up something he wanted to continue doing. In the end, a compromise had been found. Richard would take on the less dangerous cases, and she would assist him where she could. Helena had to admit that she had enjoyed putting her mind to work, helping Richard to solve the case. Even more than that, she felt quite strongly that it was something she would like to do again.

"I think we have some explaining to do," Richard declared with his signature charm, as Lady Catesby continued to stare at them both in shock.

Helena laughed again, turning back to her mother. "Mama, don't look so terrified, it was not quite as bad as all that."

"Actually, it was," Richard countered, a smile playing around his mouth. "You did save me from an almost certain death, Helena."

"I think," Lady Catesby interrupted, finally finding her voice. "That there is a great deal of explanation needed here. Could one of you please tell me what has occurred? What on earth transpired while you were in London, Helena?"

Helena glanced up at Richard, her heart filling with love for him. Turning to face her mother, she took a deep breath. "What happened, Mama, was that I found out the truth about Richard, and it made me love him all the more. I cannot imagine life without him by my side. I love him more deeply than I ever thought possible."

"I love you, my dear Helena," Richard returned, squeezing her hand. "But perhaps we should address the question in a little more detail."

Her face wreathed in smiles, Helena faced her mother and leaned forward. "Mama, let me start at the beginning."

☙❧

The End

☙❧

ACKNOWLEDGMENTS

What an exquisite ride creating a book is! While much of a writer's life is spent squirreled away in front of a computer or a notepad, that is only part of the journey from idea to what you now hold in your hands. It is not without an incredible support system of brilliant, loving, dedicated people that a book can be made and brought into the world. Thank you from the bottom of my heart to the incredible Isabel, the diligent Nicole, the loveliest ladies of Love Light Faith publishing, and my beautiful family and friends. You are incomparable, each and every one of you.

BOOK 4: LADY SOPHIA AND THE PROPER GARDENER

BOOK 4

HOUSE OF CATESBY

Lady Sophia & The Proper Gardener

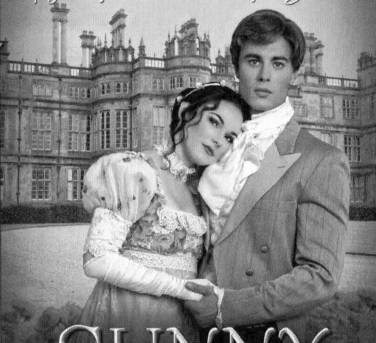

SUNNY BROOKS

FOREWORD

Always listen to your heart and don't be too quick to judge others. You
never pryule know anyone else's life journey or what they have gone
through. Trust only that you do not know the truths of others.
Our job as humans is to remember that we all come from the same
place. We were once all innocent children, we are all fragile inside, and
we all yearn to do our best, despite how we show that to the world.
Give others the benefit of the doubt and you might find that someone
wonderful lies beneath an unexpected surface.

~Sunny Brooks

CHAPTER 1

"Sophia, are you quite well?"

The book slipped from her fingers as Sophia rose from the window seat, as she gave her sister a tense smile. "Yes, of course." Her stomach swirled with anxiety as she attempted to lean nonchalantly against the edge of the window, hoping Helena would not come over to speak to her, for then she would be able to see exactly *who* it was Sophia had been watching.

Helena's face softened. "I am concerned for you, Sophia."

"Why?" Sophia asked, frowning slightly. "I am not ill."

"I know that it's just that...." Helena trailed off, walking over to stand beside Sophia. "Even before I went to town, you seemed distant and quiet." She put one gentle hand on Sophia's arm. "I do wish you would tell me what ails you."

Forcing a smile, Sophia shook her head. "I am just missing mama that is all."

"Truly?"

Sophia nodded, knowing in her heart that it was not quite true. Whilst she certainly did miss mama, that was not the only concern on her heart.

Helena sighed. "I do miss mama too, I must say. The house does seem quieter without her."

Their mother had gone to live in the Dower house, even though Francis, the new Lord Catesby, had not yet married. Their mama had said something about the house holding too many memories for her, too many old ghosts of the past. Sophia could understand that, in many ways. Every time she looked into the library or poked her head into the study to talk to Francis, she would half expect to see their father sitting there, surrounded by a cloud of cigar smoke.

For a moment, she wondered what her father would say of her current difficulty, although she could easily guess. Sighing to herself, she leaned into her sister, needing the comfort for a brief moment. She had not spoken to anyone of her heart's torment, and nor would she. It was best for everyone if she kept silent, knowing that there was no way forward. There was simply no way for her to have what her heart desired.

Helena wrapped her arm around her sister's thin shoulders, and the gesture made Sophia want to weep. She felt so alone. Francis was busy taking on all the responsibilities of the estate, their mother had relocated to the Dower house and now her closest sister, Helena, was about to marry Lord Richard Livingstone. Of course, there was Henry, her brother, and Charles' twin, but Sophia never really saw much of him. No-one did, truth be told. He occasionally ate dinner with them all but chose to spend much of his time up at night, studying the stars. Charles and Henry were both of the studious types, whereas she hated the confines of four walls.

Thankfully, her father had understood her desire for the outdoors, the need to have her fingers in the earth. Together, they had planted almost the entire garden, although Sophia had left some of the more difficult areas to the gardeners. Of course, now, her mother had taken almost the entire staff with her to the Dower house, but that meant that the head gardener had left the Catesby estate. Now, there was a new gardener, one who seemed to know what he was doing, but his arrival had caused Sophia a significant amount of turmoil.

Helena squeezed Sophia's shoulders slightly, before dropping her embrace and turning to face her. "Now, you must be honest with me, Sophia," she said, firmly. "I will not ask for your help with my wedding preparations if you do not wish to. I shall not hold it against you if you would prefer not to be involved. Whatever it is that is ailing you – for I confess that I do not believe it is just mother's absence on your mind – I do not wish for it to worsen for my sake." Helena's eyes searched Sophia's face as she waited for an answer and, for a moment, Sophia was desperate to tell Helena everything.

Instead, she simply nodded.

"You truly wish to help?" Helena murmured, softly.

Managing a wide smile, Sophia patted Helena's hand. "Of course I want to help you. That is what sisters are for, is it not?"

Joy sparkled in Helena's eyes. "It is, and I will be glad of your help. I do hope that, when you are ready, you will tell me the truth about what it is that really is troubling you so. No-one should carry their burdens alone."

Sophia knew that Helena was right, especially because she was marrying Richard who had been living an entirely secret life for a great many years. It had all been for good reason, of course, but Sophia knew that Richard felt a huge relief in being able to share his situation with Helena, even if she had forced the issue. Her heart heavy, Sophia watched Helena walk away, closing the door behind her.

Sighing to herself, Sophia resumed her position in the window seat and picked up the book she had no intention of reading. In truth, she had not read a single word thus far. Resting her head back, she lifted her knees and, ensuring her dress was tucked over her ankles, propped up the book on her lap. At least now she carried the pretense of reading.

Why did she long for this so? She knew that this would come to naught, but still, her foolish heart yearned for it. Just a single look, a single smile. Even yet, she still had not plucked up the courage to venture outside. By now, her garden must be filled with weeds. She was too afraid that she would give herself away, that she would seem entirely ridiculous and would rush back inside with heated cheeks and tears in her eyes.

Her heart caught as she looked down into the garden and, out of the corner of her eye, saw him wander into view once more. He looked to be tidying the bushes, although she was certain she had seen him do just the same yesterday.

You are being foolish, she told herself, somehow unable to take her eyes from him. *He is a gardener.*

Sophia knew that one did not fraternize with the servants. She had heard that some gentlemen liked to take their pleasure with a maid now and again, but that idea had been pronounced as vile by both her father and her brothers. So why then was she longing for a man who worked the grounds? A servant, who was employed by her brother no less!

Even worse, Sophia was more than aware that her attraction to him was based only on his physical appearance, which was utterly shallow. When he had come across her in the gardens and had taken the liberty of introducing himself, she had been entranced by the warmth in his hazel eyes, aware that he was looking at her steadily instead of dropping his gaze as a servant ought. To her embarrassment, she had struggled to find her voice, and so had turned away and walked inside. Since then, she had never dared venture outdoors again.

Without warning, the gardener stopped and looked up at the window, directly at her. Sophia caught her breath, unable to look away. Her breathing became shallow as he remained entirely still, simply looking up at her as though enjoying the view.

Then, he turned his head and walked away, back towards the stables, leaving Sophia feeling entirely bereft.

CHAPTER 2

David snipped ineffectually at a few leaves, wondering about the young lady in the window. There was something mesmerizing about her, to the point that he was unable to stop himself from studying her, even if it had been only briefly.

A small smile played around his lips as he remembered how she'd looked when he'd first met her. Her delicate hands had been encased in gloves as she pruned a rose bush, her eyes focused and mouth firm as she took great care in her task. It was obvious that she had done this before.

He had introduced himself without realizing what he was doing. He had only just managed to stop himself from introducing himself with his full title. He realized too late that he was looking into her eyes, instead of dropping his head as a servant should. She was simply too beautiful for him to look away from.

She had not replied to him, so he had not been allowed the pleasure of hearing her voice. Whether it was from the shock of him introducing himself to her, or from some other unknown reason, she had sped back into the house and had not yet come out to the gardens again.

Sighing to himself, David forced his gaze back to the bushes, even though he had trimmed them the day before. The lady intrigued him.

There was a sadness in her eyes that had him wondering, and she so often seemed to be alone. He had caught her watching him from the window on a few occasions now, and wondered what her reasons for doing so could be.

Turning his eyes back to the window, David studied her for a brief moment more before walking back in the direction of the stables. Heat filled him as he realized just how forward he was being – and he was meant to be a gardener in Lord Catesby's employ! He could not continue to behave as he once had, for surely he would then be found out. Remembering his place, that was what he had to do.

"Is that you, Hutton?"

It took David a second to respond, still not quite used to the name he had chosen. "Yes, it's me."

"Good," the groom replied, walking closer and shielding his eyes from the sun. "Lord Catesby wants to speak to you."

"Oh?" A surge of worry suddenly filled David. "Why?"

The groom shrugged. "I don't rightly know, but I'd not wait to get up there. It's not good to keep the master waiting."

David nodded his thanks and walked directly to the servant's stairs, climbing them two at a time and ignoring the frustrated squeals of the maids. Brushing some dirt from his trousers, he walked to Lord Catesby's study and knocked once.

"Ah, Hutton," Catesby exclaimed, beckoning him in as he bent his head over some paperwork. "Come in, come in."

The man did not sound angry, which was a good sign. Walking in, David remained standing a few feet away from Lord Catesby, holding his cap in his hands.

"You are settling in well, then?"

Surprised at the man's question, David nodded. "Yes, thank you."

"Good, very good. I've heard that your work is exceptional and that you do a marvellous job with the under-gardeners."

David grinned. "They are very hard workers, my lord."

Lord Catesby nodded, his face growing more serious. "I must ask you something – has my sister been outdoors?"

"Your sister, my lord?"

Waving a hand, Lord Catesby sighed. "Yes, my sister. Your response tells me she has not been working in the gardens much recently."

David did not say anything, choosing to let Lord Catesby speak.

"My sister, Miss Sophia Catesby," the man continued. "She loves to spend time in the gardens – not walking there, you understand, but working with the plants and flowers." He shook his head. "It was something she did with our father, and it concerns me that she has not been doing so of late."

Clearing his throat, David shuffled the cap in his hands, remembering to keep his gaze low. "I do hope my presence has not perturbed her, my lord."

There was a short pause. "No, I do not think it is that," came the eventual response. "Although I do intend to encourage her back into her hobby. I wanted to ensure you were aware that I would be doing this so that her presence in the gardens would not surprise you."

David bowed. "Of course, my lord. I would be more than happy to help her with anything she needs."

"Very good, very good," Lord Catesby replied, waving him towards the door. "Thank you, Hutton."

Aware he was dismissed, David walked to the door and shut it softly behind him before pausing for a moment. Taking a breath, he smiled softly to himself, delighted that Lord Catesby would be encouraging his sister to go back to working in the gardens. Perhaps he might have the opportunity to speak to her, although he had to remember that he was here as the gardener and not as the gentleman he truly was.

"SOPHIA?"

Starting with surprise, Sophia looked up from her book to see Francis walking into the library with a smile on his face.

"Francis," she smiled, starting to get up. "How nice to see you."

He gestured for her to stay seated, sitting down in the chair opposite. His face took on something of a concerned expression, making her wonder about his reason for seeking her out.

"I have not been much in your company of late, have I?" Francis said, heavily. "I am so caught up with estate business that I often take dinner in my study, never thinking that you would find yourself dining alone so often."

Realising that he must have spoken to the cook, Sophia tried to smile. "It is of little consequence, Francis. I know how hard you are working and Henry is so caught up looking at the stars that I find he is often absent when it comes time for dinner." She laughed quietly. "Even when he does join me, he is so busy thinking about his constellations that I get very little conversation from him!"

Francis joined in her laughter, shaking his head at his brother's lack of social graces. "He is quite something, is Henry."

"He will be a great astronomer one day, I am quite sure of it," Sophia declared, fondly. "In any case, neither of you intend to leave me to dine alone, you are both just caught up with important matters." Her smile grew soft as she saw Francis' brows knot together. "I am quite contented, especially now that Helena is returned."

"Helena is here now, of course," Francis said, as though he had just remembered. "Then she keeps you company."

"When she is not busy with her wedding plans," Sophia chuckled. "But yes, she is. In fact, I am meant to be helping her select the appropriate flowers for the wedding." Her voice drifted into silence as she contemplated the fact that sooner or later, she would have to venture out into the gardens.

"Do you miss mama?" Francis asked, quietly. "I only ask because I too have noticed her absence of late."

Sophia regarded her brother for a moment. "I do," she said, slowly. "But I am beginning to wonder what the reason is behind these questions, Francis." She leaned forward, studying him. "Come now, we have always been straight with one another. What is it that concerns you?"

Francis let out a long breath, a wry smile on his face. "Very perceptive, Sophia. In truth, I am concerned for you." He sat back in his chair. "It was only when I spoke to Cook that I realized just how often you are alone. Then I have heard from Helena that you seem very reluctant to return to your gardens."

Tension crept up Sophia's spine. Surely Francis could not guess about her attraction to the gardener? That would be shameful indeed!

"I know that I have hired new staff," Francis continued. "But I do hope that is not of a concern to you, Sophia. David Hutton is an amiable man who seems to have a way with the flowers and plants, in much the way our old gardener did. You need not fear that he will disapprove of your presence if that is what is holding you back." His gaze was piercing. "Unless there is something else troubling you? Are you lonely, Sophia? Is my absence, as well as Henry's and mother's, making you melancholy?"

Sophia was filled with a mixture of relief and gratitude. "I thank you for your concern, Francis, but truly, I am not melancholy."

"Then why do you not return to the gardens?" he asked, carefully. "Sophia, since father's death, you have not gone more than two days without being in the outdoors, even when there is a thunderstorm, as I recall."

Blushing, Sophia laughed a little self-consciously. "The roses needed to be secured to the trellis. Otherwise, they might have been torn to pieces!"

Francis grinned at the memory. "You looked like a drowned rat, Sophia!" His gaze softened. "Then what is holding you back from what you love?"

Sophia struggled to know what to say. She did not want to reveal to Francis her strange attraction to the new gardener, but at the same time could not find much of an excuse.

"I – I must admit, I was unsure about whether the new gardener would accept my presence there," she stammered, not quite able to meet Francis' eye.

"Then you should have asked me."

"You are busy enough," she exclaimed, truthfully. "I could not disturb you."

At her words, Francis rose and walked to sit next to her, taking her hand in his. "Sophia, you are my sister and under my care. You must never fear disturbing me for whatever reason. I want you to come to me with any concern you might have, no matter how small you think it might be." He searched her face, waiting for her to nod. "You must promise me not to keep such things to yourself any longer."

Touched by his kindness, Sophia nodded. "I will. Thank you, Francis."

"Good," he grinned. "Then I shall expect to see you out in the gardens very soon. I have already told Hutton to expect you."

"Thank you," Sophia murmured, watching as Francis left the room. Sinking back into the soft cushions, she closed her eyes and let out a long, drawn-out breath. It seemed she would have to face the gardener once more, otherwise draw more concern from her brother. Perhaps Hutton would simply leave her to work at the flowers alone, for Sophia was quite sure her throat would close up the moment she saw him.

"David Hutton," she whispered to herself. "Whatever am I to do about you?"

CHAPTER 3

"Good morning."

Sophia smiled as Helena walked into the dining room, ready to break her fast. It was a good deal later than Helena normally arose, but they had spent the previous evening talking long into the night as sisters often do. Sophia and Helena had always been close, and Sophia could barely think of the heartache that would follow when Helena finally married and moved away to live in London.

"Did you sleep well, Helena?"

Stifling a yawn, Helena nodded. Sitting down at the table, she helped herself to a piece of buttered toast and gratefully accepted a cup of tea from Sophia. "Did you?"

"Wonderfully." It was a flat out lie, but Helena did not need to know that. Were she honest enough to tell her sister, Sophia would have admitted that she had tossed and turned for most of the night, knowing that she would soon have to go out to the gardens and meet the gardener again. Try as she might, she could not stop her heart from quickening whenever she thought of him.

"What do you think?"

Blinking, Sophia realized that Helena had been speaking to her, but she had not heard a word.

"Oh, yes, I quite agree," she mumbled, hoping that Helena would not notice her lack of attention, for she could not exactly explain who she had been thinking of.

"Wonderful!" Helena's face lit up, and she clapped her hands. "Francis did say that he was going to try and encourage you to return to your gardens again, so I am very glad to hear that you are so amenable. I do so love those roses."

Sophia nodded weakly, wondering what exactly it was she had agreed to. Whatever it was involved the gardens and her roses.

"Shall we say in an hour?" Helena asked, excitedly. "Oh, I am so glad you have agreed, Sophia. I am sure that, together, we will make a wonderful wedding bouquet! Now, I must go and speak to Cook about the wedding breakfast before I forget." Still delighted, Helena picked up the rest of her toast and practically ran from the room.

Closing her eyes, Sophia let out a soft moan. By thinking about David Hutton, she had entirely missed Helena's request to put together a bouquet. She had intended to go out to the gardens in the late afternoon, knowing that the servants often took a short break around that time before the dinner gong sounded, but now it seemed she was to go with her sister in less than an hour.

Getting to her feet, Sophia lifted her chin and set her jaw. She was going to have to stop being so ridiculous and just carry on with her life, regardless of what she felt for the man. It was entirely inappropriate anyway, was it not?

Sophia sighed to herself as she left the room. She had never been in love before since they had never spent much time in London and therefore had very little opportunity to mingle with other members of society. She had never felt the loss, given that she simply adored spending time with her sisters, but now the house was growing quieter and quieter as each sibling found a love of their own. Slowly, Sophia realized that her life in the Catesby estate could not go on as it was. Once Helena married, she would be quite alone in the house, even with her two brothers occupying it. Perhaps she would ask to visit Helena at the height of the season next year, where she might finally meet a man she could care for.

Looking out of the window, Sophia wondered if she would ever feel such a fierce attraction to someone in the same way she did to David Hutton. For heaven's sake, she had never even spoken to the man, but she could barely stop herself from seeking him out every time she drew near one of the many windows in the estate. Her heart would flicker with disappointment if she did not see him, and flare to life if she did.

"You must stop being so ridiculous, Sophia," she told herself, firmly. "You cannot ever marry him, so you must stop feeling this way. Hiding from him is no way to overcome such things. You must simply carry on and, in time, you will get over what is a ridiculous infatuation!"

DAVID HEARD laughter on the wind and lifted his head at once. A broad smile crossed his face as he saw the two Catesby sisters walking across the lawn, arm in arm. He had not yet met Miss Helena Catesby, but he knew that she was the only other lady staying in the house. She was beautiful of course, but his eyes were always drawn to Miss Sophia Catesby. Her eyes were filled with laughter as they approached, the dusky pink in her cheeks making her even look even lovelier. They had not seen him yet, which meant that David allowed himself a few more seconds of simply watching the beautiful Sophia.

"Ah, you must be the new gardener."

"That I am, miss," he said, bowing to Miss Helena. "Are you both out for a stroll this fine morning?"

Helena laughed. "No, not at all. You see, my sister has a love for growing beautiful flowers, and has a special love of roses. She has been growing many different varieties for many years."

His admiration grew. "The rose garden is entirely your handiwork, miss?" he asked, directing his question towards Sophia. "It is beautiful."

He couldn't miss her blush, its duskiness matching the bloom she held.

"I thank you," she murmured, still not quite meeting his eyes. "My father and I spent many years tending them."

"And your efforts have been rewarded," David replied, honestly. They were some of the most beautiful roses he had ever seen, and his admiration for her grew. "I only wish I had some of your skills."

Her blush deepened, and she turned away to walk along the length of the trellis, studying the roses carefully.

"We are to choose some for my bouquet," Miss Helena explained. "My wedding is only a few short weeks away."

"My deepest congratulations, miss," he replied, remembering to bow deeply. "If there is anything I can assist you with, then I am entirely at your disposal."

"Thank you, Hutton," she replied, before walking away to join her sister.

David lingered near the two Catesby sisters, although he ensured they were not aware of his presence. He could barely take his eyes from the lovely Miss Sophia, finding her delicate features a pleasure to behold. If only he were not pretending to be a lowly servant, he might have the opportunity to make her acquaintance properly, and then ask to court her. Frowning, his mouth twisted as he thought about his life back in town. Were he to reveal himself, she would discover the truth and then reject him entirely. For the moment, it seemed he was only able to admire her beauty from a distance, knowing that he would never be able to reveal the truth to her.

Presently, he noticed Miss Helena walk away from her sister, holding five roses in her hand, each of a different variety. He wondered if Miss Sophia would follow after her, but to his delight, she remained where she was. His eyebrows rose as he saw the way she pushed her hands into the earth, pulling out weeds and, at times, digging for their roots with a small trowel so that they would not surface again. It was clear that she knew precisely what she was doing.

He had never met anyone like her before, for he knew not a single other lady who would be so willing to dirty her dress and her hands and work in the flower beds. They were all too 'proper' for such things. David winced as he remembered how his own mother had mocked his love for the outdoors, telling him that his title meant he should not enjoy such things. His life was meant to be one of fulfilling other people's expectations. He was meant to find a wife, marry, and produce the heir and the spare before settling down into a life pursuing hedonistic pleasures. It made him nauseous to think about.

No, he much preferred having the wind cool his cheeks and surrounding himself with the beauty of nature. Thankfully, his passion for growing all manner of things had given him the opportunity he needed to escape his mother's conniving ways, in the only way he could think of. If he told Miss Sophia the truth, would she ever be able to understand? Would she keep his secret? Or would her responsibility to her brother have her marching into the house to inform him of his lies?

Suddenly, he realized he had somehow made his way over to Miss Sophia's side, and that she was looking up at him with a slightly confused expression.

"Ah, Miss Sophia," he stammered, completely befuddled. "I was just hoping you might...."

"Might?" she prompted, slowly rising to her feet.

His mind scrambled for an answer. "Might teach me about these roses," he said, inwardly wincing at his poor response. "I confess I know very little about them." He held his breath as she looked at him, hoping she would believe his words. In truth, he would find any excuse just to be in her presence and become better acquainted with her, but only if she would allow him the liberty.

She took a breath. "Of course, Hutton. This way."

CHAPTER 4

S ophia hummed to herself as she pulled on her boots, quite prepared to go into the gardens even though gray clouds were pulling in.

"Sophia!" Helena exclaimed, finding her sister lacing up her boots. "Whatever are you doing?"

"What does it look like, Helena?" Sophia retorted, a smile playing around her mouth.

"But it is cold, and I am sure it is going to rain," Helena objected, sitting down on Sophia's bed. "I was just coming to ask you if you would like a game of cards or some such entertainment. I had not imagined you would wish to go outside in this weather."

Straightening, Sophia got to her feet. "Only last week, you and Francis were both encouraging me to return to the gardens, and now you object to my doing so?" Her eyebrow lifted, challenging her sister.

"Well, of course, but I am simply concerned about the cold," Helena spluttered, realizing she was contradicting herself. "The wedding is very soon, and I should not wish you to catch a cold."

Sophia shook her head. "Helena, I have never caught a cold from being out in the wind, as well you know. If you prefer, I will take a shawl and ensure I have warm gloves."

Helena sighed. "Very well. But you must return the moment it starts to rain."

Sophia did not reply and simply walked from the room, chuckling to herself. She would give no such promises. In truth, she had slowly begun to enjoy her hobby once more, now that she had overcome her fear of speaking to David Hutton. The gardener was both charming and helpful, and the more they had talked, the more she grew to enjoy his company. Unfortunately, that had only heightened her attraction to the man, which was exactly why Helena's concerns would not prevent her from returning to the gardens this afternoon.

"GOOD AFTERNOON, MISS SOPHIA."

Sophia felt a warm glow build up inside as she saw him waiting for her, leaning on his shovel.

"Good afternoon, Hutton," she murmured, glancing away from him. "The roses are looking beautiful today."

He smiled and fell into step beside her. "The rains have been good for the soil."

Sophia did not say another word but simply made her way slowly through the gardens. Her heart was already fluttering simply by being in his presence.

"You are quiet today, Miss Sophia."

She glanced at him, before turning away again. "I must confess, I am preoccupied with my sister's upcoming nuptials."

"I can imagine," he said, with a heaviness to his voice that surprised her. "Weddings are often large occasions."

Sophia threw him another glance, wondering at why he sounded so despondent. "You do not think of weddings as a happy occasion, I gather."

His eyes darted to hers, evidently surprised that he'd given so much of himself away. "I suppose I do not consider matrimony as wonderful as…as some others do," he finished, cautiously.

Narrowing her eyes slightly, Sophia frowned at his words, wondering why he appeared to be so hesitant in his response. It was as if he was hiding something from her, although she had no right to ask him what it was, of course.

"May I be bold enough to ask you something, Miss Sophia?"

She smiled, removing the frustration from her face. "Of course, Hutton. Although, I may be disinclined to answer it, depending on the subject matter."

He grinned at her, as warmth sparked in his eyes. "I quite understand, Miss Sophia." They wandered a little further through the gardens in silence, with Hutton showing no signs of asking his question.

Sophia kept silent, allowing him the time to consider his words. Why she was showing him such consideration, she could not explain, but she found herself keen to know what it was he wished to say.

"Does your sister love her betrothed?" he asked, quietly.

She frowned again, turning to face him as they paused in their steps. "That is a strange question, Hutton."

A deep flush swept into his cheeks. "Forgive me, miss."

Her expression gentled. "It is not impertinent, Hutton, just leaves me questioning why you would ask such a thing." She tipped her head up a little further, to see him better. "For what it is worth, I believe my sister is deeply in love with Lord Livingstone and has been for many years."

"Then you believe they will be happy together," he muttered, taking off his cap and running one hand through his hair. "I am glad for them if that is the case."

Sophia saw his frustrated expression and wondered at it. What was it about Hutton that had him asking such things? Why was matrimony such a terrible prospect for him, as though he hated the very idea of it? *And why do I feel so sorrowful over such a thing?.*

"You do not think matrimony can be a happy state, Hutton?" she asked, softly, beginning to wander away from him. "I am surprised to hear it, I must confess."

She could tell he was following behind her, very conscious of his presence close to her. Her skin prickled with awareness as she heard him sigh heavily.

"Matrimony with love is entirely different from the prospect of matrimony without," he murmured, quietly. "To be forced into such a thing is a terrible prospect."

"I quite agree," Sophia replied, looking up at him with a smile. At the same time, a slight nagging began to work its way into her mind. Hutton did not always speak as a gardener would. At times, when he became distracted, he would slip into a much more refined way of speaking. It was as if he had two sides to his character, and he could only present one at any given time. It gave her pause, realizing that she did not know the man as well as she thought. They had spent many hours together over the last week, discussing the gardens and working the soil, but their conversation had never before turned to such a delicate subject as marriage before. It was apparent that Hutton felt strongly about matrimony, which was something she had not expected.

"I had thought a man such as yourself could marry whomever you chose," she said, thoughtfully. "Unhindered by such things as class, or the need for wealth." Daring a glance at him, she saw him studying the ground with fierce concentration. "Surely you cannot find yourself in a situation where you are being forced into matrimony."

"No," came the quiet reply. "No, of course, I am not in such a situation as that." He cleared his throat, lifting his head to smile at her. "I simply know of such a predicament, and it makes my heart sorry to see it." His voice lowered, his expression softened. "One should not marry without love."

Sophia sensed her face grow warm, growing uncomfortable with the sudden heat in his eyes. Whatever it was she was feeling for this man, she needed to stop herself before it got out of hand. There could be no future for them. There was no prospect of matrimony, no children, nor a home in the country. He was a working man, lower in class than her by far, and Francis simply would not allow it, regardless of how she felt.

"I should go," she murmured, turning from him. "I – I think it might begin to rain soon."

"Wait, please," he begged, catching her hand and eliciting a gasp from her mouth. "I did not mean to speak out of turn, Miss Sophia. Please accept my apologies."

"You did nothing wrong, Hutton," she replied, her breath catching in her chest as he pressed her hand. "In truth, I am a little chilled, that is all." She gave him a wide smile but could tell that he did not quite believe her.

"You will return again to the gardens?" he asked, his eyes still searching her face.

He is a gardener, Sophia reminded herself, finding herself unable to answer such was the tumult of emotions warring in her heart. "I – I must go," she stammered, pulling her hand from his and stumbling back towards the house.

CHAPTER 5

Sophia pushed her bonnet from her head, catching it in her hands. She set it down gently, smoothing her hand over her hair. She did not want Hutton to see her with perspiration on her brow.

She had run from him before when their conversation had grown too intimate for her. It had been foolishness, of course, for she was quite sure Hutton was merely being kind. Although, she was still surprised at his willingness to be so open with her. His heart was bruised for some reason, although she did not know exactly why that was so.

Leaving her bonnet to one side, she wandered through the gardens, hoping she might catch sight of him. Usually, he would appear within minutes of her being outdoors, but she had not seen him this last hour. Her heart sank. Had her quick departure somehow made him believe that she wanted their acquaintance to be at an end?

Sophia drew in a long, shaky breath, astonished to find that she was so close to tears. She had never before felt such an affection for a gentleman, had never made herself so open and vulnerable with a veritable stranger. Could there ever be any kind of future for them both? Sophia shook her head. Francis would never allow it, of course.

But then again, he had never once shown any kind of interest in any woman so he would be entirely unable to understand her own heart. It seemed entirely impossible, yet still, deep in her heart, there was the beginning of a small hope. A hope that, despite their differences in status, there might be a way forward for them both. She did not know how to even suggest such a thing, given that she had no true knowledge of his own depth of feeling, but her heart refused to let go of that dream.

Glancing up, Sophia realized that she had walked farther into the gardens than she had intended. To her left, she saw a small path leading to what looked like an area of wilderness. It must have been left unattended for years since it was at the far end of the gardens. She and her father had been entirely focused on their roses for many years, leaving the rest of the gardens to the hired servants. Perhaps her father had said that this patch could remain as it was since no-one ever came here. It would make sense.

Thinking that perhaps she should have kept her bonnet, Sophia found her feet walking along the small path, interested in what she would find. It was completely overgrown, although the path was at least clear of branches and vines. She wandered through it, finding delight in the wildness of the place. There were flowers of all different types growing wherever they chose, the trees spreading their branches across as though reaching for one another. Ivy climbed along their trunks, adding to the greenery. It was a beautiful sight.

"Oh!"

A small, ivy-covered arbour was just to her left. A small deer rushed away as she approached, making her smile with happiness. There was more life here than she realized, hearing the birds continue their song above her. Ivy covered the roof of the arbour, trailing down over the windows and the door. It was just as well she was not afraid of spiders, for Sophia was quite sure there would be plenty of those creatures within.

Lifting the cover of ivy, she stepped inside, giving her eyes a moment to adjust to the gloom. To her surprise, the arbour held a couple of small benches, which were surprisingly clean. Even more astonishing was the small broom propped up against the wall, which evidently had been used to sweep the floor. Someone else knew of this place. But who? Francis? Was this his place of solitude, a place for him to hide away when the stresses of his title became a little too much?

Sophia did not want to intrude if that was the case. She should not remain here if it were meant for him. A keen sense of disappointment filled her as she slowly sat down on the bench, enjoying the solitude. Perhaps there might be another place she could call her own, a place to escape when she wanted to be out in the world, away from the confines of the house.

A quiet whistling broke into her thoughts, making her stiffen in surprise. Someone was approaching, and she had never known Francis to whistle before. A hand pulled back the ivy before Hutton stepped inside.

Sophia saw him physically start with surprise upon seeing her. "Miss Sophia," he stammered, as the ivy curtain dropped behind him. "Forgive me, I did not know you would be here."

Her skin prickled with awareness of just how close he was to her, and of just how alone they were. It was entirely inappropriate, but she could not bring herself to march past him and down the path.

"Excuse me," he mumbled, dropping a bow before making to turn around.

"Wait!" Sophia cried after him, her voice sounding strangled even to her. "I mean – you do not have to leave on my account. This is clearly a place you have come to often."

He dropped his hand from the ivy and nodded. "Of course, this is your brother's gardens, Miss Sophia. If you wish to come here, then I shall find another place immediately."

She saw him visibly relax as they slipped back into easy conversation. "No, I think not," she replied, quietly. "There is no reason we cannot share this place, is there? I doubt anyone else would come this far into the gardens."

His dark eyes flickered to hers.

"I did not mean to run from you," she continued, softly, aware of her sudden, desperate urge for him to remain in her company. "I was a little overwhelmed with your honesty that is all." She smiled at him, seeing his uncertain look. "Forgive me?"

"There is nothing to forgive, Miss Sophia," he mumbled, shuffling his feet. "I was the one in the wrong."

To her very great relief, he sat down on the small bench to her right, taking off his cap and placing it beside him.

"I do hope you will not stop talking with me," she replied, her fingers urging her to reach over and take his hand. "I do appreciate our conversations."

He lifted his eyes and looked at her, his features bathed in shadows in the gloomy arbour. "I thought it best to take some time away from you, Miss Sophia," he said, quietly. "If you are certain you wish to continue our acquaintance, then I would be delighted to do so."

There it was again, that unorthodox way of speaking that reminded her more of a gentleman than a servant. Sitting back, she leaned against the wooden wall of the arbor, disregarding any consideration she might have for cobwebs and spiders. Now that he was here with her, she had nothing more to concern herself with. She was back in his company, and that was all that mattered.

"Perhaps we might come here more often," she murmured, her entire body tightening as she gave him what she knew to be an entirely inappropriate possibility. "It is a beautiful place."

Hutton shifted in his seat. "I would not wish to bring any harm to you by our acquaintance," he said, slowly. "I am just a hired servant after all, and you are a lady."

Sophia tilted her head, regarding him. There was a sparkle in his eyes that excited her, as though he were trying very hard to do the right thing but was struggling not to agree to her suggestions.

"But we are entirely hidden here, are we not?" she murmured, shifting a little closer to him so that their knees were almost touching. "No-one would ever see us. Therefore my reputation will be entirely secure."

His eyes drifted from his hands up to her face, a tormented look in his eyes. "Miss Sophia," he croaked. "Please, I beg you. Don't."

She said nothing, but leaned forward, boldly placing her hand on his thigh. His muscles jumped under her hand, but she did not remove it. She was pushing him, driving their unspoken attraction forward. She could not bear to hide it any longer. She knew what he was asking of her, asking her not to open herself to him to the point that he would be unable to refuse her, but she simply did not care. What she felt was too strong.

"Miss Sophia," he whispered again, his eyes now drifting to her mouth.

In a moment, he was leaning over her, his mouth pressing against hers like a dying man living his last few moments. His hands were on either side of her, pressing down against the bench as he kissed her, sparking a myriad of sensations within her. Sophia locked her arms around his neck, refusing to allow him to step away or break the contact, her entire being coming alive at once.

To her surprise, Hutton put his arms around her waist and stood, pulling her up against him. His kisses did not stop but grew in intensity. Fire shot through her as he deepened the kiss, his fingers now digging into her hair until it began to tumble free of its pins.

"Hutton," she breathed, as he feathered kisses along her jawline. She could not say more, closing her eyes as he retraced his steps, touching her lips once more with his. Her world was alight with new sensations, as Hutton held her in his arms, fulfilling the desire she'd had for so long.

CHAPTER 6

"Miss Sophia."

Warmth spread up through her chest as she turned to see the gardener approach. A knowing look was in his eyes as he bowed to her, feigning interest in the blooms she was studying.

"Are you looking to make a new flower arrangement, Miss Sophia?"

"I am," she replied, loudly enough to ensure that her voice would carry through the gardens to anyone who might be listening. "Might you help me select some roses? I would like them to last."

His mouth curved and Sophia's breath caught in her chest.

"Of course," he said, warmly. "This way, miss."

She followed him through the gardens, knowing exactly where he intended to take her but forced herself to look as though she was simply allowing him to lead the way. Her anticipation and excitement rose with every step, her heart quickening its pace as they walked deeper into the vast gardens of the estate.

"Just this way, miss," he said, over his shoulder. His eyes caught hers, lingering there for a moment before he turned away. Licking her lips, Sophia hastened forward until, finally, they rounded the corner and came to the arbour.

The corner arbour had been their place of solace these last three weeks. The growing ivy still covered the window spaces, and the swinging vines that covered the entrance moved softly in the breeze.

Hutton pulled back the ivy curtain and allowed her to enter before him, following her quickly. The moment the ivy fell back into place, his arms were around her, and she melted into his embrace.

"Tell me that you missed me," he whispered in her ear, as his fingers brushed over her cheek and down her neck.

Sophia closed her eyes, hardly able to form words such was the effect he had on her. "I cannot tell you how much, Hutton." Her hands rested on his chest, feeling the strength beneath. It was entirely improper, of course, to have fallen in love with a gardener, but her heart wanted no-one else.

"Please call me David," he murmured, now stroking the back of her neck with gentle fingers. "Hutton seems so formal, still."

Sliding her hands around his neck, Sophia pressed herself against him, uncaring about whether her gown would become wrinkled or dirty. "David," she murmured, shivering slightly at the sensations he was building in her.

"Are you cold?" he asked, his breath tickling her cheek as he lowered his head.

She gave a tiny shake of her head, unable to form words. His breath mingled with hers, his arms tightening around her waist.

Finally, his lips met hers. Even though it was not the first time he had kissed her, Sophia felt the same explosion of feeling. It was as though the world fell away and all that was left was Hutton holding her in the way he did now. Her entire body burned with fire as he pressed at the seam of her lips, and, as she allowed him entry, she heard him groan.

Her fingers tangled into his hair, holding him fast to her. Her breath came quickly as his lips left her mouth, running along her jawline and towards her ear. Delicate kisses were pressed to her neck, making her gasp with pleasure. His hands made their way up her back, over her shoulders and slowly slid down her arms, until they found her hands.

He stepped back, and Sophia felt the loss immediately.

"Please, David," she begged, not knowing what it was she was asking for. An urgent need was burning in her core, a need that she knew only he could satisfy. "Don't leave me, not yet."

Hutton's eyes were darker than she had ever seen them before, his cheeks flushed with colour. "Sophia," he said, hoarsely, reaching for her hand but refusing to kiss her again. "I – "

He bowed his head and ran a hand over his eyes.

"What is it, David?" she asked, hesitantly. He had never stepped away from her before.

David shook his head. "Sophia, I – I am struggling with what I feel."

His words astonished her, making her heart leap with unexpected pleasure. They had never really discussed such things before, having enjoyed each other's kisses too much to give time for words. Apparently, this time was to be different.

"If you are asking me to confess that I care for you, David, then you should know that I do. Deeply." If she were honest with him – even with herself, she would admit that she was beginning to feel the first stirrings of love in her heart.

"Even though I am a servant? A hired man?" The bite of his words made her start with surprise, heat leaving her body almost immediately. He dropped her hand and moved away to sit on the small bench in the corner.

Sophia remained where she was, hating that there was sadness in his eyes. She had known from the first moment she'd seen him that he was not the right man for her, but she simply had not been able to stop herself from seeking him out.

"Hutton, I do not care that you are a hired man," she said, quietly. "My feelings for you grow with every passing day." An uneasy feeling swept over her as she realized he had not told her anything of his own emotions. Was she merely a passing fancy for him? Was there nothing deeper? Every time he had looked into her eyes, she had seen something glowing there, but as yet he had never given voice to it.

"It is not right for me to feel this way," he groaned, burying his head in his hands.

"Then, you do care for me?"

His face lifted to hers at once, surprise in his expression. "Of course I do, Sophia. How could I not? You are beauty and grace, kindness and compassion. Your gentleness and tenderness draw me to you, in a way I never expected."

Sophia swallowed, her heart beginning to fill with an overwhelming joy. "I cannot tell you how happy I am to hear you say those words, David."

He sighed, and dropped his head in his hands, covering his face. "Sophia, there can be no future for us."

"Don't say that," she begged. "I know it would be quite unorthodox, but I cannot bear to think of you not in my life." Desperation filled her chest. "Can we not continue with what we have now, and put aside fear or worry about the future?" She stepped forward, closer to him, looking down at his bowed head. The ache in her chest grew as she waited for him to say something.

Hutton did not respond, other than to rest his head against the cushion of her chest, wrapping his arms around her waist once more. Sophia brushed his dark hair with her fingers, wanting desperately to find some kind of solution for them both but struggling to clearly see a way forward.

"I think I must leave you, I must stop this."

His words stunned her, the blood freezing in her veins.

"No, Hutton," she stammered, suddenly terrified. "You must not. Please, I could not bear it!"

"This is not right, Sophia. I can offer you nothing." Slowly, he lifted his head so that he might look into her eyes and she saw there a deep sadness. What was it that he was holding from her? Was he already married? Or was it simply their difference in social status?

Sophia fought the despair mounting in her chest, blinking back hot tears. "I cannot bear it if you were to leave me," she whispered. "What would I do without you?"

His face lifted to hers, and he tugged her down beside him. "I will not pretend that I do not feel the same pain at the thought of leaving your side, Sophia, but what future can there be for us?"

"I will elope with you if you ask it of me," she whispered, her hands grasping onto his shirt as though if she held on tightly enough, he might stay. "What I feel for you now will continue to grow, I am sure of it."

Lifting one hand, he brushed his fingers along her temple, before cupping her chin. "Don't say that, Sophia. I am not worthy of your enduring affection. Not when I...." He dropped his hand and passed it over his eyes, his mouth closed as he held back the rest of his words.

"What is it, David?" she begged, fear mounting in her chest. "You have some great pain that you will not share, and I do not know what to do to get you to share it with me." Tears pricked at her eyes. "If only you would tell me, then I might be able to help!"

He shook his head, as a slight groan came from his mouth.

"If it is simply of your status, then can you not see how little that matters to me?" Sophia whispered, her heart filling with sadness and pain. "But it is more than that, is it not?"

David drew in one long breath, finally dropping his hand so he might look into her eyes. "Yes, it is more than that, Sophia, but I will not speak of it. Do not ask it of me. Already I have done more than I should have with you, but I simply cannot stop myself. Perhaps it would be best if I left this employ altogether, until I know what best to do." His fingers caught her chin once more, his thumb brushing her lips. "I want you to know that my heart belongs to you, Sophia. It is true in its affection for you."

She cried then, unable to accept that he was considering leaving her, disregarding any hope for their future together. It was too painful to even contemplate. His arm moved around her shoulders, pulling her into his chest. Sophia rested her head on his shoulder, her arm encircling his chest and resting around his neck. He held her tightly but did not speak a word to take back what he had already said. Sophia knew it was because of the depths of his affection for her, but that did not lessen the ache she felt, the deep, searing pain that came with the knowledge of the secrets he held back from her. If he would only talk to her of them, then they might forge a way together, but it seemed he was entirely resolute.

Hutton had his own secrets to keep.

CHAPTER 7

D avid pushed a hand through his hair, growing more and more frustrated with himself. He should not have allowed himself to feel any kind of emotion for the beautiful Miss Sophia but, try as he might, he could not stop his heart from longing for her. However, he had seen neither sight nor sound of her for the last few days.

Lifting the axe high, he struck at the log, slicing it cleanly in two. It was an excellent way to relieve his frustrations, although by now he was sure had chopped more than enough firewood.

He could still remember the taste of her kisses, the softness of her skin against his fingers. How much he wanted to be with her. His fondness for her was more than just a physical desire. It was a true appreciation of her character, as well as a developing affection that, if he did not check it, could easily grow into love. Growling to himself, he picked up the axe again and struck down, hard.

They had spent a lot of time together over the last three weeks, and he had found her company utterly delightful. She did not speak to him as he had expected, given that he was a servant of the house, but he had noticed the kindness in her eyes, the compassion in her character. She was always gentle, as though, by her tender persuasion, the flowers grew into their beautiful blooms. In truth, he had never heard a harsh word leave her lips and she was held in high regard by the rest of his staff.

Momentarily, David wondered what his household staff thought of him. He barely gave them more than a glance, expecting them to do what was asked without question and dismissing them if they did not. He shook his head. This experience had taught him exactly what it meant to be in someone's employ, and he was not sure he particularly liked it. There was always the fear of dismissal, the worry that their work would not be of a high enough standard.

David wondered if perhaps that was merely a concern of the newer staff who had arrived, given that the Dowager had taken the previous household staff with her to the dower house. By all accounts, the new Lord Catesby was a fair and kind man, someone he respected immediately upon first acquaintance. In fact, it had been on his mind more than once to tell Lord Catesby the truth about his situation, which would ultimately mean throwing himself on Catesby's mercy – but surely the man would understand? It would also mean that he might be able to court Sophia one day, but only if she could forgive him for his ruse and his terrible lies.

He had gone back to the arbour only once since the last time they had been together. Memories and regrets had hit him hard, coming thick and fast as he'd sat down on the bench and leaned back against the ivy-covered wall. Sophia wanted him, wanted a future with him, and yet he was forced to push her away. He could not allow her to entertain thoughts of matrimony when he was not truly who she thought he was. David knew he should never have allowed himself to touch her, for that had been the start of his downfall – but he could not get enough of her kisses. Even now, only three days since their last meeting, he was hungering for them again, like a starving man might dream of bread.

Throwing the axe to one side, David sat down on the stump and put his head in his hands. He could not risk it. If Sophia were to discover that he had been hiding the truth from her, that he was actually an engaged gentleman, then he knew he would never be able to speak to her again. The hurt and betrayal would be too great for her to endure. She would turn from him, leaving him to his disgrace and hide away from him. In truth, she would have every right to do such a thing, for what kind of woman would wish to engage herself with a cad and a bounder such as he was?

Groaning, David coupled his hands behind his head. Why was his heart so engaged with the girl? He knew he should not be speaking to her, should not be seeking out her company in order to have her in his arms again, but there was a force him that simply propelled him towards her. Why was fate dealing him such a rough hand? He had been forced to run from London, to run from his conniving mother and supposed fiancée. Only to find someone he might truly come to care for when he was pretending to be nothing more than a gardener.

"Pleased to meet you, Miss Sophia. I am Viscount David Armstrong," he muttered, wishing he could say truly say those words to her but knowing exactly what would happen, was he do to so.

Grimacing, he picked up some of the firewood and began to stack it in the shelter he had built previously. He had to remain here, for as long as he could. To return to London would be disaster itself. His mother would continue trying to force him to wed that ridiculous creature, Lady Viola Ermington.

For a long time, he had simply been enjoying his life and his title, although he ran his estates with care and precision. It allowed him to have a good balance between hard work and enjoying time with his friends at various soirees or other gatherings. Of course, he had known he would have to marry at some stage but had not considered it a pressing matter.

Too late, he had realized, his mother considered it the *only* matter of importance in his life.

He could still smell the overpowering, cloying scent of Lady Ermington's perfume. Unfortunately, when he had been introduced to her, he had taken a breath and practically swallowed the scent, forcing him to cough for a good few minutes. It had only been when he had finally recovered his breath that he had finally been able to bow to the lady. He had thought nothing of it, but soon it became clear that both she and his mother were in cahoots, planning to shackle him to Lady Ermington forever.

It was not simply the case that he did not appreciate his mother's interference in his life, but more that he found Lady Ermington singularly unattractive, in both face and character. She had cold blue eyes that did not warm when she smiled, a perfectly straight nose but a thin mouth that held a hint of cruelty. She wore far too much rouge, and batted her eyelashes once too often, making him almost nauseous in her obvious attention towards him. It was only when he had made it clear that he was not in the least interested that she had wormed her way into his mother's good graces.

Unfortunately for him, his mother had taken to Lady Ermington and, together, they had hatched a plan for his future.

Lady Ermington was respectable enough, but had gone through four seasons and, thus far, not found a single gentleman interested in wedding her. He could understand why, of course, but her interest in him reeked of desperation. Why she had chosen to sink her claws into him specifically, he did not know, but perhaps it was simply because his mother had taken a liking to her. In truth, Lady Ermington and his mother shared much of the same qualities – both were devious, sly, and extremely good at looking down their noses at others in society, regardless of their social standing.

David closed his eyes at the memory, hating that he had fallen so foul of their evil intentions. He had attended a ball celebrating the engagement between a Miss Harlington and his dear friend, Lord Darwent, only to discover that Lady Ermington was also in attendance. His attempts to avoid her had failed and, unfortunately, he had found it increasingly difficult to detach Lady Ermington from his side. At one point, he had been forced to physically remove her hand from his arm, something she had not taken too kindly to him doing. He had seethed inwardly, seeking out the quiet of the gardens for a brief moment in order to keep his temper.

That had been a mistake.

Lady Ermington had, somehow, discovered him in the gardens and had attempted to kiss him. He had been repulsed and pushed her away, only for his mother to appear and ask him, in a shocked tone, what exactly he had been doing with Lady Ermington.

It was only then that he had realized exactly what it was their intentions were. Without a word, he had strode back into the house, picked up his gloves and left, choosing to go to Whites instead of returning home. He had woken up in Whites the following morning, with gritty eyes and a thumping headache, to discover that he was now betrothed to Lady Ermington.

He had found out they had, apparently, been seen that evening in an embrace. His mother had been the one to assure the gossips that he was, in fact, engaged to the Lady but that they had kept their engagement quiet so as not to take attention away from Miss Harlington and Lord Darwent. Society, of course, had lapped it up and the town was now abuzz with the news, despite the fact that David himself had never even agreed to such a thing. So how then, had he woken to discover himself engaged?

HE HAD THROWN himself on the mercy of his friend, Lord Darwent, explaining the situation and seeking a way to extricate himself from Lady Ermington. Unfortunately, Lord Darwent had been of very little help, pointing out that he was duty bound to marry the lady now. Otherwise, he would greatly affect not only his own reputation but hers. David had been uncaring, stating that he would rather society knew that Lady Ermington was something of a conniving witch, but Lord Darwent had then pointed out that Lady Ermington had two younger sisters who were having their first and second season respectively. That had forced David to reconsider. If he broke the engagement, then her sisters would be adversely affected. Their invitations to societal events would slowly decline since they would be tainted by his actions. Slowly, he had sunk into despair, returning home to simply sit in his room, refusing to speak to his mother at all.

Eventually, he had come upon an idea. He had been forced to simply disappear. It was the only solution he could think of. If his mother could not find him, then she could not coerce him into setting a date for his nuptials. David was quite sure Lady Ermington would grow bored of his absence after some time had passed and would move onto another gentleman. She would need to marry soon, so as not to be considered entirely on the shelf. This was better than publicly breaking the engagement, knowing the shame it would bring to both him, his mother and Lady Ermington's family.

The firewood was stacked, and David realized he was completely exhausted. He had worn himself out physically and emotionally, thinking of what it was he was running from. By now, he was sure his mother would be speaking to anyone and everyone she could about her son's disappearance. He was worried that the rumours might spread to the country. Perhaps Lord Catesby would hear of them – but given that the man had only laid eyes on him twice, and barely looked at him since, David was sure that Lord Catesby would not hold any suspicion.

What of Miss Sophia?

That had him pausing in his steps, his eyes turning almost involuntarily, towards the window. Was she there, watching him? Would she guess his true identity, if notice of his disappearance reached the estate?

He had to stay away from her. He could not risk it, not now. His heart quelled at the thought of removing himself from the woman he had begun to care about, but he knew he had to remain hidden, otherwise find himself back in the clutches of his mother and Lady Ermington. He had told her that he might consider leaving the estate altogether, but his heart quailed at the prospect, forcing him to remain for the time being. He would simply have to soak her up in his memory until the time came for him to move on – whether to another estate or back to his true life.

"Hutton?"

Her sweet, soft voice drifted across the wind towards him. Turning, he saw her descend the steps leading into the garden. Pretending he had not heard her, he picked up his axe and, whistling loudly, strode across the gardens away from her. He pretended he did not feel the ache in his heart, the pain slicing through him as she called to him once more.

This was for her best.

CHAPTER 8

S ophia wept hot tears over Hutton's behaviour, aware that he was doing exactly as he had said but still hurt by it nonetheless. She had attempted to approach him, only for him to turn and walk away as though some kind of danger was snapping at his heels. It appeared he would not even talk to her and she felt the loss keenly.

Ever since the first time she had seen him chopping wood, Sophia had tried to approach him on two further occasions, leaving a day in between each, but he had been quiet and apparently uninterested in talking with her. In fact, he was more of a servant than she had ever seen him. He kept his head down, never once glancing at her with those hazel eyes of his. She found herself longing to see them, almost desperate for him to look at her again. Sophia felt as though she could hardly bear it, wishing she had the strength to drag him to the arbour and force him to tell her what it was he was hiding from her.

Wiping her face, Sophia drew in a long breath and tried her best to calm herself. There had to be some sort of solution.

"Sophia?"

Hoping that her face was not overly tear-stained, Sophia turned to see Helena walking towards her, a bundle of ribbons in her hands.

"Oh, my!" she exclaimed, scurrying forward to take them from her sister. "Whatever has happened?"

Helena shook her head. "It is best not to ask." A spot of colour appeared in both her cheeks, making Sophia laugh. Helena could, at times, have something of a fiery temper which pushed her to do the most irregular things, but this was certainly the first time she had ever seen her sister's irritation taken out on ribbons!

"Was there one you were looking for, particularly?"

Glancing up at Sophia, Helena nodded "I could not find it."

"Why are you so upset over that?" Sophia inquired, sitting down with the bundle of ribbons on her lap. "Richard is going to think you beautiful, no matter what you wear."

Richard had returned to town for a short while but was going to be joining them for this evening's dinner. Surely Helena could not be so concerned about her appearance now, not when she was already secure in his affections for her.

"I want to look my best for him," Helena muttered, throwing herself into a chair. "It upsets me when I am apart from him."

"You miss him, then," Sophia replied, calmly. "That is quite normal, I am sure."

Helena's face slowly relaxed. "Yes, I am sure it is, but I am just surprised at the great amount of feeling I have for the man. He is gone for but a few days and I am already desperate to be in his company again!"

Sophia grew uncomfortable, recognizing that her own emotions were very much in tune with what her sister was saying. Licking her lips, she ran her fingers over the ribbons and did not respond.

"I cannot wait to see him again. We have such a bond, such an ease of conversation that I find I cannot have, not even with you," Helena continued, her voice soft. "More than anyone, he understands me. The care and consideration he shows bring joy to my heart. I find that I can barely take my mind off him"

"You think of him often, then?" Sophia mumbled, her own heart beginning to quicken as her mind was filled, once more, with a vision of David Hutton.

"It sounds quite ridiculous, I know when he has only been gone for a few days, but the way he looks at me...." She trailed off, a gentle smile curving her lips. "I hope you will feel the same one day, Sophia."

Swallowing hard, Sophia ducked her head and concentrated on attempting to work her way through the ribbons. She could not be honest with her sister and tell her that she already did feel much the same way over a gardener, but she could at least be truthful with herself. What Helena described was much the same way she was feeling about David Hutton, finding herself almost desperate for his company once more. He spoke to her in such a gentle way that she found herself willing to open up to him, to tell him things that she would not mention to her sister. She remembered how they had once spoken of her sister's upcoming wedding and of her own increasing loneliness. It was, as Helena said, that David seemed to understand her more than anyone else did.

She had to admit that she could not get her mind from him, wondering where he was, what he was doing and why they could not be in conversation together. Warmth crawled up her neck and into her face as she recalled the kisses they had shared.

"There is such a thing as missing the physical affection too," Helena murmured, her fingers still working at the ribbons. "The physical intimacy between husband and wife only increases with matrimony, I have heard it said. Although apparently, mama wishes to talk to me about that." Helena glanced up and laughed on seeing Sophia's hot face. "Come now, Sophia, you cannot let such talk make you so embarrassed! You may as well come with me to talk to mama since I am sure you will be wed next."

Relieved that her sister thought her blushes were over their current topic of conversation, Sophia feigned a laugh. "Nonsense, Helena. I have no intention of marrying anytime soon."

"Nonsense," Helena replied, dismissively. "All you have to do is find a man who looks at you in a certain way, and you will be head over heels in love." She smiled and patted Sophia's hand. "Of course, he must love you in return, but I have no doubt that will happen. In fact!" she exclaimed, her eyes suddenly alight. "Once I return from honeymoon, you shall come to London and stay with me. We shall find you a great number of suitors and then you might have your pick."

Sophia tried to laugh, but the sound stuck in her throat. "Oh, Helena," she managed to say, unable to hide the break in her voice. "You have such ideas, but I am quite contented here at home."

She saw Helena frown, lines marring her forehead. "There is that melancholy again," her sister murmured, softly. "There is still something on your heart, Sophia." Frustrated, she leaned forward to catch Sophia's eye. "Why do you not tell me, Sophia? Are we not always close? Why now do you hold this from me? I want to help!"

"You cannot!" Sophia exclaimed, tears trickling down her face. "No-one can. It has all turned into such a disaster." Dropping the ribbons, Sophia buried her face in her hands and sobbed.

Helena moved to sit next to her almost at once and wrapped her arm around Sophia's shoulders. Knowing that she was going to tell Helena everything, Sophia leaned into her sister's embrace and let out all the emotion she had been holding back. It came out in a torrent, in a rush, her entire body shaking with sobs.

"My dear Sophia," Helena murmured, evidently upset by her sister's distress. "Whatever has upset you so?"

"My heart is broken," Sophia whispered, her sobs eventually lessening. "I have been so foolish, Helena. Whatever am I to do?"

CHAPTER 9

Once Helena had rung for tea and given Sophia time to compose herself, she sat down next to her sister once more and gave her a sharp look.

"Now, whatever it is that is troubling you, I must ask you to promise that you will not keep things from me any longer. I want to help you, and this is clearly distressing you more than you can bear."

Sophia nodded, knowing that Helena was right. "You will think me entirely foolish when you hear all of it, Helena," she sighed, wondering what Helena would think of her taking up with a servant. "I have fallen hopelessly in love."

Helena gasped, her eyes sparkling with sudden delight. "You have? How wonderful!"

"It is not so wonderful when you hear who it is that has captured my heart," Sophia said, miserably. "It is the gardener."

A stunned silence filled the room as Sophia kept her gaze firmly in her lap, her fingers smoothing minute creases in her gown. The maid arrived with the tea tray, and Sophia waited with trepidation as the maid placed the tea tray down and then exited the room. She dared not look at Helena, sure that there would be some kind of ridicule or exasperation there.

"And, does he return your affection?"

Startled by Helena's question, Sophia stared at her sister. "Helena, did you not hear me just now?"

"I heard you very clearly," her sister replied, softly. "And I do not think it so terrible, Sophia. One cannot help one's heart, of course. Although, it complicates matters if he returns your affection."

"He does," Sophia replied, miserably. "But now he has parted himself from me, and will not return to my side. He has decided that he cannot continue with what we started."

Helena patted Sophia's hand. "Perhaps that is for the best, though," she answered, gently. "He is attempting to do the right thing, Sophia. He is not within your sphere, Sophia, nor can he ever be. Not unless you….." Helena trailed off, her eyes widening. "Pray tell me that you are not considering matrimony!"

Knowing that this was precisely what she had been hoping for, Sophia lied and shook her head. "I know it is quite ridiculous, Helena, but my heart is broken over him."

"And I well understand that pain," Helena replied, gently. "For years I believed my love for Richard was not returned, and the agony of it almost broke me."

"Your love for him continued regardless," Sophia pointed out, not seeing any solution in her sister's words. "Which means I have very little chance of recovering from this. I know he is someone who is in the employ of our brother, but I feel as though no other man could compare to him." She shook her head, hating that tears were falling from her eyes yet again. "I believe that he is holding something back from me, something that, if he were to tell me of it, might open up a way for a future together, but he simply will not trust me."

Helena drew in a long breath. "Sophia, I love you dearly, but I must warn you that your association with a servant is not a favourable one. I know you love him dearly, but you must put him from your mind and your heart, no matter how long it takes. I am sure that, once you come to London and enjoy a few balls and the attention of various gentlemen, you will slowly forget your gardener."

Sophia shook her head as tears crept from her eyes and began to make their way down her cheeks. "I cannot forget him," she whispered, brokenly. "He understands me like no other, Helena. Not even you." Looking up, she saw the hurt cross Helena's face but did not take her words back. "I do not mean to upset you, my dear sister, but David sees into my soul in a way no one else ever has. Even though we are the closest of sisters and the dearest of friends, there is something different about him."

Helena sighed heavily, although a small smile played around her mouth. "Oh, Sophia. You have truly fallen for this man." She gave her a soft smile. "Your sentiments match with what I feel for Richard."

"Then you can see how much in earnest I am," Sophia replied, quietly. "And see how much my barren my future is without him."

"And you do not think that you might forget him in the whirlwind of London society?" Helena probed, gently.

"I can never forget him," Sophia answered, truthfully. The man she had shared her soul with, the man who had brushed her lips with his, who had shown her what it was to be alive with passion – no, she could not forget him.

"Then you must find out what it is that holds him back," Helena replied, firmly, shocking Sophia entirely.

Blinking back her tears, Sophia wiped her eyes and stared at her sister. "A moment ago, you were encouraging me to forget about him and to find myself another gentleman," she exclaimed, her voice wobbling with emotion. "And now you are telling me to seek him out?"

Helena laughed. "I had not realized just how deeply you were in love with him until just now," she replied, her eyes sparkling. "I must say that I am quite delighted for you, although I feel it my duty to warn you that the future might present many difficulties if you continue your association with him."

"I know," Sophia replied, knowing exactly what Helena was talking about. "But that still does not push me from him."

Nodding, Helena handed Sophia her handkerchief and turned to pour the tea. "Then you must find out what it is that holds him back from you and find a way through it."

"Do you think Francis will be angry?"

"Most likely, yes," Helena replied, practically. "But that is just Francis' way. After all, you are the youngest of the sisters, so it is not as though your association with a gardener will negatively influence any younger sister. You may marry the stable boy if you wish it."

Sophia could not help but giggle, suddenly filled with relief that not only did her sister understand, but that finally, she had some support in her current predicament.

"I would also suggest that you tell mama," Helena replied, lifting her teacup delicately and taking a small sip. "It may come as something of a shock to her, but I am sure she will understand."

Hardly able to believe what she was hearing, Sophia shook her head to herself and let out a soft laugh, one that was mingled with tears. She had not expected such a reaction from Helena, but her unwavering support meant the world to her.

"Well, what are you waiting for?" Helena asked, giving her a slight dig in the ribs. "Are you going to sit here all afternoon?"

"Helena!" Sophia exclaimed, glancing behind it. "It is storming thunderously outside!"

"No excuses, now," Helena replied, with a slight smile. "And what better reason to be stuck outside in the gardens – hidden away somewhere – than the rain? Should Francis ask where you are, then I shall simply inform him that you have gone out to the gardens but will be sheltering somewhere until the rain stops." Pressing Sophia's hand, her smile gentled. "Take as much time as you need, Sophia. Find out the truth and do not shy away from it. If you love him, then fight for your future together, no matter what it takes."

CHAPTER 10

A raindrop landed on Sophia's forehead and ran down her nose, as she rushed towards the rose beds, glad that she had worn her boots. The clouds were still low, filled with swirls of grey and dark blue as they poured their deluge down on her. She was going to be soaked through if she did not find some shelter soon.

She did not know where to go, nor where David might be. Her heart pushed her towards their hidden arbour, the only place she could think of. If he were not there, she would wait until the rain stopped before searching for him again. Helena was right. She could not give up this time, would not allow him to continue holding her at arm's length. The truth would have to come out so that she would know for certain whether or not there was a future for them.

The ivy was wet and glistening in the rain, the dampness brushing her cheek as she pulled the ivy curtain aside and stepped in. Her heart thundered in her chest as she looked around, only to sink into her shoes as she realized it was entirely empty. Even though she had known it was quite ridiculous, she had hoped that he would know she was searching for him and be in the arbour, waiting for her.

"Foolish," she muttered to herself, removing her bonnet and shaking the water from it. "You are a foolish girl, Sophia."

Sitting down heavily on the bench, Sophia leaned her head back against the wood wall and let her eyes close. Listening to the sound of the rain, she let her mind empty of every thought. She no longer feared about the future, did not need to worry what her mother or brother would think. Helena was right. There was no younger sibling to consider and, whilst her association with a mere servant might be considered a scandal, she was sure it could be kept fairly quiet. Who knew? Perhaps Francis might find it in his heart to bequeath a small sum on her, as well as her dowry so that they would not have to live as paupers.

"Even if we do," she murmured to herself. "I do not think I would mind it so much." Sophia knew the torment she had gone through these last days, having been separated from David. Surely life with love, even without wealth, was better than a life absent of love?

"Sophia!"

"David!"

The ivy curtain had been pulled back suddenly, and Sophia found herself looking into David's face, the astonishment she felt mirrored in his eyes.

"I – I did not expect...." he began, trailing off and beginning to back away. "I do apologize. Forgive me."

There it was again, the way his manner of speaking sounded more like a gentleman than a servant.

"Please, David," she begged, getting to her feet and catching his arm. "Do not leave me again. I have come out to the gardens to wait for you, but I could not find you anywhere."

She saw his eyes flare as he looked at her, water streaming down his cheeks from the rain he had just been walking in.

"Don't leave me," she whispered, her body suddenly coming alive with feeling. "I have been entirely miserable these last few days."

He closed his eyes, although did not pull his arm away. "Do not, I beg you."

"Do what?" she asked, confused.

"I cannot be near you," he replied, his own voice husky. "Sophia, I cannot be near you!"

Tears fell like rain on her cheeks as she found his hand, clinging to it with her own.

"I know you love me," she replied, sobs breaking through her words. "You are tearing yourself away from me, and I do not know why – all I know is that I cannot bear it. I cannot, David! I am bereft, left entirely alone." She swallowed hard, seeing the agony on his face as she spoke. "Please, tell me what it is that keeps you from me, from the future we might have together where we are bound together in love." Lifting one hand, she brushed the raindrops from his cheek, boldly capturing his face in her hands as she inched closer to him. "I have determined that I will not let you escape without the truth," she finished, her tears still falling. "I love you, David. Body and soul, I love you. Tell me that you do not feel the same way."

Her heart pounded in her chest as she looked at him, desperate to hear his answer. She felt him sag, tension leaving his body and he gazed into her eyes, emotions flickering over his face, emotions that she could not quite read.

Then, in an instant, his mouth was on hers – hot and urgent. All of her breath left her body, caught up in his sudden embrace. The tears she had cried mingled with the moisture on his face, her hands digging into his hair as his hands wrapped around her waist. They stumbled back, until Sophia felt her back against the side of the arbour, clinging to David with such a passion that it almost frightened her. She could not give a name to the feelings rising in her chest, and, to her shame, she sobbed against him as his lips left her mouth and trailed down over her cheek.

"Oh, my dear Sophia," David whispered, lifting his head and pulling her into his embrace. "How much I have hurt you."

Sophia tried to reply but could not get the words out, sobs shaking her body. It was tears of relief, she knew, her heart slowly healing as David held her.

"I have found myself almost mad without you," he continued, pouring words of love into her ear. "To see you, to hear your voice, but to have to keep myself at a distance from you...." He pulled back and looked deeply into her eyes. "It has been a torment, unlike anything I have ever known before."

"David," Sophia wept, her voice breaking. "I cannot bear to be parted from you again. My heart is twined with yours."

David rested his forehead against hers, waiting until his own breathing slowed before responding. "Sophia, I want to tell you all, but I am afraid it will push you from me forever."

"It will not," she promised, desperate to know the truth. "Whatever it is you are keeping from me, I know you are only doing so in order to protect me – to protect us." Closing her eyes, she captured his face with her hands, letting her fingers run down his rough cheeks. "Can you not see that there can be nothing for us unless you tell me all?"

For a moment, she thought he might refuse her again, the silence stretching out between them like an impassable gulf. Opening her eyes, Sophia stepped back out of his embrace just a little, so that she might see his face. What she saw there was a face lined with fear and worry, with something like guilt hidden amongst it.

"I will tell you," he said, eventually. "But you will despise me for it, Sophia."

"I will not."

He shook his head. "It must come out in the end, I suppose. But not today."

Sophia's shoulders slumped immediately, her heart sinking into her boots.

"Not because I do not wish to tell you all, but because it is growing dark and you must return to the house," he continued, catching her hands in his. "Your reputation, Sophia. Should you remain outside, there will be concerns raised at the house and perhaps even a search party." A slight smile broke out over his face. "And then what would we do?"

"You might be forced to marry me," Sophia replied, lightly.

He dropped his head, a grim look on his face. Fear lurched in her soul.

"Oh, no," she whispered, attempting to back away from him but finding herself pressed against the arbor wall. "That is what you have been hiding from me? You are married already?" Nausea rolled in her stomach as she thought of what she had shared with him.

"No, no," he exclaimed, his eyes meeting hers so swiftly that she was forced to draw in her breath. "I am not married, Sophia, I swear it." He tried to smile, but she could still see the anxiety behind his eyes. "I am free, I promise you."

Slowly, her shoulders drew down as the tension left her body. She knew he would not lie to her, trusting that what he said was the truth.

"Now go," he said, catching her hands in his once more. "I will find you here come the morrow?"

"The early afternoon, I might think about taking a walk in the gardens," Sophia replied, softly, her eyes sparkling as she saw his slow smile. "I have missed you so very much, David. I cannot tell you how glad I am that you have chosen to share all with me."

"I want a future with you, Sophia," he swore, fervently. "I only pray that you will still be able to see one with me when you know all."

Sophia did not reply but pressed her lips against his in response. Their kiss was smooth and sweet, not frantic and desperate as it had been before. It was difficult to tear herself away from him, but Sophia knew she had to return to the house.

"Tomorrow," she whispered against his lips. "Tomorrow, my love."

"I love you, Sophia," he replied, as she walked to the door. "Never forget that I love you."

CHAPTER 11

"Ah, Sophia!"

Smiling at her brother, Sophia took her place at the dinner table, aware that her hair was still a little damp.

"Helena tells me you were out in the gardens this afternoon. I must confess I was a little worried what with all the torrential rain, but she assured me you would be fine. You have not caught a cold, I hope?"

A little surprised at Francis' concern, Sophia shook her head. "No, I have not caught cold. I was a little chilled, I confess, but a hot bath has set that to rights."

"It was a pleasant walk in the gardens, I hope?" Helena asked, her eyes alight with a hint of mischief.

Sophia attempted nonchalance, although she could feel the heat burning its way up into her cheeks. "Very pleasant, despite the rain. I thank you."

Helena's smile widened. "Good. I am truly glad to hear it."

Sophia, catching Francis' slight frown, dropped her gaze to the table. Henry, of course, was nowhere to be seen. He was probably working on something in his room or in the library. That left herself, Helena and Francis to continue the conversation as dinner progressed.

Thankfully for Sophia, the remainder of the dinner passed without further comments on her activities, although Sophia did not miss Helena's inquiring glances. Just as they finished their dessert and about to leave Francis to his port, the butler entered with a note on a silver tray.

"My lord," he murmured, holding the tray out to him with a gloved hand. "This was sent as a matter of urgency."

Sophia made to rise from the table, but Francis waved her back down. "No need to rush away, Sophia. Henry is busy with his own studies, and I do not much like the idea of drinking port on my own. Perhaps tea?" On seeing her answering nod, he looked to one of the footmen. "And a port for myself, as usual."

Sitting back down, Sophia smiled at Helena as the footmen cleared the tables, soon serving them their own tray of tea each and setting Francis' port down in front of him. It had been some time since they had sat like this together, albeit without Henry. For once, Francis did not seem inclined to rush away, evidently preferring to spend some time with his sisters instead.

"How interesting," Francis murmured, his eyes narrowing as he read the note from town.

"What is it?" Helena asked, as inquisitive as ever. "Nothing bad, I hope?"

Francis threw the letter on the table. "Nothing of importance, no. It seems that Charles has some news from town and has sent a description of the man so that we might keep our eyes open. Although, I will say that a missing Earl is a cause for concern, of course."

"A missing Earl?" Helena repeated, reaching for the letter. "You do not mind if I read it, Francis?"

"Not in the least," he replied, pouring himself some port. "You may read it too if you wish, Sophia."

Sophia saw Helena's eyes suddenly round, her fingers briefly touching her lips as though troubled by what she read. How strange. Was there something about this missing earl that worried Helena? She watched as her sister folded up the letter and placed it to her left, before turning her attention to pouring some more tea.

"May I?" Sophia asked, gesturing for the letter.

"Oh, I do not think that necessary," Helena replied, lightly. "There is nothing of importance there. Francis is quite right."

That in itself made Sophia's concern grow. "Helena," she said, quietly. "The letter." Her eyes narrowed as she saw the desperate look in Helena's eyes, as she searched for a way to continue to keep it from her. When she saw that Sophia was not about to be put off, she handed her the letter with a deep sigh.

"Keep in mind it may not be what you think," she said, softly, then turned to engage Francis in conversation.

Sophia stared at her sister for a brief moment, her heart slowly sinking in her chest. Her fingers began to tremble as she opened the letter and began to read.

'My dear Francis,

I hope you are all well. I am writing to you very briefly to alert you to a concerning situation here in town. It appears that the Earl of Marching, David Armstrong, has disappeared. His mother and fiancée, Lady Viola Ermington, are utterly distraught since they have very little idea of where he has gone. Initially, it was presumed that he had simply taken some time away, but as the weeks have gone on and there has been no word from him, the belief is now that he might have found himself in some kind of nefarious situation. If you do see anyone akin to his description, please do inform me at once. He is a tall man, with light brown hair and brown eyes, I believe. I know that does not narrow it down very much, but I thought it best to inform you regardless.

I will write to you again soon.

Charles.'

Sophia finished reading, but could not lift her eyes from the page. Already, she had come to the same conclusion as Helena, but could not allow her heart to believe it. Had there not always been something about Hutton that had surprised her in the way he spoke, in the manners he displayed? At times, she had thought his behaviour to be more like that of a gentleman than of a gardener....and now it appeared she knew the reason why.

"Sophia?" Helena asked, touching her hand and making Sophia jump. "Are you quite all right?"

"No," Sophia replied, a sob catching in her throat. "I must excuse myself. I have – a sudden headache."

"Let me assist you," Francis replied, getting to his feet and coming around to her. "I must say, you look quite pale, Sophia."

Sophia shook her head, tears burning in her eyes. She could not let them fall, not in front of her brother, for then he would insist on knowing what was wrong and she was already afraid she might tell him.

Helena rose to stand beside them both, knowing exactly what it was that truly troubled Sophia. "I shall take care of her, Francis. Why don't you send up fresh tea trays to us? And perhaps a cool compress?"

Francis peered into Sophia's face, concern evident in his own. "Very well. But do send for me if you need to, Sophia. I am here for you."

"Thank you, Francis," Sophia managed to whisper, wondering if her brother knew just how much his words meant. "I am sure I will be quite recovered come the morning." Giving him a wane smile, she saw Helena quickly fold up Charles' letter and slip it into her pocket before coming to Sophia's side and take her arm.

"Come now," Helena murmured, as they left the room. "Just up to your room, Sophia, then you may weep for as long as you wish."

How Sophia managed to climb the stairs to her room without letting a single tear fall, she was not quite sure. All she could feel was Helena's arm around her waist, guiding her up to the staircase and into the welcoming warmth of her bedchamber.

"Now," Helena said, sitting her down in the chair next to the fire. "What can I do for you, Sophia?"

Sophia opened her mouth to answer, only for tears begin to pour down her cheeks, sobs racking her body. She did not know how long she cried for, only that Helena was right there beside her, murmuring soothing words of sympathy and comfort.

"It may not be him," Helena said when Sophia's sobs eventually abated. "You will have to speak to him, Sophia, to discern the truth."

"How could it not be?" Sophia whispered, recalling the words of the letter. It was as though they were all seared into her soul, tearing strips from her heart. "This tells me why I so often found him more of a gentleman in manner and tone, and why he was unable to give himself to me entirely. His inability to see a future for us, the way he pushed himself from me for a time....it is because he is already engaged." Her voice became nothing more than a whisper, her eyes unseeing as she stared blankly into the flames in the grate.

"I confess that it does seem to be the appropriate conclusion, Sophia, but you know what the *ton* is like. Rumors abound. Perhaps Charles has, unwittingly, been caught up in some and has only written what he has heard. He might well be mistaken."

"I do not think so," Sophia replied, heavily. "Charles is not like that, and neither is Abigail. I do not think they can be wrong."

A heavy silence wrapped around her for a few moments, her grief and pain almost overwhelming her.

"You will have to speak to him come the morning," Helena said, interrupting the quiet. "I will come with you if you wish it?"

"No," Sophia answered at once. "I need to be alone with him. I will know the truth the moment I tell him of what I have read. I will see it in his face."

"I still have the letter," Helena said, quietly. "Do you wish to have it?"

Considering for a moment, Sophia nodded and accepted the folded note that Helena had previously slipped into her pocket. "Perhaps I shall ask him to read it," she murmured, running her fingers over the paper. "For I do not know if I can find the words to tell him what I know."

Helena gave her a brief smile and got up to pour some tea. "I do not think you shall sleep well tonight, my dear. I will stay with you until you are ready to climb into bed."

Grateful for her sister's kindness, Sophia managed a watery smile. "Thank you, Helena."

"Not at all," her sister replied, handing her a steaming cup of tea. "I will be with you through this, Sophia. You will find a way through, I promise you."

CHAPTER 12

David paced up and down the small arbour, barely able to take more than three steps before having to turn back again. Sophia should have been here by now, for it was well past the hour when she had said she would arrive. Instinct told him that there was something very wrong, that the Sophia of yesterday would not be the Sophia he met with today, should she appear at all. The Sophia of yesterday would have been right on time, if not earlier, desperate for his kisses in the same way that he yearned for her.

He had much to think on the night before, knowing that he was now forced into telling her the truth. Over the last few weeks, he had tried to convince himself that his feelings for her were nothing more than infatuation. That they would pass in time. He had told himself over and over that nothing could come of this, only for him to start hoping that perhaps there might be a future for them. His attempts to separate himself from her had come to naught, for he had been driven almost to the brink of madness in an attempt to stay away from her.

It was only when he had identified the deep love in his heart that he'd finally realized that he could not keep the truth from her any longer. As much as he did not want to tell her of his true identity, of the reasons he had hidden away as a gardener, David knew that he had no other choice. He would throw himself on her mercy and pray that she might understand, forgiving him for his lies and deceit.

"David?"

Turning on his heel, David let out a sigh of relief as Sophia stepped into the arbour, stepping forward to take her into his arms. To his shock, she stepped away, her normally sparkling eyes not able to meet his.

His heart thudded to a stop for a brief moment.

"What is it, my love?"

"How can you call me that?" she replied, her voice barely louder than a whisper, forcing him to strain to hear her words. "When you have someone waiting for you back in London?"

Nausea rolled in his stomach at once, his jaw slackening as he took in the paleness of her cheek, her red-rimmed eyes. Clearly, she had discovered the truth.

"I do not love her," he replied, trying his best to explain. "My mother – "

"Your mother is frantically looking for you," Sophia interrupted, pulling out a note and handing it to him. "I think you had better read this before you say anything else, David."

David took the parchment from her, hating the way she jolted when their fingers brushed. He did not need to ask her what it was she had discovered, for the grief in her eyes told him that she knew everything. Unfolding the parchment, his eyes skimmed the note, feeling anger boil in his stomach.

"I do not have a fiancée," he snarled, scrunching the parchment in his hand. "This is just a scheme of my mother's, Sophia. I am not betrothed, I swear it!"

She did not flinch, her eyes looking at him with an unwavering calm that quite unsettled him. "You are the Earl of Marching, Lord David Armstrong, then?"

David swallowed, his anger evaporating in an instant. "I am."

"And you did not tell me."

"How could I?" he replied, his voice growing louder with each word. "If I had told you from the very beginning, would you not have gone straight to your brother with the news, as you ought to? If I had told you once we had fallen in love, you would have despised me for lying to you and would have left my side." He tried to catch her hand, only for her to tug it away. "I could not lose you, my love."

Sophia turned away, and he saw her shoulders shake. She was crying, and, from the redness of her eyes, had been crying for some time. Even though he told himself that he could not have told her before now, the realization that he had betrayed her began to slice into his heart. She was utterly distraught, robbed of everything she'd thought she knew about him. That cut deep.

"I – I am sorry, Sophia," he whispered, not sure what else to say. "I thought I was doing this for your protection, but perhaps I was wrong."

"You tell me that you are not betrothed," she replied, turning to face him. "But you have kept the truth of your identity from me since the first moment we met."

"I know, but –"

She held up one trembling hand, silencing him. "How can you expect me to believe you now when you tell me you are not betrothed? How can I trust a single word from your mouth?" Fresh tears filled her eyes as she gazed at him, waiting for his response.

David found that he could not give one, finding nothing to say in answer. She was quite right, he realised. Were he to find himself in her position, there would be nothing he would believe.

"So, you see," Sophia continued, when the silence became too great. "I cannot believe that you are not engaged, *Lord* Armstrong. To think that I gave you my love when you were holding such a great truth back from me, holding back your very self!" She shook her head and swallowed hard. "I think our acquaintance must be at an end, my lord."

David could not accept what she was saying, even though he knew she was being more than fair in her assessment. The thought of being parted from her, never to have her in his arms again, was more punishment than he could bear.

"No, no," he cried, stepping forward and finally catching her in his arms. "You cannot mean it, Sophia. I know I have hidden my true self from you. But nothing I felt, none of the words I spoke to you of love, none of that was a lie, I swear it."

Sophia struggled weakly in his arms, pressing her hands flat against his chest. "I cannot, David. Let me go, I beg of you."

"Sophia," he whispered, loosening his grip but still holding her tightly. "Look at me, please. I beg of you."

She stilled, her face still turned away from him.

"Please, Sophia," David pleaded, struggling against the desperate fear that clutched at his soul. "Please, just look at me. Look into my eyes. See that all the words of love I have told you are true." He could not let her go, not yet. Not until she believed that he loved her and that this revelation did not change anything about how he felt.

"What we had," Sophia said, brokenly. "It is at an end. It does not matter whether you loved me or not, for I could never be with a man who has so willingly hidden his entire past from me, and one who has run from his mother and his responsibilities."

"I have not run," David replied at once. "My mother has pushed this lady upon me, to the point of announcing my betrothal in society papers without my knowledge or consent." His own voice broke as he spoke, still desperate to cling to Sophia. "I have never loved before, Sophia, and I doubt that I will ever love again. My love for you has grown since the very first moment we met and has become so wide and deep that it fills every last part of my heart. It has rooted itself there, ever more to remain. This, I swear, is true."

Sophia looked at him then, her face still pale and eyes filled with such a myriad of emotions that David found he could not begin to decipher what it was she was feeling. He cursed himself for having caused her so much pain, so much distress.

"I should never have hidden my true self from you," he finally admitted, holding her tighter. "Believe me when I say that I struggled to think of a way to tell you the truth. That is why I chose to separate myself from you so that I would not, one day, cause this exact situation." Boldly, he lifted his hand and brushed a loose strand of hair away from her face, relieved that she did not jerk away from him. The harshness of her stance slowly softened as he trailed his finger down her cheek, guilt slicing through him once more. "I could not do anything but return to you," he finished, dropping his head in shame. "Despite knowing that I should stay away from you until my own situation was worked out, my heart would not turn you lose. I can never undo what I have done to you, Sophia, but I only pray that you will consider the love we have shared, and find, in some way, the ability to forgive me."

With bated breath, he looked down into her face, desperate to see some kind of understanding there, some kind of softness. Instead, her expression remained exactly as it was, without even a hint of a smile. Her hands pressed against his chest lightly, but there was no reaction from her. David tightened his arms instinctively, knowing he was trying to hold onto something that was desperate to be let go. Not knowing what else to do, he dropped his head and kissed her full on the mouth.

There was no response.

He lifted his head and pressed his forehead against hers, refusing to accept what he knew was going to happen.

"Goodbye, David," she whispered, putting her hands on his arms and giving them a gentle press so that he would let her go. She did not say a single word, did not give him another look, but simply stepped through the ivy curtain and walked away, walking away from him and out of his life.

CHAPTER 13

"Francis?"

Opening the door, Sophia couldn't help but smile at the sight of Francis, his head propped up on one hand but his eyes firmly closed. Her brother was working so hard that he clearly wasn't getting enough rest. It was unfortunate that she was going to have to wake him, but the truth needed to be revealed.

"Francis?" she said again, stepping further into the room and shutting the door. The click of the door woke him at once. He snorted in surprise as his elbow slipped from the table.

"I'm sorry to wake you when I can see you are quite tired," Sophia continued, moving to sit down opposite him. "But I have something I must tell you." Her heart squeezed with pain as she remembered how, only a few minutes before, she had seen David walk away from the estate, a bag in his hand. Why she had waited for him to leave before approaching Francis, she could not quite say. Perhaps it was because she did not want Francis to tear David limb from limb once he'd discovered the truth. Or perhaps it was, despite everything, she loved him still and had to, for her own good, watch him walk away. Regardless of her reasons, she was here now, knowing she had to tell her brother everything that had gone on.

"Sorry," Francis muttered, rubbing a hand over his eyes. "I've not been sleeping well."

"Something on your mind?" Sophia asked, getting up to ring the bell for tea – of coffee, given how tired her brother looked.

Francis grimaced. "Yes, unfortunately."

"Anything I can help you with?"

He shook his head. "No, although I do thank you for your concern." He smiled at her, although the frustration didn't leave his eyes. "It's unusual for you to come and seek me out. Is something wrong?"

"Yes."

He frowned immediately, leaning forward in his chair. "Please, sit down, Sophia. Whatever's the matter?"

Sophia sat down on a chair beside the fire, waiting until Francis had come round from behind his desk to sit opposite her. She opened her mouth to speak, only for the maid to come in with the tea. The concern over Francis' fate as he waited for the maid to leave made her heart swell with affection for her brother, although she was still worried about what his reaction would be.

"Now," Francis began, the moment the door clicked shut. "Whatever has happened Sophia? I have been concerned for you, of course, but I had thought that your return to the gardens signaled that you were doing much better." He leaned forward, his eyes grave. "Is it mama? Are you missing her? Are you lonely?"

Sophia lifted a hand, stemming his words. "Francis, wait."

"Sorry," he mumbled, realizing he had been talking far too much. "I am just worried, Sophia. You have never come to me like this before."

Drawing in a breath, Sophia reached to pour the tea, trying to think of the right way to tell Francis the truth. Once they both had a cup of tea at their elbow, she folded her hands in her lap and looked directly at her brother. "Do you remember that letter Charles wrote to you? The one you read at the dinner table last evening?"

A slight frown puckered his forehead. "Yes, of course. The missing gentleman."

"The missing Earl," Sophia corrected, her heart beginning to hammer in her chest. "Well, I am aware of where he is."

Stunned silence met her ears as Francis' mouth dropped open.

"I should have told you this last evening, but I had to confirm it before I came to you," she continued when he said nothing. "And, before you go in search of him, he has returned to town."

"You know who he is?" Francis repeated, spluttering slightly. "Why did I not know of him?"

Now it came to it, the crux of the matter. Sophia's heart was beating so fast she thought she might become ill. The words were on the tip of her tongue, but she could not quite bring herself to say them.

"Sophia," Francis said, a little more sternly. "Who is he?"

She licked her lips. "He is – was – the gardener, Francis."

"The gardener?" he repeated, looking utterly confused. "You mean, *our* gardener is the missing Earl?"

"Yes, that is exactly what I mean," Sophia replied, the pounding of her heart slowly lessening as she managed to tell him the truth. "The Earl of Marching has been here, working as our gardener."

Francis' mouth dropped open, the colour slowly draining from his face.

"You need not worry that you have somehow been in the wrong by hiring him," Sophia continued quickly. "He wanted to be in hiding, and this was the best way for him to do so. He has a natural inclination towards plants and the like, so his hobby became his profession." A swirl of nausea rolled in her stomach, and Francis closed his mouth and ran one hand through his hair. It was more than clear that he had not expected this in the least and a further shock was yet to come.

"How – how did you discover this?" Francis asked, his voice thin with surprise. "And if you knew of his true identity, why did you not say?"

Sophia began to fiddle with her skirts, aware that she was going to have to tell Francis exactly what her relationship with the Earl had been. "I spent a great deal of time in his company, Francis." She saw her brother frown deeply, and was forced to draw in a breath to keep her resolve steady. "He was the gardener after all, and you know how much I adore being outside."

"Your roses," Francis murmured, his frown deepening still. "Pray tell me that nothing untoward was going on between you both."

Licking her lips, Sophia looked helplessly at her brother, knowing that she could not do as Francis asked.

Francis let out a loud groan and ran his hand through his hair before pressing his forehead into his palm. Sophia felt heat rise in her cheeks, suddenly unsure about where to look. Her breath came quickly as Francis simply looked at her, saying nothing. The silence stretched between them, making her more and more uncomfortable.

"I cannot imagine how difficult this has been for you, Sophia," Francis murmured, eventually. "I assume that he did not tell you his true identity from the start?"

Stunned at the sympathy in his voice, Sophia nodded. "No, he did not."

Francis shook his head, his eyes dimming. "Then you must be heartbroken, my dear sister. To discover that, not only was he hiding his true identity from you but also was attached to another...." He sat forward and reached for her hand. "I am deeply sorry for the hurt that you have experienced."

Sophia tried to speak, but the unexpectedness of his kind words to her forced tears to her eyes. She had thought that Francis would be angry with her, furious even. Instead, he had overlooked her impropriety and lack of wisdom and had simply considered how hurt she must be. His kindness was more than she deserved.

As she began to cry, she heard Francis pull his chair closer to hers before putting one arm around her shoulders and pressing his handkerchief into her hand. She was relieved that she had managed to tell Francis the truth, but the pain of watching David walk out of her life, his lies and secrets no longer hidden, had not lost any of its severity.

And yet, Sophia knew she would love him until the day she died.

CHAPTER 14

David's return to his townhouse had spread all around town within a few hours. His mother, still prone to dramatics, had put on a great deal of shock and surprise, which ended with smelling salts being waved under her nose. David was not taken in at all, standing irresolute as his mother sagged in her chair. Once she had fully recovered, he told her curtly that his stay was not to be of a long duration. He was only there to discuss his situation with her and his so-called betrothed.

And so, it was now that he was standing in front of his mother and Lady Viola Ermington who was looking at him with a wide smile on her face.

David glared back at her, but her smile did not falter. Apparently, she expected that, due to everything that had happened, there was no way for him now to escape her clutches. What with the second announcement in the newspaper over their betrothal, Lady Ermington seemed to believe that she was soon to be his bride. David smiled inwardly. She was about to discover that he was not a man who allowed himself to be told what to do.

"I have returned, as you can see," he began, holding up a hand to still the words of delight that he was sure were going to spill from his mother's mouth. "But that does not mean that I have done so willingly."

"You are not glad to see me?" Lady Ermington cried, sounding quite astonished. "Your betrothed?"

"We are not betrothed, Lady Ermington," David replied, curtly. "As you well know. This is simply a scheme you and my mother have concocted together, and I simply will not be a part of it."

To his surprise, his mother let out a trill of laughter. "Come now, David! You know that the notice has been in society papers at least twice. All of London is talking of your engagement to Lady Ermington. You cannot break such a thing now."

"I can and I will," David replied, firmly. "I have never asked Lady Ermington for her hand, as you both know."

His mother sniffed. "That is but a small detail, David," she stated, clearly refusing to believe that he was about to break the sham of engagement. "To leave Lady Ermington now would bring shame on both her and you and to our family."

David narrowed his eyes at his mother, knowing that it had been she who had come up with the entire scheme, having found Lady Ermington, a willing partner of course.

"Mother, I am here to tell you that I have fallen in love."

She gasped and clapped her hands, her eyes bright.

"Not with Lady Ermington," he continued, seeing the light in her eyes fade almost at once. "But with another dear lady who has been badly hurt by what has gone on here. She believes me to be engaged and has torn herself from me, despite my declarations of love." He took a breath, remembering how Sophia had looked at him when he'd admitted that she was right in the accusations she'd levelled at him. Pain sliced through his heart. "I have caused her distress by refusing to tell her the truth of who I was, but her pain has doubled because she believes me already engaged. That belief *must* come to an end."

His mother's mouth was ajar as she stared up at him, whilst Lady Ermington shifted uncomfortably in her chair. David said nothing but looked back at his mother unflinchingly. He was not about to listen to one of her tirades, intended to push him back down under her wing.

She had pushed and pushed until she had pushed him too far. David vowed that his mother would never have such an influence over his life again.

"Lady Ermington," he said, turning to the lady in question. "We have never been betrothed, and you are more than aware of that. To continue with such a falsehood is both morally and spiritually wrong." To his surprise, he saw a slight sheen of guilt cross the lady's face. "You know I have never loved you."

"I do not think such a thing matters, my lord," she answered, looking directly at him and giving a slight sniff of disdain. "What your mother says is quite right. We are, by all accounts, engaged."

"Not by my account," David growled, wishing that just one of the two women in front of him would simply accept what he was saying. "I have already sent a retraction to the paper." He had done so that very morning and had been assured that it would be in the paper in two days' time, and would remain there for a week.

Two gasps of shock met his ears, as two pairs of eyes stared at him in astonishment.

"But my reputation!" Lady Ermington cried, her eyes wide. "What of that?"

David shook his head, anger rising in his chest. "Did you really think that you could simply go along with my mother's schemes and have everything go just as planned? That I would simply accept my mother's intentions for me without question? I am not that kind of man, Lady Ermington."

His mother rose to his feet, her hand shaking as she pointed one finger at him. "You are a disgraceful son," she declared, loudly. "You have disappointed me over and over again, and now you are to bring shame on Lady Ermington and on this house! It is almost too much to bear!"

"I quite agree," David replied, calmly. "That is why I have already started preparations to remove you from this house – and from my estate. As I intend to wed soon, it is fitting that you retire to the Dower House."

His mother's face paled at once, her eyes still lingering on him as she collapsed into her seat.

"I have had more than enough of your meddling, mother," David continued, quietly. "And I will not have you near my bride, should she finally accept my proposal. I should have taken a firmer hand in my affairs a long time ago. It is only because of this convoluted and, frankly, disgraceful matter that I have finally seen what I should have done many months ago. And that is to my shame." He lifted his chin and looked down at his mother, feeling no pity for her. "You are to retire to the Dower house and live quietly, mother."

"And if I do not?" she asked, her voice thin and reedy although she glared at him nonetheless.

"Then you will find yourself with a skeleton staff and very little funds at your disposal," David replied, seeing the look of defeat in her eyes. "I do not wish to threaten you mother, but after what you have done, it is no less than you deserve."

"And what of me?" Lady Ermington asked, the fight gone from her also. "I am to have the embarrassment of being a woman who has had her fiancée leave her for another. And you have sent in a retraction without even considering me."

David turned back to Lady Ermington, not feeling even the slightest modicum of sympathy. "May I remind you, Lady Ermington that you agreed to this engagement without consulting me. For the record, I have issued a retraction stating that my *mother* was the one in the wrong," he replied, quietly. "You will carry some of that shame for a time, Lady Ermington, but I am quite sure you will recover. You should never have allowed my mother to embroil you in her schemes."

Lady Ermington opened her mouth as though she wanted to reply, but could find nothing to say. Instead, she slumped back into her chair, looking utterly despondent.

"If you will excuse me," David finished, giving them both a short bow. "I have somewhere to be." Turning to his mother, he frowned heavily. "And when I return, I expect you to already be at the Dower house, mother. Do not delay in an attempt to force me to feel any sympathy for you. Do not test me." He waited until his mother gave a feeble nod before turning on his heel and stalking from the room.

CHAPTER 15

Sophia was busy with her needlework when she heard Helena draw in a sharp breath, her eyes staring down at the paper she held in her hand.

"What?" she asked, slightly interested. "Is there some more shocking news that I should know of, Helena?" One eyebrow lifted slightly. "I do hope Richard is not embroiled in some kind of dastardly scheme so close to your wedding day!"

To her surprise, Helena closed the paper and gave her a quick smile. "No, not at all. Something did catch my eye, but it is of little importance."

"Then the wedding can go on as planned?" Sophia murmured, softly.

Helena laughed, folding up the paper and placing it beside the tea tray. "Yes, I believe so. It is tomorrow after all."

Frowning, Sophia studied her sister. There was something forced about Helena's laugh, and the way she had folded up the paper and put it away told Sophia that there was something within that Helena did not want Sophia to see.

"Now," Helena said, changing the subject entirely. "Is everything ready for tomorrow? I must admit, I am more than a little excited."

"Helena," Sophia asked, slowly. "What is it that was in there?" She put her needlework down and frowned at her sister. "Do not hide it from me, sister dear."

Helena's smile became fixed. "Sophia, you are being quite ridiculous." Sophia narrowed her eyes as she saw Helena's gaze flicker towards the newspaper. "Come now, I must ensure that everything is in place for my wedding day."

Sophia settled her shoulders, folding her hands neatly in her lap. "Helena," she said, firmly. "I am quite aware that you are not telling me the truth. You have never been much good at lying. Now, if you do not tell me what it is you have seen, then I shall pick up the paper and scour every page myself until I find whatever it was that has caught your attention." She kept her gaze fixed on her sister who, after a few seconds, shook her head and sighed.

"Very well," Helena said, heavily, her shoulders slumping. "I just do not want you to become distressed, my dear sister. After all, Lord Armstrong has not left your thoughts since he left, has he?"

Wondering what this had to do with David, Sophia pursed her lips but chose not to say anything. It was quite true. She had been unable to forget the man, and the pain over what he had done had not only grown deeper but came tinged with regret over her own actions. She had given him no time to explain, had simply called to an end everything they had shared. Now that a week had passed, Sophia wished that she had given David a little more time to tell her what truly was going on. He had insisted that he was not engaged, but her heart had not wanted to believe him.

Perhaps, if she allowed him to tell her everything, she might understand why he had chosen to do what he did. After all, it was quite a desperate thing to leave one's titled status and pretend to be a servant in another lord's household. To her regret, Sophia began to feel some sympathy for David, even though he was gone from her side. She could not imagine what had driven him to take on such a façade, but realized, in hindsight, that it must have been severe indeed.

"Here it is," Helena murmured, scrunching up her face and peering into the newspaper. "Be prepared, Sophia. This may come as something of a shock to you." And, so saying, Helena laid out the newspaper on the table and pointed at one particular area.

Was she about to discover that David had married? Had she been quite wrong in feeling any kind of sympathy for him? Her eyes lingered on her sister for a moment longer, thinking that perhaps she had made some kind of mistake in insisting that she read whatever it was Helena had been so surprised over.

Drawing in a deep breath, Sophia leaned forward and looked down at the paper, her eyes landing on the article Helena was pointing to.

"Statement of Retraction:," she read aloud. "A previous notice had stated a betrothal between a Lord W. and a Lady E. It seems, however, that this was quite in error and that Lord W. and Lady E. are not engaged. It appears that Lord W.'s mother, in her fright over her son's disappearance, chose to make such an announcement in the hope of encouraging Lord W. to return home. On his return, Lord W. became aware of the erroneous notice in the paper and now seeks to correct it. He hopes that society at large will forgive the error."

Sophia stared down at the notice, her voice growing wispy as she finished reading. David had been telling the truth. He was not engaged, not in the least. Tears blurred her vision as she looked up at her sister, hope beating wildly in her heart.

"I have made such a mess of things," she whispered, an ache in her throat. "I sent him away without giving him the chance to explain why he did such a thing."

"He did hide his true identity from you," Helena reminded her, gently. "You were badly hurt and confused over his behaviour."

"But I should not have ignored his desire to tell me the truth about what had happened," Sophia replied, dashing tears from her eyes. "Oh, Helena, I have been so foolish."

Helena studied her for a moment, frowning hard. "He has written to you, Sophia," she said, quietly. "I had not thought it wise to tell you, and, in truth, I have kept the letters from you for I did not wish to cause you any further pain. Besides, I was not quite sure what you would do with them" A slight smile lifted the corner of her mouth. "You might have burned them and then where would we be?"

Sophia nodded in understanding, knowing that she would, most likely, have thrown them in the fire, unread, such had been her state of mind. "How many are there?" she asked, hardly able to trust her voice. "One? Two?"

Helena's smile was gentle. "He has written to you at least once each day since he left."

"Oh." Sophia swallowed the lump in her throat as yet more tears came to her eyes. He had not left her alone, without any kind of hope. Through his letters, he was proving that his love for her was true. She was not sure what the letters contained, but she knew that they had to be of great importance. Suddenly, Sophia was desperate to read them.

"I'll fetch them at once," Helena said, evidently seeing the emotions on Sophia's face. "I won't be long."

Sophia nodded, her fingers plucking anxiously at the creases in her skirts. Would the letters tell her everything? Explain why he had been forced to hide his true identity from her? Would she get the chance to speak to him again, to apologize for sending him away without allowing him the chance to explain? She could still feel his lips on hers as he'd held her tightly in his arms, but she had been too numb to respond. The agony in his eyes had torn at her soul but, in the end, she had stepped away from him, thinking that she would never see him again. How wrong she had been!

"Here." Helena walked back into the room, her hands carrying a small, ribbon tied bundle. "As I said, there are more than a few."

Sophia could not stop her hands from shaking as she took the bundle from Helena, pulling gently at the ribbon that kept them together.

"I will leave you in peace for a time," Helena said, softly, pressing Sophia's hand. "You need some time to read these alone, I think. Do come and find me when you are ready. I shall be in the library, I think."

Her hands still on the letters, Sophia looked up at Helena and smiled, her heart lighter than it had been before. "I thank you," she murmured, gently. "It appears there might be hope for me yet."

"Of course there is," Helena replied, bending down to kiss Sophia's cheek. "The man loves you, and you love him. Let that knowledge be your guiding light."

Sophia nodded and smiled, her fingers breaking open the first seal as Helena left the room.

CHAPTER 16

Helena knew that the groom was more than a little surprised when she requested that a horse be saddled for her, but she was not about to go in search of Francis to ask for the carriage. In fact, she could not wait a single moment more.

The letters had held more than she had ever thought possible, her heart squeezing in sympathy for him, as well as with regret for her hasty actions. Now, she could understand why he had left his home and hidden himself away, although she would not agree that it had been the best course of action. Then again, she considered, as she pulled herself up into the saddle, she had never experienced the difficulties of having an entirely overbearing mother.

"Does the master know where you are going?" the groom asked, looking a little concerned. "Not to overstep, miss but...."

"My sister does," Sophia replied, gathering the reins. "I thank you for your concern, however."

Trotting out of the stables, she made her way out of the estate gates and down the road towards the nearby inn.

The letters had spoken of David's love for her in almost every sentence he wrote. He had begged her forgiveness over and over, promising her that the love he carried for her would never be quenched. In fact, even in their parting, it had grown until it had become so much of an ache that he had been forced to return to the estate.

However, he had not come knocking on the front door or sent a calling card to Francis. Instead, he had simply told her that he was staying in the local inn, and would do so for a fortnight, in the hopes that she would send for him. David's final letter had told her that he was about to leave forthwith, and that he was afraid that, in her lack of response to him, he might not have any hope of being reconciled to her again.

Her lack of response was, of course, due to Helena's diligence in keeping his letters from her, believing it to be in her best interests. Sophia could not imagine the agony David was suffering, sending off each and every letter but never receiving a single note in return, not even when he had explained everything to her.

She should have sent for him, of course, but her heart would not allow her to wait. Instead, she had hurriedly told Helena where she was going and, without a moment's hesitation, had left the room. Sophia was quite sure Helena would understand.

Her heart began to beat frantically in her chest as she approached the inn, seeing many people milling around outside. Would he still be here, even though his hope would be fading?

Pulling the horse to a stop, she waited until one of the stable boys took the reins and helped her to dismount before leading the horse away and leaving her entirely alone.

Taking a deep breath, Sophia stepped across the muddy ground towards the front entrance of the inn and, just as she was about to open the door, Lord Armstrong stepped out.

"David," she whispered, as his eyes landed on hers, his face paling slightly. "I – I read your letters."

She saw him swallow, apparently lost for words at the sight of her. He certainly looked different, now dressed in his gentleman's clothes with his hair swept back but he was still as familiar to her as the first day they had met. Sophia twined her fingers together as they stepped back to allow another patron entry to the inn, feeling herself shaking inside.

"I cannot believe you are here," David said, so quietly that she had to strain to hear him. "When I didn't hear from you, I thought...."

"You thought I had decided against you," Sophia finished, seeing him drop his head in shame. "But I have not, I assure you. Helena, my dear sister, kept your letters from me thinking that I was already going through enough." His head lifted, and he looked at her again. "She meant well, for had I received them earlier, I would have tossed them away without a second look. It was only when I read your announcement in the paper that I realized that you had been telling me the truth." She smile trembled somewhat. "You are not engaged." Her words ended in a breathy sob, and David nodded taking her hand in his at once and placed in on his arm.

"Might we walk, my love?" he said, softly. "I believe we have much to speak of."

Sophia nodded, unable to speak as she fought tears that had come all too readily to her eyes of late. She walked beside David for a good few minutes, until the inn was left behind them.

"There is a small bench just there," he said, eventually, nodding to a small wooded area to her right. "We might sit there for a time?"

"You have been here before?" she asked, looking up at him as they walked.

His smile was tinged with sadness. "I found this the first day I came to the inn and it has become my place of solitude. A place to sit and think, or even to pray." His hand tightened on hers. "How glad I am to be able to share it with you, although it is certainly not as private as our arbor."

The mention of the place where they had shared numerous kisses brought a blush to her cheeks and a warm glow to her heart. The man loved her still, and the memory of their embrace brought gladness to her instead of pain.

"Oh, Sophia," David murmured, the moment she had sat down.

"You must know how much I have been longing to see you again." His hand brushed over her shoulder and down her back, before taking her hand again. "Tell me that you have come to save me from my agony."

Frowning, Sophia studied him. "What do you mean?"

"You have not come, I hope, to tell me that all is lost and that I should stop writing to you?" he asked, his eyes searching her face. "I could not bear it if that were so."

A glad smile crossed Sophia's face, and she brought her hand to his cheek, seeing the way his eyes closed in relief. "Of course I have not," she replied, gently. "I love you so, David."

"How can you still love me after what I have done?" he asked, putting his hand over hers. "I should never have treated you so ill."

Sophia, knowing that it was important she was honest with him, set her shoulders. "I will not say that I think your scheme to hide from your mother and faux fiancée was quite ridiculous, but I realize now that you were verging on desperation." Her smile softened. "I cannot imagine what that must have been like for you."

He groaned and looked away. "I was, in truth, utterly desperate. I did not think that my mother would do anything of the like, but it just shows you how manipulative she can be. I realize now that I should have taken her controlling nature in hand some time ago, but never did. Perhaps if I had done so, she might not have behaved as poorly." His eyes met hers, filled with regret. "I must beg your forgiveness, Sophia, for having kept the truth from you. I should not have even come near you, but you drew me to you so that I was unable to do anything but come close to you. Your compassionate nature, your spirit and your beauty of both face and heart have convinced me that I cannot live this life without you by my side."

"When you left, I was broken," Sophia admitted, hating that she had sent him away. "I should have allowed you to speak, David. I should have let you tell me the truth about your engagement."

He shook his head, holding up his hand to stop her. "No, I will not allow you to take any guilt upon yourself when it is not yours to take. Your pain, your grief and sense of betrayal were all of my doing." His fingers lingered on her cheek, running down her jawline and sparking all kinds of sensations. "I am just grateful that you chose to read my letters and believed what was contained within them."

Struggling with her emotions, Sophia gave him a somewhat watery smile. "I have never doubted your love for me, David. Not after what we shared. I realised that your character had never changed, and, now that I understand your reasons for your deception, I find that I can forgive you."

She saw David's eyes close, heard the long breath he let out slowly. Her words had brought him relief, and, that moment, her own heart healed.

"I love you, David," she continued, framing his face with her hands. "Love overcomes, does it not?"

"It does," he whispered, finally opening his eyes to look into her face.

"And our love *has* overcome," Sophia said, smiling gently. "That is how I know our love will last, for even now, it grows with every passing moment."

His lips caught hers, and Sophia could do nothing but return his kiss, running her fingers into his hair. Tears slipped from her cheeks as they had done before, but this time, they were tears of joy.

"Say you will marry me," he begged, hardly drawing his mouth back from hers. "I cannot bear to think of my life without you. I do not want to be parted from you again."

Sophia laughed softly. "You might have to discuss the entire situation with Francis, but yes, of course, I will marry you. A future with you is all I have ever wanted, David."

"Then a future I will give you," he murmured, stroking the back of her neck with gentle fingers. "A future where I will ensure that you always know how grateful I am for you, how much of a delight you are to me. A future where you will know just how much I love you, each and every day."

Thinking that she had never felt so happy in her life before, Sophia rested her forehead against David's, simply resting in his embrace.

"And you shall grow roses," he finished, his lips now brushing hers. "As many roses as you wish."

Sophia smiled. "And perhaps a hidden arbour, where we might go when it rains," she whispered, before pressing her lips to his once more.

BOOK 5: MR. HENRY CATESBY AND THE REBELLIOUS REDHEAD

BOOK 5

HOUSE OF CATESBY

Mr. Henry Catesby & the Rebellious Redhead

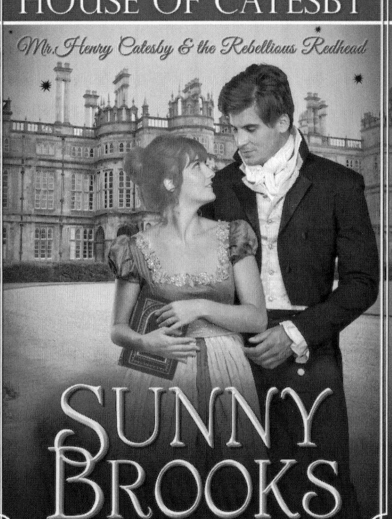

SUNNY BROOKS

FOREWORD

You are courageous, strong and worthy of happiness. Follow your heart, follow your curiosity, and stand up for what you know is best for you. I will be supporting you from afar.

- Sunny Brooks

CHAPTER 1

"Henry, I've decided that it's time for you to marry."

Henry did not immediately react, turning around slowly to view his brother Francis with a somewhat disinterested air.

"Is that so?" he muttered, putting his pencil behind his ear.

"It is," Francis declared, with a firmness that surprised Henry. "You are spending far too much time alone, doing....whatever it is you are doing....and you need a home and a family of your own."

That brought a twinge of worry into Henry's soul. He frowned, his eyes narrowing just a little. "You intend to throw me from your house, is that it?"

Francis, much to Henry's relief, looked horrified. "No, not in the least! This house is your own."

"Then why must I marry?"

"Because, as I have said, you are spending far too much time on your own and, after what happened with Sophie..."

Henry's brows furrowed. "Our dear little sister Sophie fell in love and married."

"Yes, but not without a great deal of confusion and heartbreak, which stemmed from a lack of responsibility on my part," Francis

377

declared, his expression grim. "I will not allow that to happen again. I have a responsibility to care for all of you."

"And you are doing so," Henry replied, gesturing to the house around them which had been given to him by Francis. "You need not concern yourself with me."

"You are by yourself far too much, Henry. I barely see you anymore. You need a wife to bring you back into the real world, to force you to think of something other than your studies. You are missing out on so much already."

Henry bit back a harsh retort. He was quite content with his life, with his solitude. Francis had no need to interfere in order to try and change it.

"And so you intend to force me to wed?" he asked, after a moment.

"Yes."

"What do you think will happen if I do not?" Henry asked, lifting one eyebrow. "That I shall become some kind of hermit, a family secret that everyone must keep hidden?"

Francis looked a little uncomfortable, his gaze drifting away from Henry as he evidently struggled to answer. Apparently, this was exactly what he was worried about.

Henry sighed, shook his head and turned back around to continue with his work. He was not about to become a recluse. The work he was doing was of value. At least he felt it had value, for he was in constant contact with other astrologers and they were making some excellent discoveries about the night sky.

"Henry. I mean it. If you do not start making an effort, then I will find a bride for you. At least attend some social occasion or other. It is not too much to ask, is it?"

"Oh, do go away, Francis," Henry sighed, wanting nothing more than to lose himself in his work. He heard his brother huff, muttering something under his breath but, much to his relief, Francis eventually left Henry's small study and shut the door behind him.

"Thank goodness for that," Henry said aloud, putting his pencil down and sitting back in his chair with a heavy sigh. Whatever was Francis thinking, trying to get Henry to marry? Henry was fond of his own company and therefore had always been a little off-put by the idea of marriage. Not that it was a bad thing, given how happy his parents had been, but Henry knew it was not something he wanted for himself. After all, being the third son – albeit by only a few minutes – he did not need to marry. Charles, Henry's twin brother, was married and settled and Francis, the eldest and the new Mr. Catesby would soon enough find himself a wife and heir. Why he had not done so already was quite beyond Henry, for surely Francis should be most concerned about producing an heir at the earliest opportunity rather than ensuring his brother was wed.

Then again, Henry could not pretend that Francis had not been very good to him. He had, after all, given Henry a smaller house all of his own, where he could work in peace and quiet. It was not Henry's by deed, but Francis had made it quite clear that he was to treat it as his own home. It bordered Francis' larger estate so that Henry was never too far away, yet managed to have a place he could call his own.

The only trouble was, Francis could visit whenever he chose, interrupting Henry's work. Of course, it helped that Henry was busy enjoying the stars and learning as much as he could about them, which meant that during the day, he was often asleep. When he was not asleep, Henry had found he also enjoyed cultivating plants. He was growing a wide variety of new and interesting flowers in his small greenhouse at the back of his home. Francis did not intrude on him there, at least.

Henry liked his solitude and, given that he had a rather large fortune of his own, had very little else to worry him. There was no need for him to find work, nor any need to marry and produce an heir. He was able to just do what he pleased and, instead of throwing himself into pleasures had chosen to take a more studious route. He had truly never had any kind of thoughts on matrimony or the like. The subject simply did not interest him.

"Besides, what kind of lady would accommodate me?" he muttered to himself, writing down the details of his last stargazing study. A lady who would be willing to see very little of her husband and would allow him to work, uninterrupted day or night. Henry doubted that Francis would be able to find any woman suitable for him, despite his threat of practically bringing a bride to his door.

No, there was nothing to worry about. Francis had more than enough to engage his thoughts. Henry was sure his eldest brother would soon forget about his bachelorhood altogether and focus on his own responsibilities instead. Turning his thoughts back to the papers in front of him, Henry let out a small, contented sigh and forgot about the matter entirely.

CHAPTER 2

"Laurie!"

Miss Lauren Davenport shrank back as her father, Viscount Munthorpe, stepped into the library, his dark eyes piercing the gloom.

"Laurie, are you in here, girl?" he shouted, his voice so loud it practically rattled the ornaments on the mantlepiece. "Lord Umbridge is here to see you."

Laurie winced, hoping that the curtain would hide her from his view, even though it was only partially pulled. She did not want to see either her father nor Lord Umbridge and had intentionally hidden in the window seat of the library, book in hand. Thankfully, it was a rather dreary day which had turned the room somewhat gloomy, hiding her presence even further. Laurie was glad she had chosen not to emerge in order to warm herself by the fire, even though her skin prickled with cold.

"Where is that blasted girl?" she heard her father mutter, his footsteps moving towards the door. "Lord Umbridge is a perfect match for her. If only she would see sense." The door closed with a quiet click behind him and Laurie let out a long sigh of relief.

She was more than aware that Lord Umbridge was her father's

chosen suitor, but she could not warm to the man. She had met him on more than one occasion and, whilst pleasant enough, there was something about the manner in which he regarded her that sent a wave of nausea right through her. It was as though he saw her as nothing more than a possession, something that belonged to him. Laurie leaned her head back against the dark brown wood of the window seat and let out a soft chuckle. Well, Lord Umbridge would have to learn that she was not about to acquiesce to his demands now or ever. She was quite determined that she would not have him, nor him her.

It was not as though her father was a cruel man but rather that he saw her as she truly was – a red-haired, freckled, curious soul with very few airs and graces, and certainly none of the attributes a young lady of her position ought to have. This was despite the years of training and tutoring, which had brought her no pleasure. Her watercolors were blurry, smudged things, her voice held no graceful tune, and her piano playing made the stable cats yowl in fright. No, Laurie had shunned those things the very moment her tutors had thrown up their hands in frustration – and had refused to do anything of the kind any longer.

Her father despaired after her, and that was the only thing that made Laurie grieve over her lack of accomplishments. How she wished she could prove to her father that she did not need to be able to paint beautifully in order to be seen as a successful young lady but, try as she might, he could not see her that way. He loathed the term 'bluestocking' and quite forbade her from reading any such books that might add to her own knowledge – not that she had listened, of course. She longed to learn more about the world she lived in, to find detailed descriptions of places she had never even heard of before. The only interesting place she'd visited outside of her father's country estate had been London and then only for one rather disastrous Season some three years ago now.

Cringing, Laurie tried not to allow the memories of what had occurred in London to flood her mind, but they could not be stopped. She had been so young and so innocent, entirely unaware of what a gentleman's intentions might truly be. With no mother to speak of – for hers had died in bringing Laurie into the world – she had been given a Miss Stanley as her companion, who spoke very little but watched everything. Being an unmarried spinster, she was around the age Laurie's mother would have been and ensured that Laurie was not allowed to escape her notice in any way. Even now, Laurie could still remember the sharpness of her eyes when she had found Laurie and Lord Longleat in a rather intimate embrace.

Laurie's cheeks burned. She had thought that, when they had been discovered, Lord Longleat would declare his love for her and demand they marry at once. Instead, he had just laughed in her presence, ignored her whispered pleas, and stormed back inside.

Miss Stanley had taken her home and put her to bed, speaking to her quietly and calmly, without any hint of anger or disappointment. That had been the day Laurie had learned to be careful around gentlemen. She had felt ashamed at what she had allowed Lord Longleat to do in taking her to a secluded part of the gardens and kissing her senseless, his hands roving wildly over her body. Being a little more aware of the reality of things now, Laurie concluded that he would have taken her virtue, had she let him, with very little consideration. Apparently, some gentlemen lived for such things and being as innocent as she had been, she had presented no challenge to Lord Longleat.

At least she had learned her lesson before it was too late.

Laurie let the cool air calm her warm cheeks, recalling how she had refused to return to London for another Season. Her father had been both frustrated and relieved, evidently pleased to be able to stay at his estate during the Season. Although, he had informed her that he did not intend for her to remain a spinster for the rest of her days. She would have to find a husband from somewhere.

Laurie had not taken his words with any degree of severity. She needed time to forget what had occurred and had, with great abandon, thrown herself into learning all she could about the world around her. All thoughts of gentlemen were gone from her mind, replaced with something that held a great deal more interest for her. She could not imagine Lord Umbridge allowing her to continue her own personal studies, however. He would be just as her father was, telling her repeatedly that such a thing was not for a lady of her age and inclination. There would be no more reading and studying if she were to marry him.

"Then I shall not," she muttered to herself, putting her book down and wrapping her arms around her knees. "I shall not marry him."

"Then what shall become of you?"

Laurie let out a shriek, clapping one hand over her mouth as the curtain was pulled back to display a rather disgruntled looking Miss Stanley. Her greying hair was pulled back into a tight bun as it usually was, her dark brown eyes a little narrowed as she planted her hands on her hips, clearly irritated with Laurie's behavior.

"Your father has been looking all over for you," she said, rather disapprovingly. "Lord Umbridge wishes to see you."

Frowning, Laurie pulled the curtain back in between herself and Miss Stanley, hiding away again. "I have already made it clear that I do not wish to spend any more time in that man's company," she said, firmly, refusing to listen to Miss Stanley's tut of disapproval. "He wants to marry me and father is apparently delighted by the idea, but they forget that they will need my consent if such an arrangement is to take place. I do not intend to give it to them."

"Then I ask again, what shall become of you?" Miss Stanley asked, her voice a little muffled from behind the thick curtain. "Your father will pass away one day and then where shall you go? It is not as though you have an elder brother who will take you in. In fact, I do not recall if there is any family who would care for you."

Laurie swallowed, her blood running cold. "No, there is not," she answered, truthfully. "I have not considered what I might do."

Miss Stanley slowly pulled the curtain back once more, a rather sympathetic expression on her face. "You must think carefully, Laurie. This is not something to be ignored simply because you do not like Lord Umbridge. This is about your future and what you intend to do with your life."

Laurie's shoulders slumped. "What *can* I do with my life?" she muttered, looking out of the window across the gardens. "I have no prospects other than a rather decrepit gentleman who does not care for me, and all I want to do is to explore and discover and learn!" Shaking her head, she sighed and rested her chin on her knees. "What other gentleman is there that might consider me?"

There was nothing but silence in response. Laurie felt the weight of her future resting on her shoulders and, when she turned to speak to Miss Stanley again, she saw that her companion had left.

Deciding on her future was not something Miss Stanley could help her with, in the same way that her father could not force her to wed Lord Umbridge. These were matters that Laurie had to take into her own hands and figure out for herself. But what else was there for her to do? She could not run away, for she had no fortune of her own. Her dowry came to her on her wedding day, should that ever happen, which left her with nothing but her pin money – and she could not exactly live on that!

"I don't know," Laurie murmured to herself, leaning her head back against the wall, feeling much more burdened than before. Whatever was she to do?

CHAPTER 3

"Lord Umbridge."

Having been quite unable to remain in hiding for the rest of the afternoon and having heard from her companion that Lord Umbridge was to stay about the house until she made an appearance, Laurie had not had any other choice but to walk to the drawing room to greet him.

Lord Umbridge rose to his feet at once, a lewd smile instantly settling on his somewhat repugnant face. Laurie's face burned as she curtsied, immediately averting her eyes. Lord Umbridge was much too obvious with his thoughts and she found that she disliked that intensely.

"Where have you been, my girl?" her father asked, with a smile on his face but a steely look in his eye. "I have been searching all over this house for you."

"Have you?" She put an innocent grin on her face. "I was reading outdoors in the arbor, father."

His eyes narrowed slightly. "Is that so?" he murmured, throwing a glance towards the window. "I find that most....unlikely."

She did not let her smile slip for even a second. "You know how much I enjoy reading, father."

This comment did not go by unnoticed, for her father's brow furrowed and he said nothing more, although his lips were held in a thin, tight line. It was another reminder to her of just how much he disliked her bluestocking tendencies.

"It does not matter, I assure you," Lord Umbridge said, directing his words towards Lord Munthorpe. "I am *very* glad to see you, Miss Davenport."

Laurie tried not to cringe as he took her hand in his and bowed over it. His palm was rather sweaty, making her want to tug her hand back and wipe it on her handkerchief. Praying that he would not allow his lips to touch her skin, Laurie waited impatiently for the long, lingering bow to end.

Finally, Lord Umbridge released her, allowing her to take her seat opposite both her father and her supposed beau. Her father muttered something about requiring a fresh tea tray and got up to ring the bell, allowing Laurie a few minutes to regard Lord Umbridge with fresh eyes.

She had managed to avoid him for quite some time – and would avoid him again after this particular visit. In looking at him now, she confirmed to herself that he certainly had not improved since the last time she had seen him. Being a good many years elder than she, although she could not be sure of just how many precisely, he was tall and somewhat rotund, with jowls that seemed to move of their own accord any time he spoke. His small, dark eyes were fixed on hers, that leer capturing his lips with a permanency that left her shuddering. She knew precisely what it was he wanted from her and was not about to give it to him. There was no possible way she could accept his court and certainly not his hand in marriage. She would rather be a spinster than have to warm Lord Umbridge's bed!

"My dear Miss Davenport, may I say that you look quite wonderful this afternoon."

His words were dripping with sweetness, but the taste of them made her stomach curl.

"You have such a freshness about you," Lord Umbridge continued, as Viscount Munthorpe came to seat himself again. "A vitality that lights your eyes and gives you such a brightness that one can barely look away!"

I wish you would look away, Laurie thought to herself, somewhat mortified that Lord Umbridge was still refusing to let his gaze drop from her for a single moment. Aware of her father's sharp look in her direction when she did not reply, she finally managed to say, "You are very kind. I thank you."

This seemed to satisfy Lord Umbridge, at least, for he beamed at her in delight, his hands clasped together as they settled over his chest. Apparently by her few simple words, she had somehow given him the impression that there was some sort of hope.

"Where has that tea tray got to?" her father muttered, shaking his head darkly. "I must go in search of it." Rising to his feet again, he shot a quick glance towards Laurie, who immediately felt her heart begin to thunder wildly within her chest, panic stealing away her breath. Surely her father did not intend to leave her here with Lord Umbridge? It was most improper, for one, even if he only intended it to be for a few minutes.

"I quite understand," Lord Umbridge murmured, a dark glint in his eye that made Laurie rise to her feet in fright.

"I can go, father," she stated, quickly, hurrying towards the door. "You need not trouble yourself."

"No, no," Lord Munthorpe grated, pressing one firm hand flat against the door of the drawing room, his eyes glaring at her. "I insist you remain here with Lord Umbridge. I will not be long. After all," he finished, his voice dropping to such a low whisper that she could barely hear it. "After all, you have been avoiding him for such a long time that I have no intention of allowing you another exit."

Laurie's eyes widened but she was forced to step back, knowing that she was to be denied her escape. Her father was pushing her toward Lord Umbridge with a greater urgency than she had expected. Surely he must understand why she did not want to marry Lord Umbridge! Was he truly intending to force her hand in this matter?

"My dear Miss Davenport, you are *very* kind in wishing to aid your father," Lord Umbridge murmured, as she dragged herself back to where she had been sitting. "But you need not worry. He will be back very shortly, I am quite sure."

At least he has left the door open, Laurie thought to herself, as the sound of her father's footsteps echoed down the hallway. Struggling to come up with something to say to the still leering gentleman, Laurie averted her eyes and stared at the fire burning in the fireplace, thinking that it would be best not to give him any further encouragement.

"You cannot be ignorant of my reasons to call upon you, Miss Davenport."

Lord Umbridge's voice was breathy, moving to the front of his chair as he spoke as though his earnestness would beguile her in some way.

"Indeed, Lord Umbridge, I am quite at a loss," she lied, with a slight shrug. "I thought perhaps you and my father had estate business to discuss."

Lord Umbridge chuckled darkly, apparently not taking offence. "You are much too innocent then, Miss Davenport. No, indeed, it is not business nor your father that has brought me to this house time and again. It is you."

Her stomach twisted, her skin crawling as she threw him a quick glance, trying to hide her repugnance and her fear. "I see," she murmured, not quite sure what else to say.

"I have every hope that you will one day soon become my bride," Lord Umbridge said, with a good deal of satisfaction in his voice. "*Very* soon."

"I am surprised you have such hope," Laurie replied, quickly, refusing to allow him to hold onto this belief. "I have never heard of your intentions thus far and certainly have not had time to consider them."

Lord Umbridge shook his head, his eyes narrowing. "You may play these games with me, Miss Davenport, but you forget that I know the truth already. Your father has made it quite clear that he will induce you towards matrimony and I have every hope of his success."

Before she could say a word, he was out of his chair and bending over her, his hand grasping hers before she could move. Frightened, she shrank back, seeing the fervor in his eyes.

"I *will* have you," he hissed, his face lowering closer and closer to her own. "You must understand, Miss Davenport. I intend to get whatever it is I wish. I have long desired to have you as my wife and very soon, my desires shall be fulfilled. It would be best for you not to refuse me."

Her stomach was twisting this way and that with fright but, lifting her chin, she held his gaze steadily, refusing to allow him to intimidate her.

"I think, Lord Umbridge," she stated, quite calmly. "That you will find yourself denied in this present situation. Whatever my father has said to you, I can assure you that he has not said a word to me as yet. I have no intention of agreeing to any such engagement."

Lord Umbridge's face grew dark. "We will see, Miss Davenport."

It was with great relief that the sound of her father's voice hurrying the maid along the corridor came between them, forcing Lord Umbridge to let her hand go and make his way back to his seat. Her breathing a little ragged, Laurie sat up, her head still held high, her anger beginning to burn.

Lord Umbridge might try to intimidate her, might try to force her into marrying him, but she was not the obedient, weak willed woman he thought her to be. No matter how hard he tried, she was not about to let him hold a hand of fear over her throat. She was stronger than that. She was stronger than both Lord Umbridge and her father.

"We will see, Lord Umbridge," she muttered aloud, as her father walked into the room with a broad smile on his face, acting as though he was doing her a great favor by allowing them time alone. "We will see who will be the victor in all of this. I have very little doubt that it will not be you."

CHAPTER 4

"Oh no, not today!"

Glancing out of his window, Henry saw a rather familiar figure riding towards the house and, without hesitation, grabbed his coat, pulled on his hat, and slipped out of the house using the back door.

Francis was not about to catch him today, only to rabbit on and on about Henry's need for a wife. Over the last sennight, it had become an almost daily occurrence and one that Henry could very well do without. The only time he had managed to quiet Francis had been when he had mentioned the fact that Francis himself was without a wife and should he not be leading by example. On that day, Francis had left Henry's home without another word, only to return the next day with a multitude of reasons as to why his own current matrimonial state had no bearing on Henry's.

The cool air brushed at his cheeks as he hurried outside, hearing the hooves drawing ever closer. Francis would be disappointed today. Moving quickly through the small garden, Henry slipped through the gate and into the trees that lay just beyond it. Moving through the trees carefully, he soon saw Francis slip from his horse and tie the reins to a post before walking purposefully towards Henry's front door. He knocked once, then twice more, before beginning to gesticulate wildly, exclaiming loudly that Henry was being more than a little ridiculous.

"Ha!" he triumphantly exclaimed, a trifle more loudly than he had intended. The sound echoed through the trees, making Henry shrink back into the shadows, hoping that Francis had not heard him.

Apparently, he had not.

Relaxing a little, Henry continued to peer out of the trees towards his brother, seeing Francis try the door handle. Discovering that the house was open, he disappeared inside as Henry chuckled to himself and leaned back against the tree trunk. Francis would soon discover that he was not at home and, in all likelihood, simply return to his own house and try again tomorrow.

"I'm not leaving, Henry!" Francis shouted, his voice muffled as he strode through the house. "I know you're here somewhere."

A frown appeared on Henry's brow as he waited, wondering what Francis intended. Surely he did not think to wait for Henry to return so that he could simply talk to him again about matrimony. That would be ridiculous.

"I have Miss Smythe and her father calling tomorrow," Francis called again, sticking his head out of the front door and looking all about him. "You are to attend, Henry. I know you are avoiding me, but I will not be so easily put off!" Henry shrank back just as Francis's gaze narrowed, scanning the trees, still unable to locate his brother. "A cup of tea while I wait, mayhap."

Muttering a curse under his breath, Henry took a deep breath and tried not to acknowledge the fact that he would now be separated from his work for a good hour or so. Francis did not look as though he was about to be put off, but Henry had no intention of returning to his house so that his brother would succeed in his intention of giving an invitation to join him when Miss Smythe came to call.

If he was not at home, he would have no knowledge of it. Which, therefore, meant he would not have to attend. However, his plan would only succeed if he was able to avoid Francis and that meant staying away from his home until Francis had given up and gone.

"He will find me more resolute than he expects," Henry muttered to himself, turning away from the house and storming through the trees.

Branches cracked under his feet, the sound echoing through the forest, but Henry did not care. It was a little cold, given that it was the turn of the season and heading quickly towards the autumn, but Henry simply tucked his hands under his arms and continued on his way. He was frustrated with his brother, frustrated at his insistence that Henry find himself a wife when Francis himself was still a bachelor. As far as Henry was concerned, Francis ought to look after his own matters first before bothering Henry!

He did not know where he was going, although the forest was not particularly dense. His irritation slowly began to lessen as he made his way through the trees, kicking at pinecones as he walked. His determination grew as he went further away from home. Francis would not succeed. If he had to wait even until the morning before he could return home, then Henry would do it.

The light began to grow as he walked and, looking up at the branches above, Henry realized that he was drawing near to a clearing. Pausing, Henry looked out ahead of him, only to see a small, tumbledown shack right in the middle of the woods. The trees had been cleared around it, and there was even a small garden – although it was quite wild at the moment. From the looks of it, no-one had lived here for a rather long time. There was no smoke rising from the chimney, and the front door looked to be a bit rotten.

Henry's heart lifted. Here was a wonderful space where he might escape, where he might come to hide whenever Francis tried to seek him out. Whilst the shack was on Francis' property, Henry was certain his brother would know nothing of it. It was not as though Francis often ventured into the woods. He had far too many other things to keep him busy.

Moving through the trees towards the shack, Henry smiled to himself at the discovery. The sound of rushing leaves surrounded him and a peace crept into his heart, pushing away the frustration and irritation Francis had brought him. Pausing, he listened hard for any signs of life, but all that met his ears were the sounds of the forest.

"Hello?"

His voice echoed softly through the forest, with only the occasional falling leaf rustling to the ground to capture his attention. There did not seem to be anyone else about.

Tentatively, he pushed at the door and, much to his surprise, it opened without resistance. The musty air tickled at his nose, making him wince as he stepped a little further inside.

There was no-one to be seen. Dust floated in the lazy beams of light that shone from the grubby windows, and everywhere he looked, all he could see was dirt.

His shoulders slumped. This shack needed a great deal of repair, which he did not have the skill to do. And if he were to ask Francis' men for advice, then news would surely get back to Francis, which was entirely what he had intended to avoid.

Sighing, Henry looked all about him, wandering through the three small rooms. They were each as dirty as the next, and it appeared that there were a great many small rodents who had taken up residence. Not that Henry cared about such things, although he did want to ensure that the shack would not fall down around his ears should he decide to come out here again.

Setting his shoulders, Henry drew in a deep breath and tried to regain his focus. A little dirt was not going to dissuade him, was it? Surely, if he set his mind to it, he could have this shack to rights within a week – provided it was safe, of course.

"I could have a desk here," he murmured to himself, moving towards the window that looked out over the clearing. "The natural sunlight would give me enough to see by, and I might even have a view of the stars at night." A small smile settled over his face as he continued to look around the rooms, seeing them all in an entirely new light. It would take a great deal of hard work but, should it come to rights, then it would provide him with a wonderful space all of his own.

"Away from Francis," he murmured, a slow feeling of satisfaction settling over him. "Away from his constant haranguing." Francis was not likely to come into the forest to search for him, he would simply have very little idea of where Henry was. Chuckling to himself, Henry sat down in a rather dusty chair – hoping it would not shatter beneath his weight – and when it held fast, settled back into it.

"Wonderful," he said to himself, closing his eyes as he thought of the many happy days he would spend here in privacy. "It will be simply wonderful."

A sudden thump caught his ear and, as he jerked to attention, he saw the door fly open, and a rather disheveled young lady stagger into the shack. She slammed the door behind her and leaned heavily against it, her eyes closing as she slid down to the floor.

"Good heavens!" Henry exclaimed, getting to his feet. "Whatever is going on here?"

Her eyes widened to stare back at him, dust billowing around her as it caught the gloomy light from the dirty windows.

"Explain yourself!" Henry continued, firmly. "Who are you and what are you doing in my cabin?"

CHAPTER 5

L aurie stared at the gentleman standing inside the run-down old shack, not quite sure what to say. He was clearly rather upset with her sudden entrance but there was a slight uncertainty to his gaze that told her he was not altogether sure of her.

"*Your* cabin?" she puffed, slowly getting to her feet and aware that he was not making an attempt to assist her in any way. "I do not believe that this is your cabin, sir."

He planted his hands firmly on his hips. "Mister Henry Catesby, *if* you don't mind."

Laurie took him in with a little more curiosity. "How good to meet you. Miss Lauren Davenport." She finished with a quick curtsy and slight amusement playing on her lips. "Daughter of Viscount Munthorpe."

She looked at him steadily now, not caring that she was alone with a gentleman in a broken old shack in the middle of the woods. It was not as though anyone would find them, for she had made sure not to be seen. Henry Catesby must be the brother to the new Earl Catesby since these woods were on his grounds. The grounds, however, were large, and so she had not thought that anyone would find her should she trespass onto them.

"Why are you in my cabin, Miss Davenport?"

The question was brought forth from terse lips, punctuated by green eyes that flashed as he spoke. His brows were knotted, his dark hair adding to his wrathful appearance. It was more than clear that he was not happy with her presence.

"My dear Mr. Catesby," Laurie began, brushing down her skirts so that she would not have to meet his gaze. "I was simply exploring, that is all. You see, I find my life so very dull at times, and short of my books, I have to seek ways to make it a little more exciting." She tilted her head and lifted her gaze to his face, seeing confusion slowly replace his anger. "Surely, you can forgive me for that, I think."

His frown deepened. "You appeared to be running from something."

She shrugged. "Just the rain," she explained, just as a thunderous clap rolled across the sky. "I was vastly surprised to see the weather change so abruptly and, just as the first few drops fell, I saw this cabin and hastened towards it."

The frown fell from his face and he hurried towards the windows, evidently searching for evidence that it was now raining. There was no sound of rain on the roof, nor on the windows but, as Laurie watched and waited, she heard another thunderclap followed by the steady beat of a thousand raindrops falling from the sky and hitting the earth.

"Just in time," she declared, coming away from the door and walking towards him. "Although it is about to get rather cold, I think." Shivering a little, Laurie wished to goodness she had thought to bring a coat instead of her flimsy shawl, but it had been very warm and sunny when she had first left the house.

"This is not appropriate," Henry muttered, stepping away from her. "You should not be here."

Lifting one eyebrow, Laurie studied him for a moment. "Do you really intend to throw me out of your little cabin in the middle of a thunderstorm?"

That realization deflated the wind from his sails a bit. A slightly abashed look crossed his face and he cleared his throat gruffly. "Well, no."

"Good. Then we may as well try to make a fire in the grate, don't you think?"

He cleared his throat again, looking away from her. "No, I don't think that would be wise."

Frowning, Laurie glanced towards the empty grate, only for something strange to catch her eye. With a gasp of surprise, she hurried towards it, realizing just why Mr. Catesby had been so reluctant to allow her to start a fire.

It was filled with nothing but cobwebs, spiders, and dusty old branches that she was sure would be riddled with insects. It was as if there had been birds nesting in the chimney.

A sudden thought struck her and, as she looked around the rest of the old shack, it continued to grow with certainty. The mustiness of the house, the thick layer of dust that lined every surface told her that this place had not been disturbed in a long time.

"You have never been here before, have you?" she said directly, looking at Mr. Catesby in the eye. "Is this your first time here?"

He shuffled his feet uncomfortably. "I do not think that is any of your business since this is still on my land."

"Your *brother's* land," she corrected, not caring as to whether or not he found her rude or overly blunt. "Does he know this place exists?"

Henry let out a long, frustrated breath before seeming to crumble just a little. "Miss Davenport, I would beg of you to keep this place entirely secret."

Feeling as though she were slowly peeling back a layer of Mr. Catesby's cold manner, Laurie laughed softly and shook her head. "My goodness, Mr. Catesby. If you are going to ask me such a thing, then I'm afraid you are going to have to give me a few more details."

He frowned and shook his head. "No."

"Then I find I have no inclination to keep this place to myself," she replied, airily. "I am sure my father will soon call on the new Earl, and I shall make sure to mention the tumbledown shack in the woods I stumbled across one day." Lifting one eyebrow, she saw Mr. Catesby let out his breath in a hiss, aware that she was riling him but yet finding that she somehow relished holding this particular secret over him. The truth was, she quite liked this place and found Mr. Catesby to be somewhat intriguing, even though it was clear he was very upset with her presence here. After all, had she not been searching for something new for her life, something to push her away from the quiet boredom that had surrounded her for so long?

"It does not matter whether or not I have been in this place for five minutes or five weeks," Henry said after a moment or two of thought. "It is not your property, and therefore, you are trespassing."

Laurie sighed heavily and shook her head, looking up at him with a wry smile. "It appears you are not willing to talk to me, Mr. Catesby." She tilted her head, regarding him carefully. "I shall be honest with you, however."

"If it will make you leave this place, then I beg of you to do so at once," Henry replied heavily. "I enjoy my solitude, Miss Davenport, so I would very much appreciate being left alone just as soon as you are able."

"Then we are very different in that regard," Laurie replied softly, her eyes flitting to the floor. "I am very much on my own, but find myself tired and dull because of it. My father is pushing me to marry a particularly disagreeable gentleman and so, whenever I hear he is to visit, I try my best to leave the house just as soon as I can." She gave a quiet laugh, her heart filling with a certain degree of pain. "It is just as well the weather has turned a little brighter, else I should be stuck within the confines of the house with no way to escape."

Looking up at him, she saw something flicker in his eyes, as though he understood what she meant. Her spirits buoyed just a little, she bit back a sigh and shrugged her shoulders. "It is to be inevitable I suppose, this marriage of mine, but I do so wish to try and escape it for as long as I can."

Henry studied her for a moment or two, his expression blank as he did so. Laurie felt herself being studiously examined, as though she were a puzzle he could not quite figure out.

"I am surprised to find that I understand your predicament," he admitted, after another few moments. "Although, I did not think that a young lady would be so unwilling to marry."

She laughed then, her hands on her hips. "And how would you feel, were the man your father thought you might wed looked at you as just another trophy to add to his collection?" Tugging at one of her red curls, a sad smile stretched across her face. "I know I am not a dazzling beauty, Mr. Catesby, but I am an only child, and my father has bequeathed me a large dowry. I know that this is the only reason Lord Umbridge wishes to marry me and I find myself disinclined towards him because of that."

The glint in Henry's eyes grew. "Indeed, I suppose that is to be considered. I can understand your lack of willingness in that regard."

"Thank you," Laurie replied, carefully. "That is why I am here, you see. I do not want to return home when I know Lord Umbridge is waiting. Can you not take pity on me and allow me to linger for a short time so that I might avoid his company altogether? After all, if I were to return home now, then he might think that I have hastened to meet him, giving him hope which I must then dash." She winced, looking away from him. "It is very difficult having one's life decided for them."

Glancing at Mr. Catesby, she was surprised to see that he was looking back at her with something like compassion and understanding, as though he too felt as she did. Holding her breath, she waited for his judgment to fall.

Henry sighed heavily, passing a hand over his eyes. "Very well, Miss Davenport, you may remain here for a time – although I will say that I do not much like being manipulated into doing so by threats of revealing this place to my brother."

She shrugged, not caring in the least what he thought of her but being rather glad that she was to get her way at least. There would be no need to return home as yet, and she could make the excuse to her father that she had been forced to shelter from the thunderstorm, which would take some of his anger and frustration away over her absence.

"Might I be assured of your silence on this matter?" Henry asked, folding his arms across his chest in what was either a defensive gesture or an attempt to keep himself warm. "Not that I think you will meet my brother any time soon, but still..." He trailed off, lifting one eyebrow and Laurie tried not to laugh.

"Yes, of course, Mr. Catesby. My lips shall not pass a single word about this place to anyone."

Relief etched itself across his features. "Very good, Miss Davenport." She watched him as he wandered across the room, taking in every dusty surface, every cobweb that stretched across the ceiling. It was going to take a good bit of hard work to get this place clean.

She shivered as the rain continued to pour down outside, a draft of air coming in through a crack in the window to wrap itself around her shoulders.

"Here."

She looked up in surprise as Mr. Catesby handed her his coat, leaving him in only his shirt and waistcoat.

"Please, take it," he said, not looking at her as he held it out. "You are cold."

The warmth of the coat was too much to refuse, and so Laurie took it from him and wrapped it around her shoulders at once. The relief from the cold was instantaneous, making her smile to herself as she drew it around herself.

"Thank you, Mr. Catesby, you are very kind," she said, gingerly sitting down in an old, rather dirty looking chair which he had only just now dusted for her. "Do you intend to restore this place? Set it to rights?"

Her golden-green eyes settled on the gentleman as he walked here and there, seemingly inspecting everything. He was intelligent, that was clear, given the sharpness of his eyes and the way he took everything in, considering it all carefully.

"Yes, that is my intention," he said crisply, not even turning around to face her. "Although, I do not know how long it will take."

She paused, an idea flickering in her mind. "I, I could assist you if you wish," she said slowly, seeing him jerk around to face her. "I *can* clean, after all. Although I confess, I am no good at unblocking chimneys."

He shook his head fervently. "No. It is entirely out of the question."

Rolling her eyes at him, Laurie shook her head, refusing to accept his answer. "And why is that, Mr. Catesby?"

"Because I do not want you here," he said, firmly. "Have I not made that quite clear, Miss Davenport?"

Growing a little frustrated with his tone, Laurie let out a long sigh, narrowing her eyes at Mr. Catesby. "Might you at least try to be civil, my lord? I am aware that this is not a situation you much care for but if you could at least discuss the matter with me, then I would appreciate it." She saw his face flush as he turned away from her again and knew she had hit on a weak spot. "Can you not tell that I am troubled with matters at home? Can you not see that this offer of help is not in any way an attempt to be in your company but, in fact, to bring myself a modicum of relief?"

She sighed again, aware that she was being much more frank than she ought to be, but continued on regardless. "If I were able to come here and assist you in the cleaning and restoration of this place, then for a time, it would give me a purpose in life. It would mean that I would not have to endure Lord Umbridge's company in the hope that, perhaps in time, he might give up his pursuit of me." She tilted her head, watching Mr. Catesby as he kept his back to her. "I would not even have to be here at the same time as you if you did not wish to so much as speak to me," she continued, growing desperate in her desire to convince him to let her help. "I can clean just as well with or without your presence."

"Miss Davenport."

Henry turned around sharply, his dark green eyes filled with something like anger.

"Yes, Mr. Catesby?" she asked, her chin lifted as she did all she could not to shirk from his evident frustration.

"Miss Davenport, I have neither a need nor a desire to aid you in any way," he said, firmly. "Have you never considered that it is I, in fact, who requires a place of solitude? A place where I might escape to also?"

He blew out a long, irritated breath, gesturing wildly as he spoke.

"No, you did not. You think solely of yourself and what you might gain from this rundown shack, without considering any of the consequences. What would your father think if he were to find you here? Would he be glad to know that you are spending time alone with a gentleman in the middle of the woods?" A harsh laugh escaped his tight lips. "No, indeed. He would insist that we marry and, Miss Davenport, I have no intention of marrying anyone at the present moment – and that includes young ladies who try to shoehorn me into it."

Anger burst in her like a furious fire, forcing her to her feet.

"How dare you?" she whispered, tugging the coat from her shoulders and throwing it at him. "How dare you think so little of me? It may come as a surprise to you, Mr. Catesby, but not every eligible young lady you run across thinks so highly of you. Not every young lady has a desire to marry, or to manipulate you into such a thing. You barely know me and, whilst I have spoken to you freely about the difficulties I face, it has only been in the hope that you might feel some compassion for my situation. I can see now that your heart is entirely selfish, and that it is wrapped up in thoughts and considerations only for yourself."

Storming away from him, she pulled open the door of the shack, suddenly uncaring about the cold and the rain outside. Mr. Catesby was not the kind of gentleman she wanted to be near, not after how he had spoken to her. Glaring at him, she lifted her chin, ignoring the astonished look that came over his face.

"Good day, Mr. Catesby," she said, narrowing her eyes at him. "I hope we never have the opportunity to meet again. Shame on you for how you have spoken to me."

And with that, she slammed the door hard, bringing a shower of dust down on her head, before hurrying out into the storm.

CHAPTER 6

Henry spent the next five days at the shack, only returning home to eat and to rest. He knew that Francis had been at his house on multiple occasions, having received various notes through his door, but he paid them no attention. In fact, he simply swept them aside, leaving them in a neat stack just outside the front door, held down by a paperweight. He wanted Francis to see them the next time he came calling with some ridiculous invitation for Henry to meet some eligible young lady.

The shack was nothing other than filthy from top to bottom, and Henry knew that his staff was rather astonished to find his usually pristine attire so dirty. He had taken to wearing nothing but an old shirt and pair of breeches whenever he went into the woods, not wanting to ruin any of his good jackets or cravats for the sake of a dusty old chimney.

The only problem was, however, that he could not get the ridiculous Miss Davenport out of his mind. She had left the shack in such a hurry that he had not been able to say a single word to her. He had not meant for his words to chase her out into the storm. Especially when she only had a thin shawl wrapped around herself, and to his frustration, he was concerned for her.

He hoped that she had managed to return home safely and had not taken ill from being caught in the rain. In addition, he regretted his hasty words to her, annoyed that he had refused her request so quickly and without due consideration. The truth was, he had disliked having an unexpected interruption in a place he had only just discovered. His mind had been filled with dreams of what he could do with it, what he could make it and how it could be his own secret hiding place, away from Francis and his constant haranguing.

And then Miss Davenport had appeared, resplendent in her rough beauty. He had been angry with her for disturbing his peace. In addition, he had grown angry with himself for noticing her red curls, for the way her eyes had glinted with flecks of gold as she'd looked at him curiously. He did not want to notice her, nor did he want to continue to think of her. But, yet he found that he could do nothing else. She was there regardless of what he wanted, or what he did not want. He could not get her from his mind, wanting to ensure – for whatever reason – that she was safe and well at home.

"Ah, there you are."

Henry jumped visibly as Francis walked into the room, having appeared out of nowhere. Henry, who had been busy preparing to go to the shack in the woods, ignored his brother entirely. His back remained turned until another voice sounded.

"Miss Davenport, Viscount Munthorpe, this is my brother, Lord Henry Catesby."

"How very good to meet you, Mr. Catesby."

He turned slowly, relieved that he had not, as yet, changed into his old attire to go to the woods. Miss Davenport was standing just in the doorway of his study, her green and golden eyes slightly narrowed with no smile lingering on her face.

"Miss Davenport," he said, slowly, inclining his head, before turning his gaze to the gentleman standing next to her. "And Viscount Munthorpe. Glad to meet you both, of course."

Viscount Munthorpe sniffed, a barely discernable cringe on his face as he let his eyes rove around the room. "So, you are one of those intelligent sorts, are you, Mr. Catesby?"

Henry bristled. "Yes, Lord Munthorpe," he managed to say, aware of Francis' sharp glance. "I suppose that is correct. I particularly enjoy studying the night sky."

"I see." Lord Munthorpe shrugged, clearly disinterested. "It is not really a subject that I find in any way fascinating. Not to judge, but I would much prefer a gentleman do something profitable with his time."

Francis cleared his throat, whilst Henry battled to keep his annoyance under control. "Henry assists me with the running of the estate," he said calmly, sending another glance in Henry's direction to ensure he was remaining as composed as he ought to be. "And he has written some very insightful papers that have been widely received."

Whilst Henry appreciated Francis's support, he saw that it was wasted entirely on Viscount Munthorpe, who now appeared to be bored with the entire discussion. Henry turned his gaze towards Miss Davenport, who had two spots of pink in her cheeks, clearly embarrassed by her father's behavior.

"May I enquire after your health, Miss Davenport?" he asked, hoping that he was not being too abrupt. "There has been a lot of rain this last week, and it has brought a certain chill to the air."

Her eyes remained dim. "I am quite well, I thank you, Mr. Catesby."

Swallowing, he inclined his head. "I am glad to hear it."

Francis was looking at him with a slightly puzzled expression, but Henry ignored him entirely, his mind still fixed on Miss Davenport, and wondering how he might engineer a quiet conversation with her somehow so as to apologize for his previous rudeness.

"Are you returning to the house?" he asked, turning towards Francis, who nodded in reply.

"We are to take tea with Lord Catesby," Miss Davenport said quietly, as Lord Munthorpe turned to leave the house entirely. "Do excuse us."

"Might I join you?"

Henry could see Francis' astonished expression but kept his focus fixed on Miss Davenport and ignored his brother completely.

"Of course you may," Francis replied, slowly. "I am sure Miss Davenport and her father would appreciate the addition to our company."

"Miss Davenport."

Henry offered her his arm at once, aware of the surprise that leapt into her eyes as he did. Much to his relief, she took it anyway. He escorted her out into the fresh air, making sure to leave Francis to accompany Viscount Munthorpe. As he walked from the house, Henry looked down at the lady on his arm. It appeared that she was doing all she could to turn her sight away from him.

"Miss Davenport, I must apologize to you," he said quietly, letting Francis and Viscount Munthorpe walk past so that he would not be overheard. "I have been thinking of a way to ensure that you are quite well after your excursion in the rain, and I am very glad to see that no harm has come to you."

She sniffed disdainfully and kept her head turned away.

"I know that you must be angry with me for my callous words, and can I assure you now that they were not harshly meant," he continued, hoping that she might at least glance up at him. "I was angry and upset, and I'm afraid that I allowed those emotions to overcome any consideration I should have had for you."

Laurie sighed and sent him a quick glance, her expression troubled. "You were rather rude, were you not, Mr. Catesby?" She sighed again, shaking her head. "And yet, I was also intolerably rude, speaking much too openly in the hope that you might take pity on me." She laughed sadly, her lips twisting as she did so. "Foolishness only, of course. I shall give you my apologies now, Mr. Catesby, in the hope that you might forgive me of such impropriety."

She was so different from how she had been when they had first met. There was none of that tenacity, no sign of the spark she had shown when they had talked. Instead, she was demure and proper, behaving just as an eligible young lady ought.

Henry hated it.

"Miss Davenport, might you wish to return to the shack?" he said suddenly, surprising even himself with such a question. "You indicated before that you might wish to…..spend some more time there, and I – "

"You made it very clear, Mr. Catesby, that I was not to set foot in what you deem 'your property,'" she interrupted firmly. "I must abide by that."

"I was wrong to speak so hastily," Henry countered, his frustration with himself only growing. "Please, Miss Davenport, if you would wish to return and to do what you can to help me in the restoration of the place, then I would be glad to allow that."

He held his breath as she considered his suggestion, not giving him any clear indication either way as to what she was thinking. He could not say why he had been so willing to allow her to return, after being so certain that he did not wish anyone else's presence in the shack, but he could not retract such a statement now. There was also the matter of propriety since they should not be in the shack together without the presence of a maid or some other chaperone, but he supposed that was a question that could be answered much later.

"You are something of a conundrum, Mr. Catesby," Miss Davenport uttered, as they approached the large manor house. "One moment you are ensuring me that you do not wish to so much as lay eyes on me again and the next, you are apologizing for your harsh words and inviting me back again." She turned her head towards him, arching one eyebrow in suspicion. "You have suggested that I am trying to trap you into matrimony by returning to the shack whilst you are present. Are you telling me now that you no longer believe this to be the case?"

Heat crawled up his neck, sending warmth into his face. "I was wrong to speak to you so, Miss Davenport. I can see that this Lord Umbridge – or whoever he may be – may be unsuitable for you and can understand why you seek a way of escape."

A quiet laugh escaped her. "Ah, so it is your first impression of my father that has brought you to such a decision, then?"

Henry considered this for a moment, before shaking his head. "I do not know what it is, Miss Davenport. Perhaps it is because I can understand what it is like to have the idea of matrimony thrust under your nose with the expectation that you will do just as you are told, or perhaps it is a realization that my behavior was shameful and improper." Looking down at her, he saw that her eyes no longer held the angry suspicion that had been there only moments ago.

"I was in the wrong to speak to you so cruelly and with such a lack of feeling, Miss Davenport. You are welcome to return to the shack whenever you wish, although I should say that perhaps an old, rather worn gown might be suitable if you did wish to return." He wrinkled his nose, recalling just how dusty it had been before. "My staff are having a great deal of trouble getting some stains from my crisp white shirts."

To his surprise, Miss Davenport laughed aloud, a tinkling sound that made the corner of his lips turn up. She smiled at him then, her expression open and free from all anger and frustration.

"Thank you, Mr. Catesby, I think I shall return to the shack. I have been in the doldrums these last few days, what with Lord Umbridge's constant attention and the fact that I have nowhere to escape to."

"You do now," he said, quietly. "Come and go as you please, Miss Davenport. I have taken two men with me to the shack on occasion to aid me with some of the more difficult tasks, but you may wish to bring a maid for propriety's sake, just in case our paths should cross."

Her smile spread, her eyes twinkling up at him. "Indeed, Mr. Catesby. I shall consider doing just that." Her hand tightened on his arm for just a moment. "And thank you, Mr. Catesby, for your kindness and generosity. It is gratefully accepted with true appreciation."

"But of course, Miss Davenport," Henry assured her, finally feeling a good deal more at peace now that he had finally resolved matters between himself and Miss Davenport. Perhaps, working together, they might be able to get the shack in decent order sooner rather than later. Although what she would do after that, remained to be seen.

"Perhaps I might visit tomorrow?" she asked, as Francis stood at the door of the manor house, waiting for them. "In the afternoon?"

He nodded, unable to explain the swirl of excitement that raced through him without warning.

"That would suit me perfectly, Miss Davenport," he agreed,

surprised to discover that he was already quite eager at the thought of showing her what improvements had been made at the shack already. "I look forward to it."

CHAPTER 7

L aurie smiled sweetly at Miss Stanley, who looked back at her suspiciously.

"Truly, I do not require your company for a short walk, Miss Stanley," Laurie said again, keeping her face entirely composed. "But I do thank you for your kind offer."

Miss Stanley frowned. "You are aware that Lord Umbridge is coming to afternoon tea with your father, are you not? I would hate to think that you are deliberately avoiding his company."

Realizing that her façade was not working on Miss Stanley in any away, Laurie let out a long, painful sigh and shrugged her shoulders before slumping back in her seat.

"I know you do not care for him, but he will keep you secure in your future," Miss Stanley continued before resuming her embroidery. "Besides which, you know that a lady such as yourself does not always get to do just as she pleases, no matter how much you might wish it."

Aware that her companion was giving her a little bit of a talking to, Laurie felt the old, familiar sense of frustration rising within her. "Be that as it may, Miss Stanley. I am not inclined to marry Lord Umbridge, despite my father's attempts to persuade me. I feel no regard for him and have decided, therefore, to ensure that my company is not often available to him when he visits my father." She lifted her chin, seeing Miss Stanley glance over at her. The older woman's expression showed nothing of surprise, though Laurie could see her thoughts at work as she continued her needlework.

"Miss Stanley," Laurie continued, quickly, "I know it is a great deal to ask of you but might you support me in this? You cannot truly believe that Lord Umbridge is a suitable gentleman for me, given that he is at least twenty years my senior at the very least. You know how he looks at me, how he does not particularly care about what I have to say or think, never showing me any interest whatsoever! I am nothing but a large dowry to him, another fortune he can add to his coffers."

Shaking her head, Laurie drew in another steadying breath. "I swear to you that I shall ensure you are taken care of for the rest of your days when the time comes for me to marry, but I cannot abide the thought of being wed to a man within age of my father." She suppressed a shudder, closing her eyes tightly. "I cannot bring myself to agree to such a union."

"You are not trying to manipulate me, I hope," Miss Stanley uttered, her eyes still sharp as they bored into Laurie. "You know very well that every companion's fear is what will become of them when they are too old to work any longer. But that is not something that you should capitalize on."

Laurie swallowed hard, awash with shame. "I apologize, Miss Stanley, if it appeared to you that I would only care for you should you aid me with Lord Umbridge. That is not the case. No matter what occurs with me, I shall make sure that you have a comfortable home in your elder years, whether that is in Lord Umbridge's home or in another gentleman's home entirely." She looked back at her companion with fondness, despite the embarrassment that still washed over her. "You know very well that I will always care for you, particularly after all you have done for me. Can I not ask for your help in this matter? Or have you grown tired of trying to guide me?"

Miss Stanley sighed heavily and put down her embroidery, turning to look at Laurie with those perceptive eyes of hers.

"Very well," she said after a moment. "Run along, and I will let your father know that you have gone out for a walk should he come in search of you." She frowned as Laurie let out a small shriek of delight, only for Laurie to clasp her hand over her mouth. "I think you must take a cloak with you, however, if you are not to return from your walk in the state you were in last time."

Laurie got to her feet at once, leaning down to kiss Miss Stanley on the cheek, seeing just a hint of a smile pulling at her companion's mouth.

"Thank you, Miss Stanley," she said, hurrying towards the door. "You are truly wonderful. And yes, of course, I will make sure to take my cloak."

Sometime later, Laurie approached the tumbledown shack in the woods with a degree of trepidation, which she could not quite explain. Was it because Mr. Catesby had been rather confusing the last two occasions she had met him? The first, he had been angry and frustrated with her, only to later apologize for his actions and request the pleasure of her company back at the shack whenever she wished it.

She could not quite figure Mr. Catesby out, although she had to admit that she found his apology both acceptable and well thought out. It was clear he *had* been considering her these last few days and the fact that he had been worried about her since then had to say something about him, did it not?

"Ah, Miss Davenport!"

She looked up as Mr. Catesby stepped out of the front door of the shack, which she realized, had been replaced by a new one.

"Good afternoon, Mr. Catesby," she echoed, carefully stepping over the ruins of what she assumed had once been a wall that had, perhaps, enclosed the house garden. "You have been busy, I see."

He smiled, although it did not quite reach his eyes. Laurie felt her heart drop to her toes, wondering if Mr. Catesby was, underneath it all, still rather displeased at her presence.

"Indeed I have," Mr. Catesby replied, offering to take her hand as she made her way to the front door so that she would not trip over a few large branches that had fallen from the trees above. "Would you like to come in and see?"

Accepting his hand, Laurie was surprised at the spark that shot up her arm, sending her head into a much quicker pace. She let his hand go the moment she was safely at the door, looking all about her as they walked inside.

"I have not managed to achieve a great deal in terms of cleaning the place," Mr. Catesby began, betraying nothing of the moment before. "Rather, I have been ensuring that the shack itself is quite safe. I am glad to say that it is now perfectly usable."

He gestured to the fireplace, where a small fire now burned in the grate, sending a wave of warmth towards her. "The roof has been fixed, the fireplace mended and cleared, and the windows, shutters, and front door either replaced or secured," he finished with a flourish. "Which is just as well, given that the weather is becoming a little cooler of late."

Laurie managed a small smile, still rather unsure what to make of this gentleman. "It is the autumn, I suppose."

He glanced at her, then smiled. "Yes, indeed. So it is."

They remained like this for a few moments, with neither speaking a word to the other, and Laurie felt her skin prickle with nervous anticipation. She was not certain what to say, still not sure whether or not Mr. Catesby was truly content with her presence here, but just as she opened her mouth to speak, Mr. Catesby cleared his throat and gestured to the room beyond.

"There is a key to the front door waiting for you in the kitchen," he indicated. "I have set it out next to the tea things." Seeing her surprised look, he shrugged, appearing a little abashed. "It made sense to give you a key, in case you should happen to come by and I am not yet here," he explained, his cheeks a little red. "There is a teapot, and everything else you require should you care to make yourself a pot. In addition, one of the men has found a small cellar just to the left of the kitchen, on the floor of what I think must be a pantry of sorts. He is clearing it out at this present moment, and milk can be stored down there if required. I shall bring some fresh each day, however, until it is quite ready."

She nodded slowly, tilting her head to regard Mr. Catesby a little more carefully. "Do you intend to repose here during the day, when it is quite complete?" she asked, curiously. "I know that you are interested in the stars and the like, but surely you cannot see anything much in the middle of the wood!"

He laughed spontaneously and, as he did so, his demeanor changed completely. No longer was he the serious, unsmiling gentleman who had first greeted her the day she had stepped into this place, but instead he was warm, friendly and welcoming, his eyes alight with mirth.

It was a sight that sent a sudden pang of affection deep into her heart.

"Indeed, Miss Davenport, you are quite correct," he said, laughing still. "In truth, I am not yet quite sure what it is I intend to do with this place, although I confess that it holds a great deal of delight for me as it is. To be so far away from any hindrances, any frustrating conversations and interruptions upon my time, that is a welcome thought indeed."

Her own smile faded as she realized that he was a rather solitary gentleman, which meant that once she aided him in cleaning the shack from top to bottom, then, most likely, she would not be welcome back again.

That is what you suggested, Laurie, she told herself, trying to smile at Mr. Henry Catesby. *You asked to come here in order to help Mr. Catesby in his restoration of the shack. Once that is over, you will have to return to your own life and, unfortunately, to Lord Umbridge.*

"I do not precisely know where to begin with the cleaning, however," Henry continued, looking about him with an expression of dismay. "There is just so much dirt and dust that I find I am at quite a loss to know where to start."

"And you are still willing to have my help in this matter?" she asked cautiously, wanting a little reassurance from him. "I am more than willing to do whatever I can to help, but I am still a trifle confused as to whether you truly wish for my company or not."

Henry cleared his throat, coming back to face her. "Of course, Miss Davenport, I would be more than happy for you to help me in putting this place to rights. That is why you are to have your own key so that you can come and go as you please." He looked over her shoulder towards the door, one eyebrow a little raised. "Did you bring a maid with you?"

She shook her head, a little embarrassed. "No, I did not. The less my father knows about where I am, the better."

Henry hesitated for a moment, before giving her a slight shrug. "Very well, Miss Davenport. I will admit to you that I find the whole situation a little untoward but hopefully, with my men around the place, there will be no impropriety."

"Just as long as my father does not find out where I am," Laurie mumbled to herself, catching Mr. Catesby's look of concern as he overheard her. Tossing her head, she walked past him into the kitchen, determined not to let thoughts of her father or Lord Umbridge concern her any longer.

The tea was set out on one countertop that had clearly been washed and cleaned, whereas the rest of the kitchen remained lined with dirt and dust. Laurie smiled to herself, looking over at the teapot and thinking just how much she would appreciate a cup of tea once her work for the afternoon was over.

"There is a well just outside the house, around the back," Henry said, just from behind her, making her start. "And whilst there is no stove to speak of, there is a place to hang a pot over the fire in the main room."

She nodded, suddenly aware of just how close he was to her. Turning to face him, she realized for the first time that he was dressed in nothing but his shirt sleeves, the formal attire she had seen him in on the last two occasions completely gone.

"Thank you, Mr. Catesby," she murmured, looking up into his eyes and seeing just how dark green they were, much darker than her own. His hair was still perfectly in place, in sharp contrast to her own red curls which were constantly falling out of whatever style she wore. Today's tight chignon was still having little effect on her freespirited curls, for even now she could tell that a few of them had sprung free and were dancing around her temples. She had a mad urge to rake her hands through his hair, to dishevel him completely just to see how he would react. But instead, she clasped her hands tightly in her lap, growing hot at such a ridiculous thought.

"I should leave you now," Mr. Catesby said quietly, as though he had seen her thoughts. "Do excuse me, Miss Davenport. Should you need me, I will be outside with my men, seeing to the garden wall and other matters to do with the exterior."

She mumbled her reply by inclining her head, only to raise it and see that he was already gone. Wincing, Laurie looked away from the sight of him walking towards the door, not wanting to let her eyes linger on him for any length of time. He was so proper, so correct, so formal – which was just what a gentleman ought to be, but she still found him very difficult to make out. She was unsure as to his motivations for asking her to return to the shack and was certainly at even more of a loss to decipher whether or not he truly did wish for her presence here. However, Laurie was determined to continue on regardless. After all, her main goal in coming here was to avoid Lord Umbridge and surely by the time the shack was completed, Lord Umbridge would understand that she was not at all interested in his suit. As for Mr. Catesby…

Laurie bit her lip, frustrated with herself for allowing her heart to quicken when he'd taken her hand, and for noticing just how dark his emerald eyes were. She did not need to consider him in any way and was determined not to eagerly seek his company out for any reason. Besides which, Mr. Catesby was quite obviously a solitary gentleman, looking for nothing more than his own company, his own thoughts, and his own space. There was no sense in pursuing any thought of a man who wanted to live his life alone, now, was there?

Pushing aside her thoughts, Laurie looked all about her and decided that she would begin with the kitchen, picking up where Mr. Catesby had left off. He had only cleaned one small countertop, but it was a start. Finding a basin already filled with cool, clear water, she dipped the waiting rag that sat next to it. Squeezing the water out of the cloth onto the dirty surface, Laurie let the moisture penetrate the dirt. After a second, she took up the bar of lye soap and began to scrub it through the dirt.

She had very little idea as to what she was doing, given that she was quite unused to doing such menial tasks, but surely it could not be all that difficult? Soap and water got almost everything out, as Miss Stanley had said to her on more than one occasion. Besides which, doing something like this would, at the very least, keep her mind from thinking about Mr. Henry Catesby.

CHAPTER 8

"Miss Davenport!"

Laurie jumped to her feet, suddenly aware that she was covered head to foot with dirt and soot and all other manner of things.

"Mr. Catesby," she hid a growing grin, putting one hand to her hair a little self-consciously. "As you can see, I have been hard at work this morning."

He stared at her, as though both horrified and amused at her appearance.

"But the kitchen is a great deal better, is it not?" she continued when he said nothing. "It is just the floor I am to finish and then I shall be on my way."

"You need not leave immediately, just because I returned."

She blinked, a little surprised, but gave him a quick smile. "Thank you, Mr. Catesby. That is very kind."

He cleared his throat again – a habit of his, she decided, when he was not quite sure what to say or do – then he put his hands behind his back, looking at her thoughtfully.

"My men have been busy in the garden," he relayed with slight hesitance. "The wall is to be repaired soon, and the ground turned. I am not quite sure what to plant in it as yet, but perhaps you might be able to make some suggestions?"

An unconstrained chortle escaped her before she could prevent it, startling Henry. Seeing that she would have to explain, Laurie shook her head and spread her hands wide. "I am afraid I shall disappoint you there, Mr. Catesby. I know very little about flowers or the like, although I am certain Miss Stanley would be able to give me some suggestions."

"Miss Stanley?" he enquired, looking a little calmer. "She is...?"

"My companion," Laurie explained, feeling something on her face itch as she wiped it with the back of her hand. "She will know what will take well and will be thrilled, I am sure, that I am taking such interest in flowers and the like!"

Henry colored and looked away, making Laurie wonder if she had said something untoward. He turned back, a stifled smile still evident, and gestured to her cheek, .

"You have some....dirt there, Miss Davenport."

"Oh."

Now it was her turn to blush. Whilst she knew she was in a dreadful state, the apron and her cap could be easily removed before she returned to the manor house, but smudges on her cheek or forehead would bring questions from Miss Stanley.

"Here," he offered, wringing out what appeared to be a fairly clean cloth from a bowl of water that stood on the countertop and handing it to her.

"Thank you."

She dabbed at her cheek, hoping she was reaching the stain, only for him to sigh and shake his head.

"A little higher, Miss Davenport."

Flushing all the harder, she did as he instructed. Finally, he stepped forward and took the cloth from her hand, grasping her chin gently with the other to tilt her face to one side.

Laurie froze, her stomach turning over on itself as he carefully wiped the dirt from her face, far too aware of just how close he was to her. She had not expected such a strong reaction from within herself, aware that her pulse was racing wildly as his fingers branded her skin.

"There," he said, stepping back and replacing the cloth in the bowl of water. "Now, I was to make some tea, Miss Davenport, which I know may come as a surprise to you given that I am a gentleman. But I should inform you that I am quite used to doing such a thing, given that I live a fairly solitary life."

She caught the twinkle in his eye and the way his lips curved upwards and felt herself smile back at him, her whole body warm all over.

"Might you care for a cup before you depart?" he asked, a little more softly. "I would be glad to ensure you have a little refreshment before you return home."

Nodding, Laurie felt her throat constrict as she tried to speak calmly, despite the hammering of her heart.

"Thank you, Mr. Catesby," she managed to say. "That would be very much appreciated."

Half an hour later Laurie found herself sitting in front of the small fire in the living room, sighing contentedly as she lifted the cup of tea to her lips.

"Does it meet with your approval, Miss Davenport?" Henry asked as he sat down opposite her, the chair groaning as he did so.

She laughed and saw him smile at her in return. "Yes, of course, Mr. Catesby. It is quite wonderful. I thank you." Glancing over at the dirty apron and cap which sat on the floor in a heap, she sighed again and rested her head against the back of the chair. She had done more work in this place these last three mornings than she had ever done in her life. She had struggled at times to keep going, but the sight of the kitchen as it was now made everything worthwhile.

"You have done an excellent job thus far, Miss Davenport," he said gently, as though he could read her thoughts. "It has not been too trying for you, I hope?"

Smiling at him, she shook her head. "I will confess that I am quite unused to cleaning and sweeping, but I find, to my surprise, that I am rather good at it," she replied, with a chuckle. "Although I do not think

I have ever slept as well as I have these last few nights!" She smiled to herself as she recalled how astonished the staff had been when she had requested a bath for the third evening running, but she simply could not allow herself to remain as dirty and sticky as she was after a day at the shack.

"And, do you think you will return again tomorrow?" Mr. Catesby asked, quietly, his green eyes fixed on hers. "I know there is a great deal yet to do, but you need not feel that the burden is yours alone."

She tipped her head, regarding him carefully before shaking her head.

"No, Mr. Catesby, I do not feel it is such a burden," she replied, with a soft smile. "I find that I quite enjoy my time here. It is an escape."

To her surprise, he nodded at this sentiment, as though he agreed with her. She did not say anything, despite the curiosity rising deep within her.

"My brother is attempting to encourage me into matrimony," he said, his gaze drifting away from her and towards the flames crackling over the wood in the grate. "I find that I am not particularly inclined, however, to do such a thing."

She nodded slowly, surprised that her heart was filled with sympathy for him.

"He is incredibly persistent," Henry continued, one hand passing across his eyes for a moment. "I know that he is speaking of such a thing out of concern for me, but I have very little intention of doing as he asks."

"And that is why you were so glad to find this place?" she asked, carefully, unable to remain silent any longer. "It has helped you to avoid this ongoing encouragement from your brother?"

His eyes met hers, silence stretching between them for a moment.

Then, he sighed heavily and nodded, his expression a little wry. "It seems we are both attempting to escape from the same thing, Miss Davenport," he said quietly. "Although perhaps going about it in very different ways."

There was something in that moment that Laurie could not quite explain. It seemed as though each of them perhaps understood the other. Whether it was that of a friendship blossoming, she did not know. But, a solidarity was struck up between them as they looked at one another.

Henry shrugged then, his words hesitating momentarily. "Have you any plans for what you shall do if Lord Umbridge continues with his visits, Miss Davenport?"

Tension flooded her body, and she shook her head, reaching to pour herself another cup of tea. "No, I do not know what I shall do," she said, honestly. "However, I continue to hope that my father will come to his senses and allow me the time to find a husband of my own, instead of hoisting Lord Umbridge upon me."

Henry chuckled, his face lighting up and Laurie felt warmth flood her soul.

"Is Lord Umbridge truly such an unfortunate gentleman that you would not even consider him, Miss Davenport?" he asked, his lips curving into a broad smile. "Surely there must be something to endear him to you?"

She laughed and shook her head, the tension now gone from her. "No, indeed, Mr. Catesby, there is not. He may be rich and titled, but there is no consideration for anyone other than himself. I am simply an adornment to his already wonderful fortune and manor house, and I do not intend to be paraded about on his arm. More so, the idea of having an interesting conversation between us would be utterly lost on him." She shook her head, her lips pursing. "My large dowry is all that attracts Lord Umbridge, that I am certain of. And I do not think that is a good enough reason to propose matrimony, Mr. Catesby, do you?"

Letting her eyes linger on his, she waited for him to respond, then saw something flicker in his gaze. A long exhale left his lips as he shook his head, his whole frame relaxing a little more into the chair. It was as though they were becoming better acquainted and he was not quite sure what to make of it, not quite certain that this was, in fact, something that he wanted from her.

"No, Miss Davenport," he said slowly, his eyes slowly fastened onto hers. "No, I do not think that is a good reason for marriage at all."

"Then we are agreed, Mr. Catesby," she said softly, feeling her pulse begin to quicken as she was caught by the intensity of his gaze. "Marriage should be more than just requirement, more than just expectation or social standing. It should have feeling, have friendship, and a willingness to enter into a lifelong commitment." Drawing in her breath, she smiled at him, aware that his face was a little flushed and having very little idea as to why that might be. "It is good to have someone who finally understands, Mr. Catesby. I thank you for that understanding."

He cleared his throat, pushing one hand through his hair as his eyes darted away from hers. "Not at all, Miss Davenport," he muttered, reaching for the teapot to pour himself another cup. "I am glad to have been of some comfort."

CHAPTER 9

T en days later
"Miss Davenport?"

Giving the handle a tug, Henry was surprised to discover that he felt somewhat disappointed that Miss Davenport was not in the shack, which she had affectionately named 'Tumbledown House.' It had been ten days since they had taken tea together. Ten days since he was quite sure that she would not return given the absolute state of her dress, her hands, her face, and even her hair. But, much to his surprise, she had shown great tenacity and fortitude and had returned almost every day to continue with what she had started.

Pulling out his key, he turned it quickly and stepped inside, ensuring that the door was closed tightly behind him. Drawing in a deep breath, he felt the peace he had come to expect settle over his heart as he took a few steps inside, feeling that, somehow here, he was safe.

Of course, Francis had been growing more and more frustrated with not being able to find Henry whenever he came to call, which Henry was able to surmise given the sharply worded notes that continued to come through the door whenever he was not at home, but he did not care. Francis would have to learn sooner or later that Henry had no intention of being dragged into matrimony, whether Francis wished him to or not. On one occasion, Henry had thought about writing to his mother to request her help in calming Francis' supposed determination, but he had then chosen not to do so, thinking that he was more than able to manage his brother himself.

And manage his brother he had, although not in any particularly forcible way. He had simply escaped, making sure to leave the house during the day to come to 'Tumbledown House' and then returning at night, to catch a few hours of sleep before wakening to look at and study the stars.

Francis, he knew, was always busy with estate business and the like in the mornings, which meant that he only had to remove himself from his home by lunchtime, which appeared to be working rather well. His servants were, of course, keeping quiet just as he expected them to do, which meant he had very little to concern him as regarded his brother.

A sigh of contentment left his lips as he wandered into the kitchen, amazed at just how much of a transformation had taken place, all thanks to Miss Davenport's hard work. Of course, there had been some things to fix and some things to replace but, all in all, it was looking much more like a home and less like a ruin that might fall down around his ears at any given moment! His eyes landed on what appeared to be a small covered tray and, lifting the sheet from it, Henry felt his lips pull into a wide smile.

Miss Davenport had been here before him and, as she had done from the first day she had arrived, was showing him great consideration. She had left the tea things out ready for him to make his usual pot, as he had told her he liked to do when he visited, and there was also a small tin of something he was sure would be quite delicious. His smile grew all the more as he lifted the lid, seeing biscuits and some small cakes, which Miss Davenport must have begged from her father's cook. He did not have to look to know that she would have left some fresh well water for him in a covered pot by the fire, all ready for him to heat up when he was ready. She was proving herself to be remarkably kind, even if rather improper.

Setting about lighting the fire, Henry frowned for a moment as he realized what he had just thought about the lady. Improper? That was his first thought when it came to considering Miss Davenport?

Setting the fire alight, Henry sat back on his heels and carefully began to feed it with some larger twigs and branches, before adding a few larger logs, his heart lifting as they began to crackle and burn. Miss Davenport had, only yesterday, watched him keenly as he'd set the fire. She had informed him that she wanted to learn how to do such a thing, which of course, he had found to be both charming and ridiculous in equal measure. She was a lady, was she not? So why should she have need to learn the skill to set a fire?

But nevertheless, he had shown her, and she had watched and asked questions. He had found her mind to be rather keen and had, to his astonishment, enjoyed their discussion. He had been doing his best to accommodate her without truly becoming involved, and yet the discussion he had engaged her in yesterday afternoon had sparked something in him. Something that he was not quite sure he wanted to study further.

Shaking his head to himself, Henry muttered darkly as he rose to his feet, knowing that he could not allow himself to linger on Miss Davenport's beautiful green eyes, or the way that her red curls always seemed to tumble around her shoulders no matter what she did. He did, of course, notice these things and had felt something jolt his heart as he'd watched her, but he had not allowed himself to consider what he had felt. After all, he was spending most of his time avoiding the discussion of matrimony with Francis because he did not wish to become engaged to anyone. Certainly not a red-haired young lady who was one of the most unusual creatures he had ever come across.

Leaving the water to warm, Henry looked around the room with a slight frown. It was still rather dirty, even though Miss Davenport swept the floor every day and had done her best to clean the three chairs that he had been able to salvage from what they had found. Of course, Henry had every intention of bringing decent furniture to 'Tumbledown House' once it was thoroughly cleaned but, for the time being, these would do very well.

Picking up the broom, he thought he might give the floor another do over. As he passed near one of the windows, his ear caught what sounded like someone crying.

Sobs were coming from just outside the shack and, without even having to look, Henry knew precisely who it was. It could only really be one person.

Miss Davenport.

He did not know what to do, moving a little closer to the window so that he had a clear view of outside.

Miss Davenport was sitting on the garden wall, which had only just been recently restored by his men, weeping as though her heart was breaking. Tears were pouring down her cheeks, and she was making no effort to wipe them away, even though a lace handkerchief was in her hand. Her hair was, as usual, falling down around her face. Her back was hunched, her tears falling like the rain as she sobbed, her whole body shaking.

Henry did not know what to do. A lady such as she in distress was a situation he had never been faced with before now. Given that he had very little experience in such matters, Henry felt himself grow tense. After all, even though they had been around one another more than he had anticipated these last many days, he did not know her all that well. More so, he had purposely avoided dropping his guard during their conversations, lest the chance it would deepen their acquaintance. The thought of doing so now left him feeling all the more confused.

He did not know whether to go out to her to speak to her, or whether to leave her alone. Of course, she had come here since it was a place where she could be alone, a place where she might feel the same peace as he did, but whether or not she wanted his company remained to be seen. His heart hammered wildly as he took in her misery once more, suddenly desperate to find a way to console her but having absolutely no idea what to do.

Walking away from the window and towards the door, Henry hesitated for another moment. He knew that if he took another step outside towards her, then their acquaintance, such as it was, could change forever. He would be making the deliberate choice to insert himself into her affairs. Did he really want to do that? Would it not be best for him to just continue as he was, perhaps returning to the kitchen and pretending that he had not seen her outside, should she come in? Then, at least, she could either show him her tears or hide her face until she regained her composure – which would leave the choice of furthering their acquaintance entirely in her hands.

Closing his eyes, Henry battled against the two parts of himself – the one side desperate to help Miss Davenport in her misery, and the other wanting to keep things just as they were. He had spent most of his life doing just as he pleased, living alone without the burden of others around him when he chose, and he had to admit that this was a state of being that he had come to appreciate. To speak to Miss Davenport now would be to endanger that way of living.

That makes you a selfish beast, Henry.

Wincing slightly, Henry heard the whisper of conscience in his mind, aware that he was trying to do what was best for himself as opposed to what was best for Miss Davenport. As much as he tried to convince himself that he did not need to care about Miss Davenport, he could not ignore her distress. He tried to tell himself that their acquaintance would be a short one and therefore, the less he knew her the better, but the sound of her sobs coming towards him continued to pierce his heart.

Setting his jaw, Henry turned back towards the door, put his hand on the door handle and, with a deep breath, pulled it open and strode outside. A cold wind wrapped itself around him, making him shiver. Miss Davenport did not see him at first, too lost in her pain and misery. She gave a visible start when he called her name.

"Oh, Mr. Catesby," she stammered, immediately getting to her feet and wiping her eyes with her handkerchief, turning her face away. "I did not know you were here. I do apologize if I have intruded upon your time here."

He swallowed hard, his heart aching at the sight of her red-rimmed eyes and miserable expression.

"Miss Davenport," he said gently, taking a step towards her. "Come in out of the cold. You will catch a chill if you remain out here." His gaze roved over her as she continued to dab her eyes, clearly attempting to quell her sobs. He realized that she was not wearing one of her old gowns as she had done every time before, but that her walking dress was one of good quality, her shawl thick and warm. Clearly, she had not been expecting to come out here.

"You are not disturbing me, truly," he continued, when she did not move. "Please, Miss Davenport, come inside. I can offer you a fire and a cup of tea, as well as a listening ear, should you require it."

Her pain-filled eyes looked up at him, and Henry felt the swift kick of anguish in his own heart as her lips trembled, evidently finding it difficult to speak without breaking into tears once more.

"Thank you, Mr. Catesby," she eventually managed to whisper, taking his hand with her own. "You are very kind."

His heart jolted as her fingers touched his and, for a moment, he was frozen to the spot. He found himself simply looking at Miss Davenport with a mixture of confusion and surprise at his own reaction to her. Then, as she managed a small, watery smile, he recalled what he was meant to be doing and led her into the house. As they walked into the house together he tried to quell his fear at the impropriety of being alone with an eligible young lady. He told himself that no-one else knew of this place, and that they were not likely to be discovered. He felt her shiver as she stepped into the warmth of 'Tumbledown House,' and Henry allowed the last of his concerns to drift away. Miss Davenport needed him, or at least, needed the house, the tea, and the fire. He need not be concerned about anything other than restoring her in any way he could.

CHAPTER 10

L aurie accepted a cup of tea from Mr. Catesby with a whisper of thanks, now feeling quite mortified on top of her misery. She had not expected Mr. Catesby to be in the shack, given that there were no men outside as she had approached. He had not often been at 'Tumbledown House' alone, and, besides which, she had not brought her key to open the front door. She had not intended to come here but, after the threats from her father, she had only one thought – and that was to run as far away from him and from his home as she could.

In fact, she had not even found Miss Stanley and told her where she was going, even though Laurie was quite sure that her companion would guess where she was. She had to pray that Miss Stanley would not share this news with Laurie's father, for then the game would be up, and she would be quite done for.

"Might I offer you something to eat?" Mr. Catesby's earnest voice met her ears. She looked up to see him offering her the tin of cakes and biscuits which she had brought earlier that morning during her walk in the woods.

"Thank you," she managed, her voice still trembling as she spoke to him. Picking up a biscuit, she took a small bite but found that she did not really taste it, such was her misery.

Taking a sip of her tea, Laurie felt heat come back into her hands, only just becoming aware of how cold she had been sitting outside on the garden wall. The warmth spread through the rest of her limbs as she took another sip, grateful for Mr. Catesby's kindness.

"Do you wish to talk about whatever it is that is troubling you?" Mr. Catesby asked, perching himself on the edge of the seat opposite her, which made him look more than a little uncomfortable. "I would be glad to listen, although I fear that I will not be able to offer any advice."

She looked back at him, aware that his expression was one of confusion, and yet the eagerness in his voice told her that he was doing his best to help her.

"You are too kind, Mr. Catesby, but I had no intention of crying all over you," she said slowly, as his gaze remained steadily fixed on hers. "I did not think you were here. There were no men about."

He gave her a quick smile, whilst concern still lingered in his eyes. "I thought to come here alone today. There is not much else that needs to be done that I cannot manage myself."

"I see." She did not want to say more, did not want to burden this gentleman who had already done enough for her. He had allowed her to come to his small shack despite his clear unwillingness to share it with anyone else and had even given her a key so that she might come and go as she pleased. The last ten days had been wonderful since she had been able to escape from her father's house whenever she wished. Until this afternoon, she had felt happier than she had in a long time.

There had been freedom from the unrelenting pressure her father had brought to bear in regard to Lord Umbridge. Miss Stanley had done all she could to help, and her father had very little cause to be angry with either Miss Stanley or Laurie. For the two women had simply ensured that, to anyone's better knowledge, Laurie knew nothing of her father's plans with Lord Umbridge, making it so that he could not accuse her of deliberately running away.

All had been going so wonderfully well, that it should perhaps not have surprised her that her father would react so badly.

"Miss Davenport, you are clearly distraught," Mr. Catesby said, breaking into her thoughts. "Might I pour you a little more tea?"

She held her cup out to him mutely, which he took and placed on the small tray before pouring her another cup, adding a small dash of milk. As she accepted it back from him, their fingers brushed gently, and Laurie felt that familiar warmth spread up her arm, making its way into her heart, as it had done before.

"What can I do, Miss Davenport?" Mr. Catesby asked, sounding a little desperate. "You appear to be terribly troubled, and I do wish to help you in whatever way I can."

"You do not need to shoulder my burdens, Mr. Catesby," she replied, hesitantly, not wanting to reject his offer of assistance. "This is nothing to do with you, and I know how much you value your privacy. I will not trouble you with pouring my heart out to you."

He leaned forward, his eyes searching her own. "Truly, I would not consider it a burden, Miss Davenport," he affirmed calmly, appearing to Laurie to be speaking with complete honesty. "Can you not trust me with this?"

She sighed heavily, her heart tearing asunder once again. "It is to do with Lord Umbridge. And my father, of course." Her voice grew hoarse, and she drew in a few long breaths, determined to keep her composure.

"Yes, I recall that your father was eager for you to wed Lord Umbridge," Mr. Catesby replied, sounding a little relieved that she had said something. "Is that still the case?"

Drawing in a shaky breath, Laurie tried to find a way to explain without turning into a watering pot. Unfortunately, even as she spoke, tears began to flood her vision and she felt the warmth of them on her cheeks.

"My father has betrothed me to Lord Umbridge," she let out, hoarsely. "He has decided that enough is enough, or something like that. He does not wish me to take my time in finding myself a husband and has therefore decided that Lord Umbridge will do me well enough.

There is nothing for me to say that will get him to change his mind on the matter."

There was a long silence that lasted to the point where Laurie began to wonder if she had said too much. Then Mr. Catesby cleared his throat once, twice, three times, before leaning forward and refilling his teacup, as though this was a simple conversation between the two of them.

"Is Lord Umbridge a particularly poor choice?" he posed. He casually sipped his tea, and his eyes avoided meeting hers, as if he was giving careful thought to the question. "Is your father not doing the best he can for you?"

A spark of anger shot through Laurie. "My father cares for me, Mr. Catesby, but that does not mean that he knows what is best. Lord Umbridge is *not* the kind of gentleman I wish to bequeath myself to." This was not what she had expected to hear from him, given what he had said about matrimony previously, and his words bit at her already broken heart.

To her horror, Mr. Catesby gave a small shrug. "I doubt that many young ladies get to choose their husbands, Miss Davenport. If the gentleman is wealthy, from a good family and has, at the very least, a decent character, then I cannot see what problems might arise from your match."

She stared at him, her blood turning cold in her veins. Mr. Catesby was not to be sympathetic towards her plight, it seemed. Instead, he was simply quiet and calm, thinking things through on an entirely practical level, instead of allowing any emotion to come through in his words. Apparently, he did not care for her in any way whatsoever and appeared to think that she was out of line to consider herself worthy of having personal choice.

"You think I should marry the gentleman?" she whispered, setting her teacup down carefully with a shaking hand. "Mr. Catesby, it is clear that you think me quite ridiculous being so upset over this. This is not what I expected from you, given our previous discussions!"

He winced just a little, lowering his gaze, and it was as though he had struck an arrow through her heart.

"You think me foolish," she continued, getting up from her chair on unsteady feet. "You think me ridiculous to be crying over this matter?"

He rose, holding out one hand to her as though to stop her from storming from the room. Henry shook his head, "No, I do not think you foolish for crying, Miss Davenport, but I do think that it would be best for you if you looked at this in an entirely different light."

She bit her lip, forcing herself to contain her anger.

"Your father is doing what is best for you. For you cannot remain at home for the rest of your days in the knowledge that, when the time comes for the title to pass on, you will be entirely at the new Viscount's disposal." He lifted his shoulders again, although his dark green eyes were a little wider than before, praying that she would find some way to understand him. "Lord Umbridge is a good match, Miss Davenport, and if I were you, I would simply try to find a way to accept it and move ahead to your wedding."

Shaking her head, Laurie stepped closer to Mr. Catesby, pressing one sharp finger into his chest as she looked up into his eyes. How unfeeling he was! And she had thought him so kind in bringing her into 'Tumbledown House' and making her a cup of tea.

"How dare you!" she hissed, her eyes narrowing, her tears forgotten. "Telling me that I must simply make do, that I must do what my father says without question when you are doing your utmost to avoid the very same situation."

He stared at her, his face suddenly flaming with color. Laurie realized that her hair had, as usual, begun to tumble down over her face. Tucking back an errant curl, she glared at Mr. Catesby all the harder.

"You are telling me that my father knows what is best? That I am to accept this marriage, whilst you are avoiding the very same situation as regards to your brother and his attempts to find you a wife," she continued, harshly. "How dare you suggest that you know what is best for me when you are seeking the very same freedom that I am. Why is it that you believe that you should be able to have the freedom to marry whomever you please, whereas I am forced to marry whatever completely unsuitable gentleman my father chooses for me?"

The question hung in the air, sending sparks around them both. Laurie could see that Mr. Catesby was struggling to answer as her finger still pressed hard into his chest.

And then, to her utter astonishment, his fingers reached out and touched her hair.

She was frozen to the spot. His fingers were gently tucking back another curl, whilst more fell onto his hand. There was something like bewilderment in his expression. It was as though he had not expected to be doing something as intimate as this, yet couldn't stop himself.

Laurie shivered violently as his fingers brushed her cheek, her hand dropping to her side as she looked up into Mr. Catesby's eyes. She was not quite sure why he had broken his emotionless demeanor and she was entirely unprepared for the way her heart was racing frantically in her chest as a result. His gentle touch was eliciting all kinds of feelings in her that she had never expected, her mouth going dry as he moved a few inches closer to her.

"Miss Davenport," he whispered, his eyes glazing over as he looked at her. "I….." He trailed off, his head lowering as she kept her face tipped towards his.

And then he blinked. Once, twice – swallowed hard and stepped back, his hand dropping to his side.

Laurie stared at him as he looked back at her, clearly confused and conflicted over what he had done, what he had experienced within himself.

Clearing his throat again, he gestured towards the door. "Do excuse me, Miss Davenport," he said hoarsely, his eyes no longer fixed on her but instead jumping from one place to the next. "I have some work to do back at the house. Do you have the key?"

She felt her heart break all over again and shook her head. A lump arose in her throat and she tried to force it back down. "No, I do not, Mr. Catesby, but let me make matters easier for you. I shall return home to my father and do as you have suggested." Tears stung her eyes as she looked over at him, seeing the way his lips tugged in conflict against saying more to her. "Do excuse me."

Her shoulders slumped as she walked from the room, praying that he might call out her name, that he might beg her to wait so that they could speak a little more…might explore what had just occurred between them – but there came nothing but silence.

Silence that tore her apart as she walked back outside into the cold afternoon air, the door slamming shut behind her.

CHAPTER 11

"Henry?"

Groaning, Henry put his head in his hands and waited for the unwelcome presence of his brother to enter the room. He had no wish to speak to Francis this afternoon, given that he still had Miss Davenport firmly on his mind.

"Do go away," he said, loudly, as the door to his study opened. "I have no wish to be told I am to go here or meet this young lady or that young lady, to be dragged from one place to the next. Nor do I wish for any company to be taken into my house, or to have invitations to soirees thrust into my hands. I am through with this nonsense, Francis. When will you understand that I do not wish to marry?"

"Henry."

Biting back another sigh, Henry lifted his head to see Francis looking at him with a grave expression on his face. A jolt ran through him, suddenly worried that something had happened to either his mother or one of his siblings.

"What is it?" he asked, turning to face Francis a little more. "Is something wrong?"

Francis sighed and sat down heavily.

"Henry, I know about your house in the woods."

Swallowing hard, Henry went cold all over, wondering just how much his brother knew.

"You have loyal staff, yes, but I have an equally loyal steward, who was easily able to find out what you have been doing," Francis continued, sitting down in a chair by the fire. He looked over at Henry, who rose to join him. "Are you trying to hide from me, brother?"

Henry sat down opposite Francis and took his brother in, seeing the concern in Francis' eyes.

"The truth is Francis, when I found that place it was as though a new world had opened itself up to me," he said, quietly. "A place where I can go to be entirely free of your demands – of anyone's demands, in fact." He shrugged, knowing that he would be best telling Francis the truth. "I am aware that it is your property, of course, but I did not think that you would mind, given that you were entirely unaware of its presence."

To Henry's surprise, Francis sighed heavily, shaking his head. He put his head in his hands for a moment, the atmosphere growing thick with tension.

"I have been rather intrusive, have I not?" Francis offered eventually, his head still in his hands. "I have been coming here almost every day, angry that I could not find you."

Henry couldn't help but chuckle, despite the strain in the room. "Yes, Francis, I thought you were rather angry, given the tone of the notes I received from you."

Francis groaned loudly, sitting back in his seat and blowing out a frustrated breath. "I apologize, Henry."

Henry froze in his seat, the smile fading from his face. This was not what he had expected to hear from his brother.

"I was foolish to try and force such a thing onto you," Francis continued. "The truth is, Henry, I have been trying to *encourage* you in the direction of matrimony simply because of my own worries and concerns." He shook his head, his expression a trifle sad. "I feel as though I let our sister Sophia down badly, and so I was determined not to let the same thing happen again. I went overboard, old man, and for that, I apologize."

Henry, being quite taken aback, struggled to get his breath for a moment, before nodding and stretching out his hand to shake Francis'. "Thank you, brother," he said, feeling a heavy burden roll from his shoulders. "To have that freedom is a great blessing."

"And it is a freedom you should have always had," Francis said firmly, shaking Henry's hand. "It is not my place to force you into matrimony with someone you either don't know or particularly care for. If it is one thing I should have learned from Sophia's situation, it is that love should be present if one is to have a joyful marriage. It appears that, in her situation, it has overcome the most difficult of trials."

"Yes, it has," Henry agreed, his mind suddenly filled with Miss Davenport, although he could not explain why. "I know you are concerned for me, Francis, but I assure you that I am more than content on my own."

Francis lifted one eyebrow. "Truly?"

Henry opened his mouth to respond but then shut it again, his throat suddenly closing up tight.

"You are to have that shack, you know," Francis continued, clearly not noticing Henry's inability to answer. "I am having my solicitor draw up the required documents at the moment. You are to have this house and the shack in your own name, Henry, as well as the lands that surround it." He shrugged as Henry's mouth fell open, astonished by his brother's generosity. "I have plenty to attend to myself, Henry. This is as much a gift to me as it is to you."

"Thank you, Francis," Henry breathed, staggered by what his brother had given him. "You are most generous."

Francis shrugged and sat back in his chair. "I trust you, Henry. I trust that what you are spending your time on is worthwhile. I trust that the studies you are making of the stars are going to further mankind's knowledge. But more than that, I respect the fact that you have the freedom to do as you please, without my own intentions being thrown at you every step of the way. Take a wife, or don't, it is not my affair." Francis shot his brother a quick smirk, his eyes dancing. "Although where you will meet such a lady, I cannot think, if you are to spend all of your time between this place and the woods."

Henry tried to laugh in knowing agreement, but found he could not. What his brother had said was resonating with him in a way that he had not expected. Miss Davenport had asked him why he should be chasing his freedom with one hand but, with the other, telling her that she ought to do as her father wanted. Was that fair? Was that right? And why had stating such a thing brought him so much pain?

"Besides which, I must confess that I have my own heart to consider," Francis finished, getting out of his chair and walking to the door. "Unfortunately, I have realized that in focusing all of my efforts on you, I have been ignoring my own heart."

Dragged from his own thoughts, Henry turned astonished eyes onto his elder brother, who was not looking at him but rather out of the window to Henry's left. His expression was one of confusion, his face sporting a rueful smile.

"You care about someone, Francis?" Henry asked, pushing himself out of his chair.

Francis shrugged, his gaze returning to Henry. "I cannot say, old man. It is something I have refused to allow myself to consider thus far, given that I have been entirely fixed on your situation." He sighed, passing a hand over his eyes in evident frustration. "But no longer. I will have to face up to matters of the heart eventually, will I not?"

Not quite sure what to say, Henry simply nodded, watching his brother with astonishment. He had never expected Francis to be so open, so willing to express his own thoughts and feelings, on top of his apology for treating Henry the way he had done.

"I had best return," Francis said, quietly. "Will you join me for dinner tomorrow, Henry?" Catching Henry's sharp glance, Francis chuckled, a gleam in his eye. "No, there will not be anyone else present, I assure you. What do you say?"

Henry nodded, an enthusiastic energy refilling in him. "Thank you, Francis. That would be most enjoyable."

"Good," Francis replied stoutly, clearly relieved to have everything out in the open. "Until tomorrow then, Henry. Good day."

"Good day." Henry waited until the door closed firmly behind Francis before sitting back down heavily in his chair.

He had expected to feel relieved, to feel free and unhindered, but instead, there came a heavy burden lying on his soul. It was a heaviness he could not explain. His forehead lined with frustration as he let out a small exasperation, resting his head back on the chair as he squeezed his eyes shut.

Miss Davenport.

Miss Laurie Davenport would not leave his mind. Again, the memory of what he had said to her came crashing back into his thoughts. He had told her to accept Lord Umbridge, to go on with her life as a young lady ought, whilst he had no intention of allowing anyone, Francis or otherwise, to dictate what he ought to do. Why had he spoken to her so callously? Why had he allowed his head to speak instead of listening to his heart?

Because you are afraid of what you will find there.

Henry groaned aloud again, his heart squeezing with pain. He recalled how he had reached out and touched Miss Davenport's red curls, unable to understand what he was doing or why. The shivers that had spread up his arm had gone to his whole body, and still, he had not moved away from her. Even now, he was caught by the memory of how her green eyes had looked into his. Her beauty had been so close to him that he had been unable to prevent himself from moving yet closer.

His fingers had brushed against her soft skin, sending a shock of warmth straight through him. For goodness sake, he had been about to kiss her! In that moment, he had forced himself to step back from her, realizing with horror what it was he was about to do.

If he had done such a thing as that, then he would have been tying a knot around them both, a knot that would only be strengthened by the inevitable marriage that would come soon after it. She herself had once said that not every young woman wanted to be married. The flurry of confusing thoughts had been enough to propel him away from her. He had never been one to act on emotion rather than logic, and finding his mind foggy as he shifted the curls away from her face was unfamiliar, and frankly terrifying, territory to him.

Wincing, Henry remembered just how confused, how pained, Miss Davenport had appeared, how tears had sprung back into her eyes as she struggled to regain her composure.

"Why?" he questioned aloud, getting up from his chair and beginning to pace up and down his study. "Why do you not allow yourself to *feel*?"

Francis' words floated back towards him. *'I have refused to allow myself to even consider it.'* That was the truth of the matter. He had not allowed himself to even think about what he was thinking and feeling for Miss Davenport, for fear of what it might mean. He had become so used to his own, solitary existence, and the long-held idea of who he believed himself to be: a resolutely content, academic loner. Then out of nowhere, this Miss Davenport appeared and refused to leave.

He had once longed for the day when he would be at 'Tumbledown House' alone, where he would not have Miss Davenport's presence. Only to recall how disappointed he had been to visit there and discover that she was not within. Was that what he wanted? A life without her? A life where he lived by himself, thinking only of himself and his own desires? Or did he want to let himself explore all that there could be between himself and the beautiful, extraordinary Miss Davenport?

"She is not in any way a lady," he conversed with himself, recalling just how she had struggled to know what flowers they ought to have in the garden. "Nor does she have any of the ordinary skills or talents I would expect from a lady."

He paused, catching sight of his reflection in the mirror.

"But then again, I am not exactly the kind of gentleman society would expect either."

A smile caught his lips, bringing a gleam to his eyes that Henry had never seen before. It was a freedom that he had never before experienced, a lightening of his soul that brought with it a feeling of hope and expectation. Perhaps they were two rebellious souls who were perfectly matched to one another.

He could not allow Miss Davenport to marry Lord Umbridge, not when he knew that she would never be happy with such a man. He did not know whether or not she had any true feelings for him, but he had to hope that, from her earlier reactions, she felt something. When he had touched her hair, she had not moved away, nor had she stepped back when he had almost kissed her. Surely she could not be unmoved, then? Surely he had to have some hope that, deep in her heart, there was the beginning of some kind of fondness towards him?

He swallowed, hard, finding his own feelings – now unleashed – to be rather overwhelming. It was all so new and so unfamiliar that he was struggling to think clearly. Miss Davenport had endured callous words from him, words that he now truly regretted with every part of his being.

"But by now she is betrothed to Lord Umbridge," he now calculated aloud, the smile sliding from his face as he leaned on the window sill and looked out towards the woods. "And a betrothal cannot easily be broken."

Closing his eyes, Henry let out a long breath as a slow-growing tendril of fear began to wrap itself around his heart. He had been foolish enough to send Miss Davenport back to her father and back to Lord Umbridge without any kind of hope that he would aid her in finding a way out. Where was she now? Was she at home, lost in her pain and misery, tears running down her soft cheeks as his heartless, unfeeling words came back to her time and again?

His jaw clenched, his fingers tightening on the window sill as his resolve began to grow steadily.

"I will not lose you, Miss Davenport," he said aloud, as though she were standing before him, hearing every word. "Even if I have to disgrace myself, I will not let you marry Lord Umbridge. You have my word on that."

CHAPTER 12

"Laurie?"

It took Laurie a moment to lift her eyes to Miss Stanley's concerned face, her heart sinking lower as she saw the note in Miss Stanley's hand.

"Is Lord Umbridge to call again?" she asked, dully, her eyes fixed on the letter. "Tell him I have a headache."

Miss Stanley glanced down at the letter and shook her head, folding it up carefully and putting it in her pocket.

"The note is for me," she explained as she did so, coming closer to Laurie. "Do not concern yourself with it, my dear." Bending down, she brushed Laurie's curls from her forehead, her dark eyes alive with worry.

Laurie let out a long breath, feeling her chin quiver as she struggled to maintain her composure. It had been five days since her return from 'Tumbledown House,' five days since she had been sent back with Henry Catesby's bruising words weighing heavily on her mind. Five days since she had realized that he felt something for her, that he was attracted to her, but had chosen to step back and thrust those feelings away.

Her heart broke every time she thought of it and, even now, she felt the tears threaten. How foolish she had been! She had looked up into his face and thought that he meant to kiss her. Worse, she had realized that she *wanted* him to do so, that she would have responded to him at once had he done so. Her heart had burst with a fierce passion, her desire to be in his arms almost overwhelming her – and then he had stepped away, dismissing her from his house.

She could not go back there, not again. Her time in the shack was over. Her time with Mr. Catesby had come to a sudden, abrupt end and that tore her to pieces.

"Laurie, you must listen to me."

Her thoughts shattered as Miss Stanley touched her hand, looking intently into her eyes with such a firmness that Laurie had no other choice but to pay attention.

"I can see that you are in the depths of despair, my dear," Miss Stanley said, kindly, "and for that, I cannot chide you."

Laurie could do nothing but look back at Miss Stanley, aware that her heart was filled with nothing but wretchedness.

"Lord Umbridge is your father's choice, but not your own," Miss Stanley continued, her lips pulled into an angry line. "You know that he is not right for you, just as I am aware of it. However, your father is still your guardian, and unless something happens, he is not likely to change his mind."

Laurie dabbed at her eyes with her handkerchief, finding Miss Stanley's words anything but comforting. "Why are you telling me all this, Miss Stanley?" she asked, brokenly. "You are doing nothing but adding to my pain."

Miss Stanley gave her a small, sad smile. "It is not my intention to do so, Laurie, but rather to encourage you to find a way to *make* something happen that will change your father's mind."

Staring at Miss Stanley blankly, Laurie could find nothing to say in response, no ideas coming to mind.

"You must be able to think of something," Miss Stanley persisted. "Is there not anyone else you can turn to, Laurie? Someone you perhaps met during all that time you have been in the woods?"

Laurie's shoulders slumped as she looked back at her companion, seeing Miss Stanley's lifted brow.

"You know that I was in the woods with a gentleman," she realized dully. "Well, you can have no hope or expectation there, Miss Stanley. The gentleman will be of no help whatsoever, I can assure you." She did not need to ask how Miss Stanley knew of such a thing, guessing that she had either followed Laurie herself or had sent one of the gardener boys after her. Regardless, it was entirely fruitless to consider Mr. Henry Catesby in this matter. He had made it quite clear he would not help her.

"Might you not go and make your case one more time?" Miss Stanley pressed, sounding a little desperate. "Is it not worth seeking his help again, just in case he has had time to consider, time to change his mind?"

Laurie shook her head, feeling tears trickle down her cheeks. "I do not think I can bear it, Miss Stanley. Not when my heart is...." She trailed off, not able to say more, only for Miss Stanley to take her hand.

"Tell the gentleman that you have come to care for him," she said, her words once more revealing just how much she knew about Laurie. "It may have more of an effect than you know."

"Or he may break my heart twice over," Laurie whispered, swallowing the ache in her throat. "It has only been since he turned away from me that I have realized just how much affection my heart has for him. I hate such a feeling, Miss Stanley, and yet it continues to linger."

Miss Stanley squeezed her hand. "Then go and tell him so, Laurie," she said firmly, rising to her feet and drawing Laurie up with her. "Gird yourself with strength and courage and walk back into those woods and tell this gentleman exactly what you have told me." She pressed her hand gently to Laurie's cheek, her expression gentle. "You will come to regret it if you do not, my dear. Trust me in this."

Laurie wanted to sink back into her chair. She wanted to tell Miss Stanley that she could not do as she asked, that she could not find the strength to return to the shack. But instead, she forced her spine straight and kept her mouth closed. Miss Stanley was right. She would come to regret this. One day, she might look back on her life and see the opportunity to escape from Lord Umbridge that she had refused to take.

Despite the trembling in her soul, despite the fear in her heart, she knew that she would do as Miss Stanley had suggested and pour open her heart to Mr. Catesby, whether he wanted to hear her or not. Perhaps, as Miss Stanley had said, he had taken some time to consider his words. Perhaps there *was* just a sliver of hope that she could cling on to, even with the threat of her heart being completely and utterly shattered should he refuse her again.

"You have always been strong and determined," Miss Stanley said softly, taking in Laurie's growing resoluteness. "Prove yourself to be so again, my dear. Tell him everything."

Laurie drew in a long breath, lifting her chin. "I will, Miss Stanley."

Miss Stanley's smile was bright. "Very good, Laurie. I will pray that you will have success."

❧

'Tumbledown House' did not look as tumbledown as it had done before. In fact, it looked rather pretty. The garden, whilst still empty of all plants and flowers, was at least neat and tidy, with a small wall around it. The windows shone, as beams of sunlight filtered down from the treetops, and the wind blew a little less chilly than before. It should have brought a smile to Laurie's face, but instead, she felt nothing but despair.

Walking to the door, Laurie felt herself tremble as she put one hand on the doorknob, turning it carefully, only for the door to open. She would not need her key after all. She would not need to sit inside and wait in the hope that Mr. Catesby would appear.

It seemed as though he was already within.

Trying to find the courage that Miss Stanley had told her she would need, Laurie drew in a long breath, set her shoulders and stepped inside, her eyes roving around the room.

"Mr. Catesby?" she called, in a voice that was not as firm as she had hoped. "Mr. Catesby, are you here?"

There was nothing but silence, aside from the cracking and popping of logs that were burning in the grate. A tea tray was set on the table in front of her, and as she walked towards it, Laurie was astonished to discover that there were two cups and saucers, two spoons and one gently steaming teapot. Apparently, Mr. Catesby had been expecting someone.

Caught by a horrible thought, Laurie whirled around to make her escape, suddenly terrified that Mr. Catesby was meeting someone else, someone who might see them together and jump to conclusions. The last thing she wanted was for Mr. Catesby to think she had tried to trap him into matrimony.

"Miss Davenport!"

She halted, her feet pinned to the floor when she heard his voice, closing her eyes tightly as she struggled to keep her expression composed.

"Mr. Catesby," she said evenly, turning around to face him. She was greeted with no sign of surprise, no expression of shock or dismay, but rather a welcoming smile. She could not understand it.

Gesturing toward the tray, she spoke as politely as she could. "I can see that you are expecting someone. I did not mean to intrude."

He tipped his head, regarding her. "Then why are you here?"

She scrambled for a response, relieved when she felt the key in her pocket. "I came to return the key," she said quickly, pulling it out of her pocket and holding it out to him. "Given that I have no need of it any longer, I thought it best to ensure it was returned."

Mr. Catesby said nothing, looking down at the key in her hand for a long moment. Growing frustrated, Laurie jabbed it towards him, her throat beginning to ache with pain at the thought of leaving him.

"Please," she said, brokenly. "Just take it so I can be on my way."

Turning her head away so that he would not see the tears in her eyes, Laurie was astonished when Mr. Catesby's hand touched hers, his fingers wrapping around both the key and her hand.

"No, Miss Davenport," he said gently. "I cannot let you be on your way. Not when there are so many things I have to say."

Her breath caught in her chest as she turned back to face him, seeing his eyes emote with sorrow.

"I can only apologize for what I said to you when you were here with me last," he continued, not giving her a chance to speak. "My dear Miss Davenport, I was harsh and cruel and entirely unfeeling. I did not allow myself to feel what was going on within me, deciding to return to my usual way of things." Shaking his head, his eyes dropped to their joined hands for a moment. "But I have had a chance to reconsider that now."

She could hardly believe what she was hearing, her heart beating so loudly that she was quite sure he could hear it. This was not what she had expected from him, not what she had thought he would say.

"I have been desperate to see you again, but I could not simply appear at your father's house," he said, his other hand reaching for her free one. "Not when you are engaged to Lord Umbridge. We would not have been able to speak freely there, and so I had to think of a way to have you return here."

Swallowing hard, Laurie blinked furiously as she recalled the note Miss Stanley had received.

"You wrote to Miss Stanley," she realized, her heart suddenly leaping for joy. "You asked her to convince me to return here."

Henry's smile was tender. "And I am so very glad that she succeeded," he said. "For now I am able to apologize to you, Miss Davenport." Gesturing to the chairs, he led her towards the tea tray by the fire. Laurie felt her heart quicken all the more, her nervous anticipation bubbling to the surface as she looked into his eyes. She could hardly believe what was happening. He had written to Miss Stanley, begging her to ensure that Laurie returned to the shack so that he might apologize for what he had said. Did that mean that he did not think she ought to marry Lord Umbridge any longer? Did that mean that, perhaps, he might admit to feeling *something* for her?

"Miss Davenport – "

"Laurie, please," she interrupted, feeling as though the time for propriety was well past them both.

He smiled at her then, his eyes aglow. "Laurie," he said, with such tenderness that Laurie felt herself almost melt into the chair, such was the depth of feeling he expressed. "Laurie, I do not want you to marry Lord Umbridge."

She nodded slowly, her eyes a little narrowed. "And why is that?"

"Because he does not care for you, nor you for him," Henry returned, his color a little high. "Whereas I know a gentleman who does care for you, even though it has taken him a good deal of consideration to be able to admit as much, even to himself."

Her throat constricted as he reached for her hand, shifting a little further forward in his seat.

"I am that gentleman," he continued quietly, his eyes roving over her features as though desperate to see her response. "I confess, Laurie, that I have been foolish in almost every which way. I thought that I wanted a life of my own, a life untouched by anyone else, only to discover that the thought of living a life without your presence would be one I could barely consider. Such was the horror of it." His fingers brushed her cheek gently, his eyes warm. "I swore I would not marry, but now I find the idea is becoming more and more welcome with every minute that passes."

Pressing her lips together, Laurie felt her heart heal completely, swelling with a deep and abiding affection that could only really be love.

"Will you forgive me for my foolishness, Laurie?" he asked gently, leaning so close to her that his face was only inches from hers. "Will you allow me to confess the affection that is growing steadily in my heart for you? Will you accept it from me?"

"I – I will, Mr. Catesby," she whispered, her eyes darting from his eyes to his mouth and back again, hardly able to get her breath. "And I confess to you that my own heart is full of a love for you that I have only just begun to discover."

His face lit up, his hand now gently cupping her chin. "Then might you consider marrying me, Laurie?"

She smiled at him. "I will do more than consider it, Mr. Henry Catesby. I will accept."

He did not wait but pressed his lips to hers, kissing her firmly. Laurie felt caught with passion, her breath gone from her body entirely, as she leaned into him, her heart brimming with happiness.

Only for the door to slam open and a familiar voice to fill the room.

CHAPTER 13

"Lauren, remove yourself from this gentleman at once!"

Henry lifted his head just as Laurie gasped aloud, aware that Viscount Munthorpe, Laurie's father, was standing framed in the doorway. His eyes were wide, his lips trembling with thinly veiled anger and his hands planted firmly on his hips.

"Ah, Lord Munthorpe," Henry said at once, getting to his feet and standing a little in front of Laurie. "I do apologize for the scene you have stumbled upon, but I can assure you, I have every good intention as regards your daughter."

He heard Laurie gasp again, glancing down to see her hand over her mouth, her eyes wide as she looked from him to her father and back again. Apparently, she had not expected him to speak so calmly to the Viscount but, as far as Henry was concerned, this was all going remarkably well.

"Indeed, Lord Munthorpe, I can assure you that this was all planned," said another voice which came from the kitchen, making both Laurie and Viscount Munthorpe catch their breath. "You see, my brother is deeply in love with your daughter and was unable to find a way to tell her."

Henry grinned as Francis rounded the kitchen doorway, only to stop and lean lazily against the doorframe. His brother had been more than willing to help him in this matter, and Henry could not have been more grateful.

"I – I don't understand," Laurie whispered beside him, her face rather pale. "What is the meaning of this?"

"Yes, what *is* the meaning of this?" Viscount Munthorpe repeated, looking a little less angry and a trifle more confused. "You lured my daughter here, did you?"

Henry shook his head. "No, my lord. Your daughter and I happened to run into each other some weeks ago."

The Viscount snorted disdainfully. "I highly doubt that, Mr. Catesby. My daughter is always in the presence of either myself or her companion, with only a short walk taken alone now and again. You have used trickery and seduction to lure her here in order to claim her for yourself when I am sure you are well aware she is already betrothed!"

Henry opened his mouth to reply, only for Laurie to step forward, brushing past him as she approached her father.

"Father, you know very well that I have done my best to hide from you whenever Lord Umbridge is about," she said with love, yet confidence. "You need not try to place blame on Mr. Catesby's shoulders in an attempt to secure my reputation."

She looked up at her father as Henry watched. Looking on, he was more proud of her than he could say. She had found that courage, that strength that she needed to stand up to her father in a way she had never done before. To tell him the truth about her feelings for Henry, to state to her father that she would not do as he asked and marry the man he had betrothed her to. This was the woman he loved, the one with fire and determination in her soul that only added to her ever-present beauty.

"I am not the kind of daughter you have wished me to be," Laurie continued, in a quiet voice, "but I cannot change myself in order to suit you. Nor can I marry the gentleman you have chosen for me, no matter how much you might wish it. Lord Umbridge does not care for me, nor

I for him. I do not wish to marry him, father. I wish for a life of happiness, not a life of expectation and duty."

Holding his breath, Henry kept his gaze fixed on Viscount Munthorpe, waiting to see what his reaction might be to Laurie's honesty.

"But it is done, Laurie," Viscount Munthorpe said, slowly, his thick brows knotting together. "You are betrothed."

Laurie shook her head firmly, as Henry felt his anxiety begin to rattle through him.

"I will not marry him, father. You cannot force me to do so."

"You will have nothing from me if you do not abide by my word, Laurie," Viscount Munthorpe replied, in a hard voice. "You know that I will not stand for this incessant refusal to do as you are asked."

"Then she will come to me, and I will give her all that she has asked for – and more," Henry said loudly, stepping closer to Laurie. "If you have not yet noticed, Viscount Munthorpe, I care for your daughter very much. I intend to marry her."

Viscount Munthorpe stared at him for a long moment, his mouth a little ajar.

"And I have accepted his proposal, father," Laurie said, slowly putting one hand on her father's arm. "Do not prevent this by insisting I marry Lord Umbridge, for I will not have it. Is an agreement with that man truly worth ruining the relationship we share, father? For I am your only daughter and you my only parent."

Viscount Munthorpe shook his head, the heel of his hand rubbing his forehead. "It is already agreed," he mumbled, although the fire had gone from his eyes. "Laurie, this is not what I expected of you. Your reputation…."

"Is quite gone," Francis interjected, cheerfully. "For they have been alone together here on more than one occasion and even now were involved in an intimate embrace, which you interrupted, Viscount Munthorpe." He grinned, still apparently enjoying himself. "I am here to ensure that you are aware that I give this marriage my full blessing, and also to inform you that my brother is to retain his own property on my land as well as be given this one in which we now stand, for him and his bride."

He smiled at Laurie, who looked over at Henry with sparkling eyes, her happiness evident. "And so, Viscount Munthorpe, it now stands to you as to whether or not you will allow this marriage to go ahead as everyone here intends, or whether you will insist she marry Lord Umbridge – in which case, she will end up marrying my brother regardless, although with a great deal more scandal."

Henry could barely breathe as Viscount Munthorpe looked over at him, his jaw clenched. He could not tell what the man was thinking, but by the expression on his face, Henry guessed that he was not particularly pleased with being pushed into a corner by them all. Henry did not care. All he wanted was Laurie's happiness, and this was the only way he had thought of to ensure he got it.

"Very well," Viscount Munthorpe grumbled, eventually. "I shall do what I can to smooth things over with Lord Umbridge, Laurie."

His face split with a smile as Henry watched Laurie thank her father carefully, clearly wanting to throw her arms around him and hug him tightly but restraining herself with the awareness that her father was not particularly pleased with all that had gone on.

"Thank you, Viscount Munthorpe," Henry said with respectful sincerity, stepping forward and holding out his hand. "You have done me a great honor in blessing me with your daughter's hand in marriage. I will do all I can to ensure her happiness."

Viscount Munthorpe looked back at him steadily for a moment, measuring him before sighing and shaking Henry's hand rather weakly. Henry grinned at Laurie, who was looking up at him with shining eyes, wishing that they could be alone for just a few minutes.

"Viscount Munthorpe," came Francis' warm voice. "Come with me for a moment and let us give these two a few minutes alone. In fact, have you seen the outside of this place? I would be glad to show you some of the improvements my brother has made."

Chuckling to himself, Henry wrapped a surreptitious arm around Laurie's waist as Francis, still talking, managed to persuade the

Viscount to step outside, leaving them quite alone – if only for a few minutes.

"Oh, Henry," Laurie breathed, turning towards him. "I cannot believe this to be true!"

He touched her cheek gently. "It is true, my love," he replied, softly. "We are to be wed and, should you wish it, we shall make this place our home."

Laughing, she threw her arms around his neck and held him tightly, her joyful tears dampening his cheek. Henry crushed her to him, his own eyes squeezing closed as he struggled to cope with the sheer joy that washed over him.

"I do not quite understand," Laurie continued, as he let her go. "How did my father know where to come?"

Henry beamed at her, his eyes dancing at her confusion. "Miss Stanley played her part very well, I must say," he said, chuckling as her eyes widened. "I asked her to speak to your father once you had left so that he might find us together. Of course, Francis was in the kitchen out of sight – and out of earshot I might add – just to ensure that your father was aware that he too had seen our…embrace, so that it could not be hidden away." His fingers brushed down her cheek, tickled by the red curls that had fallen around her ears. "I wanted to ensure that I would have your hand in marriage by the end of the day," he continued gently. "Francis has given us his blessing, and now your father has done the same – albeit begrudgingly."

Laurie swallowed hard, her smile dimming just a little. "I do hope he will come around in the end," she said softly. "I thought him quite disappointed in me."

Sympathetic to her concern, Henry smiled down at her, attempting to reassure her. "My dear, your father will be more than delighted when his grandchildren are living nearby so that he might dote upon them whenever he wishes."

At that, her eyes brightened, her cheeks flushing red.

"We are going to have a wonderful life together, my love," Henry continued, gently. "I feel as though I have only just begun to know you and that there is so much more for me to discover. I love that you are quite unorthodox, that you are unafraid to try new things or take on new challenges. I admire your tenacity, your courage, your determination. Without you, this place would not be what it is – and I would not be the changed man that you see before you now."

Her smile slowly returned, her hands creeping up around his neck. "You are truly changed, you say?"

"I am," Henry replied, wholeheartedly. "I once thought my life to be a life blessed with solitude, but now I see that I could never go on living without your presence by my side. You have brought such life to my staid, dull existence that I never wish to be parted from you again."

Sighing happily, Laurie threaded her fingers into his hair, her eyes glowing with warmth and affection for him. Henry felt his heart begin to burst with happiness, knowing that one day soon, they would stand in this room as husband and wife.

"And this shall be our escape whenever we wish it," she whispered, her light breath brushing against his cheek. "We can come here to hide from the world."

His mind flared with all the possibilities that lay in his future, and he could not help but tighten his arms around her waist, drawing her even closer than before.

"My world is nothing without you, my love," he breathed, beginning to lower his head. "I cannot be without you. My heart is filled with a love for you that will only get stronger with every day that passes.

"I love you too, Henry," came her sweet reply, her mouth only inches from his. "Swear to me that we will be married by the month's end. I do not think I can wait any longer!"

He chuckled, pressing a light kiss to her lips and hearing her swift intake of breath. "By the month's end," he replied, tenderly. "I promise."

BOOK 6: DILEMMA OF THE EARL'S HEART

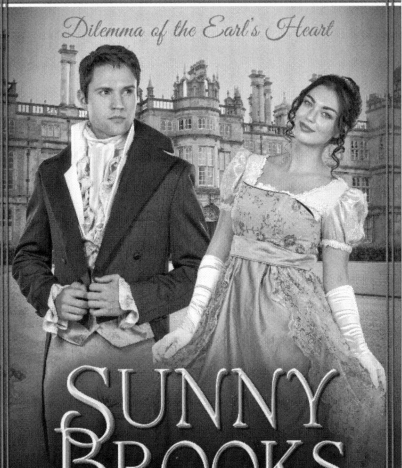

BOOK 6

HOUSE OF CATESBY

Dilemma of the Earl's Heart

SUNNY BROOKS

FOREWORD

Strength can come in many forms: whether pursuing the life you've always dreamt of, or fighting against the life you've been told you are meant to lead, be true to your own heart, persevere, and the right path will find a way to come to you.

- Sunny Brooks

CHAPTER 1

"My dear Francis, what *can* you possibly be thinking of?"

Francis, the new Earl Catesby, sighed heavily as his mother strode into the room. She had removed herself to the Dowager House which was, to his ongoing frustrations, a short distance away from the manor house. It meant that whilst she had her own abode and her own staff, she was still well able to attend the manor house whenever she wished and, somehow, was able to hear all that was going on.

"Good morning, mama," Francis murmured, getting to his feet with an effort. "Should you like a tea tray this morning? Or will you be staying for only a short visit?"

The look on his mother's face told Francis that he had overstepped just a little. Lady Margaret Catesby, the Dowager Countess, was an imposing figure. She had every appearance of elegance, with her carefully set hair only just showing hints of grey. Her refusal to wear a cap often reminded him just how strong a character she was. Her determination to live just as she pleased without the slightest care for what society thought often dug at him. With her sharp grey eyes that could be both stern yet gentle in equal measure, Francis felt himself quail under her steady gaze.

"Francis," his mother said, gently, seating herself opposite him. "I am here because I am concerned for you, that is all."

"You need not be concerned, mama," Francis replied, patiently. "All is well. The estate is doing well. I have begun to study crop rotation for the fields, the tenants are content and hardworking, and I find myself constantly busied by the responsibilities of the title."

"May I remind you, Francis, that your brother continually asked for you to remove yourself from his house, begged you to stop concerning yourself with his affairs, and yet you persisted," came the steady reply.

Francis sighed, shaking his head. "Mama, Henry's happiness was an entirely different matter. He was barely seen, was lost in his work, and seemed to have very little purpose. The sole purpose for my intervention was to ensure that he was not lost in despondency or the like."

One eyebrow slowly lifted, and Francis found himself growing hot with embarrassment. "I am not despondent, mama."

His mother nodded slowly, never once taking her eyes from his. "I can see that, Francis. But when I hear that you intend to find a new housekeeper for apparently no good reason, I find myself concerned! Whatever has come over you?"

Francis sighed inwardly, knowing that he could never explain the true reason to his mother. "Mama, these affairs are my own."

"I am aware of that," his mother said, sharply, "but you are considering yourself only, I think. Has the lady done something to upset you?"

"No, of course not."

"Then what can be your reasons for considering replacing her?"

"Miss Harrington is more than suitable," Francis heard himself admit, despite the fact that he had not intended to say such a thing. "It is simply that I feel that the house could benefit from someone with a little more experience."

This apparently, was the wrong thing to say entirely, for his mother rose to her feet in a flurry of skirts, leaning over his desk ominously.

"Are you suggesting, Francis, that Mrs. Harrington does not run your house well?"

This was not a question that could easily be answered. Francis did not want to lie and to state that yes, his house was in some sort of disarray due to the lady's lack of experience, nor did he want to tell his mother the real reason for his desire to dismiss her from her duties within his house.

"I know that this estate has been run wonderfully, both inside and out," his mother continued, when he said nothing. "I can tell that Mrs. Harrington has been doing an excellent job, Francis. After all, I would not have recommended her to you if I did not think that she would be able to do so with all skill! Why then are you attempting to turn your back on her?"

"I will give her an excellent reference," Francis mumbled trying to find some sort of excuse. "She will not be without work for long."

The dowager glared at him, her lips in a tight line. "You are being much too difficult, Francis. I know that you are not telling me the truth as to why you wish to find a new housekeeper. Therefore, I must question whether or not you are truly being fair to the lady."

Francis spread out his hands. "Mama, Mrs. Harrington is much too young to be a housekeeper." When it had come time to hire a new complement of staff for his estate, so that his mama could take the staff she knew and loved back with her to her new home, he had struggled to know how and what to do. For his mother to suggest a lady named Mrs. Harrington as housekeeper had been, at the time, a wonderful relief. He had heard what his mother had to say about the lady, had read her references, and had sent her an offer of employment before he had even clapped eyes on her. The moment she had appeared at his house, Francis knew he had made a dreadful mistake.

"Does her age or supposed lack of experience have any bearing on the work she is doing now?" his mother asked, clearly unwilling to drop the matter. "Do you find her lazy? Incompetent? Foolish?"

"No!" Francis exclaimed, slamming one hand on the desk as a burst of anger caught him. "No, mama, she is none of these things and yet –"

"And yet you wish to remove from her the safety and security of a position in your home," the dowager replied, with a sad smile. "Do you even consider what such a thing will do to her, Francis? The people who work here, they rely on you in ways you cannot even imagine. They have no home of their own, no money save for the income they earn here. To be let go from a position simply because it is a whim of yours and not because of anything they have failed to do will stain their reputation for a long time."

Biting back another sigh, Francis waited until the anger he felt began to wane. His mother was speaking the truth, and he could not answer to it. There was no particular reason as to why he intended to let the lady go, save for the one thing he was finding more and more difficult with each passing day.

He could not get his housekeeper from his mind.

The unfairness of what he was doing struck him, hard. He *was* considering himself only and never once thinking of what such a decision would do to Mrs. Harrington. He was thinking only of his comfort, his happiness, and his contentment. He did not want to keep thinking of Mrs. Harrington, did not want to even consider her for another moment and yet his heart and mind would not let her go. Therefore, he had come up with the idea of ending her employment here at Catesby House, simply so that he would not have to struggle any longer.

That was entirely wrong of him. Mrs. Harrington had not done anything wrong. She had not failed in her duties, nor been lazy or uncooperative. In fact, his house was running quite well. He had no real complaints. Everything he had told his mother was simply an excuse.

"Francis?"

His mother's voice was gentler now, as though she knew very well what was going on in his mind.

"Yes, mama?" he replied, heavily.

She smiled at him gently, putting her hand on his for a moment. "I do not mean to interfere or upset you, Francis, but I do so want to ensure that you are being a fair and respectful master. You may be the new Earl, but that does not mean that you can simply do as you please without considering the consequences." Her expression grew a little concerned. "I know very well that you *are* that kind of gentleman, which is why I am so surprised to hear such things."

Aware that his mother was only seeking his best, Francis managed a small smile in her direction. "You are quite correct, mama. I was being foolish."

She stepped back and smoothed her skirts, her intentions having clearly been fulfilled. "Indeed you were, Francis. But not any longer, I think."

"No," he grated, hating himself for his thoughts towards Mrs. Harrington and his inability to stop such inappropriate considerations other than to think of removing her completely from his house.

"You will not continue on this path, then?" the dowager asked, pulling on her gloves. "You intend to keep your housekeeper?"

Francis tried to smile. "If it will prevent you from appearing at my door in such a whirlwind, then, yes, mama, I will retain her."

This did not appear to upset the dowager in any way. In fact, she appeared more than satisfied. Nodding to him, she walked to the door, bid him goodbye, and walked out, closing the door softly behind her.

Francis put his forehead on the desk and groaned loudly. Had his mother not heard of his intentions, then he might now be speaking to Mrs. Harrington and informing her that he could no longer give her a position here. Instead, he had agreed to retain her and had, even more than that, allowed his heart to feel the pain and sorrow she would experience should he do precisely that.

His mind was full of her once again, even though it ought not to be. An Earl did not have affection for his housekeeper! A titled gentleman did not think of none other than one of his staff! It was simply not the done thing. Such was his embarrassment that he kept all such feelings to himself, refusing to mention a single word to his mother despite the fact that, had he told her the truth, she might have then encouraged him to remove Mrs. Harrington from his house.

"Or she may have encouraged me in it," Francis muttered darkly to himself, knowing that his mother was a little less bound by the propriety of late. Lifting his head, he rose from his chair and, despite the early hour, poured himself a decent measure of brandy. Today had started off rather badly, and he was not convinced that the remainder of it would go any better.

CHAPTER 2

"Mrs. Harrington?"

Rebecca turned as the dowager walked into the kitchen, immediately curtsying as the rest of the staff followed suit.

"Yes, my lady?" she asked, in a quiet voice.

"Might I have a word with you, Mrs. Harrington?" the dowager said at once, with a kind smile to all of the other staff who were now staring at her as though they could not believe that a Dowager Countess would be below stairs. "I think your parlor will suffice."

Swallowing a lump in her throat, Rebecca nodded and walked quickly towards her own rooms. "But of course, my lady. This way, if you please."

She was aware of the rest of the staff watching intently, the butler included, as the dowager stepped inside. Glancing back at them, she saw the butler give her a small, encouraging smile and, feeling a small flicker of relief, stepped inside and closed the door.

"Oh, my lady!" she breathed, as the dowager smiled softly at her from across the room. "You need not have come downstairs. I would have gladly come to you, as I have done before."

The dowager waved a hand, seating herself carefully on one of the thin wooden chairs that were, at least, cushioned. "You are tired enough already, and I would not ask you to do such a thing again. I think once a week is more than enough – although you need not call upon me this week if you do not wish it since I am here now."

Rebecca sank into her chair, lacing her fingers in her lap. "Well?"

"Well," the dowager replied, with a warm smile. "I have spoken to Francis – I mean, Lord Catesby – and he will not be ending your employment here. I have had his word on that."

Tears immediately came into Rebecca's eyes. "Truly, Lady Catesby? That is wonderful news," she breathed, blinking rapidly. "I can never thank you enough."

The dowager shook her head, her expression a little grim. "I have not yet ascertained as to the reason for my son's reluctance in keeping you on but have no doubt, I will find it."

Nerves swam through Rebecca's stomach. "You do not think that he suspects that – "

The dowager laughed. "Francis? No, indeed. He has nothing but estate matters to consider. You need not worry, my dear."

Letting out a long breath, Rebecca tried to return her breathing to normal, having been somewhat anxious to hear whether or not Lord Catesby intended to retain her or would let her go, as she had been gently informed by the butler only last week.

"You have no real idea as to why he would wish me to depart from this place?" she asked, the question having dogged her mind ever since she had first heard it from the butler. "I have questioned myself over and over. I have looked at my work and strived to discover where I might be failing, but I cannot see where it is I am going wrong. Lord Catesby, certainly, has never said a word and so I am quite at a loss as to what it might be."

The dowager shook her head, her expression now somewhat thoughtful. "No, my dear, I cannot tell you for I do not know. What I will say is that it has nothing to do with your work or your expertise, for Francis, from his own lips, confessed that he was more than content with you. I cannot tell what it might be." She shook her head again.

"But it is not all that long until you can return to your position in society now, is it? How long until you can gain your fortune?"

Swallowing hard, Rebecca tried to smile, but the thought of her late father brought tears to her eyes. "My father's will states that I must be the grand old age of five and twenty before I can possess the fortune in its entirety. If I wed before then, my fortune goes to my husband, as my dowry."

The dowager nodded slowly, her eyes glittering with faint anger. "Your cousin is a wicked man indeed, my dear. I am just glad I was able to provide you with such assistance when you wrote to me and asked for it. Although I still do not understand why you did not wish to reside with me instead of taking on the role of housekeeper – although I confess that you do it very well. I must admit that I find it rather difficult to refer to you as 'Mrs. Harrington' when I know you as Miss Patterson."

Rebecca smiled softly. "I confess, it took me some time also to acknowledge and respond to my change of name! I am glad, however, that you feel I am doing well in my role here."

"Your cousin does not know of your presence here, it would seem," the dowager murmured. "My son has not received any correspondence from him, from what I know. I cannot imagine that he would pursue you all the way here, my dear girl."

A slight shudder shook Rebecca's frame. "With all due respect, my lady, you do not know my cousin. He would try anything in order to get what he wishes. When he did not receive my father's title as he had hoped, given the reappearance of my brother from overseas, he made it more than plain that he would do all he had to in order to gain some kind of wealth. I knew that he would use me against my brother, or my brother against me, in order to achieve his aims. That was why I had to become anonymous."

"And what can be more anonymous than a housekeeper working for a lord of the realm?" the dowager murmured, gently. "I am truly glad that you came to me for aid, my dear. Your mother was a very good friend of mine, and I am honored to be able to assist you."

"And I can only thank you for your generosity," Rebecca replied, quietly. "You have done more for me that I have ever hoped for. I need only wait a few more months until I am of age and can claim my fortune. Then it belongs to me regardless of whether I marry or not."

The dowager frowned. "And do you believe that your cousin will refrain from chasing you at that time?"

It was a question that had dogged Rebecca's mind for some time. "I must hope so," she said, slowly. "For hope is all I have."

Sighing to herself, the dowager looked back at her steadily for a moment. "I must hope so also, my dear. If it comes to it, however, I know that my son will do what he can to help you. I can well understand your reasons for keeping such things from him at this time, for the less who know the truth of your identity, the better, but do not push Francis from your mind entirely. He may still be able to assist you, in time."

Rebecca, who wanted to do nothing more than get on with her work and have as little notice from the master as possible, tried to smile. "Thank you, dowager. I will, of course, remember what you have said, and I must thank you again for all you have done for me thus far. Had you not been able to offer me such help then my life might be very different from how it is at this present moment."

The dowager nodded, smiled and rose to her feet. "Do be careful, Rebecca," she said, softly. "I know that you have said before that your cousin is a dangerous man. Always be on your guard. Of course, I will keep watch as best I can."

The knot of fear that Rebecca had constantly been forcing away now returned to her stomach. "I will, Lady Catesby. I thank you."

The dowager held Rebecca's hand for a moment, her expression a little strained. "Very good. Do come and see me next week, if you can."

"Of course," Rebecca replied, knowing that her weekly visits to the dowager always lifted her spirits. "I look forward to it, Lady Catesby."

With a swift goodbye, the dowager was gone, leaving Rebecca alone with her thoughts. Despite the fact she had duties to attend to, Rebecca sat back down in her chair for a moment, her head heavy with thoughts. She did not know why Lord Catesby had thought to remove her as housekeeper and, even though the dowager had assured her that it would not happen and that she was quite safe, the matter still pierced her heart.

She sometimes felt a little guilty over her deception in the face of Lord Catesby's apparent willingness to take her on even though she did not have a good deal of experience. Her references had been quite made up, although the dowager had taken care of those for her. But to be given that freedom had been an opportunity she could not pass up. She had been offered the chance to escape from the fears and worries of living with her brother whilst their unfortunate cousin, the Honorable Stephen Jefferson, had an extended stay with them.

She could still recall how Stephen had warned her, in no uncertain terms, that she would wed him or it would be all the worse for her brother, Mark, the newly titled Viscount Rapson. That had been the day she had known she needed to leave. Having told her brother some of the story, she had begged him not to look for her until she had come of age, telling him to rid his house of their cousin. How much he had hated letting her go, but he had seen her reasons for it. Having been as good as his word, he had not once tried to contact her, and she had received not so much as a note in the months she had been here.

Sighing heavily, she rose from her chair and made her way back towards the kitchens. There were duties to take care of and, sooner or later, she would have to speak to Lord Catesby about the menus for the week as well as another few matters. For one, they needed to hire some new maids since two had recently accepted a post with Lord Catesby's younger brother, Henry, which now left the Catesby House short.

She hated how flustered she became whenever she spoke to him, although he had never commented on it, of course. Whether it was because he was the master of the house and her now the housekeeper, or because he unsettled her with those sharp blue eyes of his, she could not say. Her awareness of him was always there deep within her, her skin prickling whenever he was nearby. It was ridiculous to have such reactions as these to her employer, and she always fought to keep herself composed whenever she was in the same room as he.

Wondering if that was the reason for his consideration of removing her from his house, Rebecca sighed to herself as she chivvied the maids up the stairs. Perhaps it would be best simply to ask Lord Catesby outright what it was she was doing that caused him so much discontent. It would take a good deal of courage but, mayhap, that would bring an end to her wondering and an end to his dislike of her. She could only try.

CHAPTER 3

"Lord Catesby?"

Francis turned slowly, seeing Mrs. Harrington in the doorway. "Ah, Mrs. Harrington," he said, in a voice that fractured for no particular reason. "Do come in. I thought to ask you about the dinner I am to host on Friday."

She nodded and came a little further inside, standing a little uncertainly in front of the fire.

"Please," he continued, hating that his heart was quickening all the more. "Do sit down, Mrs. Harrington. You need not stand when this will be a prolonged conversation."

To his surprise, she paled at once, seating herself quickly. Her hands were tightly clasped together, her papers set neatly on the table beside her.

"You need not fear me, Mrs. Harrington," he said, slowly, seating himself opposite and ensuring there was a good distance between them.

She nodded, a wane smile on her face. "Of course, my lord. I just hope that I have not displeased you in some way."

The tremor in her voice gave him pause. Looking at her steadily, he realized that mayhap she had found out that he had been considering removing her from her post. His heart dropped to his toes, feeling a weight of guilt settle on his shoulders. Of course, she would have heard of such a thing! It was not as though this house was without rumor and gossip, despite his best attempts to quash such a thing amongst his staff.

"No, indeed, you do an excellent job as housekeeper, Mrs. Harrington," he said, firmly. "I am sorry if you have heard anything other than that." A slight flush made its way up his neck, and into his cheeks and he contained his embarrassment with an effort. "I know the way staff can talk, Mrs. Harrington but I can assure you that your position here is quite safe."

She nodded, her cheeks now a little less pale. "I thank you, my lord."

"Now," he continued, briskly, wanting to move onto more polite conversation. "Might we discuss the menu?"

"Of course, my lord," Mrs. Harrington murmured, her cheeks now a dusky pink. She began to talk through what the cook had suggested, which included a good number of his favorite dishes. Francis felt himself focusing less on what she said and more on how her beauty caught his attention. She was, as usual, wearing her dark gown which was perfectly pristine. Her long dark hair was tied up in a neat bun with nigh a hair out of place. She ought to be entirely nondescript, entirely unremarkable and for whatever reason, he could not stop himself from looking at her.

Her full lips brought the urge to kiss her senseless, her beautiful blue eyes filled him with longing and a slow-growing affection for the lady. It was as though he wanted to know her better, wanted to have her sit with him and discuss matters of all natures, simply so that he might know her thoughts, know her feelings, know her heart. It was ridiculous indeed, of course, and he knew he ought not to even entertain such feelings, but he was entirely unable to prevent himself from doing so. His heart was calling out for her more and more, which had been the only reason he had thought to dismiss her from his employ.

"Does that satisfy you, my lord?"

With a start, he realized he had not been paying attention to what she had said. Flushing, he reached for the paper in her hand. "May I see it again?"

She handed it to him with an uncertain look in her eyes, her whole body jerking as their fingers brushed. Feeling suddenly alive from the briefest of touches, Francis cleared his throat again and forced his eyes down on to the paper, struggling to focus on her handwriting for a moment.

He caught his breath.

"Goodness, Mrs. Harrington, I did not realize you had such a wonderful script," he commented, taking in the ornate handwriting. "Beautiful."

She blushed, and he smiled at her, glad to see that she no longer appeared quite so uncertain.

"Thank you, my lord," she murmured, dropping her gaze. "You are most kind."

His smile lingered as he let his eyes rest on her for a moment longer before returning to the menu. "Yes, this all looks quite wonderful," he said, finally. "Thank you, Mrs. Harrington."

Reaching for the menu, she took it from him and rose to her feet. "Thank you, Lord Catesby. Is there anything else I can assist you with whilst I am here?"

Hesitating for a moment, Francis nodded. "Might you seat yourself once more, Mrs. Harrington?"

She did as he asked almost at once, her eyes now a little rounded with concern.

"I simply wanted to take the time to apologize to you for the rumors that have circulated about this house. The rumors came from me, I will confess, but it was only a moment of madness."

Blushing furiously, Mrs. Harrington looked away. "You need not explain yourself to me, my lord."

"But I wish to," he replied, fervently. "I should never have thought such a thing. Your work here is impeccable. I have no complaints as regards to that. I wish you to know that, Mrs. Harrington."

Finally, her eyes lifted to his and such was the warmth in her gaze that Francis felt quite lost for words. His breath caught, his body burning with a sudden awareness of just how drawn he was to her. Struggling to regain his composure, he cleared his throat harshly, rising to his feet and seeing her follow suit.

"Thank you, Mrs. Harrington. I must return to my correspondence."

She nodded, inclined her head and retreated towards the door.

"Oh, I quite forgot," Francis called after her, seeing her turn towards him. "For the dinner party on Friday, we are to host an old acquaintance of mine, who wrote to me only yesterday to signal his arrival to the area."

"Of course, my lord." Mrs. Harrington turned back towards the door, only to pause and look back at him. "Might I ask who it is, Lord Catesby? It is simply so that the place settings are in order."

"Lord Rapson," he replied, remembering the gentleman from the time he had spent in London. "Viscount Rapson, you understand. He has only recently gained the title and wishes to seek my advice on some matters as regards his estate." He did not know why he was telling her this but found that, as he looked back at her, she was staring at him with a mixture of horror and fear in her expression. He started towards her, suddenly worried that she was about to collapse, only for her to start, straighten herself and incline her head once more.

"Thank you, my lord," she whispered, her chin trembling slightly as she held onto the door handle with one hand, as though using it to steady herself. "I will ensure that the place is set for him."

Frowning, Francis took a step towards her. "Are you quite all right, Mrs. Harrington? Is something the matter?"

Her smile was tight. "I am quite all right, my lord, I thank you. I just felt a little weak for a moment, but I am quite sure a drink of water will set me to rights. Do excuse me."

She bobbed a quick curtsy and stepped from the room, pulling the door closed behind her. Francis looked at the closed door for some time, his brows furrowing all the more as he considered Mrs. Harrington's strange reaction. Was she unwell? Or was it the mention of Lord Rapson's name that had her behaving so strangely? A sudden, protective urge rose up within him. He felt the strange need to ensure that Mrs. Harrington was kept quite safe from Lord Rapson, even though he knew that the gentleman was well respected and kind.

He had known him before he had gained his title but had never been blessed to meet the rest of the gentleman's family, nor even his father who must have passed away given that he was now Viscount Rapson. His year of mourning must have come to a close were he to be travelling to London and, despite Mrs. Harrington's rather strange reaction to this news, he was quite looking forward to seeing his acquaintance again.

"Why do you consider what it is Mrs. Harrington thinks of it all, anyway?" he muttered to himself, shoving one hand through his brown hair and disordering it completely. "You must stop thinking of her!"

His stern talking to did nothing whatsoever to relieve his considerations of the lady. Instead, for the rest of the day, Francis discovered that, no matter what he did, he could not remove the lady from his thoughts, growing all the more angry with himself at his continued inability to forget her.

CHAPTER 4

The rest of the week dragged slowly. Rebecca found no time to go to the dowager's home in order to tell her this new development that had taken her completely by surprise and, therefore, found herself growing more and more anxious with each day that passed. Her brother had known where she was coming to and had sworn not to say a word to another living soul. He had promised not to so much as write even the shortest of notes, but now here he was, apparently ready to call on Lord Catesby and take dinner with him.

Not only that, but since that information had been told to her, she had now discovered that Lord Catesby had offered her brother an extended stay in Catesby house and that her brother had accepted. She could not understand *why* Mark was to come to Lord Catesby's home now. Why had he suddenly decided to come to the one place where she was meant to be staying hidden. The speculation brought her a good deal of anxiety.

He was not coming to speak to her directly, of course, which was her first reason for concern. She was to remain in her role as housekeeper whilst he was here as Lord Catesby's guest. Why was he still making sure to keep her secret whilst still coming to reside at Lord Catesby's estate?

On top of all of this, she had been keenly aware of just how truly apologetic Lord Catesby had been when he had explained to her she would not be sent away. Even though she knew that it was certainly more than a simple rumor, even though she knew that there was a good deal of truth in the idea that he wanted to remove her from her position for whatever reason, she accepted his apology and the promise that such a thing would not happen. Yet, she was still entirely unsettled. She did not know what to think and struggled to focus entirely on what she was doing. The dinner on Friday consisted simply of the dowager, Mr. Henry Catesby and his wife – Henry being Lord Catesby's brother - and now, her own brother, Viscount Rapson.

Rubbing her eyes, Rebecca tried to focus on what she was doing. Even though she had been in Lord Catesby's presence many times, she had still forgotten to speak to him about the matter of the maids. They needed to hire two more and whilst the butler was more than happy to secure those they would need, Rebecca still required Lord Catesby's approval. Why she had not yet been able to ask him was quite beyond her. Perhaps it was because she had so much on her mind as regarded her brother that she simply didn't recall.

Quietly entering the library - Lord Catesby's usual haunt come this time of the evening, she rapped quietly on the door but heard no response. Pushing the door open further, she stepped inside but saw no-one. Setting her candle down, she saw that the fire was burning brightly and let the heat wrap around her for a moment, chasing away the dark thoughts she had let spill all through her. The maids had not yet managed to tidy the library, however, since there appeared to be papers everywhere, with a few books stacked haphazardly here and there. She sighed to herself and began to tidy the room, knowing that it was not the maid's fault that such things had been forgotten, not when they were short of staff.

"I did not think such things were your remit, Mrs. Harrington."

An astonished cry fell from her mouth, and she turned on her heel, her heart hammering painfully.

"Oh, Lord Catesby," she breathed, trying to catch her breath. "I must apologize, my lord. I did not see you come in. I will remove myself at once."

He held up one hand, stopping her exit. "Continue with what you were doing, Mrs. Harrington. I will not prevent you."

She saw the easy smile on his face, took in the way his eyes almost glittered in the shadowy light and felt her stomach swirl with a sudden warmth. Her face flushed darkly as she turned her head away, astonished at her own reaction to him. He appeared a little less formal than before, looking at her in such a way that brought with it a shiver of awareness.

You are the housekeeper, she reminded herself, quickly stacking the books one on top of the other before picking them up from the bottom. *You cannot act as though you are a lady of society.*

"Careful, there," Lord Catesby said, his words a little slow, seeming to stretch out across the room. "Here, let me help you. I insist."

She realized then that he had been drinking, given the smell of alcohol on his breath and the way he attempted to help her but, instead, managed to knock into her and push the stack of books from her hands. Closing her eyes, she drew in a long breath and felt herself a little frustrated. For a moment, she had allowed herself to become affected by Lord Catesby's presence, seeing him as a little more relaxed than usual – and now it became apparent as to why that change had occurred. He was in his cups.

"Goodness," Lord Catesby muttered, looking at the books on the floor. "I am something of a fool. Here, Mrs. Harrington, allow me to help you."

"No, please," Rebecca replied hastily, bending to pick up the books so that he would not help. "I am quite able to – ouch!"

Unfortunately for her, Lord Catesby had leaned forward just as she had done and their foreheads had collided. It felt as though she had been hit across the head by a large rock. Stars sparkled in her vision as she rubbed furiously at the growing lump on her forehead, seeing Lord Catesby do the same, albeit with a lesser intensity.

"I am truly sorry," he said, his voice muffled through his shirt sleeve as he rubbed his forehead. "I thought that I was assisting you, Mrs. Harrington."

"I do not require your assistance, Lord Catesby," she replied, as firmly as she could. "Why do you not seat yourself and I will find you something to drink?" Seeing him nod, she let out a small sigh of relief and picked up the books again, despite the ache in her head.

Suddenly, she found herself desperate to be away from him. At another time would she look into her heart and find out why she was feeling such things for the lord of the manor. A jumble of frustration, irritation, and a growing confusion over the sudden warmth she had felt when he'd smiled at her made her head ache all the more. Setting the books on the shelf, she turned to see Lord Catesby still standing, looking at her with a puzzled frown.

Her heart turned over.

"Might I assist you into a chair, Lord Catesby?" she asked, thinking she ought to, at the very least, pretend to be helpful. "Do you wish for another brandy? Or I could fetch you a tray of coffee if you would prefer it?"

Grunting, he let her help him sit down, his hand catching hers as he did so. When she rose to stand, he did not let it go but rather looked at her for a long time, considering things carefully.

"You are unhappy, I think," he said, patting her hand. "And I think that has a very good deal to do with me."

She shook her head, not quite sure what to make of the heated sensations running up and down her arm as he held her fingers tightly. "I am quite content, my lord."

"But not at peace, Mrs. Harrington," he stated, firmly, his eyes drifting closed for a moment as he tried to look up at her. "You have not found contentment, just as I have not. You are struggling with something." His eyes opened again and the intensity of them burned into her soul all over again. "Pray tell me, what is the matter, Mrs. Harrington? I am quite sure I will be able to help you should you wish to discuss the matter with me."

Rebecca made to dismiss the question outright, only for her to find a moment's pause. There was sincerity in his expression, despite his slightly drunken state and for a second, she found herself desperately longing to tell him everything that was on her heart. It was foolish to even consider it, of course, for she was nothing more than a housekeeper to him and she could not tell what he would do with such information should she tell him.

But despite her fears, the urge was there. It grew steadily as she looked down into his face and felt his fingers grasping hers tightly. He was no longer the calm and collected gentleman who said very little and often appeared to be ill at ease with her, but rather his expression was open, his small smile appearing genuine as he looked up at her waiting for her response.

"You are very kind, Lord Catesby," she said, slowly, "But I feel as though such matters are not for your consideration. You have more than enough to deal with, I am quite sure."

He shook his head firmly, although his eyes took a moment to refocus on her. "No, indeed, Mrs. Harrington, you are quite mistaken. I wish to know what troubles you. I saw it in your face the moment I mentioned Lord Rapson. Is there something wrong with that particular gentleman? Do you truly fear him? Is that it?"

A little unsure as to what to say, she hesitated for a moment, only for Lord Catesby to speak again.

"I cannot remove you from my mind, Mrs. Harrington," he said, hoarsely, his voice and expression now terribly earnest. "Release me from my torture. Tell me what it is that troubles you. I can assure you I will do all I can to aid you in this."

Her smile became sad, her heart slowly dropping down to the floor. "You are very gracious, Lord Catesby, but I am afraid that such matters do not require your input. Lord Rapson, I know nothing of. I believe what you are speaking of was when I was simply feeling a little overwhelmed by all that was to occur. I am so afraid that I shall not have the dinner as perfect as you hope it will be. The additional guest was a little…. surprising, I will admit."

She had not meant to speak too plainly but given just how open Lord Catesby appeared to be at this very moment, she had found the words tripping from her tongue regardless. Blushing furiously, she made to tug her hand from his but found that he held her fast.

"I did not inform you of Lord Rapson's arrival in due time, did I?" Lord Catesby murmured, sounding most apologetic. "Tell me, is cook utterly furious with me? Did she begin to throw flour all over the kitchen in anger? Did you have to dodge a swipe of her rolling pin?"

A little astonished at Lord Catesby's carefree and mirthful comments, Rebecca struggled to keep her face expressionless. "Cook is quite content, my lord, I assure you."

His eyes glinted with humor, his lips curving into a wide grin as he retained hold of her hand. "Are you quite sure, Mrs. Harrington? You did not need to have a glass of wine and a lie down after telling cook the news that there would be one additional guest?"

She could not help but laugh, despite the awkwardness of the situation. Cook was, in fact, known to have a dragon-like temper and could put fear into any man's soul should they anger her, but Rebecca knew that the lady would never once show such a failing to the lord of the house. And yet, the picture he had drawn her with his words made her laugh. It echoed around the room and had the surprising effect of allowing her to look at Lord Catesby in a very different light. It was almost with fondness that she took in his grinning face, his bright blue eyes and disheveled hair. This was a very different Lord Catesby from the gentleman she was used to.

"You are quite remarkable, Mrs. Harrington."

His words cut her laughter dead, seeing something burning in his eyes that both confused and unsettled her.

"I confess that I find you quite.....extraordinary," he continued, his voice now a little thick. "What am I to do with you, Mrs. Harrington?"

She could not breathe. Her chest was tight, her throat constricting as he slowly got to his feet to gaze down into her eyes. The air was crackling with tension, the heat from the fire washing over them both and seeming to set her body alight.

"You impossible, impossible woman," he whispered, tugging her even closer. "Why can I not forget you?"

His lips were brushing hers before she could react. Her body froze stiff, her arms down by her sides as he held her there. What was she doing? Why was *he* doing this? What did he mean that he was unable to forget her?

Slowly, her body began to relax, his lips a little more persistent as he kissed her again. The stiffness left her frame, warmth slowly unfurling in her belly as one of his hands slipped about her waist.

And then the reality of what she was doing crashed over her like an icy wave.

She was kissing Lord Catesby, the gentleman who was both her employer and, in a way, her protector, even though he did not know it. This was not a good situation. He could easily turn around and tell her that he had made a mistake and did not want her to remain here any longer under his roof.

She jerked away from him, one hand pressed to her lips as horror sank into her bones. Was he doing this purposefully, so that he had a reason to ask her to leave? It would not be the first time a gentleman had attempted to press his attentions onto his staff – and more the fool her for allowing herself to become so caught by his advances.

"What are you doing?" she whispered, backing away from him. "Lord Catesby, I –"

His face was flushed, his eyes boring into hers without a single hint of regret within them.

But why would he regret it, if this was his intention all along?

"Excuse me, please," she whispered, turning on her heel and practically running from the room, tears filling her eyes as she stumbled away, torn apart by her own foolishness and regret.

CHAPTER 5

F rancis woke on Friday with a blinding headache. It did not dissipate even though he drank copious amounts of coffee and it was only when he was in his study, attempting to read some of the papers that were requiring his attention, that it began to fade.

The throbbing behind his eyes was still painful and, despite the fact that it was a little less agonizing than before, he rang the bell in order to request a cool compress. He was in no fit state to greet his brother and his wife, his mother and now Lord Rapson, for which he had no-one to blame but himself. In his struggle to prevent himself from considering Mrs. Harrington, he had turned in desperation to the one thing he knew would wipe his mind completely – brandy.

Clearly, he had drunk far too much of it. Last evening was almost a blur, although he was quite certain he had spoken to the lady in question at some point. The last thing he had recalled was staggering into the library, not quite sure where he was going or what he was doing. Had Mrs. Harrington been within? Was that when he had seen her?

"Ah, Mrs. Harrington," he mumbled, as she answered the bell pull. "No, it is not more coffee that I require. Might you, in fact, fetch me something cool to put across my brow?"

To his surprise, his housekeeper seemed incredibly ill at ease. She was jittery, moving from foot to foot as though something was terribly wrong. He did not know what to make of this and looked at her through slightly narrowed eyes. "Is something wrong?"

Mrs. Harrington stared at him for a moment, frozen in place with wide eyes. "N – no, my lord," she managed to say with an effort. "It is just that I thought….." Trailing off and with a look of pure relief on her face, she turned from him and made her way back through the door. "I will fetch you something at once."

The minutes ticked by slowly. Francis closed his eyes and tried *not* to think of the lady who had just left his presence, reminding himself that this was how he had managed to get himself into such a sorry state in the first place. How much time he had wasted either chastising himself for thinking of her or allowing his mind to return to her again!

She had such a quiet beauty about her that it almost drew him towards her, almost forcing him to have her near him. They had talked many times but always about nothing of importance – menus, maids, staffing, guests. There was nothing of significance, not really. Of course, for a lord of the realm, that should not make any particular difference. What gentleman *wanted* to talk to those beneath him? And yet, he could not remove the desire from himself. She caught his attention like no other lady before.

Frowning, Francis opened his eyes as a memory tried to make its way into his mind. A memory of Mrs. Harrington standing near him. It began to piece itself together with such slowness that he wanted to scream, feeling it burning in his mind with more fierceness than he had expected. For whatever reason, his heart began to quicken, his stomach knotting itself painfully as he tried to remember.

"Here you are, my lord."

Mrs. Harrington stepped back into the room with a small bowl and a wet cloth.

"I have tried my best to have it as cold as could be," she continued, her feet faltering just a little as she moved towards him. "Where shall I place it?"

A small smile tugged at his mouth, the memory gone altogether.

"Here," he said, pointing at his forehead. "Would you mind terribly, Mrs. Harrington? I know I ask a lot of you, but my head is aching terribly, and I fear that if I move, it may fall from my shoulders altogether!"

Her lips quirked but soon returned to the thin, tight expression that she had worn ever since she had come into the room. "Of course, my lord," she murmured, wringing out the cloth carefully so that the remaining water stayed in the bowl. "If you would just lean back in your chair."

The way she moved closer to him had his breath catching. The fragmented memory of last evening began to return to him, and he stared at her, seeing the uncertainty in her eyes and finding that such a look brought him a sense of awareness, as though he should know something.

"Mrs. Harrington," he said, holding up one hand to stop her approach, ignoring the stab of pain right between his eyes. "Did I…?" He trailed off, not quite sure what to say and saw her step back just a little, her cheeks paling.

"I was rather drunk last evening," he continued slowly, seeing her glance away and lick her lips, evidence of her nervousness. "You were present, I think."

A jerky nod.

"Did I treat you terribly?"

All of a sudden, her face was aflame. "Indeed not, my lord. You cannot recall last night, it seems, so I hardly think that it matters."

That was not an answer at all, he realized, growing coldly aware that whilst he had either done or said something he ought not to have done, Mrs. Harrington was not about to tell him what it was. That was the thing with staff. They always were to ignore their employer's less than perfect behavior, even if they had been injured in some way.

Closing his eyes tightly, he let his breath shudder out of him, feeling suddenly lost and a little afraid. "Did I hurt you in some way, Mrs. Harrington?" he asked, hoarsely. "Please, say I did not bring you any kind of injury!" He could see her now, in his mind's eye, looking down at him. What had he been doing? Had he fallen? Had she come to his aid in some way?"

Mrs. Harrington's face was still a delicate shade of pink. "My lord, pray do not ask me any more questions. You did not injure me in any way, I can assure you."

A small wave of relief crashed over him, despite the frustration that he still was quite unaware of what he had done. "Very well, Mrs. Harrington," he muttered, shaking his head at himself. "If you will not tell me and I cannot recall, then it appears we are at an impasse. Whatever behavior I exhibited, however, I must beg for your forgiveness, for I can see that it affected you somewhat."

Mrs. Harrington did not deny this, her eyes darting from here to there before continuing on with her task of laying the cool cloth on his forehead.

The reprieve was immediate. Sighing heavily, he closed his eyes and let the coolness take some of the pain away. "Thank you, Mrs. Harrington," he murmured, lifting his hand and accidentally catching hers with his fingers. He did not jerk away from her, however, even though he knew he ought to. Instead, he lingered for a moment, feeling the softness of her hand and marveling at it, given that she was a housekeeper and not an elegant lady.

It was she who stepped back first. "Of course, my lord," she replied, in a hoarse voice. "Is there anything else I can get you? The staff is all hard at work preparing for this evening, and I am quite sure that everything will go to plan."

He did not open his eyes, feeling the warmth flood his soul at what had been the briefest of touches. "Thank you, Mrs. Harrington. No, there is nothing more. You may go."

Waiting to see if she would respond to him, he was filled with disappointment to hear the door close quietly behind her. It irritated him that he could not recall what he had done, upset him that he had somehow upset Mrs. Harrington, and still the desire to have her in his arms and in his life continued to grow steadfastly.

The ache in his head intensified with such thoughts and so, with a good deal of strength, Francis pushed the lady from his mind. He had to recover quickly so that he would be able to meet his guests. They would soon be here, and he could not exactly be found lying in the study with a cool cloth over his eyes, although silently, Francis vowed not to drink so much brandy again. It had done him no good – and done Mrs. Harrington no good either. Perhaps, with his friend Lord Rapson here, he would be able to forget about Mrs. Harrington entirely, and all would go on as normal, just as he had always intended.

CHAPTER 6

"Mark!"

Rebecca stumbled towards her brother, tears pouring down her cheeks unabated. It had been some months since she had last seen him, but the complete separation had been difficult to bear. She had seen his carriage arrive and had allowed him to see her from a distance, pointing towards the gardens so that he would know where to find her. At last, he was here.

"My dear sister," he said, grasping her hands before holding her close for a moment. "My dear, brave sister. How are you?"

She shook her head, trying to wipe at her eyes with the back of her hand but finding it almost impossible to do so such was the sheer number of them. "I am well, brother. Whatever are you doing here?"

The jut of his jaw had her stomach tensing.

"Our dear cousin has made it plain that he intends to pursue you no matter where you are," Mark replied, darkly. "He wants your fortune, Rebecca. I have offered him a sum of money to stay away from the both of us, but he refused it outright."

Rebecca closed her eyes tightly, refusing to cry over a cruel man's actions. "I see. That was good of you, Mark. You did not need to do so.

I am quite safe here I am sure, and it is only a few months until I am of age. I shall have my fortune and will be able to live wherever I please."

To her chagrin, her brother's expression did not change. There was not even a hint of a smile on his face.

"He intends to pursue you regardless of whether or not you have your fortune in hand," he said, slowly. "Wed to him, you will be forced to give up your wealth. You know how the law sees husbands and wives."

Unfortunately, Rebecca did know. She had seen it all too often – a downtrodden, mistreated young wife who was seen as nothing more than her husband's property, to do with as he pleased. To be married to Stephen Jefferson would give him the liberty to treat her in any way he saw fit. She did not have to imagine what that would involve.

"But why have you come here?" she asked, hoarsely, not understanding the reason for his presence. "I was quite safe here."

He shook his head. "Cousin Jefferson is doing all he can to try and force me to reveal where you are. The last thing he did was attempt to burn down my home."

Her hand flew to her mouth. "A fire?"

"Fortunately, it was put out very quickly," he said, calmly, one hand on her arm. "You need not concern yourself, my dear, the damage was not great. However, I thought it best to avoid the manor house for a time. I need to secrete myself away and, in addition, I needed to warn you about Jefferson's heightened determination. I confess I am quite at a loss as to what to do. I called him to a duel, but he simply laughed and refused to meet me. He does not care about his reputation, of course, for all he wants is you and your money."

"But I will not marry him," Rebecca whispered, her voice not strong enough to speak with any firmness. "I cannot. I will not."

"After seeing what he can do and what he intends to do, I would suggest that you are on your guard, my dear sister," her brother replied, darkly. "Together though, I am certain we can find a way through this. We can find a way to set Jefferson apart from us for good – but I could not think of a way on my own."

Closing her eyes, Rebecca dragged in air, trying to keep her thoughts in careful order. There was so much he had said, so much she would have to try and take in, and yet it was difficult to see past the lurching fear that now filled her.

"We can ask the dowager also," her brother continued, trying to reassure her. "She has been more than helpful already. And," he finished, looking a little awkward. "We ought to tell Lord Catesby also. He may be able to advise us."

"No."

The word shot from her mouth like a speeding bullet. Shaking her head fervently, she shut her mind off from considering what Lord Catesby would do should he discover her deceit.

"Why ever not?" her brother asked, with a frown. "He is a good man, Rebecca. Good and kind-hearted, with a steady character and true moral compass. You need not shirk from him."

She shook her head again. "No," she replied, with as much firmness as she could muster. "Here, I am safe. What if things become worse and all and sundry in this house know the truth of who I am? That will make things all the more difficult for both of us, even for the dowager. Besides, we cannot guess at Lord Catesby's reaction."

Given that she was quite sure he was still attempting to remove her from her position in his house, Rebecca did not want to imagine what he would think or say or do should he find out the truth, not when it was so apparent that he was dissatisfied with her already. Even now, she believed that he wished to get rid of her in whatever way he could, finding herself waiting for him to dismiss her.

Her brother shook his head, clearly disagreeing with her decision. "Very well, my dear sister. If you wish to remain as you are, then I cannot disagree with you. However, if the time comes to tell Lord Catesby the truth, then I will not step back from that."

"If, as you say, our cousin does not yet know of my whereabouts, it is not quite likely that he has followed you here."

At that, her brother shook his head fervently. "When last I saw him, he was blind drunk in the gatehouse by our home. I took the opportunity to leave soon after. The staff knows only that I intend to go to London and have no knowledge of my intentions to come here. I do not think that you need worry, my dear."

A slightly frustrated look crossed his face, as though he had been unsure as to what to do when it came to their cousin and, putting one hand on her shoulder, he dropped his head. "In truth, Rebecca, I was afraid for my life. I had no knowledge of how you fared, and the attempt on my life made me afraid for you." Sighing, he lifted his head and looked into her eyes. "I will need your wisdom when it comes to dealing with our cousin once and for all," he finished, hopelessly. "Everything else I have tried has failed utterly."

For a fleeting moment, Rebecca recalled what it had been like to have Lord Catesby kiss her. She considered if there was anything in his kiss that could possibly be the answer to their difficulties. But then she remembered that not only had he been drunk but that she believed it to be a reason for him to dismiss her. Why he had not used it as yet, she could not understand. Thinking to herself she wondered if either he simply had not recalled it or that he was holding it carefully in his mind until a more suitable time – mayhap after his guest had gone. Whatever the reason, she was still uncertain around Lord Catesby, despising her own reaction to him, her body growing warm, whenever he drew near.

Her brother was looking down at her and, with an effort, she drew herself back to the present.

"We will think of something," she said, carefully, looking up at him and trying to smile despite the fear in her heart. "I am just glad that you are safe." He leaned down to hug her again, and she felt her heart lift just a little. How much she hated that her brother had been forced from his estate, simply to ensure that his life was not in danger from their cousin! She would marry Jefferson if that was what it took to keep her brother safe, but she knew full well that Mark would not allow her to do so. There was a strong bond between them and oft times she was grateful for the kindness and affection of her brother. It was not every lady who had such a sibling, and for that, she was truly grateful.

"I suppose I had best let you go," Rapson murmured, as she stepped back from his embrace. "It will be very strange seeing you as the housekeeper, I think." He took her hands and smiled at her. "Mrs. Harrington, is it?"

"Yes," she replied, with a small chuckle. "It is. Mrs. Harrington took a little time to become used to, but it comes very naturally now. Not that you will see much of me, I do not think."

Her brother frowned. "But I must see you again. How will we speak?"

She bit her lip, hesitating for a moment. "I can sometimes meet in the library. We are short of maids at this present moment, and often I go in there to ensure everything is as it ought to be." She tipped her head, thinking quickly. "Perhaps tomorrow evening, a little after supper?"

He nodded. "Yes, of course."

"It will give me some time to consider the matter of our cousin and attempt to come up with some kind of solution," she said, shaking her head a little. "Thank you, Mark."

Letting go of her hands, they turned together to walk back into the house – only to see a figure coming towards them. Rebecca stiffened at once, seeing it to be Lord Catesby. Had he seen them talking together?

"Ah, Lord Rapson," Lord Catesby said, ignoring Rebecca completely. "I can see you have met our staff." He threw a curious look at Rebecca, who blushed furiously. It was a little strange to see the housekeeper out of doors at this hour.

"I had a few minutes and thought to take a turn outside," she explained, hastily. "I have greeted your guest, of course."

Lord Catesby shrugged. "Of course. Come, Rapson. My brother and his wife have only just now arrived, and I would be glad to introduce you."

Rebecca stayed where she was as her brother and Lord Catesby walked back towards the house, feeling her heart break just a little. It was difficult to be the housekeeper, difficult to remove herself from her former station – particularly now when her brother was here.

Consoling herself with the fact that she would soon be able to speak to him again, Rebecca quickly made her way towards the servant's entrance and tried to push the worry about her cousin from her mind. She had the dinner to think of now. The rest she could consider later.

CHAPTER 7

*T*hree days later
Francis was not altogether pleased. There was something very strange going on between his housekeeper and Lord Rapson, although he was not quite sure what it was. When Lord Rapson had first arrived, Francis had come upon his friend walking with Mrs. Harrington, which was in itself somewhat surprising, but even more so to see her smiling up at him. That had irritated him a good deal, although he had dampened such a feeling down.

And then, only last evening, he had heard voices coming from the library and had listened hard at the door, which had been slightly ajar. Having expected his friend to be in the drawing room, which was where he had been going, to hear Lord Rapson and Mrs. Harrington's voices from the library had stunned him. They were talking with a good deal of familiarity although he had been unable to quite make out what had been said. Hearing Lord Rapson state that he would have to return to the drawing room, Francis had torn himself away from the library and sauntered to the drawing room to await his friend, feeling not even the smallest fragment of guilt over listening to what had been a private conversation.

When Lord Rapson had entered the drawing room, he had apologized for being late by stating that he had thought to search for a novel with which he might read in his bedchamber during the early hours of the morning, should he waken. This was not, perhaps, a lie, but there had been no mention of Mrs. Harrington, and Francis had not yet found a way to ask his friend about her.

Frowning hard, Francis rubbed his forehead with the back of his hand, groaning aloud as he saw his mother's carriage pull up the graveled path. She had not been about for a few days since their dinner together and, as much as he hated to admit it, he had rather enjoyed her absence. She had kept Lord Rapson entertained with good conversation over dinner, however, he did have to confess.

He had not recalled that Lord Rapson had known his mother from a prior acquaintance but, then again, Francis had been forced to admit that he had no great knowledge of his friend's acquaintances nor even his family! When his mother had expressed her sorrow over Lord Rapson's late father, he had colored hotly, realizing he had not done such a thing himself – not that Lord Rapson seemed to mind.

Francis' frown deepened, recalling the rest of the conversation. He had asked Lord Rapson what family he still had, and Lord Rapson had seemed quite ill at ease in answering him. Finally, he had stated that his mother had passed away some years ago and that he had a sister, a Miss Rebecca Armitage. For whatever reason, this had appeared quite difficult for Lord Rapson to say and Francis got the distinct impression that the man did not want to speak of her.

Shrugging to himself as he walked back to his study table, Francis sat down to look through the sheaf of papers on his desk that required his attention but still the matter of his guest and Mrs. Harrington dogged his mind. Why was it that Lord Rapson was able to have Mrs. Harrington laugh and smile within a few moments of meeting her, whereas he struggled to garner nothing but fear and anxiety whenever they spoke? Even though some days had passed since the night he had been rather drunk, Mrs. Harrington still eyed him with slight suspicion, as though waiting for him to do or say something terrible. What made it worse was that Francis found himself longing to take her in his arms and reassure her that everything was quite all right. Worse, he dreamt of placing his lips on hers as she looked up at him, finally able to fulfill his greatest longing.

It was quite ridiculous. He ought not to be so upset over Lord Rapson's ability to ease Mrs. Harrington into conversation and laughter. It was foolish to consider it so deeply. Mrs. Harrington was simply a little ill at ease with him for whatever reason.

His hand curled into a fist, and he thumped the desk. "I must know why that is!"

His words echoed around the room, filling him with a sudden determination that had not been there before. He *would* find out Mrs. Harrington's reasons for behaving as though he was a tiger crouching in the reeds, ready to attack her at any moment. Perhaps then he would be able to press such questions away from his mind.

"Lord Catesby?"

The door opened slowly, and Francis realized that Mrs. Harrington had evidently knocked and had assumed that his loud mutterings to himself were, in fact, a call for her to come in.

Never mind, this could simply be the opportunity for such a conversation.

"Mrs. Harrington, sit down."

She stared at him for a moment, the color leaving her cheeks as he rose to his feet.

"Please," he added, trying to gentle his tone. "I would like speak to you."

Slowly, she shut the door behind her and came to sit down in the seat he indicated by the fire. Her eyes looked up at him with anxiety, faltering a little as he sat down opposite. He noticed that her fingers were almost white as she clasped them together in her lap, evidently frightened about what he was to say. His frustration grew. He had to discover why she was so afraid.

"Mrs. Harrington," he began, in rather more of a harsh tone than he had intended. "Why is it that you appear to be shaking whenever I ask you for a simple conversation?"

Keeping his gaze steady, he watched her closely as she took in his question, although she did not immediately answer it. Instead, something flickered in her blue eyes, her lips pulling tight for a moment.

"I – I am not afraid of you, my lord," she replied, slowly. "I apologize if I have led you to believe such a thing."

This was not the answer he wanted. Rather, this was the answer he had expected for a servant did not ever question the master.

"No, Mrs. Harrington, that is not true," he said, slowly, leaning forward in his chair just a little and seeing her shrink back. "There is something that you are not telling me, and I wish to know what it is. Why are you always so afraid to speak to me? What is it you think I will do?"

To his surprise, two spots of color appeared in her cheeks, and she looked away, her gaze resting on the fire. "You do not intend to let me go then, my lord?" she asked, in something of a flat tone. "From what has occurred, I fully expect you to do so, and I cannot understand why, as yet, you have not done so."

Confused beyond words, Francis took a moment or two to think carefully, letting Mrs. Harrington's words enter his mind and settle there. He had already reassured her, had he not, that he had no intention of removing her from his employment, so why was she still under the impression that he would do so?

"Mrs. Harrington," he replied, softly. "I do not have any plans to remove you from your post. I thought I had made that point clear."

She looked at him disbelievingly. There was no smile of relief on her face, nothing to suggest that she was glad of his words.

"Lord Catesby, if I may speak plainly for a moment, I am well aware that there is a good deal of truth in the supposed rumor that you intended to find another housekeeper and what has clouded my mind for many days is that I do not know *why* you intend such a thing." Her expression grew somewhat frustrated, as well as a little scared. "I cannot tell what it is that I have done to offend you, what I have done to bring you to such a conclusion, but I know that the intention is still within you. Why, only last week, you attempted…." Trailing off, her eyes widened, and she clapped one hand over her mouth, as though she had said too much.

Francis let out a long, slow breath, trying to keep a hold of his temper as he realized that, yet again, he had no understanding of what it was Mrs. Harrington spoke of.

"Mrs. Harrington, I can *assure* you that I have no plans to remove you from your post," he said, firmly, striking the flat of his hand on his knee for added emphasis. "I considered the matter at one time but have discarded it."

"But why?" she asked, softly, her hands now back in her lap. "Why did you consider removing me from my station here?"

It was a question he could not answer, not truthfully at least. As he looked at her, he saw that, for the first time, she looked as confused as he felt. The anxiety was no longer there, the fear was gone completely – and that opened her expression all the more. His heart lifted, filling him with a new appreciation for her. *My goodness, she is beautiful.*

Clearing his throat, he passed one hand over his eyes in order to give him a few more moments with which he could consider his answer. "Mrs. Harrington, the reasons are of little consequence. I –"

"They are not of little consequence to me," she interrupted, showing a good deal more spirit than he had ever seen from her. "Am I failing you in some way, my lord? Or is it simply that you have taken a dislike to me?" Her words were coming faster now, accentuated by anger. "Is that why you tried to shame me? So that I would have a reason to leave of my own accord and, if I did not, you could use that reason to force me out?"

Helplessly, Francis spread his hands. "My dear Mrs. Harrington, I have very little idea of what you are speaking of."

Her mouth closed tightly. "I see. I should be grateful that you have either evidently forgotten or have chosen not to use it against me. I cannot tell which one to believe."

"Why do you think so poorly of me?"

Francis was on his feet in a moment, his anger bursting to life.

"I have not harmed you, I have not shamed you, and yet you speak as though I am some sort of conniving rogue who....." Trailing off, he saw her wide eyes and slowly, so slowly, a memory came back to him.

A memory of the night he had been drunk. A memory that had only been fragments and shards. A memory that told him he had done something altogether foolish.

"Oh....."

Slowly, he sank back down into his chair, seeing Mrs. Harrington watching him with a good deal of astonishment on her face. His cheeks colored at once as he finally remembered what he had done that night. He had not injured her nor brought her to harm, which was a relief, but rather, he had kissed her. Kissed her soundly.

"You remember, then," she stated, bitterly. "Am I to be sent from your house, Lord Catesby?"

Groaning aloud, he put his head in his hands. "No, Mrs. Harrington. No, you shall not be sent away. That was my own foolishness, my own drunken idiocy. There is no blame for you in that unfortunate circumstance."

Daring to send a glance in her direction, Francis was surprised to see that she was blinking back a sudden flurry of tears.

"I am truly sorry, Mrs. Harrington," he said, slowly, meaning every single word. "What a terrible position for you to be in. I can well understand why you have been so troubled. I should never have so much as mentioned to the butler that I was thinking of replacing you. It was my own foolish thoughts, and I deeply regret ever allowing myself to consider it as an appropriate solution.

As for –" he struggled to get the words out, heat creeping up his spine and into his face. "As for kissing you, Mrs. Harrington, I can only apologize again. I should not have done so. This is nothing to do with you, and I would not ever ask you to depart from this house based on my own disgraceful behavior."

Sitting up, he cleared his throat before glancing at her again, seeing tears on her cheeks and felt guilt slam into his heart. "I do not know if you can forgive me, Mrs. Harrington but I do beg it of you. My inhibitions were evidently lowered – if not absent altogether, and so I must have given in to my desires without even realizing them."

If it had not been for Mrs. Harrington's swift intake of breath, Francis might not have realized what it was he had just said. Ice clung to his limbs, making it impossible to move. He stared at Mrs. Harrington, who was looking back at him with utter astonishment.

"I –"

There was nothing he could say to explain what he had meant. Having just told her outright that he had given in to his desire to kiss her, he could not easily explain it away.

"I – I think I should leave you, Lord Catesby," Mrs. Harrington murmured, her face pink and eyes roving around the room in a desperate attempt not to look at him. "Do excuse me."

"Mrs. Harrington."

He had risen to his feet without really knowing why, looking at her directly as she turned back slowly to face him.

"Mrs. Harrington," he said again, slowly beginning to realize what it was he wanted to say and trying to find a way to say it. "I do not want you to think that I am a gentleman intent on seducing his staff simply to satisfy his own fleeting whims." He saw her blush and felt his own cheeks warm, but continued on regardless, determined to speak the truth to her as though, in its own way, it might save him from his embarrassment. "I do not do such things. It is not my way. Rather, I will confess to you that I have been quite unable to get you from my mind ever since you have come to my house."

Her eyes were rounded, staring at him, whilst her mouth hung a little ajar. Evidently, he had astonished her completely.

"I tell you this because it is the truth, Mrs. Harrington," he continued, refusing to shy away from it. "That is the only reason I have attempted to remove you from this house, and it was wrong of me to do so. I do not want you to go simply because of my own struggles. That would be entirely unfair. However, I will confess that I continue to desire to know you better, to spend time in conversation, to talk and laugh and share – but such a desire is quite ridiculous. I am aware of that. I am a lord of the realm, and I would not sully your reputation by forcing my desires on to you. I should not have done so then, and I will not do so again."

Breathing hard, he finished his little speech with a feeling of both relief and a sudden awareness of just how honest he had been with her. He had never said such things aloud but now that they had been spoken, his heart felt a good deal lighter.

Mrs. Harrington, however, was looking entirely stunned – and he could not blame her for such a reaction. She had one hand to her heart, her eyes glistening with sparkling tears and, suddenly, Francis felt himself jolt with fear.

"You will not leave the house because of what I have told you," he said, as though stating a fact rather than asking a question. "You cannot, Mrs. Harrington, that would not be fair." He realized immediately that in saying what he had done, he was practically forcing the lady from his home. That had not been his intention. He had wanted her to understand why he had been so conflicted, but by being so forthright, he could now have opened the door for her to leave of her own volition.

Tears fell onto her cheeks. "Oh, Lord Catesby," she breathed, clearly struggling to get the words from her lips. "You have astonished me entirely. I did not think that you would have such a depth of feeling for one such as I."

She did not look either angry or upset at what he had confessed. In fact, there appeared to be almost a lightness about her, as though what he had said now brought her some kind of relief.

"I will not ruin your reputation or your standing by doing anything I should not," he promised, going against everything that he longed for. "I will remain as I ought, and you can continue your duties regardless of what I have said." A small smile caught his lips, tugging them ruefully. "I did not mean to confess all of this to you, Mrs. Harrington, but I could not bear your distress any longer. I will not have you afraid of me."

She shook her head, her eyes dropping to the floor for a moment. Francis closed his eyes and took in a steadying breath, refusing to let himself reflect on the significance of what had happened that evening in the library. If his memory was correct, Mrs. Harrington had responded to him in her own way. She had not slapped him and run from the room but had grown soft and warm under his embrace. But no, he would not think on this, would not allow himself to consider, to dream. He had said and done enough already.

"Lord Catesby, I think there is something I must tell you," Mrs. Harrington stammered, her cheeks now cooling to a dusky pink. "I –"

The door opened just as she was about to speak, admitting the butler.

"I am terribly sorry, my lord," the butler apologized, ignoring Mrs. Harrington completely. "I knew you were talking to Mrs. Harrington and thought to step in. You have an unexpected visitor."

Francis, rather irritated by such an interruption, sighed heavily and picked up the card from the silver tray. "Who is this gentleman?" he asked, waving the card about. "I do not recognize the name."

The butler lifted one shoulder. "I cannot say, my lord, although he claims to be the cousin of Lord Rapson. Apparently, he is looking for him for I believe there has been some sort of upset back at the estate."

That brought a frown to Francis' face. "Very well," he stated, waving the butler away. "I will see him. Just bring him along here and send for the tea tray."

The butler withdrew, leaving only Mrs. Harrington remaining. Francis turned back to her, expecting for her to continue, only to see her turn puce.

"Mrs. Harrington?"

"Lord Catesby," she whispered, coming towards him and grasping his arm with one hand. "Has the honorable Stephen Jefferson come to see you?"

Astonishment shot through him. "You know the gentleman?"

She swayed slightly, and for a moment, Francis thought she might collapse where she stood. "You must not tell him that Lord Rapson is here," she replied, hoarsely. "Please, my lord, do as I ask. It is for Lord Rapson's safety."

Knowing that he could not delay in order to demand how Mrs. Harrington knew of both Mr. Jefferson and Lord Rapson, Francis put one hand over hers. "I will not pretend to understand, Mrs. Harrington, but you appear to be quite in earnest."

"I am," she pleaded, her eyes boring into his. "He must not know, my lord."

"Very well, very well," he said, softly, although he was entirely unsure as to why she could have asked him such a thing. "Although I will expect an explanation from you as regards this matter forthwith."

She nodded, no smile or even flash of relief on her face. "Thank you, Lord Catesby. I must go."

Francis watched her leave the room, feeling more confused than ever. Mrs. Harrington had been more receptive to his confession than he had thought and now, it appeared, there was more to her than he had first believed. How did she know Mr. Jefferson? And what did Lord Rapson have to do with it all?

"The honorable Stephen Jefferson, my lord."

Jerking in surprise, he saw the butler standing at the open door, standing to one side to announce Francis' guest.

"Mr. Jefferson," he said at once, hoping the gentleman had not seen his lack of preparation. "Do sit down and tell me at once what it is I can do to assist you."

CHAPTER 8

Rebecca's breathing was ragged as she hurried from one room to the next, desperate to find her brother. Jefferson was here. Mark had to be warned.

How he had found them, she did not know, and she could not believe that it was simply happenstance. Mark had promised her that no-one knew of her whereabouts. He had promised that not even his staff knew that he intended to come to Catesby House, and yet here Jefferson was.

Whilst she had been able to talk with her brother on more than one occasion, she had not been able to come up with any particular solution as to how to remove Jefferson from their lives for good. She had thought they would have more time, that they would be able to talk with the dowager who, as yet, they had been unable to visit together. Angry, frustrated and afraid, she turned into the dining room to find her brother busy finishing a late luncheon.

"Rebecca!" he exclaimed, looking delighted to see her. "Have you come up with something?"

Closing the door tightly, she leaned against it for a moment before shaking her head. "No, Rapson, I have not."

His expression changed at once, evidently seeing her demeanor. "Is something the matter, Rebecca?"

"Jefferson is here."

His knife and fork clattered unceremoniously, on the plate. His face went sheet white as he stared at her, his smile fading at once.

"You told me that your staff knew nothing of this," she said, hoarsely, walking towards him on trembling limbs. "How, then, has he found us both?"

Her brother did not say anything for some moments, his eyes glazing over as he looked at her, clearly thinking about what he had said and who could have told their cousin.

"Jefferson may have found a way to gain entry into the estate," he murmured, eventually. "I never once let him in, and the staff was told to refuse him, but I am quite sure he could have easily wheedled his way in using one of the more impressionable maids. He is, as you know, a particularly persuasive man."

She didn't understand. "But what would that matter? You did not tell any of the staff where you were going."

"But I did keep my correspondence in my study," he admitted, quietly, his gaze faltering as he looked at her. "If he found a way in there, then he might easily have discovered the letter I received back from Lord Catesby welcoming a visit from me."

Her breath caught. "Oh, no, Mark."

He dropped his head. "I should have burned the letter," he lamented regretfully. "But truly, I did not for one moment imagine that he would find a way into the manor house if that is what he has done. I am sorry, Rebecca."

She shook her head. "It is not something you could have anticipated, Rapson. Our cousin is more devious than either of us ever expected."

"But what are we to do?" he asked, hopelessly. "I feel so very useless, Rebecca. I am meant to be protecting you, but without realizing it, I have managed to lead our cousin directly to us." His eyes caught hers, and she was caught by the lack of hope that was within. "I am failing in my duties, Rebecca. I have been unable to protect you, and even now when the danger has loomed even closer, I find myself entirely at a loss."

Rebecca drew in a long breath in an attempt to steady herself. "I have begged Lord Catesby not to say a word about your presence here," she began, seeing a flicker of light in her brother's eyes. "He agreed, I am glad to say, but it will require an explanation from us both." The way Lord Catesby had spoken to her before the news of Jefferson's arrival still warmed her, the sudden anticipation catching her off guard. "I cannot predict what his reaction will be, but I pray that he will be able to help us."

Her brother nodded. "I could send a footman to fetch the dowager also," he murmured quietly. "It is a little discourteous given that we are guests in Lord Catesby's home, but she will need to talk of her part in all of this, especially if we are to convince Catesby to help us."

Rebecca leaned heavily on the table. "I think that would be wise."

She waited quietly whilst her brother called for a footman, dictating a short note which would be taken at once to the dowager. Whilst she waited, her mind turned back to her employer. What Lord Catesby had revealed to her already, only a few minutes beforehand, had quite taken her by surprise – and now she was to reveal something of her own to him.

To hear him speak of affection, of his desire to be close to her and how he could not remove her from his thoughts had forced her to see him in a very different light. Suddenly, his reasons from turning from her, for considering that he ought to remove her from her position and replace her with someone entirely new, all began to make sense. He had been afraid of what he had begun to want, turning away from the overwhelming sense of longing that he had spoken to her of.

A lord of the manor might have whichever of his staff he chose, given that he was of a much higher station than they. But she knew that Lord Catesby was not that kind of man. He was a gentleman.

He had thought to send her away rather than disgrace her or soil her reputation. That spoke of kindness, of consideration and of a strong sense of what was right and what was wrong. Her brother had been correct to state that Lord Catesby was a trustworthy fellow, with a good, strong moral compass. At the time, she had thought that entirely incorrect, believing that Lord Catesby had kissed her in order to ensure that she could not remain in his employ for very much longer, but she had been wrong on that count. Very wrong. Lord Catesby was, all in all, a very good man.

"There we are," her brother muttered, thrusting one hand into his hair as he began to pace the room in a state of agitation. "The note is sent. The dowager will be here shortly, I hope. Although it will take us some time to explain it all to Lord Catesby, I think."

She gave him a rueful smile. "I do hope that he will not be too angry with me."

"Angry with you?" Rapson repeated, looking astonished. "My dear sister, I am quite sure that Lord Catesby will understand. He will not be angry with you, not when, as I understand, you have been doing such a remarkable job in managing the household."

A small blush crept into her cheeks. "Did he say such a thing?"

"On more than one occasion," her brother said, firmly. "You cannot imagine how proud I was to hear it. You have done remarkably well, Rebecca. I am only sorry I have been unable to do more."

She shook her head and caught his hand, preventing him from walking away again to pace the floor. "You did all that you could, Mark. You even called him out, but he refused to meet your demands. That is hardly your fault." She squeezed his hand gently. "You were willing to put your life on the line for me. Even worse, you have been chased from your home by the crazed attempts of a gentleman desperate to have what he has long desired, despite having no claim to it."

Shaking her head sadly, she looked up at him again. "You and I are both at as much of a loss as the other when it comes to dealing with our cousin. Aside from having him shot, I can see no easy solution to our present difficulties – unless…." She trailed off, an idea sparking in her mind. If she were to marry another, then Jefferson would have not only herself and her brother to contend with, but also her husband. It would mean giving up her fortune to her husband but if she found a good man, then would that be as much of a trial as she feared?

Her mind filled with the face of Lord Catesby. She could not pretend that there was not a small amount of feeling that filled her soul when she thought of him, burning all the brighter now that she knew the real reason for his thoughts of sending her away. He was a good man, was he not? If she gave him her fortune by wedding him, she was quite sure that he would not withhold anything from her that she desired. It was not as though she knew any other particular gentleman, given that she had only just finished her half year of mourning before she had been forced to run from her home.

But, then again, Lord Catesby might not have any thoughts of matrimony. That was a foolish hope and certainly not one she could cling to.

Letting out a long sigh, she looked up into her brother's anxious face, knowing just how much he wished to help her and just how little they were able to do. "We will think of something, Rapson. I am quite sure we will be able to come up with something, once we have the assistance of the dowager and Lord Catesby."

"I do hope so," he murmured, clearly very despondent. "I have done nothing of use thus far."

She embraced him, trying her best to draw up her courage and strength whilst reassuring him also. He hugged her back, murmuring yet more apologies as frustration radiated from him.

Just as she was about to step back, the door opened, and Lord Catesby stepped inside, stopping dead as he looked at them both, an angry glint in his eye.

CHAPTER 9

"Whatever is the meaning of this?"

Francis knew his voice was loud and held a good deal of anger, but to walk in and see Mrs. Harrington in the arms of Lord Rapson was more than he could tolerate. He had just bared his soul to the lady and, whilst he had not expected her to run to him, he certainly did not think she would then be in the arms of another gentleman! On top of all of this, he had just come from a very confusing conversation with Mr. Jefferson, who had apparently been searching for Lord Rapson in order to inform him about some terrible news which, for whatever reason, he could not divulge to Francis himself.

It had been as though Mr. Jefferson knew that Lord Rapson was within and had been trying to force Francis to admit it. Francis had not liked the gentleman, and for this reason, finding Mr. Jefferson's sharp hazel eyes and slightly menacing smile a little disconcerting. But, as he had promised to Mrs. Harrington, he had not mentioned a word about Lord Rapson's presence, even though the gentleman had persisted with his questions for some minutes.

"Lord Catesby," Mrs. Harrington stammered, stepping back from Lord Rapson. "Is Mr. Jefferson still here?"

He frowned, finding himself growing angry with her lack of consideration for what he had just stumbled upon. It was as if he did not really know the lady before him. Upon retrospect, he began to question what he really knew of her. He had thought her sweet and kind, gentle and respectable, and yet here she was with her arms around Lord Rapson's neck!"

"I think you need to explain yourself, Mrs. Harrington," he grated, coming a little further into the room and closing the door with a little too much force, making Mrs. Harrington jump. "Whatever are you doing here with Lord Rapson? I did think that something strange was between the two of you, but I never once considered that it could be.....*this*." He emphasized the last word, arching an eyebrow as he regarded her, seeing her flush a deep red.

"Now, see here," Lord Rapson said, firmly, stepping forward. "There's more to this than you understand, Lord Catesby. Don't suggest something foolish."

"Foolish?" Francis exclaimed, waving a hand at Mrs. Harrington, who was now standing a little further away from Lord Rapson. "Do you have any idea what has just passed between myself and the lady? I have told my housekeeper, my *housekeeper,* if you can imagine, that I am half in love with her and that I cannot remove her from my thoughts. I have begged her forgiveness for kissing her and have asked her to remain within this house in her position here, promising not to give in to any of my own desires ever again. And then, some minutes after baring my soul, I walk in to see her standing with you!"

A dark flush burned in his cheeks, his expression growing angry. "Evidently, Mrs. Harrington is not the lady I thought her to be! If you wish, Lord Rapson, I suggest you take Mrs. Harrington with you when you leave. I am quite sure she will make a *warm* companion."

Lord Rapson took a step forward, his face filled with rage – only for Mrs. Harrington to step forward and tug at his arm, begging him not to harm Lord Catesby. Francis' lip curled.

"I do not require your assistance, Mrs. Harrington. In fact, I do not require you at all. Go and collect your things. You are dismissed."

Much to his surprise, Mrs. Harrington did not look either

astonished or regretful, as he thought she might. Instead, she looked at him calmly, her hand still on Lord Rapson's arm.

"My dear Lord Catesby," she said, in a clear voice. "You must excuse my brother. He is most protective."

Francis's heart stopped dead. His smirk fell from his lips, replaced with an open-mouthed gape. His eyebrows practically vanished into his hair as he saw Lord Rapson give him a small, apologetic smile. This lady, the lady he had thought of as his housekeeper, the one he had been battling to forget, battling to ignore, was not a servant after all. In fact, she was the daughter of a nobleman and the sister of a viscount!

It was some moments before he could speak and even then, his voice was thin and wispy, his whole body feeling as though it had been filled with ice.

"But – but why?" he asked, hoarsely. "I do not understand."

Mrs. Harrington – or whatever her true name was – shot him an apologetic look. "I had no other choice, Lord Catesby. Your mother was so willing to help that I could not –"

"My *mother*?" Francis repeated, interrupting her. "Do you mean to say that my mother has been aware of this situation for…." He trailed off, recalling just how interested his mother had become in his life of late. "I see," he muttered, feeling as though he were adrift at sea with no way of getting to dry land. "She has been involved in this matter, whatever it be, since the beginning."

"Indeed," Lord Rapson agreed, quietly. "I do apologize, old boy, but I couldn't tell you the truth, for my sister's sake. It was imperative that she remained hidden."

A dull ache began to form between Francis' brows. "Why is that?" he asked, glancing from one to the other. "Is this something to do with Mr. Jefferson?"

"Our cousin," they both said together, making Francis all the more astonished.

"Your cousin who came to call to tell me that he has been eagerly searching for you, Lord Rapson, to tell you of some terrible news," he said, slowly. "Am I to understand that this supposed news is nothing of importance?"

Lord Rapson shook his head. "I think it nothing but a ruse, Lord Catesby," he replied, with a small shrug. "Should we, perhaps, seat ourselves around the table? There is a good deal to explain, and I believe your mother will be joining us shortly." He cleared his throat, glancing away from Francis for a moment, evidence of his embarrassment. "I do apologize, Lord Catesby, but I sent a note and asked her to join us."

Mrs. Harrington smiled tightly. "We could not be sure of your reaction to this news, Lord Catesby. We thought it best she be present also."

Francis felt as if he had woken up in a dream and was able to walk about in it. Nothing seemed to make sense. Mrs. Harrington was not, in fact, a housekeeper of the lower classes, but was a lady of quality. Lord Rapson had not simply come here for a brief stay, but evidently had come to ensure the safety of his sister, for whatever reason. And his mother, the dowager, had apparently facilitated all that was going on without saying a word to him about it.

Why had he not been informed? What possible reason could there be for a young lady of the *ton* to hide in another gentleman's estate? Anything might have occurred that could have brought Mrs. Harrington harm, and he would not have known how to help her.

"May I ask," he said, as he sat down in a chair by the dining table. "What is your real name, Mrs. Harrington?" He looked at her seated across from him, seeing her gentle features and feeling his heart fill with confusion and doubt. Was what he felt for her finally able to come to some sort of conclusion? Was he now able to allow himself such a depth of feeling without chastising himself completely? It should have brought him a sense of happiness, but he felt nothing but bewilderment.

Letting out a small sigh, Mrs. Harrington settled back into her chair, folded her hands in her lap and smiled at him. "I am Miss Rebecca Patterson, my lord. Daughter to the late Viscount Rapson."

He inclined his head almost without thinking. "I am glad to finally make your true acquaintance, my lady."

She flushed a deep, rich red. "I cannot tell if you are teasing me or if you are genuine, my lord, but for my part, I will say that I did not enjoy deceiving you. There was, however, no other way."

Clearing his throat, he took in her sad smile, her burning cheeks and the flash of hope in her eyes. She was praying that he would accept her, he realized, just as she was. Did she not understand that such a sudden change in her circumstances meant that he did not have to continue preventing himself from allowing his heart to fill with her, that he was free of the desperate longing to rid himself of her from his mind?

"Oh, Francis."

Turning his head, Francis saw his mother walk into the room, her face a picture.

"I am terribly sorry you had to find out this way," she said, with a shake of her head. "But it was all for the best, you understand."

He closed his eyes for a moment, keeping his frustration under control. "So everybody keeps telling me, mama, but as yet I have received very little explanation as to why this was the case." He looked at his friend, Lord Rapson, who was seemingly very interested in the painting hanging on the wall just behind Francis' head. "If anyone cares to start from the beginning, I should very much like an explanation."

"Of course," his mother replied at once, soothingly. "Just let me ring for tea, my dear. It has been a rather trying afternoon for you all, has it not?" Her eyes flickered to Miss Patterson. "I understand your cousin is here?"

It was not Miss Patterson who answered, however, but her brother.

"He is," he replied, heavily. "And I must have made the mistake of thinking him unable to discover where I was headed. Thankfully, Lord Catesby was able to do as my sister requested and give him no information as regarded my presence here. I am sure he is quite well on his way by now."

A slow sense of dread began to fill Francis, starting from his stomach and going all through him. His blood began to roar in his ears, his mouth going dry as he saw Miss Patterson's face fall.

"Oh, no," she breathed, one hand at her heart. "What has occurred, Lord Catesby?"

He tried to clear his throat, tried to appear matter of fact, but the words stuck to his lips.

"Mr. Jefferson is to reside here overnight," he said, with a fair amount of difficulty. "He explained he was to continue on to London come the morrow and it would not have been proper for me to ignore such a matter. Of course, I offered him a room."

For a moment, there was nothing but stunned silence. Francis let his eyes rove around the room, taking in his mother's horrified face, Lord Rapson's astonished expression, and Miss Patterson's fearful gaze.

"What is it I have done?" he asked, feeling the burden of responsibility settle onto his shoulders as he spoke. "What is so terrible about Mr. Jefferson that I ought not to have offered such an invitation?"

Miss Patterson sat a little further forward in her chair, piercing him with a suddenly fierce gaze. "Because, Lord Catesby, he has threatened the lives of both myself and of my brother. Because he is nothing more than a scoundrel and a villain. Because I have spent months hiding from him, only to now find he has discovered us. Is that enough of a reason for you?"

CHAPTER 10

"Lord Catesby?"

It had been some hours since Lord Catesby had discovered the truth about her identity and about Mr. Jefferson and still, the guilt on her shoulders had not yet dissipated, not even slightly. She ought not to have spoken so sharply to the gentleman, to the one man from whom the truth had been hidden. And yet, hearing that he had offered Mr. Jefferson a place to stay had sent both fear and anger through her, and she had spoken from the feelings within her heart.

He half turned. "Mrs. Harrington – I mean, Miss Patterson. Good evening."

She bobbed her curtsy as usual. "I think, given that I am to remain as your housekeeper for the time being, you ought to refer to me as before."

A rueful smile caught his lips. "Is that so?" he muttered, turning his back on her to walk closer to the fire that was burning in the grate. "I confess I am finding this all very difficult, Miss Patterson. I do not know what to call you, and I certainly think it rather terrible that you are still under the guise of a housekeeper when you ought not to be anything of the sort."

Rebecca gave him a half smile. "It is for the best, Lord Catesby. I am quite sure."

They had discussed the matter at some length that evening, quite uncertain as to what Mr. Jefferson's plans and intentions were. Lord Catesby surmised that the gentleman wished to ensure that the house was, in fact, entirely free of Lord Rapson and so, from that, a plan had been formed. It was by no means a very good plan, for there was a good deal that could go wrong and even the dowager had looked somewhat perturbed. She had suggested that Rebecca and her brother relocate to her smaller home, but Rebecca had not agreed. This was not the way forward. They had to face this together and stop Mr. Jefferson altogether. Running and hiding was no longer something she was willing to continue.

"Mr. Jefferson retired early," Lord Catesby continued, in a flat voice. "I am quite sure he intends to squirrel all through the house once we are all abed and, even if that is not what he has thought to do, I am quite sure that George, the footman, will make certain to put the idea in his head – just as we have intended, of course."

Her stomach turned over, even though she knew this was what had been planned. "I am a little frightened, I confess," she replied, quietly. "I do hope my brother will not be in danger."

Lord Catesby did not smile. "You can trust me," he said, softly. "You know very well that he will not deal with your cousin alone."

"Yes, I know," she said quietly, shutting the door tightly behind her so that it closed with a soft click. "I do trust you, my lord."

Lord Catesby looked at her then, his eyes filled with the flames of the fire. There was a deep intensity to them, a burning that seared her very soul.

"I am sorry," she said, knowing that she had already apologized more than once. "I did not mean to deceive you."

He held up one hand, turning his face away. "Enough, Miss Patterson, I beg you. I have had enough apologies for one day. I hold no anger nor regret in this matter. I can understand why you have run from your cousin and why your brother has felt so helpless. To be facing a man who does not care about his reputation, nor about your own lives, must be difficult indeed."

She nodded and moved away from the door, her body humming with a mixture of anxiety and anticipation. "My brother did all he could, going so far as to call Jefferson out, but my cousin ignored him. I believe he has lost his mind somewhat, growing so obsessive over what he long desires that he will do anything to have it."

"Your fortune," Lord Catesby murmured, looking a little more relaxed. "He would take it by force."

She shook her head slowly, feeling the agony and the fear she had been so used to wrap around her again. "I knew he would use my brother against me and so I left. I thought that if my cousin could not find me and if my brother remained on his estate, then the matter would come to an end. I never imagined that my cousin would make an attempt on my brother's life in order to force him to reveal my whereabouts." Filled with sadness, she closed her eyes to prevent tears from falling. "What else could I do? What could Rapson do? We are at the mercy of a madman."

When she opened her eyes, she found Lord Catesby standing by her, having moved closer to her in seeing her distress. His eyes sought her own, searching her face as he managed a small smile.

"I am here with you now," he assured her, touching her hand with his own. "I know why you did not say a word to me, why you kept your identity a secret from me, but I do wish that you had told me from the very beginning."

Rebecca shook her head. "Your mother was a little unsure as to how you would react," she replied, quietly. "You have been caught up with all manner of estate business, and there have been so many weddings to deal with that even I did not want to bring more of a burden to you. After all, you have nothing whatsoever to do with my family. Why should I bring my difficulties into your life?"

His lips curved gently. "Mayhap because I would have been entirely willing to have helped you," he suggested, his fingers still capturing hers. "From the moment I saw you, Miss Patterson, you burned into my very soul. Had I but known the truth, then I would not have spent all this time berating myself, forcing my heart to forget you, only for it to fill with you all over again."

His breath brushed across her cheek and, for a moment, Rebecca forgot completely about Mr. Jefferson and her very reason for being in the library with Lord Catesby. "I have confused you, I know – and in turn, I suppose, you have confused me, but even with only a few hours consideration, I know that I care for you still, Miss Patterson. I wish to know you better, although I am quite certain that your kind and gentle nature is truly who you are." He glanced around the room at the books before returning his gaze to her. "There are so many things I wish to discuss with you. Miss Patterson, my desire is to know everything I can about you, to allow my heart to feel all it wishes. Can you understand that?"

She swallowed hard, her throat dry. "I – I can, my lord," she replied, hoarsely.

"When I kissed you," he continued, making her face flame with heat, "You did not turn from me, I do not think. If I remember correctly, you remained as you were and allowed me to do so. I distinctly remember you returning my kiss, Miss Patterson."

She closed her eyes tightly, overwhelmed by the awareness of him. "I did not think you would recall such a thing, my lord."

"But I did," he replied, gently. "Might I hope, my lady, that there could be some return to my affections?"

Going quite still, Rebecca looked into his eyes. Her heart and mind were full of a great many swirling emotions and thoughts, all wrapped up in one another and now he was only adding to them.

"My lord," she said slowly, trying her best to put her colliding thoughts into words. "I do not know what to say, nor what to think. You are right to state that I returned your kiss, but I will admit to being rather surprised by my own response." Even now, the touch of his fingers on hers was sending streaks of excitement up into her heart, a heart that was clouded by the knowledge that Mr. Jefferson was not only present in this house but would soon be seeking either herself or her brother. "I do not think that there is a lack of feeling, my lord, but only that it is very slight," she confessed, seeing the light in his eyes begin to fade. "There has been so much happening of late that I do not know what I truly feel about anything."

He touched her face with one finger, sending a shiver straight through her. "And once Mr. Jefferson is dealt with?" he asked, his voice low and warm, wrapping itself around her. "What then, my dear lady? Will you consider your heart again? Might you permit me to court you?"

She smiled at him then, relieved that he understood. "I can promise you, Lord Catesby, that I would be more than delighted to receive your court," she confessed, making his smile widen. "But as to my heart, allow it some time to be free from the fear and the worry that has held it for so long. As you may recall, I accused you of kissing me simply so that you might turn me out of your house!"

Rubbing the back of his neck, Lord Catesby looked at her ruefully from under his brows. "I can understand why," he admitted, quietly. "My goodness, we have both been wrapped in uncertainty and suspicion, have we not, Miss Patterson? Although I will admit a certain relief in being able to speak to you so freely."

Her heart lifted all the more. "I thank you for your consideration of me, Lord Catesby. I would have you know that I am truly appreciative for all you have done for me thus far – and all you will do when it comes to Mr. Jefferson." The reminder that her cousin was within the house sent shivers down her spine, and she stepped away from Lord Catesby for a moment, rubbing her arms as though to ward off a chill. Out of the corner of her eye, she saw the smile fade from Lord Catesby's face, replaced with an almost grim appearance, as though he too had only just recalled why they were in the library. "Ah yes, of course. We are to take on your adversary together, are we not? When did your brother say to be ready?"

"Within the hour, Lord Catesby," she replied, glancing at the grandfather clock in the corner. "Come now, I suppose we must prepare."

Lord Catesby chuckled, his eyes darting to hers and causing her to blush all the more. "I must say, I find that I am rather expectant with this part of my mother's plan, Miss Patterson. What say you?"

She stepped closer to him, the heat from the fire warming her completely. "I find that I am a little anxious, my lord," she replied, her voice a little thin. "What if it is all to go wrong? What if my cousin does not believe you?"

He patted her shoulder before resting his hand there for a moment, running it down her arm so that he might catch her fingers. "He will," he stated, firmly, giving her not even a single moment to disagree. "It will all come out in the end, my dear. You will be safe; your brother will be able to return home, and you shall have your fortune in its entirety when the time comes."

She let out a long, slow breath so as to ensure she remained composed and calm. "I hardly care about that any longer, Lord Catesby. Just so long as my brother is safe, then that is all that matters to me."

This seemed to please him. "Which is just as it should be, Miss Patterson."

CHAPTER 11

"I hear footsteps."

Francis looked down at Miss Patterson and saw her cheeks flush with heat. Her eyes were flickering with both fear and expectation, akin to his own swirling emotions. Believing it to be Mr. Jefferson who was to come into the room, having been prompted by Francis' footman, Francis took Miss Patterson in his arms, holding her tightly against him. Her back was to the door, and he let his hands slip to her waist, her hands linking behind his neck.

Her breath quickened, matching his own. This was both a delight and torture, giving him just what he desired whilst anticipating that he was to be encountered found at any moment. George, Francis' footman, had been told to speak to Mr. Jefferson about the presence of Lord Rapson within the house, making sure to appear as though he ought not to be speaking so candidly. He was also to mention that he knew Lord Rapson often enjoyed spending his evenings in the library, which was just where Francis intended to be 'discovered' with Miss Patterson.

"Are you quite ready, my dear?" he murmured, seeing her eyes burn with a sudden fire.

"Quite," she whispered, moving all the closer.

He had not intended to kiss her but, much to his surprise, Francis realized that this was precisely what he was going to do. His mother had suggested that he and Miss Patterson stand close to one another, embracing with a tender affection, but had never once suggested that there be anything more than the holding of hands. And yet, somehow, he had lowered his head and captured her lips with his own, forgetting entirely about the reason for their closeness.

"Good gracious, Lord Catesby! I did not know you had a mistress within these four walls!"

Miss Patterson lurched away from Francis at once, and it was only the fact that he held her tightly around the waist that kept her from moving away entirely. The fear in her expression was immediate, and Francis felt his own heart tug with both anger and dread.

"Mr. Jefferson," he said coolly. "I was not expecting you. I thought you had retired for the evening." Francis was relieved to see that Miss Patterson had recalled what she was meant to do and had kept her back to her cousin, refusing to reveal herself to him.

Mr. Jefferson eyed her carefully, before turning his sharp gaze back onto Francis. "I thought to come and fetch a book or two," he explained, lazily. "Couldn't sleep."

"Is that so?" Francis murmured, lifting a brow. "Well, if you will just excuse me for a moment, I ought to –"

"Is this your wife?"

Francis lifted his chin, glaring at Mr. Jefferson's impertinence. "Mr. Jefferson, I hardly think it is of any importance to you whether or not I am wed. These affairs are entirely my own."

This harsh reprimand, however, only appeared to make Mr. Jefferson's interest all the more apparent.

Mr. Jefferson took a step forward. "Of course," he muttered, whilst still casting a sharp eye over the back of Miss Patterson's head. "It was just that we did not dine with anyone else and I did wonder if you had any other guests present."

Francis' eyes glittered. "Again, Mr. Jefferson," he stated, firmly. "None of this is of any importance to you and I would kindly –"

Mr. Jefferson gasped, one hand to his mouth whilst his eyes widened. "Good gracious! Rebecca!"

Miss Patterson, who had half turned her head so that her cousin would be able to make out her profile, drew a little away from Francis, who let one hand slip from her waist, pushing her behind him.

"It *is* you," Mr. Jefferson continued, sounding utterly thrilled. "My, my, my. However, did you end up here?" His dark eyes flickered to Francis and back again whilst a wide grin spread across his face. "Came to him for help, did you?"

Miss Patterson lifted her chin. "I am the housekeeper, Mrs. Harrington."

Mr. Jefferson let out a shout of laughter. "Is that what he calls you, is it? Keeps you here as the housekeeper but makes sure you know *precisely* what your role is – your nightly duties."

Francis' body rippled with anger. "Steady, Mr. Jefferson. That's quite enough."

Mr. Jefferson ignored him, however, seemingly aware that Miss Patterson was in something of a difficult situation.

"My goodness, Rebecca, how unfortunate that you have been discovered! And here I am looking for your brother, only to discover you here! My, my. Your reputation is quite ruined now, you know. What will you do now?"

Miss Patterson stepped away from Francis entirely, crossing her arms across her body in a defensive gesture. "My dear Mr. Jefferson, I care very little about my reputation. I have my fortune, as you know."

Mr. Jefferson chuckled. "And what of your brother and his future, Rebecca? To have a sister so soiled, so defiled – well, that will make his chances of finding a suitable bride almost impossible! No-one will want to align themselves with such a family now, will they? What are the chances for your brother to then find himself a wife and produce the required heir?" His eyes glittered, and he took a small step forward. "Very little, do you not think?"

Francis said nothing, despite the growing urge to step forward and smite the man hard across the face. They had known that Mr. Jefferson would use what he had seen against Miss Patterson, just as he had done. He was immensely proud of Miss Patterson, seeing her standing there with a firm stance and cold, sharp eyes that glared at her cousin. She was not showing him even a modicum of fear, despite the fact that she was probably trembling inside. After all, had he not felt her shudder in his arms but a few moments ago?

She glanced up at him and, for a moment, Mr. Jefferson's smile slipped. Francis knew what he was thinking. Should Francis offer to wed the lady in order to save her reputation, then there would be very few consequences. In fact, Miss Patterson would do her family line the world of good in marrying an earl. This was where he had to step in, where he had to show his disdain for the idea of marrying the lady, even though it was quite the opposite of what he felt.

"I am sorry, Miss Patterson," he grated, his hands curling into fists as he forced himself to steady his resolve. "But you can receive no help from me." Shaking his head, he let his eyes drift away from her, placing an arrogant expression on his face. "After all, a gentleman does not marry their mistress."

A small cry of glee escaped from Mr. Jefferson's throat. "So, you see, Miss Patterson, you can have very little option *but* to do as I have asked," he said, as Francis slowly began to make his way towards the door, feigning disinterest. "What say you to that?"

Francis heard Miss Patterson take in a shuddering breath and felt himself curl with rage. He wanted nothing more than to throw himself at Mr. Jefferson and beat the man until he knew nothing but the welcome arms of unconsciousness, but he had to continue on with this façade. After all, that was what it was, he reminded himself. Play acting. A disguise. A falsehood that would lead to Mr. Jefferson being outsmarted and disgraced.

"Ah, Lord Rapson," he said loudly, pushing the door open to admit Miss Patterson's brother. "I'm afraid I have something to confess to you."

Mr. Jefferson swung around as Lord Rapson stepped inside, his face paling a little as he looked from one gentleman to the other.

"It seems Mr. Jefferson had stumbled upon myself and your sister in a rather...intimate embrace," Francis continued, in a somewhat apologetic tone. "I do apologize for keeping her presence here a secret, but she came to me *begging* for help and urged me not to let a single person know of her whereabouts, not even you." He saw Mr. Jefferson's mouth swing open in surprise. "I know you have been looking for her."

Lord Rapson played his part wonderfully. He let his eyes trail from Miss Patterson to Mr. Jefferson before turning dark, angry eyes onto Francis.

"Do you mean to tell me, Lord Catesby," he said, harshly. "That you have been keeping my sister here all along?"

Francis shrugged. "She has been the housekeeper," he said, truthfully.

"Amongst other things," Mr. Jefferson added at once, putting his hands firmly on his hips. "And unless you want all and sundry to know of what else your dearly loved sister has been up to, you'll hand her over to me, Rapson."

Lord Rapson started as though he had been slapped and it was only with a sharp warning look from Francis that he prevented himself from swinging around and punching Mr. Jefferson hard across the face. Closing his eyes for a moment, Lord Rapson drew in a long, calming breath before turning away from Francis and facing Mr. Jefferson.

"You've been looking for me," he said, slowly. "Why?"

Mr. Jefferson chuckled. "I am not to be outdone, Lord Rapson. I know what I want, and I intend to have it."

Lord Rapson shook his head, putting one hand to his brow. "You want money. I will give it to you."

A sneer crossed Mr. Jefferson's face. "Not enough. I want your sister's fortune – and having her as my bride, and as one of my possessions, will make me more than satisfied." His sneer spread as he looked at Lord Rapson with a hard look in his eyes, ignoring Francis completely. It was as though the man had forgotten that he was even in the room, focusing entirely on Lord Rapson.

"Else," Mr. Jefferson continued, firmly, "everyone in good standing will know of your sister's disgrace. Think of the damage that will do to your good name, to your attempts to secure a bride. Your name will be tainted, your children unable to escape the shame brought on them by *her*." He spat the last word, shooting a glance at Miss Patterson who was still standing tall.

Lord Rapson said nothing for a moment, swaying slightly. "How did you find me, Mr. Jefferson?"

Francis stepped back into the shadows, allowing the scene to play out in front of him. Mr. Jefferson had a gleam in his eye that made him think Miss Patterson had been quite correct to suggest that Mr. Jefferson had gone mad. He appeared almost crazed with the desire to have what he had long sought. He was speaking with such freedom, seemingly so unconcerned at Francis' presence in the room, that Francis felt himself grow tense. There was no certainty about what Mr. Jefferson would do once he discovered that this had all been nothing but a ruse.

Mr. Jefferson chuckled. "One of your maids is very easily persuaded, Rapson. A little bit of attention and she gave me whatever I wanted. *So* sympathetic, truly." Leaning lazily on the back of the chair, he gestured towards Miss Patterson as he spoke. "No-one knew where your sister had gone to, but I soon found out that you had been corresponding with someone of late. Took a little bit of persuading but that stupid maid soon brought me your last piece of correspondence with Lord Catesby." Shaking his head with a touch of wryness about his expression, he looked at Lord Rapson with a degree of satisfaction. "Those maids are so easily persuaded and, as I have said before to you, Rapson, I always get what I want."

"And you want me."

Mr. Jefferson did not so much as glance at Miss Patterson. "I want your fortune," he said, with a small sneer. "You ought to have given it to me the moment I asked for it. Your father always promised I was to have something!"

"And you did, did you not?" Lord Rapson interrupted, darkly. "But it was not enough."

"It is *never* enough!" Mr. Jefferson shouted, his face suddenly going a dark, blood red. "I was to have the title! I was to be the heir! And then suddenly *you* reappeared!" Something flashed in Mr.

Jefferson's hand, and Francis felt his heart stop dead. This was not something they had ever considered.

Lord Rapson shook his head slowly. "There was a misunderstanding, that was all, Jefferson. News was brought to my father that I had been taken gravely ill and, of course, a good many people presumed I had died as often happens. It was not the case, as you can see." Shaking his head, Lord Rapson let out a long breath whilst fixing his cousin with his gaze. "You have no claim to anything, Jefferson."

Mr. Jefferson looked all the more crazed. "I *need* the money, Rapson!" he shouted, clearly growing desperate. "I must have it, else —"

"Else, what?" Lord Rapson interrupted, loudly. "Your creditors will come to your door, to take away all you own? All the money you claim you require is simply due to your own lack of sense, Jefferson. Your vices, your follies, are all your own. You can try to claim my sister to seek her fortune, you can even attempt to kill me in order to gain the title – but it has all come to naught. Indeed, it will not be my sister who is disgraced but rather it will be *you*."

This appeared to be too much for Mr. Jefferson to take. Before Francis could move, he leapt wildly at Lord Rapson. It was as though it all happened slowly, for Francis could not move, could not even speak as he watched Miss Patterson let out a shriek and twist her body to prevent Mr. Jefferson from reaching her brother.

CHAPTER 12

The two bodies fell together with a thump on the carpeted floor, just as the dowager burst into the room. Francis had ordered her to remain outside with the footmen and butler ready for his order but having heard the scream from both Mr. Jefferson and Miss Patterson, had been unable to wait any longer. Francis, finally free of the ice that had filled his limbs, rushed forward with his mother towards Miss Patterson and Mr. Jefferson, who was being dragged to his feet by one furious and terrified Lord Rapson.

"Hold him," Francis ordered, as Mr. Jefferson was thrown towards the footmen and butler. He bent down by Lord Rapson, seeing a dark stain begin to seep through Miss Patterson's gown. His throat ached with fear.

"I am quite all right," Miss Patterson replied, her voice weak. "It is just my arm, that is all. Do help me sit up."

"This was not what we had intended," he whispered, as Lord Rapson tried to help his sister up carefully. "We thought to –"

"Never mind that," the dowager snapped, grasping his arm. "Help her up and seat her here." She turned to the butler, telling him to fetch the doctor at once and ordering hot water, cloths, and bandages. "Goodness me, Miss Patterson, whatever were you thinking?"

Francis, still on his knees, shuffled towards Miss Patterson, looking at her arm with concern. It was bleeding, evidently and he could not tell how deep the wound was.

Lord Rapson pulled a chair over to his sister and sat down heavily, clearly shocked by all that had gone on. He took her free hand and held it tightly, his expression tight. "You did not have to do that, Rebecca. I —"

"I could not let him hurt you," Miss Patterson interrupted, gently, as the dowager carefully pulled the torn sleeve away from Miss Patterson's arm, revealing the wound to her forearm.

Lord Rapson swallowed hard, shaking his head and raking one hand through his hair over and over as he attempted to speak. "You could have been gravely injured, Rebecca."

"But she is not," the dowager replied, practically. "You must have raised your arm in defense of your person as you jumped in front of your brother, Miss Patterson, but I do believe you saved your life by such an action." She smiled at the young lady, clearly relieved and yet upset at what had occurred. "You are quite remarkable, truly."

Francis was utterly relieved to see Miss Patterson manage a small smile, though her face was rather white. She was not going to die, it seemed, and his heart finally broke free of the terrifying worry that had torn through it the moment he had watched Miss Patterson leap in front of Mr. Jefferson's knife.

"What shall I do with him, my lord?"

Slowly, Francis got to his feet, turning to see Mr. Jefferson sitting, white-faced, in his chair. The man had appeared to shrink into it, as though only just realizing what he had done. Anger coursed through him, urging him to move forward and strike the man hard but it was only by sheer force of will that he remained exactly where he was.

"Send for the constabulary," he grated, harshly. "This man made an attempt on the life of Lord Rapson and, in doing so, has gravely injured Miss Patterson, the viscount's sister. In addition, I believe he is very badly in debt and will be wanted by a good many others."

Mr. Jefferson let out a low wail of fear, no longer the arrogant, haughty gentleman who believed he was owed everything.

"And take him below stairs and secure him tightly," Francis finished, as two footmen hauled Mr. Jefferson out of his chair. "You are to stand guard over him until he is taken away. Send the constabulary to me the moment they arrive. We all will have a good deal to say to them, I am quite sure."

Mr. Jefferson whimpered, a pathetic creature now. "Please," he whined, looking at Lord Rapson desperately. "I did not mean – surely, you cannot….it may be the gallows!"

Lord Rapson turned his head away from Mr. Jefferson, clearly disgusted by the fellow. "Take him," he muttered, as the men moved towards the door. "I have nothing more to say to you, Mr. Jefferson."

Finally, the door shut behind the offending gentleman and the occupants of the room gave a collective sigh of relief. Francis felt his legs a little weak and immediately offered them all a brandy, which was accepted, although the dowager insisted on having a tea tray also sent, despite the hour.

"This was not what we had intended, as you know," Francis murmured, handing Miss Patterson a small brandy. "I was meant to reveal to Mr. Jefferson that this had been nothing more than a ruse. He was meant to realize that he had revealed his hand not only to me but also to my mother waiting outside. Our influence and our threats were meant to be enough to send him away and, if that had not been the case, then I would have settled his debts with his creditors and taken them on myself. That would have been enough, surely, to stop him from –"

"My lord."

Miss Patterson put her good hand on his arm, preventing him from finishing his sentence.

"You need not go over it again, my lord," she said, gently. "What happened was not what any of us expected, I will admit, but we have brought Mr. Jefferson to justice regardless." She glanced down at her bloodied arm, which the dowager was carefully cleaning. "I may have sustained an injury, but I will recover fully, in time, I am quite sure. You need not feel any guilt, my lord. I am glad it is all at an end, and I am glad that I was able to protect my brother."

Lord Rapson shook his head. "I ought to have been the one protecting you, my dear sister."

Francis, who had been unable to take his eyes from Miss Patterson, finding her both extraordinary and utterly wonderful, let out a sigh of relief that took the tension from his limbs. "You were both in danger from a very dangerous man. I know he cannot hurt either of you again and that does bring me a good deal of relief, I will admit."

Miss Patterson smiled at him, wincing just a little as the dowager dabbed at the wound. "Thank you for all you have done, Lord Catesby. I am sorry that I did not come to you from the first. Mayhap I should have done."

The dowager glanced up, her expression a little guilty. "And mayhap I ought not to have encouraged Miss Patterson not to do so, Francis. I thought you too caught up with all other manner of things."

Francis shook his head, a small smile capturing his lips. "Mama, you too need not worry. I think that it has all ended quite well, Miss Patterson's injury aside. I just pray that this may mean that you shall begin to absent yourself from my house and my study a little more?"

His mother laughed, brightening the mood all the more. "Indeed, Francis, I shall. Thank you for your understanding."

At that moment, the door opened, and the butler announced both the doctor and the constabulary had arrived. Both parties clearly willing to answer the summons of an Earl with the greatest of speed.

"I shall leave you with the good doctor," Francis murmured, as Lord Rapson got up to speak to the two men from the constabulary. "But I think it best if you remain at Catesby House for some time, in order to recover yourself. What say you?"

Her eyes glowed despite the pain. "You are most kind, my lord."

His smile grew slowly. "I believe we have some things to say to each other, my dear Miss Patterson. Perhaps tomorrow?"

She nodded slowly, her cheeks a little dark. "Tomorrow would suit me very well, Lord Catesby. I thank you."

EPILOGUE

Despite the urging of her brother and the dowager, Rebecca did not wish to remain in her bed for any length of time. She had slept wonderfully well, even though she had refused the doctor's suggestion of laudanum, her thoughts no longer worried over Mr. Jefferson and what he might do next.

She did not regret for a single moment her actions of last evening. She had seen the knife, seen Mr. Jefferson lunge for her brother and had reacted out of instinct. The pain of the knife slicing into her arm had taken her breath from her body, the sheer weight of Mr. Jefferson landing on her as they had fallen to the floor adding even more to her distress, but within the hour, everything had seemed to be a good deal brighter. Her arm had been cleaned and dressed, her brother and Lord Catesby had talked to the constabulary about all that had occurred, and she and the dowager had sunk back into their chairs and drank a nice hot cup of tea, finally free of it all.

"Do stop worrying, Mark," she muttered, seeing her brother hesitate in the doorway of the drawing room. "I am not an invalid. My arm is already improving. You see?" She lifted it and attempted to wave at him, only for a stab of pain to shoot through her. Wincing, she set it down gently in her lap, seeing Mark's concerned expression.

"Are you sure you are quite all right?" he asked, gently, coming to sit by her. "After last evening, I thought you might be quite overcome with exhaustion."

She smiled into his anxious face. "I feel quite free," she replied, quietly. "My heart is glad; my mind is filled with nothing but delight. I do not have to worry about Jefferson any longer. He can never come near us, never attempt to hurt either one of us ever again."

Her brother nodded, his expression a little rueful. "Indeed. Although I shall have to find out which maid it was that was so willing to tell Mr. Jefferson such details and to go through my personal things in order to give him the information he required."

Rebecca nodded her expression a little sad. "Foolish girl. I do not believe she had any true understanding of what she was doing."

"Regardless, I will have to send her away," Mark said, firmly. "No references, nothing. I will not have such disrespect shown to me."

Understanding, Rebecca patted his shoulder gently. "I know, Mark. Now, why do you not go in search of a good book for me to read since I am supposed to be resting?"

He chuckled and got to his feet. "You really do not wish to be fussed over now, do you?"

"No," Rebecca said, sternly. "I do not. Now, off with you."

Her brother laughed and quit the room, promising to be back in a few minutes with at least four books for her to choose from. Rebecca laughed softly and closed her eyes to enjoy the peace for a moment – only for a gentle hand to touch her shoulder.

Jumping, she opened her eyes expecting to see her brother had sneaked back in to again ensure she was all right, only to see Lord Catesby looking down at her. His expression was one of tenderness, sending a flurry of warmth all through her.

"My dear lady," he murmured, quietly. "Might I sit with you for a moment?"

Her throat was suddenly dry. "But of course, Lord Catesby," she replied, in a voice that did not sound like her own. So much had changed over the last two days, so much had developed within her own heart, that she felt almost nervous to be alone with him.

Sitting down next to her, Lord Catesby glanced at her arm. "How are you this afternoon, my dear?"

Smiling at his caring expression, she looked into his eyes and found him looking back at her with a soft smile on his face. "I am doing very well, I thank you," she replied, her eyes drifting to his lips for a moment as a flush went straight through her. "You have been quite wonderful, Lord Catesby, truly."

"No." He picked up her good hand and brought it to his lips, placing a kiss to the back of it. Sparks shot through her.

"You are wonderful, Miss Patterson."

"Rebecca," she found herself saying, suddenly desperate to have such an intimacy from his lips. Lips she had already kissed a good many times. "Please, do call me Rebecca."

The delight in his eyes glowed. "Rebecca," he murmured, softly. "I did say to you last evening that I had a good many things to say to you, but now that I am with you, I find my heart filled with one single desire that eclipses all other."

Swallowing, her stomach filled with butterflies. "If it is that you wish to court me, then I will gladly accept," she replied, her voice barely audible. "I believe I have already made my affection for you more than evident."

He chuckled softly. "I believe I too have done the very same," he replied, his hand now holding hers tightly. "And yet now that you are to remain here until you have recovered, I find the idea of letting you return to your brother's home almost torture. It pains me to think of you leaving my side, not when we have experienced so very much." Smiling at her still, he drew in a breath and ran his fingers down the curve of her cheek, forcing her to catch her breath. "I would rather it, Rebecca, that you would never leave."

Her heart burst from her chest, soaring towards the skies. It was as though, with the departure of Mr. Jefferson from her life, that she could finally see what it was that she wanted, what it was she desired. This gentleman here, the one who had clearly loved her for so long despite his determination not to do so, was becoming more and more to her with each passing minute. Her emotions were stirred every time he came into the room, every time his lips pressed to hers. She did not want to leave, she realized, but that would mean....

"I would have you as my wife, Rebecca," Lord Catesby finished, quietly. "If you wish it, you can reside with my mother until the time passes for your fortune to become your own. I know that is important to you and I would never ask you to wed me before that time."

She shook her head immediately, and the light faded from his eyes. He thought she was refusing him when the opposite was quite true. "My dear Lord Catesby," she replied, leaning a little closer to him. "My fortune matters not. It is no longer what I think of, no longer what I fear I must protect. My heart has begun to call for you. You asked me to trust you, and that is what I am doing. I know you will treat me with all kindness, with all care, and therefore my fortune matters not a jot."

His eyes widened for a moment before his lips tugged into a smile. "Does that mean, then, that you will marry me, Rebecca?" he asked, hope filling his expression. "Will you be my bride? My heart has been filled with none but you since the first day I saw you. No longer do I have to hide my heart and ignore my feelings. They are all for you, my dear lady. I love you with every part of my being."

Wishing she could fling herself into his arms, Rebecca contented herself with pressing his hand tightly with her own. "I love you in return, Lord Catesby. I will be your bride. I will be your wife. And I will love you every day of my life."

BOOK 7: THE SCANDALOUS DOWAGER COUNTESS

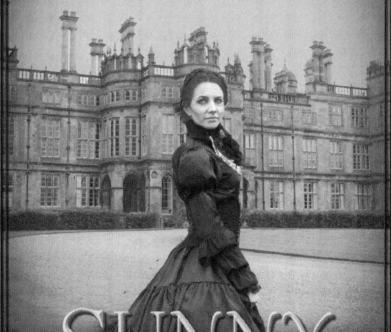

BOOK 7

HOUSE OF CATESBY

The Scandalous Dowager Countess

SUNNY
BROOKS

FOREWORD

Never let it be said that the young have all the fun. Let's embrace life at every age, after every setback, during every chapter of our lives!

Live your best life and know that you deserve to be happy and loved.

From my heart to yours!

- Sunny Brooks

CHAPTER 1

L ady Martha Catesby, wife to the late Earl Catesby, looked around with a satisfactory air. She was to go to London and, having spent the last six years in this quite wonderful and yet often lonely house, she was looking forward to a little more excitement.

"Mama," her daughter, Emily, said in a slightly unconvinced tone. "Are you quite sure about all of this?" She frowned at her mother's smile, clearly not as delighted as she that Martha was to go to town.

"Yes, yes, I am quite certain," Martha replied, patting her daughter's shoulder. "Believe me, each of my children in turn has done their best to convince me that I ought to remain here in the dower house, but I feel as though I deserve a little more enjoyment from life." Seeing Emily's startled look, Martha regretted her quick words. "That is not to say that I do not greatly enjoy your visits, Emily, dear, and especially now that you have such a beautiful son of your own, but almost everyone else is so very far away." She smiled sadly, hoping that her daughter would understand.

"Francis and Henry do not live more than a few miles from here!" Emily protested at once. "You cannot mean to tell me that you live too far for you to visit whenever you wish?!"

Martha laughed, knowing that Emily was quite right. "No, indeed, that is not at all what I am suggesting. However, what I am trying to say is…" Sighing, she took her daughter's hand, knowing that she would have to be truthful. "My dear girl, when one's children marry, then it is quite right for their lives to move on in a very different way from one's own. I know that I am always welcome to see Francis and Rebecca, and indeed, to call upon Henry and Laurie, but I am also keenly aware that they all require the space and time to enjoy their own lives together. It would not do for me to intrude too much, although I know they are all most generous in their willingness to see me at any time and for however long I wish it." She smiled, seeing Emily's shoulders soften, a sign that she was beginning to understand. "Besides, almost everyone is with child—or has just had a baby! That is a great adjustment, although I will be glad to visit you when your time comes."

Emily flushed bright red, her eyes widening as she stared at her mother. "How did you know?"

Martha laughed. "Because, my dear girl, I have borne six children and am well aware of how one looks and feels near the very beginning. I have not seen you this pale and tired since you were first told you were carrying Joseph." She was referring to Emily and Thomas' son and heir who, at almost four years of age, was precocious and utterly charming. Thomas had taken him outside to the gardens for a time, so that Emily and Martha might have a chance to talk, although Martha was still suspicious that Emily was trying to convince her to remain at home.

"You are very insightful, Mama," Emily admitted with a small sigh. "The truth is, I have been feeling quite terrible these last few weeks, although I have had a ravenous hunger."

Martha lifted an eyebrow. "I felt the very same way when I was carrying your brothers." She saw Emily's face pale but patted her hand gently. "There is always the chance of twins, my dear girl, but it is nothing to fear. As I said, regardless of whether it is one babe or two, I shall be with you should you need me, just as I have been for everyone else thus far." A small smile crept over her face as she recollected just how many brows she had mopped, how many hands she had held, and how many baby cries she had wept over. She now had six grandchildren, starting with Joseph, who had been swiftly followed by Matthew, the son of Charles and Abigail. Thereafter had come the birth of Hugh, son to Helena and Richard. Charles and Abigail had then delighted her further with a daughter of their own, whom they had named after Martha. Sophie and David had been blessed with twins, Sarah and William, and now both Laurie and Rebecca were soon to go into confinement. It appeared that Emily would not long be behind them.

It was all so very wonderful, and yet Martha had been unable to remove from herself the desire to return to London, to reacquaint herself with some of her old friends. For so many years of her life, her time had been entirely taken up with her children and her husband, whereas now she had time to do whatever she wished. Of course, her children and grandchildren were a joy and a delight to her almost constantly, but that still did not take away from the small stab of loneliness that would attack her most evenings—a loneliness that seemed to be growing steadily.

"Very well, Mama," Emily said with a sigh, breaking through Martha's thoughts. "If you must go to London, then I see that I shall not be able to prevent you."

Martha chuckled, patting her daughter's hand. "You have learned of your mother's stubbornness very quickly, I see. I promise I shall not be long in town. A month or two, and then I shall return home." She smiled as her daughter frowned, evidently thinking that two months was much too long for Martha to be away. "Laurie and Rebecca may need me then."

Emily nodded, although she said nothing more by way of trying to convince Martha to change her mind. "When do you leave?"

"Tomorrow," Martha replied, looking about her bedchamber and finding things to be quite satisfactory. "The maids have packed everything I will require and Francis has been very kind in allowing me to stay in the townhouse there."

Emily snorted in a most unladylike fashion. "*Allowing* you, Mama?

It is your townhouse as much as his, which he is well aware of. Although I hardly think he agreed to it so easily, given that he is not entirely content with you leaving."

Martha laughed, rose to her feet, and walked to the door. "Indeed, he was not. However, your brother knows me well enough to understand that I will not allow my mind to be altered by mere pleas."

"Just as I have learned," Emily mumbled darkly, taking her mother's arm. "Well, then, shall we take tea together since I shall not see you for some time?"

"Of course," Martha replied warmly, thinking that she would dearly like to talk of other things instead of her trip to London. "And I must remember to promise Joseph that I will bring something wonderful back for him from London. What do you think he would like?"

Managing to successfully move Emily onto another topic of conversation, Martha let out a small sigh of relief as Emily began to come up with suggestions of what Martha might buy for her grandson. This trip to London seemed to have caused more trouble than it was worth, given that each and every one of her children did not seem to want her to go.

But, then again, they could not understand what it was like to lose one's husband, to feel the world you had known and come to love now crashing down around your feet. They could not understand the loneliness and pain that came with a life lived alone, instead of a life shared with someone else, and for that, she did not begrudge them.

Six years, she thought to herself, as she walked towards the drawing room with Emily still chatting by her side. *Six years I have been without him. Six years since he left for a place I cannot yet follow him to. Six years of living alone.*

Silently, Martha wondered if that would ever change, or if this was the life she was destined to lead for the rest of her days here on this earth.

CHAPTER 2

Heading towards London seemed to bring Martha nothing but painful memories, which was something she had not expected. Having spent a good deal of time in London over the course of her life, she had not expected this trip to become something more agonizing than enjoyable.

She could remember all the times she had joined her husband and children in their carriage—although they had required to take two of them in later years—as they had driven towards London for the Season. She could even remember being in London as a debutante herself, never once thinking that she would be wed by the end of it.

A stab of pain brought both a small smile to her face and a tear to her eye. She had been so young to marry, only just out and enjoying her first Season at the tender age of seventeen, never thinking that she would find herself a suitable husband during her first year. The second year, her mother had reassured her, would be much more likely. She was simply to enjoy herself that first year. She was to make acquaintances, dance, converse and spend as much time as she could savoring every single indulgence.

And then, her father had introduced her to Joseph, the new Earl Catesby.

Even now, the memory of their first meeting had never left her. He had appeared so severe, his thick, dark eyebrows burrowing over his eyes, his mouth set into a thin line as he had surveyed her. She had disliked him intensely, comparing him to Lord Blackford, who had been showing her a particular interest of late, and finding Earl Catesby to be falling quite short. It did not help matters that the earl appeared to be a good deal older than she, and that he seemed quiet, gruff and quite stern in his character. She later learned, through conversation with her acquaintances, that the earl did not often make an appearance in London and certainly had not ever sought an introduction to a debutante. Everyone had thought that he found London society to be as dull and staid as they found him, but now that he had been given the title, perhaps, they had considered, he realized that he now needed a wife and a child whom he might make his heir.

Martha had prayed that she would not be sought out to be his bride.

But it had not been her choice to make. Within a fortnight, she had discovered herself to be betrothed to Earl Catesby, even though she did not know him at all. They had been introduced, and had conversed on only two prior occasions, but apparently that had been enough for the earl. Her father had been delighted with the match, her mother singing the earl's praises, whilst Martha had withered silently within. Lord Blackford had stated his congratulations with a look of sadness in his eyes, and she had wanted desperately to explain that it had not been her choice but that of her parents, but nothing had come to her lips.

And so, within the month, she had been married. The earl had not said a good deal to her on their wedding day, although he had been kind and gentle during his visit to her bed. What a shock it had been to discover she was soon expecting a child! She had felt almost a child herself, hardly prepared to be both a wife and mother—and yet the babe had arrived a month before her eighteenth birthday.

From that day on, Joseph had changed from a gruff, severe gentleman into a man she barely recognized. It was as though holding the child in his arms had made him soften completely, breaking apart the hard, coarse shell that he had built up around him. He had become tender in his affections, to the point that Martha had found herself falling in love with him and he with her. The difference in ages between them—a matter of almost sixteen years—no longer seemed to hold any particular importance. She had loved him for the man he was.

And thus arrived the rest of their children, with Francis as the eldest, followed by Emily, then the twins, Charles and Henry, Sophia and finally, Helena. She had birthed six children in eight years, which meant that by the age of six and twenty, she had well established her husband's household. With each child, Joseph had become even more loving, even more compassionate and caring, spending as much time as he could with his children and refusing to send them to boarding school at seven years of age, insisting that a tutor would do for his children until they were older.

He had been proven correct. Francis has grown up to be wise, kind and considerate, much like his father, and was doing marvelously well as the new Earl Catesby. Martha was quite sure that his father's influence was the reason for Francis' good heart, just as she believed was the case for the rest of her children.

She could see Joseph's influence everywhere, making her miss him almost every day that passed. It had been six years since he had died, leaving her alone in the world with six unmarried children—the youngest of them not yet eighteen—and all the grief and pain that came with losing the husband she had loved so very dearly.

But now, that grief had loosened its grip on the house of Catesby. Every single one of her children had married, finding love and affection with their chosen partners, and she could not have been more contented for each of them. The children borne thus far brought her so much joy that, at times, she could barely contain her happiness, but still underneath it all, had been a yearning for a life of her own.

The dower house was warm and comfortable, but it did not have the companionship that she had always found in Joseph. It was not, of course, that she was going to London in the hope of finding herself another husband, which, at the age of almost one and fifty, was quite ridiculous, but more that she hoped she might find good company there. Perhaps some of her old acquaintances might have returned for the Season, possibly with children of their own whom they would need to accompany, which would give Martha the opportunity to reacquaint herself with them all. Mayhap, in time, they would come to visit her, perhaps with a few having an extended stay at the dower house. That was the hope, at least.

Martha smiled to herself, her head resting back against the squabs as the driver called to her that they were only a few hours away from London. The last three days of travelling had wearied her but she was looking forward to being in town again. How much would have changed? Would anyone be there who might remember her?

A quiet laugh escaped her as she closed her eyes. Her son, Charles, his wife, Abigail, and their two children, Matthew and baby Martha, also resided in London and she was quite sure that she would often be invited to spend time in their home—most likely so that Charles could report back to his siblings on how their mother was doing, although Martha did not intend to give all that much away. This was to be her time and she did not feel the need to share the details of what she did with anyone, least of all, her son!

"Stop there!"

A gasp ripped from Martha's mouth as the carriage suddenly came to a shuddering stop. The sound of horses' hooves caught her ears, making her press her hand against her heart as she realized what was happening.

"Open that door!"

Martha wanted to scream, looking out of the window and seeing a figure dressed all in black, sitting astride a black stallion. He had a grey neckcloth tied over his face so that only his sharp, dark eyes could be seen.

"No, I cannot!" the driver shouted, refusing to leave his seat. "That be my mistress and you will not touch her!"

The horseman waved his pistol menacingly. "Would you prefer to be shot or shall I run you through?"

Knowing that it was not just her driver who was at risk of losing his life, but the other servants who accompanied her, including the maid who was still sound asleep in the opposite corner of the carriage, Martha held her breath. She did not want anyone to be hurt but the way this fellow was talking, she feared that she soon might have an injured —if not dead—servant on her hands.

"That is quite enough."

Throwing open the carriage door, Martha summoned all her courage and rose to her feet, looking at the man directly. "You will not harm anyone here."

The man dressed all in black looked back at her with an almost baleful gaze. "If you give me what I wish, then I have no need to harm anyone."

Martha shook her head, growing angry despite her fear. "None of what I own is yours to take," she said clearly, despite the urgent whispering of her maid behind her, who had apparently woken up on hearing Martha's loud voice. "You are attempting to rob me."

The man chuckled darkly, sending a tremor through Martha's body. "Some of us must make a living in any way we can, my lady," he said, with a small inclination of his head. "I apologize for the interruption to your journey, but for me, it is quite necessary."

She glared at him. "What is it you want, sir?"

He shrugged. "I do not mind particularly. Whatever it is of value that you can give me, my lady. Gold, coins, jewels." He examined her with a calculating eye. "That necklace you wear, and mayhap the ring on your finger. That would be enough to secure you safe passage."

Anger burned in her chest. "No," she replied, her heart suddenly beating wildly. "I will not give you my ring, but my pendant you may have without question."

A ripple of harsh laughter wafted towards her. "You cannot believe that you are able to bargain with me, my lady."

"I will not give you my ring," she repeated, without wavering. "I have gold, coins and jewels as you can see here." She lifted her pendant from her throat as it sparkled in the sunshine. "But the ring is mine."

The man slid from his horse, his pistol held loosely in one hand.

"I think, my dear lady," he said, his voice now somewhat quiet and gentle, as though he were speaking to a friend, "that I shall have to take your ring, given that it is so very precious to you." He tipped his head, his dark eyes sending a shudder through her. "It must be priceless if you cling onto it so, although, of course, I will take the rest." He held out his hand and she, somewhat unwillingly, gave him her ruby pendant and the small reticule she had in the carriage.

"The ring," he demanded, holding out his hand. "At once."

Despite the fear clamoring in her heart at his nearness, Martha lifted her chin and looked him steadily in the eye. "This ring will not bring you any great price," she stated with as much conviction as she could. "It is not the worth of it that matters, sir. It is my wedding ring. The one my late husband gave to me on the day I became his wife."

The fellow snorted, evidently refusing to believe her.

"I will not take it off, nor will I give it to you," she continued, ignoring him. "The only way you will have it is if you pry it from my cold, dead fingers."

The man's eyes narrowed, and Martha wished she could see his expression for she could not guess what he was thinking. Her spirit threatened to wilt within her but she remained strong with an effort, silently praying that he would give her a reprieve.

"What is your name?" the man asked after a moment, his head tilting slightly as though he might see her better.

"Lady Catesby," she replied, wondering what difference it would make if he knew her name. "My husband was the late Earl Catesby. This ring was his gift and, for the love of him and for the dear memories I have of him, I will not give it to you."

Silence fell. It was as though every living thing was waiting to see what would happen next, although Martha was quite sure the man could hear the frantic beating of her heart.

Then, much to her astonishment, the man turned away. Walking back towards his horse, he thrust the jewels into one of the saddle bags and then mounted his horse. With a jaunty tip of his hand, he turned the horse around and rode away, leaving her standing, utterly shocked, as she watched him disappear down the road.

CHAPTER 3

M artha was nervous.

Returning to London had been a good deal more trying than she had expected. First of all, she had been held up by the scoundrel on the black horse, who had taken her reticule and her ruby pendant, although, at least, he had not insisted upon taking her ring also. Thereafter, she had only just settled herself in her town house when Charles had called upon her, although he had not taken Abigail and his children with him. She had been forced to recount what had occurred and Charles had been quite horrified, especially when she had told him that the stranger had asked for her name. He had been quite certain that, in doing so, she had managed to bring down a good deal more trouble on her head, for what was to stop the fellow from finding her in London and robbing from her again? He had tried to insist that she come and live with them all, but Martha had refused, thinking Charles a little too dramatic. She lived here with her staff, did she not? And the butler was not about to let in any man from the street, simply because he claimed an acquaintance with her, surely? She had managed to convince Charles that she was quite all right and could very easily be left alone, and, eventually, her son had relented, although he had made her promise she would join them for dinner two days hence. It had been Martha's joy to accept, for she had been very much looking forward to seeing Abigail and the children again.

After a restful night, she had received her first invitation, which was quite remarkable given that not many knew she was in London. She had opened it to discover that she was invited to a small gathering at Lord and Lady Drake's home, which Martha was quite sure would involve cards, songs and other delightful forms of entertainment. It was the first event she had attended in some time and therefore spent a good many hours ensuring that she looked quite the part.

Her lady's maid had done quite well, but even though she knew that her gown was fine and her hair done wonderfully—albeit more liberally streaked with white than she liked—her stomach was twisting itself in knots as the carriage began to approach the Drakes' home. Lady Drake had been Miss Heatherstone, from what she remembered, and had been enjoying her second year in society. She had become engaged to Viscount Drake whilst Martha had been getting her head around the fact that she was to become a countess, and that was the last time they had been in one another's company, although Martha had written to her from time to time. It was kind of Lady Drake to invite Martha to her little soiree, though Martha was still rather unsure as to how the lady knew she was in town.

"Here we are, my lady."

The footman opened the carriage door and held out his hand towards her, which Martha grasped quickly, feeling the need to steady herself. Was she truly this anxious about returning to the society that she had once loved? She felt almost like she had stepped back into her debutante days, when she struggled with both a growing excitement and a nervous fear. What if she said something out of turn? What if she did not recognize someone who knew her? What would the *beau monde* think of her then?

"Thank you," she murmured as the footman closed the carriage door behind her. Taking in a deep breath, she pressed one hand lightly against her stomach as she walked towards the house, wishing she did not feel as nervous as she did. She was no longer a debutante, she was almost to be esteemed by those young ladies given her age and experience, but that thought did not bring her any sort of relief. Suddenly, she became more aware of her aloneness than she was before, her heart aching over the lack of her husband's arm offered to her. Joseph was not here with her. He never would be again.

Tears sprang to her eyes as she climbed the stone steps, forcing herself to blink them back rapidly as she put a bright smile on her face. It would not do to break into weeping at this very moment, for she would surely have to mention her late husband a good many times over the course of this evening. Many would express their sympathy and pass on their condolences at her sad loss and she could not allow herself to lose her composure.

"My dear Lady Catesby!"

Lady Drake, older yet still quite recognizable, had evidently been waiting for Martha's arrival, for she greeted Martha with such warmth and fervor that Martha immediately felt her spirits lift.

"Lady Drake," she began, as her old friend clasped Martha's hands. "It is very kind of you to invite me."

"Oh, please, you need not thank me!" Lady Drake exclaimed, her once blonde hair now white, although her blue eyes were still as alive as ever. "You cannot know how glad I was to hear of your return to London." She smiled at Martha's questioning look. "My husband is acquainted with your son and they often meet in Whites. That is how I discovered it."

Martha smiled. "I see," she replied, truly glad over this lovely welcome. "I confess that I was a little anxious about returning to London, but I do hope it will be a wonderful few weeks."

Lady Drake nodded understandingly. "It can be difficult to return when one is no longer a debutante!" she replied with a quick smile. "But it is also quite delightful. The debutantes for this Season are quite lovely, and it is interesting to see who might court whom. Already there have been whispers about possible matches!"

Martha did not find this particularly interesting but did not want to say so.

"Of course, there are a good many of our acquaintances from our debutante days here now," Lady Drake continued, as a few more guests gathered to wait behind Martha so that they might greet their host and hostess. "Most with their own daughters, you understand, but I am quite sure you will recognize a few. You will not be without friends tonight, my dear Lady Catesby."

"No, I think not," Martha replied, feeling a good deal more reassurance. "Thank you, Lady Drake. I shall leave you to your other guests now, of course."

"Until later." Lady Drake pressed Martha's hands, bestowed on her another smile and left her to greet Lord Drake before Martha removed to the drawing room.

The house was large and the drawing room itself wonderfully ornate. There were at least twenty-five other guests there already, spread out across the room in small groups that were caught up in conversation and evident merriment. Martha did not immediately recognize anyone, despite Lady Drake's promises, and so wandered slowly towards a quieter corner of the room, allowing herself to slide in amongst the shadows and nestle there. The darkness covered her quite well as she let her gaze rove over the other guests.

"That is Lady Johnston," she murmured to herself, recognizing someone she knew. "And I would think that to be Lord Mulford."

"And you would find yourself quite correct in that," said a voice nearby, making Martha jump violently. A flush hit her cheeks as she kept her eyes away from the gentleman who had spoken so quietly, his figure hidden in the dark next to her. She had not realized that anyone was nearby, else she would not have spoken aloud.

"Forgive me, you must think me terribly rude to be eavesdropping," the voice continued quickly. "It is just that you came to join me here first, although I do not think you saw me hiding here."

"No, sir," she agreed, still not looking at him. "No, I did not."

The man chuckled softly but Martha did not react. "That does not matter. My apology still stands. I ought not to have overheard, or if I did, I ought not to have commented."

"Not if we are not acquainted, sir, then no," she stated, lifting her chin and praying that the gentleman would not see her as a willing widow, as she knew was the reputation of many rich widows here in

London. She was not about to chase after any gentleman's affections, physical or otherwise, for that was not her intention in coming to London. "And I do not recall ever being introduced." Shooting him a quick glance from under her brow, she took the gentleman in, a little surprised that he was older than she had expected. He had a strong jaw, however, with broad shoulders that showed no sign of bowing, and was a good head taller than she. His eyes were alive with good humor, although she could not make out their color as they stood together in the shadows. His face was not heavily lined, although his hair was somewhat grey and a little thinning near the temples. For a moment, Martha had the impression that she had been wrong to state that they were not already acquainted, believing that they did know one another, but then the thought was pushed away as the man smiled at her. No, she did not know him.

"You are quite right," the gentleman said eventually with a small smile as she turned her head away. "You must inform me of at least one name here that might introduce us properly, for I fully intend to make your acquaintance before the evening is over."

Martha arched an eyebrow, a little unused to the gentleman's almost flirtatious way of speaking, and certainly very surprised at the compliment. At her age, she had not expected to ever receive such compliments again and was a little unsure as to whether or not she appreciated such things.

"You must be acquainted with our host, that I can be certain of," the gentleman continued when she did not reply, smiling at her when she glanced over her shoulder at him. "But surely you must know a few others here, unless you are hiding in the shadows because you do *not* know many at all and must be introduced?" The sly note in his voice sent a wave of heat all through her, starting from her toes and making its way up to her cheeks. It was not from embarrassment nor a reaction to his voice, but rather it came from anger. Anger that he was attempting to persuade her to find a way to have her introduced to him, when she had not made any such suggestions. It was as though he expected her to want to become acquainted with him without ever considering that she was doing quite well without his company.

Besides which, suggesting that she was somehow afraid of being introduced, or was worried that she would be lonely and without company, was a suggestion she could not quite accept in good humor —most likely because there was an iota of truth in his words and she was not inclined towards revealing that to anyone.

"If you will excuse me, sir," she murmured, aware that her face was burning and praying that, as she stepped back into the crowd of guests, no one would be aware of it.

"Pray, wait!" the gentleman exclaimed, moving quickly towards her. "We must be introduced!"

Martha spun on her heel to face him, lifting her chin and pinning the gentleman with a fierce, unrelenting gaze. She was not inclined towards this fellow at all, whether he wished to be acquainted with her or not. His manner was leaning towards rudeness, his flirtations unwelcome and his urge to become introduced doing nothing more than pushing her away.

"I think, sir, that there is no great need for us to be introduced at all," she stated, finding the courage she needed to speak to him quite plainly. She was no debutante and did not need to find herself a husband, so she did not need to be terribly careful over what she said and how she spoke. She was quite able to speak her mind and was inclined to do just that. "I have a good many acquaintances here already." Seeing a twinkle in his eye only sent another burst of anger shooting through her heart. "I was taking a moment, that was all. You need not think that I am some poor, lonely creature who requires your help, for I assure you that I need no such thing." Seeing the gleam fade from his eyes sent a swirl of warmth through her, allowing her a small sense of triumph. "Now, *if* you will excuse me, I must go speak to Lady Crawford." Choosing not to curtsy nor show any sign of deference or respect, Martha made her way through the throng of guests and left the rather rude gentleman behind her, aware that his eyes were fixed to her back as she walked away. He had not expected her to speak so, she was quite sure, but that did not matter to her. There came such a sense of freedom in being the older widow that she found herself quite reveling in it, a smile nipping at the corners of her mouth as she made her way towards Lady Crawford.

Lady Crawford, at least, knew at once who Martha was, for they had been reacquainted only a few years ago, when Martha had last been in London with one or two of her daughters. She was somewhat thicker than Martha remembered her, although her smile was almost jolly as she greeted Martha. The lady's rounded cheeks were bright red, her eyes sparkling with the delight of being part of London society once more. Martha recalled just how much Lady Crawford enjoyed being in town, often complaining bitterly to Martha that it was much too short a time for her liking and bemoaning the fact that she would soon have to return to her husband's estate in Cheshire.

Martha had never felt the same way, although it was quite obvious to her that Lady Crawford was in raptures at being back in town, which did make Martha smile.

"Oh my! Lady Catesby! How wonderful to see you!" Lady Crawford grasped Martha's hands tightly. "I am truly delighted." She smiled broadly as Martha murmured something in the same vein. "Are you here in town with your children?"

Martha shook her head. "No, I am not, although Charles is here in town with his family, of course." Seeing Lady Crawford's interest, she smiled hesitantly and tried to explain herself. "I thought to come to London to reacquaint myself with my friends and to have a few weeks of enjoyment," she clarified as Lady Crawford nodded excitedly. "I have so many wonderful things at home, of course, but I do miss my old friends, such as you, Lady Crawford."

"And I have missed you also," Lady Crawford said emphatically, catching Martha's hand and pressing it again. "My goodness, it seems an age since we were debutantes ourselves here in London!"

Having only been vaguely aware of Lady Crawford—or Miss Merriweather, as she had been at the time—during Martha's debutante days, Martha could only smile and nod, knowing that she and Lady Crawford had become friends during the years that had followed their marriages. "And yet here we are again," she murmured with a small smile as she looked out at the other guests.

Lady Crawford leaned in conspiratorially. "You are not here to find yourself another husband, are you?" Seeing Martha's shocked look, she giggled as though she were a schoolgirl and not an older lady of quality. "A gentleman caller or two, then?" she asked, making Martha catch her breath with horror. "You think me rude to speak so plainly, but you would not be the first widow to come to London in search of such things. And given who you were speaking with, I cannot think that—"

"I have been speaking to no one save our host and hostess!" Martha exclaimed, looking around quickly to ensure that no one had overheard Lady Crawford speak. "Goodness me, Edith, you must ensure not to speak so."

Lady Crawford, who had long ago encouraged Martha to call her by her Christian name, such was the depth of their friendship, laughed again and patted her friend's arm. "You need not worry, no one will think the worse of you for conversing with that fellow. He is almost always here in London during the Season, although he has never taken an interest in anyone in particular, I must say. No, he has never married but does tend to ensure he knows and is acquainted with almost every single lady here in London! Right from the very youngest debutante to the oldest, most refined lady of quality." She smiled, the corner of her eyes crinkling. "He is, of course, much too flirtatious for my liking, although I can understand why *some* of our set find him so charming." Her lips quirked. "It is not often that a lady of our years is engaged in flirtatious conversation!"

Slowly, Martha realized who Lady Crawford was talking about. "The gentleman you saw me talking to is a gentleman I am not acquainted with," she confessed as Lady Crawford chuckled. "I was informing him of such a thing and that was all that was said."

"Oh, but you *are* acquainted with him!" Lady Crawford protested with a gleam of mischief in her eye. "Although I must say, I am very surprised that you do not know him, given that he has almost always been here in London during the summer months. But, then again, you were always very much inclined to focus all your attentions on your daughters and that is quite understandable."

Growing a little frustrated with Lady Crawford's evasiveness, Martha closed her eyes and settled her inner irritation. "Edith," she said evenly, "who is he?"

Lady Crawford grinned as Martha opened her eyes. "You do not remember him, Martha? Why, that is the gentleman whose heart you broke into pieces the day you became engaged to Lord Catesby."

Martha felt shock ripple through her, her face going pale as ice began to form down her spine, sending shivers across her skin. "That cannot be."

"But it is," Lady Crawford insisted, evidently enjoying herself enormously. "That is Lord Percival Blackford." She eyed Martha for another moment, her smile still spreading. "So, you see, my dear friend, you *are*, in fact, already acquainted with him. And I do not think that he has ever been able to forget you."

CHAPTER 4

Over the course of the following week, Martha had done all she could to avoid conversing or even meeting Lord Blackford again. Lady Crawford's explanation of who the gentleman was had quite shocked her and she had been unable to compose herself fully for some minutes that night, but thereafter she had become quite determined to ignore the fellow completely. She did not like Lady Crawford's comment that Lord Blackford had been unable to forget Martha, nor did she think it wise to seek out an acquaintance with him, for he was not at all the sort of gentleman she wished to consider a friend. He was much too flirtatious, she had decided. Much too easy in his manner, much too confident. She did not like the way he had spoken to her.

And yet, she had been quite unable to forget him. Every time she had gone to a ball, a soiree or even a walk in the park, Martha had found herself always on her guard, her eyes searching for any sign of him. It was as if, in trying to avoid him and thereby evade any further introductions, she was placing him firmly in her thoughts.

How very different he was to Joseph. He was, of course, a good deal younger than Joseph would have been, had he still lived, for from what she could remember, Lord Blackford was only a few years older than she, whereas Joseph had been close to sixteen years older. Not that such a difference in years had mattered to her, for she had loved him completely regardless.

Her eyes began to burn. She did not like having her heart and mind filled with another man, even though her heart was anxious rather than eager to see Lord Blackford again. She had always had Joseph settled there, although she did not think of him as often as she once had, putting that down to the fact that she was so caught up with her children and grandchildren, who brought her such joy that she could not linger on her grief.

And yet, now, she was struggling to think of anything else.

"You are being quite ridiculous," she told her reflection, surveying herself with slightly narrowed eyes. She had never considered herself beautiful, although she was glad that her grey eyes were still bright and not dull, as she had feared might come with age. Her hair was long and thick, which meant that the maid had no trouble in putting it into a most respectable yet fashionable style, although Martha did, on occasion, mourn the loss of her light brown tresses which Joseph had always found so wonderful. She was not grey there, for her hair had decided to turn white, albeit very slowly. At the same time, Martha considered, it did give her an appearance of respectability for, as Lady Crawford had suggested the last time they had taken tea together, it was now their role to appear as proper and as refined as they could, for the sake of the young debutantes who would be looking towards them for guidance. Martha had not quite believed her, only for Lady Crawford to point out just how many young ladies were watching them both as they conversed at the ball thrown by Lord Hastings only two days ago. Martha had realized then that Lady Crawford knew a great deal more about society than she did, feeling almost a little lost as she attempted to make her way through the *beau monde.*

At least society is still inclined towards the theatre, she thought to herself, rising to her feet and making her way towards the door in preparation for Lady Crawford's arrival. *I will not have to worry about Lord Blackford there, at least!*

Lord Blackford, regardless of whether or not he would be at the theatre, would not be able to attempt to speak to her, nor would she have to avoid him. Her only danger would be during the intermission, when there was the opportunity for conversation and the like. She would have to make sure that she was quite caught up with someone else, even if it was Lady Crawford herself. Lady Crawford had been very good at ensuring Martha had been introduced—or, sometimes, reacquainted—with other members of the *ton*, although she had insisted that Martha always tell the story of the thief that had stopped the carriage as she had come into London. Martha had wanted to forget it entirely but had not yet been able to, given just how much delight Lady Crawford seemed to gain each and every time Martha told the story.

"My lady?"

Martha turned to the butler, who had just now come into the room. "Yes? Is Lady Crawford here?"

"She sends her apologies."

An unfamiliar voice filled the room, as the butler was forced to step out of the way of a gentleman who walked directly into the room without being invited.

"She has asked me to accompany you to the theatre tonight, in her place."

Martha's stomach tightened, looking into the face of the one man she had been trying to avoid. What had Lady Crawford done?

"Lord Blackford," she stated coolly.

Chuckling, he bowed deeply. "I see that you have recalled me at last," he declared, making her flush with embarrassment. "Although we have not yet been formally reintroduced, which I must beg your pardon for."

She lifted her chin, no smile on her lips. "Pray, what is wrong with Lady Crawford? And why was I not informed of it?"

He smiled, the lines by his eyes thickening for just a moment. "I was visiting with Lord Crawford," he began to explain, spreading his hands as though to evidence his innocence in all of this. "His estate is but a few miles away from my own and we have been discussing the merits of crop rotation—but I digress." Clearing his throat, he put his hands behind his back and smiled at her. "Lady Crawford happened upon us, for she had been in search of her husband to inform him that she was not feeling quite the thing and was, therefore, worried about what she ought to do as regards the theatre this evening. I queried what she meant and she informed me that she was to come for you this evening so that you might enjoy a little Shakespeare together." His eyes twinkled, although Martha felt nothing but irritation. "Naturally, I could not help but offer my assistance, given just how troubled she was. I did not want her to make herself any more unwell and therefore insisted that she remain at home to rest and allow me to accompany you." He shrugged, as though this was all the explanation she would need. "And so, here I am, Lady Catesby."

She struggled to think of an adequate response, finding the idea of going to the theatre with Lord Blackford to be most unwelcome. "I do not want to trouble you, Lord Blackford. I am quite content to remain at home this evening."

"But I am not," Lord Blackford countered easily. "I do so like a little Shakespeare and Lady Crawford informs me that it is something of a favorite of yours." He took a few steps towards her, his eyes now a little pleading. "You need not remain at home just because Lady Crawford is unwell."

"It would not be seemly," she replied, knowing that a good many rumors might begin from such a thing. "I could not."

To her surprise, Lord Blackford laughed, although it was not cruel by any means. "My dear Lady Catesby, have you not yet learned that society does not consider widows in the same way that it considers debutantes? You need not worry about your reputation or such things over a simple trip to the theatre! No one will think the less of you for it."

Martha shook her head. "Regardless, *I* would not feel at ease."

Lord Blackford was incredibly persistent. "And why is that?" he asked, his voice dropping to a more gentle tone. "Am I truly that terrible, Lady Catesby?" Seeing her faint blush, he nodded as though he knew precisely what was going on in her thoughts. "Yes, I have been aware that you have been doing all you can to avoid me, Lady

Catesby. Why is that, might I ask? Did I make such an unfavourable impression upon you that you cannot bear to speak to me?"

Refusing to be cowed by such questions, Martha looked back at Lord Blackford without malice or embarrassment. "Indeed," she said plainly. "I found you rather forward, Lord Blackford."

This did not seem to insult him. "Yes, I think that I am," he agreed. "That is why you find me here, seeking to accompany you to the theatre, instead of leaving you to spend the evening at home, in your own company. Perhaps a better gentleman than me would have stayed away, would not have offered his help, given just how obvious your dislike of me is, but I am not that way inclined."

Something stabbed at her heart. Was it guilt? "I do not dislike you, Lord Blackford," she replied slowly, wondering if she was, in fact, being a little unfair towards him. "It is more that I am uncertain as to whether such a connection would be beneficial. I am not, in any way, seeking a courtship nor an agreement from any gentleman here in town." She felt heat climb up her spine and crawl into her face, but she did not allow her gaze to drop from his. He had to know precisely what it was she was saying.

Lord Blackford inclined his head. "I quite understand," he said quietly, his eyes slowly lifting back to hers. "I apologize, Lady Catesby, if I was overly familiar the first time we met. I confess that I recognized you almost at once." He smiled gently. "The years may have gone by but you are still the same."

She waved a hand, hating that she was blushing, and at her age, too! It was quite ridiculous. "You can spare me your compliments, Lord Blackford, for I fear that I cannot return them given that I did not immediately recollect you."

He chuckled, and much to her surprise, Martha found herself smiling. Perhaps they could, in fact, enjoy one another's company, just so long as he ceased his flirtations and his compliments. She had made herself quite plain, had she not? She could continue to be firm with him if it was required, making him see that she would not accept any such nonsense from him.

"You are more sharp-tongued than I remember, however!" Lord

Blackford laughed, shaking his head. "Although there is a greater strength within you than before. I am glad of that."

Her heart twisted. "My parents arranged my marriage, as you know, Lord Blackford. As a debutante, it was quite impossible to turn against their wishes." A smile crept over her face at the memory. "Although now, I confess that I am very glad that they chose my husband so well."

Lord Blackford remained silent, although his eyes were shadowed.

"I cared for my husband very much," Martha continued, as though she had to give some sort of explanation to Lord Blackford. "He was quite wonderful in almost every way. I miss him terribly."

Lord Blackford cleared his throat, his voice now a little gruff. "How long since he passed, if you do not mind me asking?"

She shook her head. "Not at all." Her voice was thin with pain. "It has been six years since we buried Joseph, six years since my son, Francis, took the title. And yet, sometimes, it feels as though it were only yesterday."

Lord Blackford nodded, his expression becoming wretched. "I quite understand the pain, Lady Catesby."

Her eyes narrowed, sending him a sharp glance as she recalled that Lady Crawford had told her Lord Blackford had never married.

"I see that you do not understand," he said softly. "It may not be the long, firmly established connection such as you had with Lord Catesby, but I, too, lost someone who had become very dear to me. I lost her only a short time after we had wed. Five months only." His eyes darkened with memories and Martha felt her heart swell with sympathy. She knew he was not lying, for she could see the same pain in his expression that she constantly carried with her.

"I am sorry," she said, surprised to find that she no longer felt so disinclined towards him. It was as though this sharing of their pain had allowed her to feel some sort of kinship with him, bringing down the walls between them. "When was this?"

Lord Blackford's laugh was harsh, biting the air between them. "It was only two years after you wed Lord Catesby," he said with a shrug, as though such a thing was quite ridiculous. "So a good many years ago—and yet the pain still lingers. I do not think that it will ever completely leave me."

"No," Martha agreed, a little taken aback at just how open Lord Blackford was being, when they were only just reacquainted. "And perhaps that is how it is meant to be, Lord Blackford. We remember them, do we not? They have helped to form the person we are today and one cannot simply forget all that has gone before."

"Indeed." Lord Blackford's voice was gruff, his eyes now looking away from hers. Martha swallowed the lump in her throat as she allowed her mind to drift back towards Joseph, finding both the joy and the pain that came with her memories.

With an effort, she put a small smile on her face, brushing aside her sadness. "Well, then, Lord Blackford, shall we go to the theatre? I should not like to miss the first act."

Lord Blackford's head shot up, his expression one of complete astonishment. "You intend to allow me to accompany you there?"

"I do," Martha replied, praying that she was not making a mistake in doing so. "Although I will not stand for any flirtations or the like, Lord Blackford. And I have my own box."

A broad smile began to spread across Lord Blackford's face, chasing away the darkness that had lingered in his eyes. "I quite understand," he stated with a small bow. "Thank you for allowing me such a privilege, Lady Catesby, I—"

"That is precisely what I mean, Lord Blackford," Martha interrupted, walking past him towards the door. "No such nonsense, if you please. I do not hold with frilly compliments, not at my age." She smiled to herself as Lord Blackford hurried after her, feeling quite in control and finding that she rather enjoyed being able to speak her mind without fear of the consequences. "Do come along, sir."

Lord Blackford hurried after her, making Martha smile quietly to herself. She was quite able to ensure that her acquaintance with Lord Blackford was seen by the *ton* as nothing more than that—a simple acquaintance. She would speak sharply if she had to and would not allow any such flirtations to escape from his mouth. If he persisted, then it would be quite easy to simply bring an end to their acquaintance, for it did not matter a fig to her whom she spent time with during the Season here in London.

Although, she considered, as she climbed into the carriage, there was that sudden connection between them now, which she had not expected. It had come from Lord Blackford's openness, his willingness to allow her to see his loss and the pain that came with it. That had brought an understanding between them, she thought, managing a small smile in his direction as Lord Blackford came to sit down opposite. Perhaps she had been foolish in her attempts to avoid him. Perhaps this might be the beginnings of a friendship.

"Lady Crawford will be quite delighted that I have managed to persuade you," Lord Blackford said lightly, as the carriage drew away from the house. "Although I will, of course, tell her that I did nothing of the sort and that you were fully convinced in your own mind regardless of what I said or did."

Despite herself, Martha laughed. "Indeed, Lord Blackford, I expect you to say just that. Lady Crawford knows me well enough to understand that I will not be pushed and pressed in one particular direction any longer."

Lord Blackford's smile did not quite reach his eyes, his gaze becoming almost contemplative as he looked back at her. "Indeed you will not," he murmured, as though this was something new to consider. "You are quite changed from the girl I once knew, Lady Catesby."

"We all change, Lord Blackford," she replied, wondering why she suddenly felt quite so anxious. Her stomach had tightened, her breathing had quickened and she was suddenly a good deal more aware of his presence. "I cannot believe that all change is a bad thing either."

"It is not, of course," he agreed quickly. "And certainly not in your case, Lady Catesby. I think you quite remarkable, more than I have ever done before."

CHAPTER 5

"Tell me, what of your children?"

A little surprised that Lord Blackford would show any such interest in her life, as well as the fact that she had not known he was aware of her family, Martha stared at the gentleman for a moment, nonplussed.

Lord Blackford chuckled. "I am not as ill-mannered as all that, Lady Catesby," he commented, as though he had known what she was thinking. "Yes, I am aware that your son has taken on the title of his father and that he is recently married. I am also aware that you have four—or is it five?—other children."

"Five," Martha replied faintly, barely aware of the buzz of conversation from the other theatre-goers around them. "Charles remains here in town."

"Ah yes, of course," Lord Blackford murmured, his eyes alight. "I am acquainted with him, I think, although I gather he finds his time quite taken up with his occupation and his family."

"Indeed," Martha agreed, managing to find her voice again amidst her surprise. "They have two children."

Lord Blackford smiled, his expression kind. "Then you are a

grandmama twice over, Lady Catesby. How wonderful for you and for the children."

A little unsure whether this was one of the compliments she had warned Lord Blackford against, Martha studied the man's expression and decided that he was being both genuine and kind. Her mind went back to when they had first met, which seemed so long ago now. Lord Blackford had appeared to be quite wonderful in her eyes, for he had not been brusque nor overly flirtatious, but had good conversation and, from her limited experience at the time, had seemed quite eager to hear what she had to say. He had not lost that trait, it seemed, although he certainly had become more carefree with his compliments. Silently, Martha wondered why he had never chosen to marry again, given that his first marriage had been so long ago and of such a short duration.

"Grandchildren are a blessing most wonderful," Lord Blackford continued softly, his head turned away from her and now looking towards the stage, as though he were speaking to himself.

"I have six grandchildren," Martha murmured quietly. "And they are all quite adorable, although one or two can be something of a trial at times."

Lord Blackford's eyes twinkled as he looked back at her. "As children are inclined to be," he said, as though he knew what he spoke of, although she could not understand where such knowledge came from. After all, he had only been married to his first wife for five months, had he not? And he had not mentioned any children.

"You—you do not have any children?" she asked haltingly, not wanting to appear rude or improper in any way. "It is just that the way you speak of them makes me believe that you—"

"Should you care for some refreshment?" Lord Blackford was on his feet, her question torn from her lips and flung into the air before she had even had a chance to finish speaking. "Goodness, how rude of me to sit here conversing when the time is fast slipping away from us! What should you like, Lady Catesby? Champagne?"

"That would be sufficient," Martha uttered, terribly surprised at how brusquely he had thrown her question aside and changed the subject. "I thank you."

Lord Blackford was gone from the box in a moment, leaving Martha sitting quite still, her shock mounting with every second. Evidently, there was something Lord Blackford did not wish to talk about with her and she was quite willing to remain silent on such a matter, but the way in which he had ended the conversation had rubbed at her angrily. She felt almost bruised, quietly chastising herself for being quite so forward with her questions. An acquaintance long forgotten could not simply be brought back to life again with only a few hours spent together!

"Mama!"

Jumping in surprise, Martha turned to see her son, Charles, enter the box with his wife, Abigail, on his arm.

"Goodness!" Martha exclaimed, a glad smile on her face as she rose to greet them both. "I did not know you would be in attendance this evening."

"Nor did we know you were here," Charles replied with a chuckle. "It was Abigail who spotted you from our box." Something dark flickered in his eyes. "Who was it you were sitting with, Mama?"

"Oh, that is Lord Blackford, an acquaintance from when I was a debutante," Martha answered with a quick smile, refusing to allow her son any sway over who she chose to spend her time with. "It has been quite wonderful to spend so much time here in London with those that I consider to be my friends, both from years ago and more recently."

Abigail smiled, pressing Martha's arm and making her quite aware that she, at least, had nothing of concern in her mind when it came to Martha sitting with Lord Blackford. "I am glad for you, Martha," Abigail smiled, sitting down in one of the chairs near to where Martha stood. "Have you nothing to drink? Charles will go and fetch you something, if you wish." She gestured for Martha to sit down, evidently eager to speak to her.

"Lord Blackford has gone in search of something," Martha replied, a little lamely, as she saw her son's gaze flicker yet again.

"Then, in that case, I require something," Abigail said briskly, looking pointedly at her husband. "Champagne?"

Charles rolled his eyes. "We have both just—"

"Yes, but I am so very hot," Abigail said with a small smile in Martha's direction. "If you would, Charles, I would be very much obliged."

Charles sighed heavily, although Martha saw the smile in his eyes as he reached for his wife's hand. Dropping a kiss to the back of her hand, he bowed grandly as though they were just being introduced.

"Anything for my fair lady," he said, with a broad grin that made Abigail blush. "Do excuse me."

Martha watched fondly as Charles left the box, knowing that he adored his wife and finding her heart swelling with happiness for them both. Abigail was a strong-willed woman, much like Martha herself had become, but she brought out the best in Charles. She was loving, kind and yet absolutely firm in her decisions. Martha thought the world of her.

"Now," Abigail began, tilting her head. "I think, Martha, that there is something I must tell you so that you are not left entirely unawares."

A stone dropped into Martha's stomach, sending her into a whirlwind of anxiety.

"Do not fret so," Abigail laughed kindly, reaching to take Martha's gloved hand. "It is not at all to do with you but more of the company you keep."

Martha's eyes widened. "Is it something to do with Lord Blackford?"

Slowly, Abigail nodded.

Martha's stomach tightened. She could feel herself growing tense, her breathing a little ragged as she watched Abigail carefully.

"You know very well how rumors and things go in London," Abigail said gently. "And it may very well be nothing, but the rumor is that Lord Blackford's estate is not doing particularly well at all. In fact, some say that he is quite poor and is therefore looking for a rich widow or even a lady with a large dowry that he might marry." Her eyes grew keen as she leaned forward to look directly into Martha's eyes. "You must understand that I am not accusing you of caring for Lord Blackford in any way, for I have only just seen you in his company this evening, but you must be on your guard."

Martha's breath left her all in a rush, relief pouring into every part of her. "Oh, is that all? You are quite mistaken, my dear girl. I am not in any way inclined towards Lord Blackford in that sense. We have only just picked up our acquaintance this very evening!"

Abigail nodded although she did not appear to be entirely convinced. "It is no crime if you begin to care for someone new," she said slowly, evidently choosing her words with care so that she would not offend Martha. "I know that you love your husband still, but to care for another soul does not mean that your love for him grows cold."

It was Martha who went cold at this, a trickle of ice making its way down her back. "This is not something you can speak of with any certainty, Abigail," she said, as kindly as she could. "You have no experience of it."

Abigail did not seem to take offence, a small smile catching the corner of her lips. "I have experience of love," she said gently. "I know that I loved my first child so dearly that I was quite afraid that I could not love another in the same way. Of course," she continued, her smile softening, "I found myself to be quite mistaken in that. I love both my children with such a fierceness that at times, it quite takes my breath away. Loving one does not stop me from loving the other."

Martha swallowed.

"I am aware that this is not the same as what you have endured, Martha, and I know that you have said you came to London with the express intention of seeking out your old friends simply to bring that part of your life back again, and that is, of course, wonderful. However, if you should find yourself considering something new, then I do hope you will not fear it, that you will not turn from it. None of us will think the worse of you."

A harsh laugh escaped Martha's lips before she could stop it. "I hardly think that is so, Abigail," she said darkly. "I know my children. I saw my son's expression when he mentioned who it was I was sitting with this evening. You cannot truly believe that my children will not consider me foolish, if not betraying their father, if I were to even *consider*—"

Abigail had taken both of Martha's hands in her own, her expression determined.

"Martha," she said firmly, interrupting her. "Stop. Your children love you. *I* love you. Charles may find the idea of your happiness with another to be quite unsettling, but that does not mean that he will not be glad for you should that situation ever arise. No, they will not think ill of you. They will not think you a betrayer and nor should you think of yourself in such a way. I cannot tell you how glad I was to see you talking with Lord Blackford in such a way that brought a smile to your face and a lightness to your eyes. Do not shun that, Martha, not out of fear, at least."

Martha realized that the ache in her throat had been building slowly, to the point that the pain was sending tears to her eyes. She looked back at her daughter-in-law, wondering when the girl had become so wise. It was not that simply conversing with Lord Blackford had brought back any sort of feelings of affection or the like, for she could not simply forget the years of love and devotion she had spent with Joseph, but rather that she had found herself enjoying his company and his conversation but had been chiding herself inwardly for doing so. Abigail was correct to state that she had been shunning the idea of continuing her acquaintance with Lord Blackford, for she had no intention of spending any further time with him. Why had that been, she wondered? Was it because she was afraid of what might come of it? Or was it because she had quite set herself against the idea of ever considering another gentleman ever again? Was she truly determined to live out the rest of her life as a widow, even though the opportunity for companionship and even affection might be open to her?

"You will think about what I have had to say?" Abigail pressed gently, seeing the other theatre-goers quickly arriving back to take their seats again.

"Yes," Martha replied, her voice hoarse with the strength of her emotion. "I will."

Abigail gave her a warm smile, and her eyes twinkled. "And do not worry about Charles, I will be able to talk him into accepting almost anything!" she laughed, and Martha could not help but smile in return, chasing away the tears that still threatened.

"I am sure you will," she agreed, just as Charles and Lord Blackford reappeared in the box. "Thank you, Abigail."

Her daughter-in-law pressed her hands again before letting them go, urging her husband to return to their box with haste so that they would not miss the second half. She greeted Lord Blackford kindly, but then took her leave, almost dragging Charles along with her.

"My, my," Lord Blackford murmured, handing Martha a glass. "Your son does not appear to like my presence here with you, Lady Catesby." He frowned as he sat down again. "I would not like to bring you any sort of trouble, of course, so if you would prefer, I can easily find somewhere else to seat myself for the duration of the performance."

Martha, recalling what Abigail had said, shook her head. "You must forgive my son," she said with a fond smile. "He is, I think, a little perturbed to see his mother in London for the Season, simply to enjoy myself. He is much more used to me being at the dower house, making calls or inviting my family to stay." She took a sip of her champagne, her mind working furiously. There was so much going on within her that she could not quite sort everything out, although she was certainly not concerned with Charles' behavior. Whether he liked or disliked Lord Blackford was not of particular importance. What *did* matter was just how much *she* was enjoying Lord Blackford's company.

Lord Blackford cleared his throat, suddenly appearing to feel a little awkward. "Then, might I ask if you would care to accompany me for a short walk through Hyde Park tomorrow? Or St. James' park, if you prefer? I have been assured that it will be quite a fine day."

Martha considered this for a moment, her stomach twisting this way and that. Lord Blackford was looking at her from under lidded eyes, appearing almost boy-like in his nervous anticipation of her answer. His gaze was darting this way and that, his feet shuffling uncomfortably on the floor of the box as his lined brow furrowed all the more. She could not leave him in such a state, struggling to find her answer.

"Yes," she found herself saying, surprising them both, it seemed. Lord Blackford's eyes widened slightly as he looked at her, making Martha laugh.

"My goodness, Lord Blackford, this cannot be the first time a lady has accepted an invitation from you, surely?" she smiled, as he let out a breath of relief. "You look quite done in."

He shrugged, his eyes twinkling, the deep furrows gone from above his eyes. "I thought you would be quite set against me, Lady Catesby."

"I thought I would be also," she stated truthfully. "But it seems that my first impression was, perhaps, incorrect."

Lord Blackford looked both gratified and relieved. "That is generous of you to say," he said, although his eyes darted away from hers for a moment as though he were hiding something from her. "Shall we say tomorrow afternoon? A little before the fashionable hour?"

"A good time *before* the fashionable hour, if you please," Martha replied with feeling. She did not want to be caught strutting about the park at her age, for the idea of it had never really enticed her. "I would much prefer a quieter walk, Lord Blackford."

He grinned at her, evidently pleased with this answer. "Then a quieter walk it shall be," he said with alacrity. "I am looking forward to it already."

CHAPTER 6

Martha smiled as Lord Blackford offered her his arm, feeling somewhat awkward as she accepted it hesitantly. This was now the fifth outing they had enjoyed together since that night at the theatre, but she was still rather uncertain about it all. She could not get Joseph out of her mind at times, fearing that he was almost looking down from above, disapprovingly. She had no particular feelings of affection for Lord Blackford, she told herself repeatedly, every time she felt such a way. She simply enjoyed his company, his conversation and the way he could make her laugh at a moment's notice. She would return to the dower house at the end of next month, leaving her filled with such happy memories of her time in London.

"You still are a little uncertain around me, Lady Catesby," Lord Blackford commented, a little dryly, as his eyes caught hers. "Why is that, I wonder?"

She shook her head. "I am not uncertain," she refuted immediately. "You are quite mistaken there, Lord Blackford."

"Am I?" he queried, making her laugh. "I cannot allow you to disagree with me without evidence, surely? I offer you my arm quite regularly and every time, there is a moment or two of hesitation before you accept." His brow lifted, although no smile caught his lips. "That must speak of uncertainty, surely."

Seeing the seriousness in his expression, Martha allowed herself to speak honestly and openly. "I am glad of your acquaintance, Lord Blackford, truly. I was wrong, as I have admitted before, to shun you as I first did. Lady Crawford should be thanked, I suppose, for choosing to have a dreadful headache that night of the ball!" She was disappointed that he did not even chuckle at this comment, realizing that he was truly in a very serious frame. "I confess to you, Lord Blackford, that I am constantly on my guard, wondering what the rest of the *beau monde* must think."

Lord Blackford frowned. "But that should not matter, Lady Catesby. You are a widow, with means of your own and a wonderful reputation. No one speaks ill of you, no one would even dream of remarking on anything you choose to do, unless, of course, it was quite scandalous. I might add that accepting my arm is by no means scandalous, Lady Catesby, in case there was any confusion there."

This last sentence was spoken with such sharpness and irony that for a moment, Martha was quite taken aback and did not know what to say. Lord Blackford's expression was darker than she had ever seen it before with all trace of joviality and good humour gone.

"I apologize," she said slowly, not quite able to look at him. "I apologize if you think I have wronged you in some way by my hesitation, Lord Blackford. It was not intentional, of course. This is all quite new to me in so many ways, even though I was once here as a debutante." Her heart ached suddenly and she felt the urge to step away from Lord Blackford, to drop her hand from his arm—but with an effort, she remained exactly where she was. "To be here again in society as a widow, and not as either a debutante or a married lady chaperoning her daughters, has been something that I have struggled with, Lord Blackford."

He sighed heavily, rubbing one hand over his eyes, appearing suddenly a good deal older than she had ever seen him before. His face almost drooped, the lines in his forehead and beside his eyes seeming to grow heavier as he sighed again.

"You are much too good, Lady Catesby," he grated, not looking at her. "It is I who must apologize. I have not considered things from your perspective, of course. I can see that now." There was a moment or two of silence as they walked, leaving Martha with the feeling that Lord Blackford was not yet finished speaking. She was correct in her assumption.

Lord Blackford stopped walking, dropping her hand from his arm as he turned to face her.

"I must apologize, Lady Catesby," he said heavily, his eyes still fixed on the ground by her feet. "I have been rude and that is quite uncalled for. You have every right to do exactly as you wish, regardless of what I should want."

Martha felt her heart quicken at his words, silently wondering what it was, exactly, that Lord Blackford wanted from her.

"I apologize," he said again, finally looking into her eyes. "I have had some news that has brought me some pain and I have let that come out on you."

Martha raised her eyebrows, a little surprised at his confession. Lord Blackford was not the sort of gentleman to speak about himself a great deal, she had come to realize, for he did not often speak of his life, his family, his estate or the like. She had been forced to draw him out when she could, finding him to be something of a challenge which, Martha had to admit to herself, she had found almost enjoyable. Here, now, stood another opportunity for her to do just that.

"If you wish, Lord Blackford, you are welcome to share your news with me," she suggested, as calmly as she could. "You are, of course, quite within your rights *not* to do so, but I would state that such pains shared with another can often bring about a good deal of relief."

Lord Blackford smiled sadly. "You have found that to be the case, have you?"

"I have indeed," she stated quietly. "My children and I shared our grief with each other over the loss of Joseph, and that helped us comfort one another." Silently, she wondered if he had never told anyone about his own grief and pain when it had come to the loss of his first wife, considering that he might have carried—and continued to carry it—entirely on his own.

Lord Blackford ran one hand over his eyes. "Then I shall speak to you," he said aloud, as though confirming the idea to himself. "Although might we continue to walk?"

His eyes were filled with worry and she nodded at once. "But of course."

For some minutes, they walked in silence. Martha's heart was beating a little more quickly than usual, worrying about what it was that troubled Lord Blackford so much.

"Did I ever tell you that I have a son?"

Martha caught her breath, stumbling just a little as she struggled to take in what she had heard.

"I take it I have not told you this before," Lord Blackford continued, a touch of humour in his voice. "No, I have not. That is not surprising. His presence is not particularly well known amongst society. In fact, it has never been well known amongst society, for I have made sure to keep it that way."

Martha struggled to know what to say, both astonished and confused. Had not Lord Blackford stated that he had lost his wife at only five months after their marriage?

"His mother died giving life to him," Lord Blackford continued, as if he had been able to see where her thoughts were directed. "The pain that came with such an event... well, I cannot tell you of it for there are not words to describe what I endured," he finished thickly.

"Indeed, I quite understand," Martha said softly, wondering how such a young man as Lord Blackford had been could have endured the loss of a wife and the birth of a son at the same time. The emotions that would have torn at him must have been fierce and unrelenting.

"For a long time, I did not want anything to do with the child," Lord Blackford admitted darkly, not looking at her. "I blamed him, I suppose. The wet nurse had full charge of him, then the nurse thereafter. It was not until he was three years of age that I finally began to spend some time with him." A harsh laugh poured from him. "The regret that came to me at that moment has never quite left me. I should never have blamed the boy, I realized. What had I missed in turning away from him at such a young age?"

Martha placed her free hand on his arm, unable to prevent herself from wanting to encourage him in some way. "The boy would not have been old enough to know that you were absent from the first few months of his life," she said gently. "And you spent time with him thereafter, did you not?"

"As much as I could," Lord Blackford stated firmly. "I am more proud of him than I can say."

Martha smiled at this, recognizing the pride of a father over his son. Joseph had often spoken that way of his own children.

"He is not yet wed but does not wish to come to town and find a bride," Lord Blackford said with a half-smile. "He has been courting Lady Crawford's youngest daughter, given that our estates are close enough to one another." He chuckled at her astonished expression. "Lady Crawford has not been forthcoming about this, I presume? I quite understand. I think she hopes that her daughter will forget about Theodore soon enough." His hazel eyes flickered with good humour. "I doubt it, however. Theodore is singular in his affections towards Miss Catherine."

"Theodore?" Martha asked gently. "That is your son's name?"

"The Honorable Theodore Hornby," Lord Blackford smiled, although his face was still somewhat shadowed. "Yes, that is his name. He is gone to the continent, to see what is left of my holdings. However, I have had news that they are just as unprofitable as ever." His face fell, the frustration evident. "I have done all I can for my son, but I cannot give him an unprofitable estate."

Frowning, Martha came to a stop. "Your estate is unprofitable? Surely, that cannot be? You told me only a last week that you were speaking to Lord Crawford about your crops and the like."

Lord Blackford looked wary, as though he were a rabbit about to be snapped at by a wily fox. "I spent so many years leaving it to wilt and ruin," he said slowly, "that the estate has never quite recovered."

"You left your estate?"

"Yes," Lord Blackford said harshly, turning away from her. "When my wife died, everything became meaningless. I left my estate, turned my tenants out and spent every moment I could in London, doing whatever I could to forget the grief and the pain." He closed his eyes, his head hanging low in apparent hopelessness. "What else could I do? And then, when I came to my senses and spent some time with my child, my only son and heir, a little light began to come back into my life."

"I am glad to hear it," Martha said slowly. "But as for your estate—"

"I did not return to it until my son was almost six years of age," Lord Blackford interrupted miserably. "The tenants' houses were almost entirely ruined, the fields waterlogged. The money I should have spent on it all, I had thrown away in my grief."

"I see," Martha said quietly, wondering just how difficult life had been for Lord Blackford, shouldering all of his grief and responsibilities alone. She did not think ill of him for having reacted in such a way to the death of his wife, for pain such as that almost seemed impossible to bear at times.

"It has taken years of work to restore the estate to what it should be," Lord Blackford finished, his eyes haunted as he looked back at her. "I have kept my trials to myself, not wanting anyone to see my struggle, not wanting to shame my son, but I am leaving him with such a small fortune that I am almost ashamed of it." His eyes closed tightly, his voice jarring. "What sort of father am I that would leave my son and heir with the consequences of my own actions?"

Martha did not know what to do. Lord Blackford had never spoken to her with such openness before, for she felt as though he were bearing his very soul to her, revealing the deep wounds and scars that lay within him. She wanted to find something of comfort to say, wanted to be able to bring him some relief and reassurance, but no words came to her mind.

"He does not think little of me," Lord Blackford whispered, his eyes still closed. "But he ought to. He does not know it all."

"I know that he will be certain that you love him," Martha said, feeling entirely inadequate. "You have made that clear and I know that that is one thing a child will always seek from their parents."

Lord Blackford smiled sadly, opened his eyes and looked at her. "You are much too good for my acquaintance, Martha," he said gratefully, the sound of her Christian name on his lips sending a shiver down her spine. "You do not know me at all and yet you speak with such kindness."

She managed a small smile, wondering at the quickening of her heart and the urge to draw him close to her to bring him comfort and relief. Why did she have such a yearning to do such a thing? It would be most improper and certainly ought not to be something she was allowing herself to consider.

"I am here as your friend," she told him. "I am here if you wish to speak of the things that trouble you. You know that I can understand your grief and your pain, do you not?"

"Yes." His hand reached for hers and she gave it willingly, her heart suddenly fluttering as his fingers intertwined with her own. "Yes, I know that, Martha. You have always had such a generous and kind heart."

She could not speak, her mouth going suddenly dry as she looked up into Lord Blackford's face and found his eyes fixed on hers, burning with such an intensity that she wanted to look away but could not. Pressing her lips together and ignoring the butterflies that were pouring into her stomach, making her feel as though she were a foolish girl accepting her first attentions from a gentleman, she tried to smile and speak calmly.

"I am glad to be considered your friend," she said, reminding herself that this, after all, was everything she had wanted to pursue with Lord Blackford. "I am sorry for what has occurred with your holdings but I am quite sure that, no matter what it is you are able to present to your son when he comes to claim the title, he will not consider what it is you have burdened him with, but rather all you have done to ensure he has everything that you have been able to give him." She was not even sure that her words made sense but, to her relief, Lord Blackford smiled, a heavy sigh escaping him.

"I think you must be an angel, Martha," he said quietly, his expression warm as he studied her, his hand still holding hers. "An angel sent to comfort me in my hour of need." Something flickered through his gaze, a pain that she could not quite make out. "Thank you."

She smiled and gently tugged her hand free, refusing to allow herself to consider what was going on within her own heart, not when it confused her so. "But of course, Lord Blackford," she said, turning towards the path again. "Now, shall we continue to walk? We must be quick if we want to avoid the fashionable hour."

He laughed, breaking the air of sadness that had seemed to settle over them both. "And we cannot allow ourselves to be caught up in that now, can we, Lady Catesby?" he commented with a broad smile. "Although what say you to a short visit to the bookshop as we return back to the house?"

She smiled at him, knowing that he was doing so just because she had expressed a love of reading to him earlier in the week. His thoughtfulness did not go unappreciated. "I think that quite a wonderful idea," she said, looking up at him.

"Then might I offer you my arm again, Lady Catesby?" he asked with a playful smile.

"Of course," she laughed, accepting it at once without even the smallest flicker of hesitation. Something had grown and blossomed between them both this afternoon, something that brought her a good deal of contentment and yet a good many questions with it. Questions that she was going to have to consider the very first moment she was alone.

CHAPTER 7

This was to be her first hosted soiree since she had come to London, and Martha could not help but feel both nervous and excited. She had invited only a few guests, with Charles and Abigail amongst them, as well as Lord and Lady Crawford. She had not hesitated to invite Lord Blackford, who had promised eagerly to attend, and Martha had found herself almost glowing with the excitement of it all.

Taking one last look at herself in the mirror that hung above the drawing room fireplace, Martha smoothed down her gown and told herself that she had no need to feel so anxious. It was not as though there was anything that could go wrong this particular evening, for she had both refreshments and entertainment already prepared.

So why did she feel so terribly anxious?

Her mind immediately went to Lord Blackford, recalling how, earlier that week, he had talked so openly about his son—the son she had never known he'd had. One question had lingered in her mind and she had allowed herself to consider it once she had returned home: If the baby had been born after only five months of wedlock, then that meant that the child had been conceived beforehand. It was quite scandalous, of course, but now that they were decades past such a time, it no longer seemed to carry quite as much weight. Perhaps that was why Lord Blackford had chosen to keep the news of his son fairly quiet. She was glad that he had both an heir and a family, although she was sorrowful that he had lost his wife at such a difficult time.

The way Lord Blackford had been so open with her, the way he had chosen to reveal his deepest wounds to her, had had an impact upon her heart that she still could not easily explain. It terrified her, though she had forced herself to consider it all as rationally as she could. Abigail's words came to mind over and over again, helping her to remember that she was not betraying Joseph by beginning to have a gentle affection for another gentleman. She still loved Joseph desperately, still grieved for him and had him in her thoughts every day, but there was the beginning of something new growing in her heart. Something for Lord Blackford.

Martha did not know whether or not she welcomed such feelings, still confused over all that she felt and wondering what this could mean for the rest of her life. Would her children react as Abigail had suggested, not holding such a thing against her but rather being glad for her happiness? It might not come immediately, she realized, sitting down rather heavily in a chair by the fire, but perhaps they would learn to accept such a situation.

"What situation?" she muttered aloud, pressing one hand to her forehead in order to rid herself of such ridiculous thoughts. Lord Blackford had not made any advances towards her and she had certainly not done so towards him. They were, as she had said to him herself, very good friends, and for that, she was truly glad.

But it was a friendship she did not want to lose. To return to the dower house now, to turn her back on society, on London and even on Lord Blackford seemed quite impossible. He had become part of her every day and to return to a life where he was not present brought her a sense of pain that she could not easily remove from herself.

"Oh, Joseph," she said aloud, as though he could hear her. "Am I doing you wrong?"

The scratch came at the door, making her jump with fright, only to realize that it was the first of her guests arriving.

"Lady Crawford, my lady," the butler said grandly, as Lady Crawford stepped into the room, looking resplendent in a dark red gown.

"My dear Edith," Martha greeted her. "Thank you for coming. Where is your husband?"

Lady Crawford waved a hand. "He was lingering over his cravat so I came without him. The blessings of having been long married—one does not have to wait for one's husband! One can simply tell him that the carriage will return for him and his cravat in a few short minutes." She chuckled as Martha laughed, shaking her head. "He is becoming quite ridiculous in his old age, I'm afraid."

"Oh, do not say that," Martha sighed heavily. "I do not feel old and yet my appearance tells me that I grow older every day."

"Nonsense," Lady Crawford proclaimed with a good deal of firmness. "You look quite wonderful, Martha. Indeed, I believe you have looked all the better these last few weeks." She smiled, a knowing look on her face. "Yes, I am referring to Lord Blackford, my dear. I am not ashamed to speak directly."

"Lord Blackford and I are friends," Martha insisted, not allowing her friend to make any sort of accusation. "That is all."

Lady Crawford's expression gentled. "And is that all you wish for him to be, Martha, my dear? You cannot tell me that you have not found his company to be anything less than enjoyable."

Martha hesitated. "He is a kind man, yes."

"And I have not seen him spend so much time with any one lady in all my years in London society," Lady Crawford added, sending a blush to Martha's cheeks. "There, you see!" She grinned triumphantly. "I knew you had something of an affection for him."

Groaning, Martha prayed silently that her friend would not continue to speak so openly when the other guests arrived. "My dear Edith, you must not be ridiculous. I am in my sixth decade and am no longer a debutante."

Lady Crawford snorted. "I hardly think age is of any particular concern when matters of the heart are involved, Martha. If you have any sort of affection for Lord Blackford, then I suggest you pursue it."

Martha shook her head, her confusion mounting. "I loved my husband."

Lady Crawford's eyes filled with sympathy almost immediately. "I know that, my dear friend," she said, reaching for Martha's hand and pressing it gently. "But you do not need to spend the rest of your life in abject sorrow simply because you are widowed. You loved your husband, yes, and you love him still—but that does not mean you cannot find happiness with another."

"It is not as simple as it might seem," Martha said heavily. "How can feeling such a small amount of affection for a gentleman feel as though I am being condemned for doing so at the same time?"

Lady Crawford took both of Martha's hands in her own. "Because you are a loyal creature," she said gently. "You are devoted and unselfish. Your torment is your own self battling against what it feels. You may let yourself feel, Martha, my dear, without allowing the guilt or the worry to take hold. It may take some time, of course, and there will undoubtably be moments when you will think yourself quite lost, but you must not hold yourself back. There is no shame in taking a hold of one's future and finding a little light where there was once only darkness."

Martha swallowed hard, feeling tears threaten. Her friend spoke with such compassion and consideration that it was as though she had looked into Martha's heart and was tugging out her concerns one at a time.

"Now, do not begin to weep, for it is most unseemly for ladies of our age and standing," Lady Crawford said, a good deal more briskly. "For if you begin, then I shall have no other choice but to join you in your tears, and then what shall your other guests think?"

Reaching for her friend, and unheeding as to whether or not her gown would become crinkled, Martha hugged Edith tightly, battling her tears as she did so.

"You are quite wonderful, Edith," she said hoarsely. "I do not know what I should have done without you."

Lady Crawford smiled and squeezed Martha's hand before letting it go. "You are quite welcome, my dear," she replied kindly. "I only want to see you happy and if Lord Blackford is the one to bring that to you, then I can have nothing but praise for him."

Martha laughed. "I hear his son is courting your youngest daughter."

"Yes," Lady Crawford stated with no smile on her face. "Catherine, who would not even come to London for the season! I had to send her to my sister's in order to assure the girl that I would not force her to find another."

"And is Lord Blackford's son not a good match?" Martha enquired, wondering why Lady Crawford had not warmed to him. "Even though Catherine must be quite devoted to him."

Lady Crawford laughed and rolled her eyes. "They are both very strange creatures, in their own way," she said with a small shrug. "Neither wishing to go to town, to dance and acquaint themselves with a good many others. No, you are quite right to say that there is nothing wrong with Hornby, it is more that I wanted to make sure that Catherine was quite certain about her feelings for the gentleman. I thought if she came to town, she might be swept off her feet by an earl or some such thing, instead of a mere viscount... but then again, she is the daughter of a viscount and I confess that I can be somewhat ridiculous about these things." Martha laughed, aware that Lady Crawford had always loved London and the society that came with it. It must be very unusual for her to have a daughter that rebuffed the very things Lady Crawford loved.

"Ah, here is Lord Crawford," Lady Crawford exclaimed as the door opened again to reveal her husband with his perfectly tied cravat. "And your son. How wonderful." She smiled at Martha, who felt a sudden swirl of butterflies in her stomach as she waited with anticipation for Lord Blackford to arrive. "This is going to be a wonderful evening, I am quite sure of it."

SOME HOURS LATER, Martha had to admit that she was somewhat disheartened. The evening had gone wonderfully well, just as Lady Crawford had predicted, and her guests had seemed to enjoy the refreshments and the entertainment. Now, a good few were sitting to play cards of some sort, whilst others were still deep in conversation, enjoying the champagne that the footmen continued to serve.

But Lord Blackford had not appeared.

Martha smiled tightly as her son drew near.

"This has been a lovely evening, Mama," Charles said, smiling at her. "You were not nervous, I hope?"

"No, not at all," Martha lied, knowing that she could not tell her son that she had been anxious about Lord Blackford's arrival. "I think it has been most enjoyable."

Charles' smile faded. "You have not enjoyed it yourself?"

She put a bright smile on her face. "Of course I have, Charles!" she exclaimed, pressing his arm. "I confess that I was somewhat anxious over my first social event without your father being here, but I am delighted it has gone so well."

A shadow crossed Charles' face. "I thought you might be thinking of him, Mama."

"I am," she admitted quietly. "But not in the way that you might think, Charles."

Her son looked at her, a steadiness in his gaze that told her he already knew what it was she was going to say.

"I will always love your father, Charles," Martha began, her hand still on his arm. "But I confess that I have begun to find a new happiness with another."

Charles did not so much as blink, although his eyes flickered with something akin to worry or concern. "With Lord Blackford, then."

"This does not surprise you."

Charles shook his head. "No, it does not," he said slowly. "I have spoken to Abigail about this previously and she has a remarkably different view from my own, I confess. I will not pretend that I do not find the idea difficult, Mama, but I must admit to my own selfishness with such a view." He smiled at her, his expression no longer troubled. "I cannot imagine what it must be like to have lived so long with so many of us around you, and then to start life alone in the dower house. There is nothing to hold against you if you choose to pursue happiness with Lord Blackford, Mama. You will have no complaints nor murmurs of disapproval from me."

Martha let out a long breath of relief, only just realizing just how troubled she had been over her son's reaction to such news. "That means a very great deal to me, Charles. I want you to be assured that I will never stop loving your father, for he blessed my life in more ways than I think I can ever express. But I confess that it can be lonely to live in the way you have described, more lonely than I think I realized before I came to London. I have so many joys in my life, but I cannot pretend that I do not long for a companion to share my days." She smiled as Abigail came to join them, not afraid to speak openly to them both. "I cannot promise that Lord Blackford is to be that companion, but there is the start of something growing between us that I am still trying to comprehend!" Laughing gently, she shook her head as a slow sense of contentment filled her. "Your reassurance means the world to me, Charles. As does yours, Abigail."

Abigail took her husband's arm. "I am glad you have both had the opportunity to talk. Now, I think Miss Graham is willing to finish this evening with a few songs, Martha, if you would like her to take her seat at the pianoforte?"

Martha smiled. "That sounds wonderful, thank you."

CHAPTER 8

Martha did not rise early the following morning, finding herself quite at her leisure. She was rather tired after a very late evening, although she was truly delighted with just how well the occasion had gone. The only thing that troubled her now was just why Lord Blackford had not appeared.

Resting in bed, with her breakfast tray at her elbow and her recent novel on the table beside her, Martha let out a small sigh of contentment, trying not to allow her mind to linger on why Lord Blackford had been absent. She felt a good deal more at peace over what she had begun to feel for the gentleman, given her discussion with first Lady Crawford and then her son and daughter-in-law. She knew that she did not need to fear this affection that was growing within her heart, for it did not take away from the love she still had for her late husband and, from what Charles had said, would not make her family distressed in any way. Yes, it might take her children some time to accept that she was being courted by Lord Blackford—if he were to ask her, that is—but they would come to approve of it soon enough.

"You are most ridiculous, Martha," she said aloud, reaching for her cup of tea. "The gentleman has not yet even made mention of such a thing as courtship!" A small smile lingered on her face as she considered this, aware that all they had been doing of late, with their many outings and time spent together, might well be considered a courtship by any other person aware of their continuing acquaintance! Mayhap Lord Blackford was less than inclined towards considering a possible courtship with her because of how firm she had been at the beginning of their acquaintance. She would have to find a way to reassure him that she did not feel that way any longer.

Of course, there was always the chance that Lord Blackford was not disposed towards her in such a way as she hoped, but given how he had been with her, Martha was not inclined to believe that. There had been those long glances, the vulnerability of his heart towards her own, as well as the laughter and good conversation they had shared. Their friendship did not show any sign of diminishing and it was this that gave Martha hope. Lord Blackford wanted to call upon her, wanted to remain in her company for a good deal of time each day—aside from the fact that he had not shown up at her soiree last evening.

Biting her lip, her brow furrowing as she let her mind drift onto that particular matter again, Martha shook her head to herself and let out her breath slowly, aware of the tension that was filling her. She had no need to be concerned. Lord Blackford had, most likely, become caught up in something of importance and would write to her very soon with his apologies, if he did not call upon her instead. There was nothing to be anxious about.

"My lady?"

Just as Martha had settled her mind, the bedchamber door flew open and, much to her surprise, the maid hurried in with a note in her hand.

"Goodness, whatever is the matter?" Martha exclaimed as the maid bobbed a curtsy and handed her a note. "There is no need to come bursting into the room in such a way, surely!"

"I was told it was a matter of great urgency, my lady," the maid replied, looking as though she were about to burst into tears. "Should I remain here with you, in case you have need of me?"

Martha frowned, then nodded. "Very well." Looking at the letter, she turned it over to examine the seal but found none there. It was tied with a bit of ribbon and not sealed as she would expect of a letter from any of her children, which was something of a relief.

Pulling aside the ribbon, she unfolded the letter and began to read.

Her heart seemed to stop in her chest.

'*Lady Catesby, my master has asked me to send for you. He is in need of aid and states that he can trust you. If you might spare the time to call just as soon as you can, Lord Blackford would be most appreciative.*'

There was no signature on the note to tell her who had written it, but it was quite apparent to Martha that this had come from one of Lord Blackford's staff, although what had occurred that would require her help, she could not say.

The maid had picked up the breakfast tray and had set it aside, leaving Martha free to throw back the covers and swing her legs over the side.

"I must dress at once," she said, no longer irritated with the maid. "You were quite right to bring that to me at once. It is of the greatest urgency."

"There is a carriage waiting for you, my lady," the maid whispered as she hurried to help Martha into her things. "The footman who brought the note is below."

Martha said nothing, her heart pounding wildly. She had very little idea as to what had occurred with Lord Blackford, but the fact that he had his servant write the note instead of writing it himself did not bode well for him. She had to get to him at once.

Hurrying the maid to dress her hair into a simple chignon, Martha sat quietly for a moment and looked at her reflection in the mirror. She looked pale and weary, her eyes wide with apparent fright and a slight tremble about her lips. There was no doubt in her mind now. She was afraid for Lord Blackford.

ARRIVING at Lord Blackford's home seemed to take an inordinate amount of time, making Martha more and more fractious with each minute that passed. Finally, the carriage door was opened and she stepped out into the street, before hurrying up the stone steps that led to Lord Blackford's front door.

It opened for her at once, the butler appearing just to her left as she walked inside.

"Thank you, my lady," he said, bowing slowly. "Might I take your things?"

Martha found herself almost throwing her hat and gloves at the butler, growing desperate to seek out Lord Blackford. "What has happened?" she asked hoarsely. "Where is he?"

The butler cleared his throat as the footman closed the door behind her. "He is in the study, my lady," he said, beginning to walk away from her. "If you will just come with me."

She did not hesitate but hurried after him, her heart beating so frantically that she could barely catch her breath.

"In here, my lady," the butler said, opening the door. "Shall I send up some tea? Although mayhap you will need something stronger."

"Both," came Lord Blackford's voice from inside the room, flooding Martha with such relief that she almost collapsed where she stood. "And some more hot water and bandages, if you please."

Walking into the room on unsteady legs, Martha tried to make out where Lord Blackford sat, wondering why the drapes were still closed on what was a quite lovely summer morning.

"I must have some light," she said, bumping into something solid. "Do you mind?"

Lord Blackford let out a heavy sigh. "I suppose I shall have to allow it," he said in a voice that rasped with either pain or irritation. "Thank you for coming, Martha. I did not know who else to turn to. This is the first time such a thing has occurred and I doubt it will be the last, should I choose to continue. Not that I think I will, however."

The depth of pain in his voice had her practically rushing towards the drapes, doing her best to avoid the heavy oak table and then the chair that seemed to deliberately be in her way. Pulling them back, she fastened them quickly and then turned to look at Lord Blackford.

He was sitting, slumped, in a chair by the fire, which only had a few glowing embers remaining. He was in his shirt sleeves, with a large red stain covering the top of his right arm.

Martha caught her breath.

"Yes, it is as you see," Lord Blackford said heavily. "I have been shot." His eyes met hers, a rueful smile twisting his lips as he kept his agony hidden behind his eyes. "Twice, in fact. The other one has nicked my ribs, although it is nothing more than a flesh wound. This one," he indicated his right arm, "has the bullet still embedded in my flesh, I fear. You can understand why I was unable to write to you myself, I think."

Martha was, by this point, leaning heavily on the oak table, trying to draw in enough breath to stop her head from spinning. She was quite overcome with what she saw and had heard from Lord Blackford. He had been shot? On two occasions? It was almost impossible to take in.

"I know this is all most awkward," Lord Blackford said in a gentler voice. "And I know I shall have to explain to you why such a thing has occurred, but for the moment, I must have this bullet taken from my arm so that I might sew it up and bind it thereafter."

"Then a surgeon," Martha breathed, closing her eyes tightly. "You require a surgeon."

"No." Lord Blackford's voice was sharp. "I cannot. They are prone to talking about what they have seen and what they have done and I will not allow them to endanger me... even though, I confess, I would most likely deserve any punishment that came my way."

Martha looked at him, confused, trying to keep her eyes averted from the large bloodstain that covered Lord Blackford's shirt. "Punishment?"

Lord Blackford cleared his throat and, for the first time, Martha realized just how pale he was. "As I said, my dear lady, I will explain it to you all much later but I cannot do so now. This arm of mine is a more pressing matter and I fear that my staff will not be of much use. I have only told a few of them what has occurred—the butler, housekeeper, maid and footman—and I pray that they will be able to keep what has occurred secret, known only to themselves. However, I am well aware that this may be wishful thinking on my part. After all, that is what London runs on, is it not? Rumor. Gossip. Intrigue." He shrugged. "Your presence, however, could prevent such a thing. I will not need to send for a doctor or a surgeon if you are able to assist me."

Martha closed her eyes, rubbing her forehead with the back of her hand. "I do not understand, Lord Blackford."

"Here." He held out his hand to her and, unwillingly, she went towards him, thinking quietly to herself that this was not at all what she had expected and that she certainly had no skill when it came to doctoring! She wondered why he had not sent for the doctor, her eyes taking in the stain on his shirt which still appeared to be wet with blood. The injury had not stopped bleeding, then.

"Martha, I know that I ask a great deal of you, but might you be able to help me in this matter?" Lord Blackford asked, his voice serious and his eyes filled with desperation. "I promise that I shall tell you everything you wish thereafter, and I shall not be at all angry if you should choose to turn your back on me."

This sounded rather ominous but Martha knew she could not refuse. "I do not know what it is I am to do," she said, her voice shaking. "What if I hurt you further?"

Lord Blackford managed a tight, hard smile. "Most likely, you will, but it will be worth it given that the bullet will then be removed from its resting place. You need not fear, Martha, I will tell you exactly what to do and when. You are not inclined to fainting, I hope?"

"I have not fainted yet," Martha replied with a small sense of pride. "In all my years, I have never once swooned or anything so ridiculous."

Lord Blackford nodded, his face contorted with pain. "Then I hope this will not be the first time," he said with a sigh. "Now, you will need the whisky and that knife that I have set on the table. Bring them both to me. The butler will bring more bandages very soon, but we have no need of them as yet." He managed to smile, his hand tightening on hers. "Thank you, Martha."

She nodded, her anxiety rising too high for her to either speak or smile back at him.

"You will do wonderfully, I am sure."

. . .

HALF AN HOUR LATER, Martha was doing her very best not to cast up her accounts in the middle of Lord Blackford's study. The bullet was resting safely on the floor somewhere and she was now attempting to sew up the wound, which she found more trying than anything she had done before.

Lord Blackford had looked away as she had begun, having already let out a yelp of pain when she had been forced to delve into the bullet wound with the knife, in an attempt to find the bullet. She was sweating all over, feeling hot and ill at ease as she pushed the needle through the edge of the wound and pulled it as tightly closed as she dared.

Lord Blackford let out a hiss.

"It is almost over," she said quickly, attempting to be encouraging. "You need not worry."

"Splash it all liberally with whisky when you are finished," Lord Blackford instructed. "Do not worry about wasting it, for it is suggested that such a thing will prevent infection."

She did not question this but accepted it as she had done with everything else. Finishing the stitching, she filled a small glass with a mouthful of whisky and poured it down over the wound. Lord Blackford cried out, his face screwed up tightly with the pain of it.

"Again," he said, through gritted teeth. "Do not fear hurting me, Martha. This is for my own good."

Martha made to do so, only to pour herself a second, smaller measure in another glass which she then picked up and threw back, allowing the heat and the smoke of the whisky to ignite her very being, capturing her breath and bringing her fresh wakefulness and awareness. She then did as Lord Blackford had instructed, until, finally, he allowed her to bandage his arm.

His ruined shirt was soon on the flames as the butler helped Lord Blackford change into a fresh shirt, whilst Martha kept her back turned. Her mind was filled with questions, her worry growing steadily. What was it Lord Blackford had been doing?

CHAPTER 9

"Y ou cannot know how much I wish to keep the truth from you," Lord Blackford murmured once the butler had quit the room and Martha had seated herself opposite him, a tea tray to her right. "I have been considering this matter ever since I first knew you had arrived back in town."

Martha tried her best to remain completely silent, despite the many questions that came to her lips, burning her lips and tongue as she left them unspoken. Her stomach was knotting, her heart beating wildly as she looked at Lord Blackford, wondering what it was that he had to say to her. Why had he wanted to keep this from her? Was it something so terrible that she would not be able to forgive him?

Lord Blackford sighed heavily, his face haggard. His eyes were heavy, with deep shadows beneath them. His forehead was wrinkled, his brow furrowed. Whatever it was he had to say, it was bringing him a great deal of distress.

"I will tell you this, Martha, although I cannot expect you to believe me, that I have only ridden out on three occasions. Yours was my second attempt and I have done nothing with the things I took."

"Took?" Martha repeated, not understanding him. "I do not know what you mean."

Lord Blackford closed his eyes and ran a hand over his face, before looking at her directly.

"The day you came to London," he said slowly. "What was it that occurred?"

Martha frowned, wondering what he meant. "I came by carriage."

"Out on the road," he said, leaning forward in his chair. "Do you recall? Lady Crawford insisted you tell it on multiple occasions."

Martha's eyes widened. "You mean, the rogue who stopped my carriage and threatened to shoot my men?" she asked, her heart slowing as she realized what Lord Blackford was saying. "The man who did not take my wedding ring from me but took gold, coins and a ruby pendant?" That had not meant much to her, she had to admit, for she had been so very relieved that she had been allowed to keep her wedding ring that she had not thought twice about the pendant or the money.

Lord Blackford nodded. "Yes, that is what I mean, Martha. That rogue, that man who stood in your path and threatened to shoot your men—that man was I."

Martha stared at him, her breath gone from her chest. Her world began to tip sideways, a loud buzzing in her ears as she fought to keep herself from fainting. This could not be so. Lord Blackford could not have been the man who had stolen from her in such a terrible way.

"I did not do anything with your coins or your pendant," Lord Blackford continued, his head dropping so low that his chin almost rested on his chest. "They are in a locked drawer in the table." One hand reached out and pointed to the large oak table behind her but Martha did not look at it. "I should never have taken them."

Martha rose unsteadily to her feet, surprising Lord Blackford entirely.

"You are not leaving me?" he asked, suddenly sounding quite desperate. "I know I have done terrible things but there is more for me to say, Martha. I want to explain."

She shook her head, holding out one hand to him in order to silence him. "Pray, give me a moment, Lord Blackford."

She walked towards where she had left her glass of whisky, praying that she would not collapse before she reached it, such was the shock coursing through her. Lifting it to her lips, she threw back the rest of the whisky in one smooth motion, letting the fire bring life back to her veins.

Setting it down, Martha drew in her breath and pressed one hand firmly against her stomach in an attempt to calm herself.

"My pendant," she said, turning around to face Lord Blackford, who was staring into the flames in abject misery. "Where is it?"

Lord Blackford closed his eyes. "The key is in the lock," he said, gesturing towards the table. "I have thought of returning it to you on so many occasions but I found I could not, not when you would wonder why I had such a thing in my possession."

Martha ignored this, walked around the table and found the small drawer that Lord Blackford had been talking about. Turning the key, she opened the drawer and found not only her ruby necklace, with a few gold coins scattered underneath it, but also a ring or two, pearl earrings and what appeared to be a rather large emerald.

Lord Blackford was a thief.

He must have seen the look in her eyes for as she came back to join him—reluctant as she was to hear his excuses for becoming a vagabond—his face fell and his expression grew desperate.

"When I came upon your carriage, Martha, I did not know what to do," Lord Blackford said urgently. "I saw myself as if for the first time, saw the depths of what I had allowed myself to become."

Martha, realizing that she had not said anything as yet, took in a steadying breath, settled her shoulders and looked at Lord Blackford with as much calmness in her expression as she could. "You stole from me."

Lord Blackford did not argue with this. "Yes."

"You threatened to shoot my men."

"Yes."

"You would have done so?"

Lord Blackford shook his head firmly. "N0, indeed, I would not. My pistol would not have fired, even if I had wished it. I am not that sort of gentleman, Martha. Surely you must know that."

Martha shook her head slowly, sadness seeping into her every pore. "I do not know what to think, Lord Blackford. I have spent so many days trying to work out what it is I feel for you but now I fear that all that time has been nothing more than wasted, for the man I believed you to be is not, in fact, the man you truly are."

"But it *is*," Lord Blackford exclaimed, leaning forward and then wincing as his arm pained him. "I did not want to become such a rogue as all that, and yet in my desperation, I felt I had no other choice."

Martha wanted to tell him that this was poppycock, that there was no good reason for anyone to turn to a life of crime, but there was something in Lord Blackford's eyes that made her hesitate. Did she not owe it to him to allow him an explanation? After all, he had been most kind and generous to her, as her friend, over these last weeks.

Looking down at the ruby pendant in her hand, Martha sighed heavily, her shoulders slumping. This was all so very foolish. She had been battling with her feelings for Lord Blackford, relived that she had finally come to a decision that she was both glad and relieved about, only to discover that Lord Blackford was not the gentleman she thought him to be. Her mind went back to that day she had been travelling to London—had he not struck fear into her heart? Had she not been afraid for her servants?

And yet, had he not allowed her to keep her wedding ring? Had he not shown her kindness in that? Yes, he had taken what was not his, but she had not given the pendant nor the coins any more thought since they had been taken. They were not of particular importance to her— but to Lord Blackford, they had obviously meant a good deal.

"Why did you steal from me, Lord Blackford?" she asked solemnly. "What could be your reason for doing so?"

Lord Blackford's eyes drove into hers. "My son," he stated quietly. "It has been an attempt to rectify my estate for my son."

Something dropped into Martha's stomach. "What do you mean?"

Lord Blackford sighed and ran one hand through his greying hair, evidence of just how difficult he was finding such explanations. His eyes turned away from hers, towards the fire that burned beside him.

"As you know, I have made a rather unfortunate mess of my

estate," he began slowly. "At the death of my wife, I lost myself for some years. I have been trying to bring my estate back to its full capacity since then, have been trying to regain some of the wealth I did not care about at the time." He sighed, shaking his head. "My son wants to marry Catherine, Lady Crawford's daughter. It was this news that made me consider what it was I could do in order to add to my coffers, feeling almost desperate in my attempts to do so. That is why I chose to steal from those who have a good deal already." His eyes slid back towards hers, a deep sadness lingering in them. "It was foolish and ridiculous, yes. It was also wrong, but such was my desperation that I threw all that to the side." A small, wry smile caught his lips. "The first time I was fairly successful, for the rest of that box is what I took from the unfortunate inhabitants of the first carriage." He shook his head. "I wrestled with what I had done for some weeks, only to convince myself that not only could I do it again, but that I could slowly begin to accumulate wealth for my son and his future. And then, I encountered you."

Martha let out her breath, not realizing she had been holding it. That was why the gentleman had ridden away when he had asked her what her name was. He had recognized her and had been filled with such horror that he could not have lingered.

"I was so very ashamed of myself, Martha," Lord Blackford continued, his voice thick with emotion. "I was doing all I could to be callous and detached and yet when you spoke of your ring and your husband, I could feel my own heart crying out in understanding. How could I take such a precious thing from you?" His eyes caught hers and Martha found that she could not look away. "But I told myself that a thief such as I was trying to be would be cruel and hard of heart, and so I tried not to allow my emotions to hold sway over me. In the depths of my mind, I felt as though I knew who you were, which was what brought me to ask your name. When you told me, I felt as if I were about to fall through the ground in shock, my heart beating wildly with both fright and disgust at myself." Shaking his head, he rubbed his forehead with the back of his hand. "I have been so afraid that you would recognize me."

"And that is why you wanted to spend time with me?" Martha asked, finding, to her horror, that tears were beginning to pool in her eyes.

"No! No!" Lord Blackford was on his feet in a moment, his arm forgotten as he flung himself towards her, on his knees before her as though he were a desperate man looking for a reprieve. "I told myself, Martha, that I should stay away from you, but I could not. You have become so very dear to me that this burden only increased in weight with every passing moment."

She sniffed and pulled out her handkerchief, dabbing delicately at her eyes. Her heart was breaking and she did not know what to do about the pain.

"I have wanted to tell you that I feel more for you than I had ever expected to, but I could not allow those words to pass my lips while I carry this weight with me," Lord Blackford explained, his eyes wide and his expression pained. "It is all my own fault, of course, and I do not even attempt to pass the burden onto any other. This was my own choice, my own responsibility and my own foolishness."

Martha wiped her eyes and looked at him. "And yet it did not stop you from attempting to do so again," she pointed out, looking at his arm. "You were shot."

Lord Blackford hung his head. "I will never do so again," he said hoarsely. "That is enough. I have been foolish long enough."

A short, heavy silence rose between them.

"But why?" Martha asked, trying her best not to cry. "Why would you do such a thing when you know that it is both wrong and unwise? Why did you go out again?"

"Because of news of my holdings," Lord Blackford muttered, his shoulders slumped as he knelt before her. "It is all borne from desperation, from fearing that my crops will not yield as much as they ought, that I shall have to take more money from my accounts in order to improve the estate. Money that my son shall have to struggle with when it comes time for him to take the title." His eyes darkened and he looked away. "I wish to goodness that I had never allowed my grief to drive me to such foolishness," he finished, looking for all the world as though he had quite given up on ever regaining her trust or her understanding again. "But it did. I behaved in a most selfish and irresponsible manner and even now, years later, I am bearing the consequences of what I have done."

Martha closed her eyes, almost battling against the wave of sympathy that threatened to crash over her. Lord Blackford had admitted that he had been wrong to do as he had done, had confessed to his reasons for doing so and had told her the entirety of what he had done without hesitation—although she knew he had been keeping it from her since they had first met. She found that she wanted to understand, that she wanted to express to him that she knew why he had behaved in such a way and that she did not hold his actions against him, but found that she could do no such thing. Not yet. The shock of his revelations had been too much.

"I think I must leave you," she said softly, trying to rise to her feet without brushing against him. "I do hope your arm recovers quickly, Lord Blackford."

Lord Blackford did not look up, evidently having expected or simply accepting that this was the course of action she had chosen to take.

"I will write to you very soon," she promised, making him glance up at her. "This is not the end of our acquaintance, Lord Blackford, but I must do some thinking."

He nodded, eventually pushing himself from his knees to a standing position, although his body remained hunched over, his guilt and shame evident.

"Know that everything I have said to you, Martha, is the truth," he said without looking at her. "If I had any hope of your acceptance, I would press you for your agreement to let me court you, but I know that what I have done would not allow for such a thing. I quite understand, of course. I am just glad that you know the truth now."

Her heart ached terribly but Martha said nothing, one hand pressed against her chest as though she might prevent the pain from increasing.

"I have enjoyed every moment in your company, Martha," Lord Blackford continued, his head still bowed low. "This has been one of the most delightful seasons I have ever had, and that is all down to you. Your company, your conversation, your generous heart has called out to me and I have reveled in all of it. Whether or not you choose to continue our acquaintance—and I would not blame you if you do not— I have been glad to know you again, Martha, after all these years. You have brought light back into my dark existence. I have found happiness —and love—growing within my heart."

Martha caught her breath, her whole body alive with a sudden, fierce joy that she could not quite explain.

"I know you must go and I will not beg you to stay," Lord Blackford finished, turning away from her. "I am grateful for this opportunity to share my heart and my disgrace with you. It has freed me in a way I did not expect. My apologies are heartfelt, Martha. I should never have done such things, neither to you nor to the others I stole from. I swear I shall do so no more."

Martha nodded, closed her eyes and forced herself to draw in a steadying breath. She was battling against her own desire to fling all that he had done aside and run to him, to confess that her own heart had found an affection for him that she had not expected either, but the pain of what he had done still lingered in her mind. Opening the door, she looked back at him for another moment, but found that his back was still towards her. Without another word, she slipped out the door and walked towards the entrance of the house, leaving Lord Blackford behind.

THE END

Martha had not slept.

Instead, she had spent the night tossing and turning, her mind filled with questions and her heart both joyful and despondent in equal measure.

She could not forget Lord Blackford's confession of both his wrongdoing and his love for her. They battled against each other, making her struggle to understand what it was she felt and what it was she wanted to do.

One thing was quite certain, however. She did *not* want her acquaintance with Lord Blackford to come to an end, no matter what he had done. He had reignited her heart in a way she had never thought would ever occur again. Yes, she still grappled with what she felt for Lord Blackford and the deep love for her late husband that ran through her, but slowly she was beginning to find a way for them both to run alongside each other in contentment and understanding. She loved Joseph still, but she was beginning to love Lord Blackford also.

She loved a man who was a thief.

Closing her eyes, Martha rubbed at her forehead, aware that she had deep shadows smudging underneath her eyes. Breakfast had not been particularly appetizing and now, even though she had barely eaten anything, she was still not hungry for the tea tray that had been set before her. There was a small arrangement of various sweets, but none caught her interest. How could she eat when she was in such confusion?

Pouring herself a cup of tea and praying that it would calm her somewhat, Martha stirred it carefully before sitting back down in her seat by the small fire. The day was rather dull and not particularly warm, adding to her feelings of discontent. Looking into the flames, Martha questioned whether or not she could understand *why* Lord Blackford had chosen to behave in such a brutish manner... and to her surprise, found that she could.

She knew all too well what grief was like. She knew how it troubled one's soul, to the point that it seemed to be all that one could feel. The misery, the pain, the distress that came with it almost every waking minute could drive anyone to distraction—and Lord Blackford had dealt with it in a way that had brought ongoing consequences. He had, as he had said, been trying to rectify that for decades, but the damage he had done had obviously been severe. Trying to heal those wounds, financial or otherwise, was quite honorable, although using theft and robbery to do so was not something she could accept. At least, on that point he had admitted as such and had only done so on three occasions—with one of those occasions being her own. If he could return the jewels to their respective owners, then that would be the start of a way to make amends, would it not?

Sipping her tea, Martha let a sigh shake her frame, aware of just how much he had been offering her by confessing the truth about his feelings. He loved her, which was something equally extraordinary and frightening. She had not expected such feelings from him, although she could now understand why he had not spoken to her of them before. Now that he was free of his burden of guilt, he had been able to tell her the truth about his heart—and she had found herself drawn to him with such desperation that she had almost wanted to fling herself into his arms right there and then.

"Is that what you will do now, then, Martha? "she asked herself aloud, a frown creasing her brow. "Will you go to him? Or will you return home?"

Home. That word did not bring her the joy she had thought would come with it, realizing that she would be quite alone once more, although her family would soon ensure that she was kept busy, of course. But there would not be the pleasant conversation after dinner, the laughs and smiles at the breakfast table that she had once enjoyed with Joseph and now found herself longing for again. If she turned her back on Lord Blackford, if she chose to tell him that she could not forgive this nor allow her understanding to show him any sort of compassion, then she would be resigning herself to a life without his company.

Her stomach twisted, just as a knock came at the door.

"Yes?"

The butler cleared his throat. "My lady, Lord Blackford has arrived. He says he will not stay if you do not wish it, but he has come to take his leave of you."

Martha blinked, her heart quickening dramatically. "To take his leave?"

"Yes, my lady," the butler repeated, his face stoic. "That is what he said."

Martha got to her feet, her tea forgotten. "Send him in at once."

She began to pace up and down in front of the fire, her fingers twisting together as she held her hands in front of her. Take his leave? What did that mean? Was Lord Blackford leaving London?

Another scratch at the door. Martha forced herself to stand still, her eyes fixed on the door as it opened.

Lord Blackford stepped inside, his eyes only lingering on her face for a moment before they dropped to the floor. "Thank you for seeing me, Martha. I was not sure you would and I am—"

"Are you leaving?" Martha asked, interrupting him. "Are you leaving town?"

Lord Blackford nodded, his eyes heavy with grief. "I think it best," he stated quietly, pulling out a small parcel from his pocket. "This is yours, I think." He made to hand it to her, only to pull his hand back and set the package on a table, as though he did not want to touch her. "It is what I took from you, Martha. I have sent the Egertons their own monies back also, although they will not know who has sent it, of course."

Relief flooded her heart. "That is wonderful, Lord Blackford."

A wry smile pulled at his lips, his eyes finally lingering on her face. "It is the end," he said slowly. "The end of my foolishness. I have made amends, I have paid for my actions." He gestured to his arm. "And now I think I must return home, where I can oversee all that goes on at my estate. I must make it as profitable as I can for my son."

Her heart sank to the floor. "You are leaving?"

"I think I must," Lord Blackford replied, turning away towards the door. "Although I will be sorry to leave you behind."

Martha shook her head, her stomach roiling as she took a few steps towards him. "Wait. Lord Blackford, please."

Slowly, Lord Blackford turned back to face her, his expression confused.

"I do not want you to go," she told him, lifting her chin. "In fact, I do not think I can allow you to do so."

Lord Blackford frowned, confusion etching itself across his expression. "You cannot let me go?"

"No, Lord Blackford, I do not think I can," Martha replied, her mouth going dry as she saw the look in his eyes. "I have spent a good many hours considering what it is you have said, letting myself think over what has occurred and what the future might hold should I either refuse to continue our acquaintance or allow myself to forget everything that has happened." She saw his eyes flare, a glimmer of hope appearing within them. "If anyone can understand the part that grief has played in your actions, Lord Blackford, then it is I."

Lord Blackford let out a long breath, shaking his head in apparent disbelief. "You cannot think that what I did was right."

"No, indeed!" she exclaimed, a small smile on her face. "It was quite wrong, but you have confessed it to me and have returned what is mine." Her hand was trembling as she settled it on his arm, the enormity of what she was doing coming home to her as she looked up into his face. "I cannot forget all that we have shared, Lord Blackford. You have become quite dear to me, although I confess that I have been struggling with what I feel."

Lord Blackford did not move, as though to either move or speak would prevent her from saying more.

"I love Joseph," Martha continued, her voice hitching as she thought of her dear husband, who had been so wonderful to her during their marriage. "Even though he is gone, I love him still. And yet, within my heart, I have felt the beginnings of a second love. A love for you, Lord Blackford."

Lord Blackford swallowed hard, his face seeming to pale as he placed his hand over hers. "You make me feel as though I am a young gentleman again, seeking to claim the hand of the most beautiful creature he has ever set his eyes upon," he murmured, his tender words bringing a light to her soul. "I have not felt such things for years."

"Nor I," Martha admitted. "Joseph has been buried almost seven years now, and I have found my life to be both wonderful and lonely in equal measure. I came to London in the hope of pursuing old friendships, never thinking that I would find my heart lost to another." She smiled up at him, taking in his lined face, his hazel eyes that were still vibrant and filled with light. "I do not want you to leave London, Lord Blackford, not unless you intend on taking me with you."

She laughed as his brows shot up towards his hairline, aware that she had been more than obvious about what she expected their future to be.

"You cannot mean it, Martha," Lord Blackford whispered, evidently overcome with what she was offering him. "Not after what I have done."

Martha placed one hand on Lord Blackford's chest, the other still holding his hand. They were closer than they had ever been before and yet she felt no guilt or awkwardness about it. This felt right, as if this was where she had meant to be ever since she had returned to London.

"I do not intend to think of what has passed any longer, Lord Blackford," she replied truthfully. "You have made amends, you have told me the truth and I have chosen to accept it, forgive it and set it aside. My heart will not allow me to forget the love that has begun to grow within it. To separate myself from you now would only bring me pain and struggle, and I have had quite enough of such things, I think." She smiled as he nodded, his eyes fixed on her own. She knew that he understood everything she was saying. "I have wealth, Lord Blackford. Wealth enough to share with your estate so that your son will have a good future with his wife."

Lord Blackford framed her face with his hands, his eyes searching hers. "I would not marry you for your wealth, Martha."

"Then what would you marry me for?" she asked, her heart beating wildly with all that she felt.

"For love," Lord Blackford said, his expression gentling as her hands ran over his shoulders to twine around the back of his neck. "I confess this to you now, Martha. I love you desperately. Terribly so. I love you more than I think I can ever express."

Martha smiled up at him, knowing that this was the beginning of something truly wonderful, something she had never expected to occur at this stage of her life. She had found a new love with Lord Blackford, a love that she knew would only continue to grow with every day they spent together.

"And I love you, Blackford," she murmured as he began to lower his head, his hands falling to her waist so that he might hold her close as he kissed her. She leaned into him, her fears and her doubts falling aside as she gave her heart to the man who had lost so much, who understood her grief and who, ultimately, had come to be more precious to her than she had ever expected.

ENJOY THIS BOOK? TRY THIS SERIES!

If you love Hallmark movies and HGTV home design shows, you will fall in love with Sweetwater Island Ferry! Read this popular, **Bestselling** trilogy in its entirety today~

The Sweetwater Island Ferry Book Trilogy

Includes:

For Love…and Donuts (Book 1)

To Love…and Renovate (Book 2)

With Love…and Reality TV (Book 3)

READ & REVIEW

If you enjoyed this Collection, please consider leaving a Review!

Every single review makes a tremendous difference. We cannot express how much we appreciate that you took the time to read this series.
With love and appreciation,
~The Love Light Faith family

Leave a Review on the platform of your choice, including:
Amazon
Bookbub
Goodreads

ABOUT THE AUTHOR

Sunny Brooks may seem mild-mannered, but she secretly craves the dramatic! For years she worked in the theater, producing period plays and productions on everything from scrappy little stages to sold-out amphitheaters. Through it all she found that one thing stays the same: a great story is always compelling, regardless of budget, production quality, or costumes.

Sunny now brings those stories of inspiration, suspense, heartache, redemption, strength and overcoming adversity to an even wider audience through her books.

With a true love and devotion to story-telling, she aspires to bring her readers on a journey culminating in HAPPINESS and HOPE.

When she is not writing she tries desperately to master the art of baking pies, and spends a whole lot of time reading (you guessed it) romantic novels!

To find out about more great books visit:
www.LoveLightFaith.com
Sunny@LoveLightFaith.com

❦

Please join the Love Light Faith Mailing List
to be notified of upcoming releases and promotions!
Visit our website for many additional titles!
www.LoveLightFaith.com

Printed in Great Britain
by Amazon